MICHAEL GREGORIO

Days·of·Atonement

D1114716

MINOTAUR BOOKS ♏ NEW YORK

A THOMAS DUNNE BOOK FOR MINOTAUR BOOKS.
An imprint of St. Martin's Publishing Group.

DAYS OF ATONEMENT. Copyright © 2007 by Michael Gregorio. All rights reserved. Printed in the United States of America. For information, address St. Martin's Press, 175 Fifth Avenue, New York, N.Y. 10010.

www.thomasdunnebooks.com
www.minotaurbooks.com

The Library of Congress has catalogued the hardcover edition as follows:

Gregorio, Michael.
    Days of atonement / Michael Gregorio. — 1st ed.
        p. cm.
    ISBN-13: 978-0-312-37644-4
    ISBN-10: 0-312-37644-8
    1. Police magistrates—Germany—Prussia—Fiction. 2. Murder—Investigation—Fiction. 3. Kant, Immanuel, 1724–1804—Influence—Fiction. 4. Prussia (Germany)—History—1806–1815—Fiction. I. Title.
PR6107.R447D39 2008
823'.92—dc22

                                                                                2007050681

    ISBN-13: 978-0-312-54517-8 (pbk.)
    ISBN-10: 0-312-54517-7 (pbk.)

First published in Great Britain by Faber and Faber Limited

10 9 8 7 6 5 4 3 2

Days of Atonement

Also by Michael Gregorio

Critique of Criminal Reason

For our parents,

AGNES

and

WALTER JACOB,

ROSINA

and

GIUSEPPE DE GREGORIO

For the thing which I greatly feared is come upon me, and that of which I was afraid is come unto me. I was not in safety, neither had I rest, neither was I quiet, yet trouble came.

Book of Job, 3.25–26

Days of Atonement

· 1 ·

'OCTOBER THE FOURTEENTH . . .'

Helena's voice faded away, her figure partly hidden by the heavy drapes of green velvet. She was looking out on the garden, where evening was turning rapidly into night. I did not need to see her face to know that she was deeply offended. Like every other Prussian, she was wounded by the reduced state of our nation, by the changes that the French had forced upon us, as defeat followed defeat, and rout followed rout. It had all begun in October the previous year.

'Jena?' she insisted. 'Is that what they mean to celebrate?'

The invitation from Count Aldebrand Dittersdorf had arrived by post ten days earlier. Before the war, the annual dinner and ball had been as fixed a point on our calendar as the falling of the autumn leaves. Should we go, or might it be wiser to stay at home? I had spent hours debating the question. Helena had not been out of the house in more than two months. Her third pregnancy had been difficult, the weeks leading up to the delivery had tried her strength greatly. She had lain in for a month afterwards, though the daily sight of little Anders—a plump look of satisfaction on his tiny mottled face as Helena tucked her swollen breast away inside her wet-smock—had more or less restored my wife to her former bloom. When the embossed card from the Dittersdorfs arrived, I instinctively pushed temptation away behind the large Dutch clock on the oak mantle-shelf in the kitchen.

But the fateful day was almost upon us, and the question had to be faced.

Memories were still strong of 13 October the year before, when we had all risen heavily from the Dittersdorf dinner table and made our way home cheerfully beneath a brilliant starlit sky, unaware of the fact that our troops were manoeuvring into position to face the French at dawn.

'I suppose *they* will be there in force,' Helena murmured, pressing her nose up against the glass, frowning out at the darkness, as if that were the true cause of her indisposition.

'Probably,' I answered.

'There is nothing probable about it, Hanno,' she corrected me pettishly. 'They will certainly be there.'

'It is certainly most probable that they *will* be there,' I replied with a sigh. 'They are everywhere else in Prussia. And Count Dittersdorf is the District Governor. He can hardly hold a secret dinner party for Prussian nationals alone. Our safety depends on peaceful coexistence with the invaders.'

Helena turned to stare at me. The cut-crystal bulb of the Bohemian oil lamp on the side-table cast delicate diamond patterns on her cheeks and forehead.

'Can you offer me no more comfort than that, husband?' she whispered. The proud tension had gone from her voice. 'One hears such terrible stories of those who are foolish enough to socialise with the French. The rebels care not for peaceful coexistence. They show no pity.'

'We are in no danger,' I reassured her, stepping close and taking her hand, which was cold and unresponsive to my touch. 'There are armed patrols everywhere, and we will have a permit to stay out after the curfew. If we decide to go, that is.'

I kissed her gently on the forehead. She was thinner than before, though whether from the strain of childbirth, or the state of constant nervousness that had possessed her since the occupation, I could not tell. Dark shadows had etched themselves into hollow cavities in her cheeks. The broad brow, high cheekbones, and slender lips that constituted the essence of her beauty had shifted in their delicate relations, and a dark furrow appeared on either side of her mouth on the rare occasions when she chose to smile. Her eyes alone remained unaltered. They were large, intelligent, enquiring, defiant, the warm chocolate brown of chestnuts. My new son had inherited those eyes, and I was glad of that. I could only pray that one day Helena would recover the fullness of her beauty, and that those two worry-lines would fade away with the slow passage of time.

'Are you suggesting that the French will save us from our fellow countrymen?'

I shook my head, and looked away. 'I only meant to say that we have to begin again, my love. Dinner at the Dittersdorfs is as good a place to start as any. Of course there are dangers, but nothing untoward has ever happened here in Lotingen. I do not see why the situation should change this Saturday evening.'

I caressed her chin with my thumb and forefinger, and gazed into her eyes, determined to change the subject. 'I was hoping that you would be more worried about what to wear.'

'What?' she echoed, knitting her dark eyebrows, glancing up.

'Your gown was always a matter of great concern as the autumn season approached. There is fierce competition between the ladies, I believe.'

She smiled, timidly at first, her eyes glistening ever more brightly, like coals in the blacksmith's forge when the boy works the bellows. That smile had conquered my heart at our very first meeting. Thank heavens! I thought. Count Dittersdorf was right to revive the old customs. The autumn feast was just the thing to mark a vital change for the better. My taste buds surged at the welcome vision of the honeyed side of pork that would dominate the table. As Helena smiled back, contemplating the prospect of the dinner— with feelings similar to my own running through her head, I imagined—the dark clefts on either side of her mouth seemed to fade away to nothing.

'I shall wear the one I wore last year,' she said quietly. It was a declaration of a sort, though I had no intuition of what was coming. 'That pretty ball-gown will serve as an emblem, Hanno. As if these past twelve months had never been. In my heart of hearts, the field of Jena will always be a gentle rolling plain, where birds sing and marigolds bloom in the spring. But that will be *our* little secret.'

The clock struck seven and Helena retired upstairs to feed the baby. I sat down by the fire, intending to read through the Court House proceedings, happily distracted by my wife's soft voice in the room above. The lullaby she sang was one that I had known since the cradle. *Im zoologischen Garten* spoke of a family visit to a menagerie, something that I had never seen. One day, perhaps, I would take Helena and my children to Berlin on such an outing to see the exotic animals and wild beasts. Before going upstairs that night, I opened the window, as I always did, and stuck my head outside to check the weather. Nature had been as dour and unforgiving as the occupying French in the past two months. Cold, tumultuous winds had gusted down from the Arctic circle throughout the month of August, turning the melancholy green waters of our Baltic shore wild and black, sending huge white-capped waves crashing in upon the seashore. September fog had shrouded the flat countryside, the smell of salt impregnating every shrivelling ear of spelt and corn. Then, the worst had arrived: ice and frost, glazing the world like the sugar coating on a cake.

But that night, the wind had changed direction. The air was considerably warmer, heavy with damp. The unexpected thaw was a welcome sign for the days to come. The crows would have his eyes once the crust of ice encasing them dissolved away. Rats would venture out along the gallows arm, and shin down the rope with the careless skill of able seamen, ripping and tearing at the flesh and guts of Adolphus Braun-Hummel. Helena had not been to town since spring. If the weather continued mild, I thought gratefully, she might hear of it, but she would never need to see that sight.

A lance corporal in the *Alt-Larisch* battalion of royal Prussian grenadiers, Adolphus Braun-Hummel was just twenty-two years old when he was rounded up after the capitulation of the Erfurt garrison. In a fit of youthful passion, he had more recently attempted to stab a French prison guard with a spontoon. The unwieldy spear had been ripped from his hands in no time, but his intentions were clear. He had been court-martialled, found guilty in the course of fifteen minutes, and hanged within an hour. The French had stripped him of his black leather knee-boots and fine uniform before the execution. He had been stiffly swinging from the gallows for two weeks now, his regimental sash of blue-and-white silk tied to his wrist, the rest of his body naked, the sex and the buttocks frozen black, a warning to us all. Well, I thought with grim satisfaction, stretching my hand out into the night, feeling the warm caress of fine drizzle, he won't be there much longer. The French would be obliged to cut the body down and have it hastily interred. If the sun should shine for an hour, the stench would settle like a miasma on the town before noon.

Yes, they would certainly cut him down.

I secured the parlour window, and prepared to go to bed with a lighter heart than I had felt for quite some time, hoping against hope that for a month or two, we might be spared the grim humiliation of another Prussian dangling from a hangman's noose. If the corpse were removed before the feast, it might be easier for us all to sit down and share a meal with the French.

HELENA CAME SKIPPING lightly down the staircase at a quarter to seven. A delicate shade of rose-pink greeted my eyes, and my thoughts flashed back to the last occasion when she had worn that gown. The night we had dined and danced at the home of Count Aldebrand and Countess Dittersdorf, the previous year. The final waltz, so to speak, before calamity fell upon the nation. The colour set off Helena's pale complexion to perfection, and she had allowed herself to suffer Lotte's hot irons in taming her hair. Those wild wiry locks had been miraculously transformed into a curtain of tightly bunched ringlets.

As she turned her bare shoulders to accept the heavy cloak that I held out, I closed my eyes, touched my lips to the crown of her head, and filled my lungs with the sweet, powdered perfume of her hair.

'Nothing has really changed, my love,' I murmured, almost drunk on the scent of honey and roses, happy that we had decided to go, glad beyond belief to see her looking so well.

The children were sleeping in their cots protected by their own dear

Lotte, Helena and I would be absent for a few hours, a short walk away, eating our share of roast pork and drinking ruby-coloured wine from the Dittersdorf cellar. Life in Lotingen would go on, as it had always done. What danger could there be that we had not already faced and overcome?

We left the house and took the gravel road in the direction of the mansion, which stood on a slight rise within visible distance of our gate. The cold had come on again—it was sharp, stinging. The moon was low, and there was still a trace of daylight in the sky on the western horizon, though the garden was dark. Curfew had been set for seven-thirty after recent skirmishes by roaming bands of starving rebels in the province, but I was not unduly concerned. The foreign troops were heavily concentrated around Lotingen, and together with the dinner invitation from Count Dittersdorf, there had been enclosed a late-night pass signed by Lieutenant Mutiez, the recently arrived officer of the guard. He was reputed to be a revolutionary gentleman of the new French breed, and I was expecting to meet him at the dinner table that evening.

Along the way, we were stopped on three separate occasions by Frenchmen on patrol. They emerged suddenly out of the woods, muskets at the ready, their bayonets fixed, demanding to see our papers. I felt Helena cling more tightly onto my arm as I told them who we were, and handed over the protective note. I felt reassured by this vigilant foreign presence, and I did not share my wife's anxiety about the rebels.

My sympathies went out to the defeated remnants of our own poor army, of course, but I wanted everything to go off without a hitch that night.

The autumn feast promised a new lease on life.

· 2 ·

THE RECEPTION ROOM was hot and crowded.

It was a humiliating sight to see the white Prussian mess-jackets mingling with the dark blue field-coats of the French officers. But mingle they did. Ceremonial swords rattled, and scabbards sometimes clashed by accident, but no blade was bared. That scene had been repeated in every country conquered by Napoleon Bonaparte, which meant nine-tenths of Europe. 'A necessary act of reconciliation,' Count Dittersdorf had tritely called it when he informed me of his intention to invite the French.

I peered out through the tall glass doors of the long gallery which gave directly onto the terrace and the garden beyond. A sheet of solid ice had covered the flagstones during the afternoon, reflecting the dancing warmth of the hundreds of candles inside the house. At least *that* tradition had been respected. Whenever Count Dittersdorf spoke of the annual event, he used an expression that had become something of a formula and a joke in Lotingen: 'You must gobble my roast pork before Jack Frost freezes your jaw.' Walking to the house that evening, I realised that his prediction had been fulfilled: the ground crackled beneath our shoes, we might have been walking on eggshells. After the short thaw, winter had arrived with a vengeance.

Three or four waiters in the purple family livery moved among the assembly, offering a welcoming glass of seasoned *kabinett* to one and all, myself and my wife among them, while other retainers swiftly lowered one of the magnificent glass chandeliers and replaced the candles which were in imminent danger of dripping hot wax onto the heads of the assembled company.

'Procurator and *Frau* Stiffeniis, what a pleasant surprise!' Count Dittersdorf was the first of many Lotingeners to turn his kind concern on Helena that evening. 'It is so good to see you up and about again, my dear. And looking so well. Now, tell me all about the baby!'

Before Helena could tell him very much, the dinner gong sounded, the double doors to the banqueting room were thrown open, and the whole company began to shift out of the reception hall, as if the smell of dinner were irresistible. As indeed it was. I took my wife by the arm, waiting for the crush to disperse before we entered the crowded room. No place-names had been set, so we made our way to the bottom end of the long dining table, where four or five chairs still stood empty. I was not put out by this informality. Dittersdorf had let it be known that if a man found himself sitting next to a French officer, he should make the best of it, as the French would be obliged to do. 'All friends together' was the particularly unhappy turn of phrase that he had coined for the occasion. But there was a weakness to the scheme. The French officers were all men, and very young for the most part, bachelors, or single by force of circumstance. The women were Prussian without exception, and French compliments were lavish. It was a potential minefield.

Helena took the empty place next to Professor Krazman, a retired teacher with silvery grey hair who had once held the chair of Ancient Greek Philology at the University of Königsberg, and I made myself comfortable beside her. The cook went round with a huge tureen of soup on a cart with wheels, and still two places remained vacant at the foot of the table. I was raising the spoon to my lips to savour the mutton broth when the latecomers arrived. They were Frenchmen, one wearing a uniform, the other dressed in an ankle-length leather cape. As comments were made about the excellence of the soup and the toasted particles of bread floating on the surface—a refinement that had only recently come into fashion in Prussia—I cast a furtive eye on the new arrivals.

The soldier who had taken the place next to mine was a handsome young man in his early thirties. Well-groomed, with shoulder-length hair tied up in a bow, and flashing black eyes, he identified himself as Lieutenant Henri Mutiez. He seemed little disposed to mingle with the company. All his attention was directed towards the slightly older man who had seated himself at the foot of the table. This person was of a most singular appearance. His nose had been broken at some time in his life, and poorly set. Even so, he was handsome in a striking fashion. Clear blue eyes of a sharp, intelligent cast darted around the table as he digested the substance of his dinner companions. With a mass of silvery hair, which seemed to have been roughly cut around his ears with a knife, and a large silver ring that dangled from his left ear every time he moved his head to his wine glass, he might have been a cut-throat privateer, though he announced his name and title as Colonel Lavedrine. He seemed to start as I gave my own name, but after smiling in a particularly ingratiating manner at Helena, he turned abruptly to his young companion, and spoke rapid French with a Parisian inflection.

All eyes were attracted by the main course as it entered the room. The servants carried in a large pewter tray, where a roasted pig of the most

7

gigantic proportions had been laid out on a bed of chestnuts, a cooked apple in its mouth, its skin peppered with black chives. As tradition required, this splendid sight was greeted with loud cheers and clapping, before it was set to rest on a side-table at the top end of the room. Count Dittersdorf then began to hack and saw, heaping slices of pork onto the plates of his guests, which were taken up empty from the table, two at a time, by the servants and carried to their master, before being returned to the fortunate recipient.

Seated at the very foot of the banquet, our appetites sharpened by the mountains of carrots and beetroot in trembling gelatine, the steaming plates of boiled potatoes set down at intervals along the table, this ritual was destined to take some time. In the lull that naturally followed as we waited self-consciously for our turn to come, watching enviously as other guests received their loaded plates, and ours remained empty, I was grateful when Professor Krazman boldly chose to invent a topic of conversation.

Whether from politeness or genuine interest, he leaned out over the table, and directed his attention towards the two newcomers.

'The Emperor has travelled a great deal, has he not?' he said in a quaint, delicate manner, pronouncing each foreign word with carefully controlled accuracy, the general effect of his schoolboy French made almost comical by the exaggerated volume of his quavering voice.

The Frenchmen exchanged a quizzical glance, then Lieutenant Mutiez replied in an artificially slow and measured tone: 'Indeed, he has, sir.'

Professor Krazman smiled warmly, and seemed to congratulate himself on being understood. Indeed, he felt encouraged to venture further. 'And you, good sir? Have you travelled with him?'

The young man smiled as he replied, 'Indeed, I have, sir!'

Professor Krazman was drawn inevitably deeper into discourse. Having asked a leading question, the curt reply obliged him to ask another, which came after some moments. 'To Egypt, too?'

The young lieutenant laughed heartily, glancing at his companion, who smiled a more languid smile. 'I was still in swaddling clothes in '98,' he quipped. It was a blatant lie, but who would dare to question his humour? He swept his hand in a sort of theatrical bow towards the older man, as if desiring to draw him into the conversation. 'But Colonel Lavedrine was in Egypt. He'll tell all you wish to know, I'm sure.'

This must have been a more than adequate introduction for any man, no matter how distinguished, but it did not suit this Colonel Lavedrine. He did not speak, merely nodded assent, as if that should be answer enough for any man's curiosity.

Thus Professor Krazman was obliged to step even further out onto the thin ice of his scholastic French.

'How I send you!' he declared ecstatically.

Everyone sitting nearby laughed gleefully. Professor Krazman had chosen wrongly from his small stock of vocabulary, substituting the word *envoyer* for *envier*.

'Professor Kazman envies your good fortune, sir,' I said, stepping in to right the wrong. 'Not many men have been to Egypt. And of those who went,' I added, 'not all came back in one piece. The Mamelukes are renowned for their ferocity. Even here in Prussia.'

'I had to swim at Abukir,' Lavedrine replied offhandedly, making no attempt to excuse the naval defeat at the hands of Nelson and the British fleet.

'You are a lucky man!' I said, turning to the servant at my elbow, watching as he made his way up the room towards Dittersdorf, my plate in one hand, Helena's in the other.

Colonel Lavedrine stared hard at me.

'You are yourself, sir,' he said at last.

'I beg your pardon?' I returned, my eye bewitched by the mountain of food on Professor Krazman's plate. I had seen nothing like it since the feast the year before. Blighted potatoes and boiled nettles had been the staple ingredients of our meagre diet. The harvest had been all but lost in the aftermath of defeat, and the invading French army had snapped up everything that survived the pilfering and destruction.

'You mentioned earlier that your name is Hanno Stiffeniis. You were acquainted with Immanuel Kant, were you not?' He nodded kindly in the direction of Professor Krazman, and repeated the lexical error which had amused us all three minutes earlier: 'How I *send* you, sir!' he said.

I gaped at him. Was my history an open book to every Frenchman who chanced to pass through Lotingen?

'Professor Kant?' I repeated uncertainly, saved from saying more by the arrival of the servant and the plates of food for Helena and myself. I jabbed hastily at an over-large piece of pork and stuffed it into my mouth, chewing rapidly, tasting nothing. My mind flew back to Königsberg, recalling the last occasion I had seen Immanuel Kant: laid out in the coffin in his living room, the day he was buried. That day, I had been obliged to face the final, unimaginable twist of his philosophy.

Suddenly, I realised that Colonel Lavedrine was addressing me.

'. . . a most remarkable man. I had a short, but fruitful, correspondence with him.'

I set my knife and fork down, managing to swallow the lump of pork that seemed to have clotted on my tongue, while Lavedrine continued to fix me with those clear blue eyes. There was something hawk-like and rapacious in his stare, as if he knew far more than he was prepared to say, and was waiting for me to fall into some snare.

'You corresponded with Kant?' I asked, the good things on my plate forgotten.

'The man himself,' Lavedrine replied.

'Were you a student of his?'

'A student?' Lavedrine echoed with an ironical smile. 'It would be truer to say that Professor Kant was a student of *mine*. For a short while, at least.'

I made an elaborate show of racking my memory for the name of this man who claimed to have tutored Immanuel Kant. 'I did not catch your name,' I said.

'Lavedrine,' he answered. 'Serge Lavedrine. Of Paris.'

'Which aspect of philosophy are you interested in, Colonel?'

'Philosophy does not interest me,' he said dismissively, wiping his mouth with his napkin. 'Some years ago, I was working on a report that had been commissioned for inclusion in the revision of the *Encyclopaedia*. But my master died, and I was left with the papers unfinished in my hands.'

'Your master?' I asked curiously.

'Monsieur Diderot was my tutor at the Sorbonne,' he said. 'I studied the new science of social anthropology under him. *The Apology for Man*, as he himself defined it. I was, and I am, particularly interested in criminal behaviour.'

'This was . . . when?' I asked, attempting a show of ingenuous interest.

'Diderot died in 1784, but I continued with my studies, and published a short pamphlet, *L'assassin rural*, at my own expense in 1793. Professor Kant wrote to me a few months after the work appeared. Despite the fact that half the sovereign states of Europe were at war with France, at least one copy must have reached Prussia,' he said, appearing to be amused.

I took another forkful of pork, and chewed more slowly, saying nothing. There was something patently false about this tale. Was this French upstart trying to gain credibility for himself by inventing a learned correspondence with Immanuel Kant, the greatest mind in the whole of Prussia?

'*L'assassin rural*,' I murmured. 'I've never heard of it, I'm afraid. What was the topic of your research?'

'Murder,' he said quietly. 'Within the context of the French peasant family. You'd be surprised how many deaths in rural areas are less than timely.'

'Kant? Murders committed by peasants?' I asked too sharply, raising my wine glass to my lips to cover my acidity of tone.

'Most certainly,' he replied. 'Professor Kant was interested in just about everything under the sun.'

'Everything under the sun,' I answered more mildly, 'but *not* crime.'

'I would hardly have expected it myself,' he replied smoothly. 'But one day I received a most intriguing letter from him. It spoke of nothing else.'

Now he had gone too far. Immanuel Kant was at the height of his public fame in 1793, all of his greatest works—the *Critiques* that would make his name immortal—published and acclaimed. Could one really imagine him writing to an unknown student in Paris to enquire about a vulgar pamphlet that the man had been obliged to publish at his own expense? It was a ludicrous suggestion. I determined to treat this provocation with the disdain that it deserved, and say nothing.

'His intuitions went far beyond anything I could have imagined,' Lavedrine continued aggressively. 'But you know what Professor Kant was capable of. And it is wrong to say that crime did not interest him. He made such acute critical suggestions that I was obliged to open up a line of reasoning that had never occurred to me before. I simply could not ignore the possibility.'

'Which possibility?'

Like Professor Krazman before me, I had been drawn into a conversation from which it would be difficult to escape. The topic was one that I would have preferred to avoid.

'What inspires murder, in your informed opinion, Herr Magistrate?'

The sarcastic tone of voice, and the gesture that accompanied this question, were unthinkably rude. He shook his forefinger at my face as if it were a duelling rapier.

'Life is sacred,' I said. 'When anger, jealousy, greed, or the mistaken desire to right an action that is perceived to be wrong, take hold of the mind, there is no anticipating the consequences. If a lethal weapon happens to be on hand, we may expect the worst.'

'Yes, yes, yes,' Lavedrine replied with a dismissive flick of that offensive forefinger. 'Correct, sir, but *banal*. There is a less predictable side to the human heart, as Herr Professor Kant was quick to point out.' "The bent wood of humanity," don't you remember? I believe he was thinking of a particular case when he wrote those words.'

'A criminal case?' I said. 'That is impossible! He had never shown the slightest interest in crime until the final year of his earthly existence. And even then,' I paused, weighing my words with care, 'he became involved against his will. The peace of Königsberg was threatened, the police were helpless, and so, despite his declining health, he attempted to resolve the question for them. But his efforts were wasted. The murderers were identified by myself in the end, shortly after Professor Kant's death, though they were never captured.'

Colonel Lavedrine smiled and looked away, gently touching the forearm of his young companion, as if to suggest that he should listen attentively, that some telling comment was about to be heard which would successfully conclude the argument in his own favour.

'You misunderstand me, Herr Stiffeniis,' he said. 'Or else you have a less informed view of Professor Kant than you would like me to believe. I tell you again, and I can prove to you, if necessary, that Kant was interested— passionately—in the nature of criminal behaviour a decade before that spate of murders in Königsberg led him to search out the doer with your assistance.'

'And I say again, sir. You are wrong. You pretend to possess knowledge in fields in which you are probably a novice.'

Helena placed her hand on mine, and whispered calming words in my ear, but I did not hear a thing she said.

Lavedrine's youthful companion stretched forward in his chair.

'Be very careful, sir!' he warned. 'Colonel Lavedrine is a guest of this house, and this nation. I can hardly believe that any Prussian would be so foolhardy as to doubt his word. Every man in Paris has heard of his capacities. I see no reason why this Professor Kant of yours should not have heard of them, too.'

Lavedrine sat back in his seat, a thin smile on his lips, stroking his chin with his thumb and forefinger. He seemed to be scrutinising me, curious to hear what my reply would be.

'If Colonel Lavedrine can prove the truth of what he says,' I returned, glancing between my accuser and the man I had accused, 'I will apologise with all my heart. And if that apology does not satisfy him,' I added, leaning back in my chair, shrugging my shoulders, 'the prison cells are waiting for Prussians such as me, who are obliged to have guests such as you!'

I suddenly realised that the room was silent.

All eyes had turned towards our end of the long table. Not one knife or fork moved. Wine settled untasted in fifty goblets. The joys of the table were forgotten in the unexpected thrill of the moment.

'Come, come,' Colonel Lavedrine said gently, smiling warmly, standing up and taking his faithful friend by the arm. 'If I have taken umbrage, Henri, I am old enough to settle my own scores! I assure you, I have taken no offence. My apologies to you, Herr Stiffeniis. Perhaps I have spoken of a subject which is close to your affections? I did not intend to belittle the memory of a man whom all the world admires. I simply meant to point out that even in the field of criminology, an activity in which Professor Kant was only marginally concerned, he was able to teach something to a man such as myself, who is interested in little else.'

He raised his glass and held it up to the room.

'To the memory of Immanuel Kant!' he cried.

All present lifted their glasses to the toast.

I waited a moment longer. I wanted Lavedrine to understand that although I had not been taken in by his fine words, I was willing to accept the olive branch of peace that he was holding out to me. Helena's hand tugged fitfully at my sleeve. I raised my glass, and added my voice to all the others.

'Very well, Monsieur Lavedrine,' I said, as the cheering died down, sitting back, resting my elbow on the table, as if I might be prepared to listen to whatever he wished to tell me. 'I wonder what Immanuel Kant might have been able to teach to an expert such as yourself? Which door, exactly, did he open?'

'The door marked "Affection".' Lavedrine's eyes flashed, his voice was heavy, intense. 'Love, if you like. All of us fight for the things we love most dearly. We fight, and we die, if necessary. Or we kill to defend them. Sometimes, too, we kill what we love.'

He narrowed his eyes and furrowed his brow, as if involved in a private process of the most serious reflection. 'Professor Kant had something specific in mind, I think, because he asked me whether I had ever come across a crime that was motivated by sincere affection. He wanted to know what might be the *modus operandi* chosen by a person who kills for such a reason. He was interested in details.'

I was speechless.

If I had deceived myself into thinking that no correspondence between Kant and Lavedrine concerning the question of murder could possibly exist, I was now obliged to accept that it did. Lavedrine suggested that they had been in touch in 1793. That year I had made a pilgrimage to Königsberg. That year I had sought the philosopher out, confessing my tangled feelings as I watched my brother die, unwilling and unable to save him. Was Professor Kant thinking of me when he spoke of motives which might lead to the death of a loved one? Had he asked this 'scientist of crime' to explain *my* unnatural behaviour?

'Ladies and gentlemen,' the voice of Count Dittersdorf thundered, 'the moment has arrived for us to sample the first pressing of this season's cider!'

All those who were 'in the know' expressed their enthusiasm. The newcomers, many of whom had never tasted Prussian cider, were curious, carefully watching every move that Count Dittersdorf made, as he stirred the contents of a huge silver salver, then served out a helping of this nectar, which gave off a smoky vapour as it settled heavily in the waiting cut-crystal goblets, and was handed out to the assembled guests. Everyone turned excitedly to his or her neighbour, commenting on the fine colour of the liquid, and the delicious aroma that began to settle like a perfumed cloud over the long table.

When Dittersdorf held up his glass, inviting us all to drink to the Fruits of Autumn, a second cry went up, and I believe that it was first heard from the lips of my wife: 'Long live dear Count Aldebrand!'

As I drank to both these toasts, looking around the table, intent on sharing my appreciation of the cider with the other guests, my eye settled on Colonel Lavedrine. He was staring at me, oblivious to the feast.

'I hope that we will have the opportunity to speak further,' he murmured, taking a brimming jug of cider which the waiter brought to our end of the table. 'More cider, Herr Stiffeniis? Hold up your glass, Henri! And for you, *madame*?'

Helena thanked him graciously, but a vein was pulsing nervously in her temple.

We rose from the table shortly afterwards, the faces of the men inflamed by the final glass of Bischoff's cordial that our host had pressed upon us to ward off the cold. The Dittersdorfs took their customary places by the door to thank their guests, an air of satisfaction clearly stamped on Count Aldebrand's large face. His habitual expression of stern severity had been replaced by a milder one. He appeared to consider the evening a sort of personal triumph, as if the 'reconciliation' of Lotingen were no longer just a hope, but a fact. I prayed to God that he was correct, only too well aware that the rebels of our own defeated forces had not been invited to the feast. They were still capable of causing untold damage.

'Thank heavens no blood was spilled,' I heard him whisper to Helena as he bowed to kiss her gloved hand.

She turned to say goodbye to the Countess, who seemed more evidently relieved that the evening was over, and that nothing worse had come of it. 'Sometimes the fact that we speak our different languages is a blessing in disguise,' our hostess said with a nervous smile.

'Your guests may have exchanged pleasantries in each other's tongue this evening, ma'am,' Helena replied, as she buckled her mantle, 'but what they may have said between themselves, or thought in private, is anybody's guess.'

From the tone of her voice I realised that she was frightened by something.

'Procurator Stiffeniis, may I wish you a good evening?'

The voice was low, hardly audible above the general clamour, but I knew who it belonged to before I turned around.

'Colonel Lavedrine, you may, indeed,' I replied with a smile that was as cordial as I was able to manage.

'Frau Stiffeniis, my most sincere compliments,' he continued, placing his hand on his heart and bowing his shaggy head to my wife. Then he glanced back at me. 'There are a thousand questions I would like to ask about the investigation you carried out with Professor Kant in Königsberg. As a criminologist, of course, I made a point of reading your report. It was flawless from a bureaucratic point of view, but I would rather hear the details from your own lips.' He hesitated an instant, then added: 'For the sake of my studies.'

Helena took hold of my arm as if to warn me to be on my guard.

'Unfortunately, I shall be leaving in a day or two,' he continued, his German truly excellent. 'I am not a soldier, as you will have realised. I hold the rank of a colonel, but the battles I fought in the back streets of Paris earned me that respect. I'll be going eastwards soon, towards the Russian border. I must admit, that prospect worries me a little. Our hold on the border territories is still not entirely established.'

'Is that why you are going there, *monsieur?*' Helena proposed with a show of candour. 'To secure the area?'

'A country can be ruled without a French soldier sitting on every single clod of it.' He laughed. 'Besides, the explanation is simpler. There is a hospital for the insane which is of great scientific interest in Bialystok. I mean to speak to some of the "guests."'

Helena relaxed her grip on my arm.

'*Bon voyage, monsieur!*' she said lightly.

'*Merci,* Frau Stiffeniis,' Lavedrine murmured with a smile that seemed to light up his face. But his mind was elsewhere. He stretched out his hand and laid it heavily on my shoulder.

'You possess information that is precious to me, sir. I came this evening for no other purpose. I am interested in knowing Kant's thoughts about murder. I feel certain that he must have left some detailed notes on the subject. You are one of the few people who might know.'

I knew the writing he was searching for. I had torn the pages into shreds with my own hands, and thrown them into the mud-brown waters of the River Pregel in Königsberg. They swirled and sank again in my mind's eye.

I shook my head.

'Professor Kant died suddenly,' I said. 'He had never shown the slightest interest in crime before.'

'Yes, yes, so you said,' he interrupted impatiently. 'And yet, I am convinced . . .'

'Unfortunately, Hanno cannot help you, Colonel Lavedrine.' Helena stepped between us. She smiled with captivating warmth, her hand on my arm, pulling me away. 'I hope you may find more interesting material for research on your travels.'

The road was thick with French soldiers as we made our way home.

The sky was crystal-clear above our heads.

The constellations shone in all their glory as we walked in the direction of our house. But the sight did not provoke my admiration, as it had once worked its magic on Immanuel Kant. On the contrary, that unsullied sky promised cold weather in the foreseeable future. If any more Prussians were hanged, their frozen corpses would shadow our days until spring.

We were not alone as we walked through the night. Other guests were making their way home along the same path. We heard their comments in tinkling French and the low, guttural German of the coastal lowlands.

Language had driven its wedge between us once again.

· 3 ·

I sat bolt upright in bed.

Wide awake, I turned to Helena, unable to see her in the darkness. Her breathing was deep and regular. Beyond her, the sleeping child let out a whimpering sigh.

Was that the noise which had disturbed my rest?

I listened attentively. Outside, not even the hoot of an owl breached the peace. But I felt no easier. War robs a man of his tranquillity. With exaggerated care, I pulled back the coverlet and slipped down off the high bed. Stepping to the window, the rough-hewn floorboards cold beneath my feet, I lifted back the curtain and looked out over the rear of the house. The garden was a formless black pit. The hazel trees marking the edge of our domain were a solid wall, the starless sky tinged an impalpable shade of violet. At the break of dawn, farmers' carts would clatter past our gate on their way to market, men driving cattle to the slaughter with their dogs . . .

A low moan sounded somewhere in the house.

I moved towards the door, grabbing the first garment that came to hand, throwing it around my shoulders against the icy cold, as I stepped out onto the landing. I looked down the stairwell, where a figure in a white shawl was hovering in the hall, holding up a candle, as if transformed into a pillar of salt. Nothing moved, except the flame. Then, that strangled sound escaped once more from lips that I could not see.

A hand brushed by my ear, and came to rest upon my shoulder.

'What is it, Lotte?' my wife called in a whisper.

Like an imp, her bare feet and slender ankles stretching forth from beneath the hem of her nightgown, Helena skipped down the stairs. The wild thicket of her untied hair bobbed before me as I followed in her wake.

Lotte turned, her eyebrows arched, eyes wide.

'Soldiers,' she hissed, causing the flame to flicker.

Edging Lotte aside with my shoulder, I raised the brass thaler and exposed the hole that I had drilled in the oak the day the news of the defeat at

Jena reached Lotingen. At the time, I had convinced myself that this spy-hole would provide an advantage against any unwelcome caller armed with evil intentions. But hard as I tried, all that I could see outside was as black as pitch, and the cold air streaming in caused my eye to water. As I peered out from my fragile fortress, I prayed that Lotte had been mistaken.

Just then, the garden gate swung open with a creak, pushed back too hard on its ancient hinges. There was a click, and a lantern was raised. Three men huddled on the path in a tight group. I recognised the uniforms: two privates in trenchcoats, an officer wearing a black leather *képi* with a tall white plume, their faces etched in stark chiaroscuro by the lamplight. They were consulting a piece of paper.

This is the moment, I realised with a start. If Lotte took the baby in her arms, and Helena led Süzi and Manni out by the back window, I might be able to hold them off for a minute or two.

'Don't think of it!' Helena had read my intentions as surely as if I had shouted them out at the top of my voice.

'They seem uncertain,' I said, my eye glued to the spy-hole. 'Perhaps they are seeking a fugitive . . .'

The officer swung around and took a pace forward, his face filling the spy-hole. The shock of recognition flashed upon me. I had seen the man at Dittersdorf's feast. I had argued with him. Was that why he had come? There was a determined set to his face, the number '7' writ large in gold lettering on his *képi* above the peak.

Helena's voice was amazingly calm.

'Open the door,' she said. 'We have no choice.'

Her face was close to mine, our noses almost touching. She seemed so cool and calculating, as if some scheme had formed in her mind. Pulling the mantle from off her shoulders, she twirled it around and held it out to me.

'You wouldn't wish to be seen like that,' she said.

I was wearing her lemon-coloured dressing gown, the first thing that had come to hand in the dark. Whatever was about to happen, Helena had decided that I must face it with the dignity befitting a true Prussian. She thrust the mantle into my hands, stretching out to remove the feminine garment from my shoulders.

'Lotte, run upstairs. Anders will sleep, but the other two will wake. I will hold the candle, Hanno. You remove the bar and open the door.'

I shifted the wooden bar, slid the well-oiled bolt, and pulled back the door with such rapidity that it seemed to stop the soldiers in their tracks. All three took a step backwards, eyes wide, mouths open. The squaddies pointed their muskets, but did not shoot.

Cold air rushed into the hallway.

'Are you looking for me?' I asked, surprised by the firmness of my voice.

The officer's eyes flashed. He had recognised me.

'I know you,' Helena said. 'We met last week at dinner.'

'Lieutenant Mutiez, *madame*. Seventh dragoons,' the officer said in heavily accented German, touching the peak of his cap.

I took a deep breath, and held his gaze. Nothing induced me to relax my guard. These foreigners were dangerous. More dangerous, now that the door was open wide.

'*Le papier, vite!*' he urged, turning to one of the privates. His eyes dropped to the paper in his hand: 'Procurator Stiffeniis . . .'

Helena gasped out loud.

This was how the military behaved when instructed to take up a man who was destined to disappear. The time was right, the hour before dawn, when human resistance is at its lowest ebb. The physical and mental capacities of the condemned man were reduced to a minimum by terror, and the unexpected interruption of sleep.

'Yes?' I prompted him.

'You must come with me, sir,' Lieutenant Mutiez responded.

'God save us!' Lotte cried from the top of the stairs, her shrill voice echoing in the hallway.

'What do you want with my husband?' Helena demanded, stepping in front of me, facing them with a ridiculous show of bravery. 'Has the victorious French army nothing better to do?'

I placed one hand on my wife's shoulder, and told her roughly to be quiet. My other hand reached down and grabbed her wrist, holding her back. Fear or frustration seemed to have taken possession of her senses. If Helena insisted on spitting venom in their faces, those men might slit every throat in the house. No one would punish them for it.

'Lieutenant Mutiez,' I said quickly, 'what brings you here? If some false charge has been brought against me, knowing what it is, I'll be better able to defend my name.'

'Herr Stiffeniis,' Mutiez replied, his voice softer than before, 'it is cold out here, very cold. For the sake of these ladies and yourself, sir, allow us to step inside.'

I stepped back two paces.

The Frenchmen advanced to the same degree. To my surprise, Mutiez removed his hat, an expression of relief, or something similar, stamped clearly on his face.

'This is for you, sir,' he said, holding up the paper. 'See for yourself, it is an order.'

I took it from him, glanced at the contents. There was very little written there. My name, my address, and another address that I did not recognise. No mention was made of an arrest.

'You must come with me,' he repeated. 'I have my instructions, sir.'

'For what reason?'

Helena snatched the note from my hand.

'I'm going with him!' she cried as she tried to make sense of it.

Lieutenant Mutiez turned on her quickly. 'Do you have children?' he asked, his mouth moving energetically as he forced his tongue around the foreign words.

Helena stared at him, then nodded.

'It would not be wise,' he added, glancing at Lotte, who was halfway down the stairs, 'to leave them alone in the house with just this person to protect them.'

'Why not?' Helena demanded.

He did not reply, but turned to me. 'Be quick, sir. Get dressed to face the cold. It's a night for wolves . . .'

'The only wolves in Lotingen wear uniforms like yours!' Helena hissed.

I held my breath. This insult must be the final straw.

Instead, a smile began to form itself on the lips of Lieutenant Mutiez.

'Believe me, *madame*,' he said with a polite, ironic bow, 'I would rather be in my own warm bed. And in my own home town. We have no wolves, and the winter is warmer in Arles. The sooner we leave,' he added more gently, 'the quicker the business will be done.'

'Helena, would you help me find my clothes?' I said to break this deadlock.

Then I turned to Lotte. 'Please, show these gentlemen into the day-room.'

As the intruders made their way into the parlour, Helena and I returned upstairs. Tight-lipped and nervous, my wife made haste to lay out my clothes. I rinsed my hands and my face with cold water from the ewer. One thought was racing through my mind. I ought to hold her, kiss her, assure her of my love. The sight of little Anders sleeping in his cot on the far side of the bed, the knowledge that Manni and Süzi were safe in the next room, brought a lump to my throat. I longed to hold them all. But even that small comfort was denied me. Helena would interpret such a gesture as a final farewell.

She handed me my shirt, my heaviest trousers, a thick woollen over-vest, knee-length boots, seal-skin jacket, and woollen cape.

And not a single word was said.

I left the house, believing that I would never see her and the children again.

· 4 ·

If Bonaparte brought anything new to Prussia, it was fear. That night I prepared myself for a good dose of it.

A black carriage was waiting out in the lane, the horses giving off clouds of steam, as if they had been driven hard. Mutiez followed me down the path, urging me to climb aboard. He jumped up and took his place on the bench without saying a word to explain himself. The privates were obliged to brave the cold outside: one at the front, driving the pair of horses, the other standing guard behind.

As the vehicle pulled away, I noted the direction that it took.

We began ominously, driving towards town. The road was icy, and the horses would not be rushed, despite frequent cracking of the whip. Whenever the vehicle approached a bend in the road, met a rise, or followed a dip, the animals would slow down of their own accord, much to the anger and irritation of Lieutenant Mutiez, who rapped fitfully on the wooden roof, urging the soldiers and the horses on, shouting, 'Vite! Vite!' as if it were the only phrase he knew.

Soon, we would be passing through the market square, taking a left turn after the cathedral, aiming for the high tower of Bitternau, the medieval stronghold where the French authorities had installed themselves. All the dangerous prisoners were held in the dungeons, which was where the interrogations took place. I was convinced that Mutiez had played a more courteous role than the situation required, in the hope that I would offer no resistance. His tense silence was clear proof of the cowardly trick that had been played on me. And he seemed studiously to avoid catching my eye. No doubt, when we reached our destination, I would be arraigned, then thrown into a prison cell. Physical torture was a possibility, though I was not so frightened at the prospect as I ought to have been. I was more concerned about the safety of my wife and children. How would they survive without me?

Suddenly, I was thrown hard against the coachwork as the vehicle swung left onto the Pieniezno highway and began to race southwards into the countryside, leaving Bitternau fortress and Lotingen behind.

What did this change of direction signify?

Did they intend to murder me without a trial?

We had not gone a mile when the horses drew to a slithering halt. Lieutenant Mutiez threw open the door, kicking down the folding step. He jumped out, then turned back to face me.

'They are waiting,' he announced.

I climbed down in the violet penumbra of the dawn.

The coach had stopped in the open countryside. Armed soldiers were milling around in the half-light, each with a long musket and his bayonet fixed. They seemed to be protecting two more black carriages which were parked hard up against a stand of trees, where a narrow lane disappeared into the wood.

Something had happened. Or was about to happen.

'You must enter that carriage, *monsieur*,' Mutiez ordered, pointing to the vehicle on the left.

The fear was physical, debilitating.

I wanted, more than anything else, to relieve the weight pressing down on my bladder. I had been abducted for reasons unknown; now I was to be interrogated in an unmarked coach on an isolated country road.

The blinds of the vehicle were down. Even in stronger light it would have been impossible to see the occupants. The French soldiers clustering around seemed tense, wary. It made a harsh contrast with their usual air of contemptuous unconcern. They held their firearms as if they meant to use them. As I mustered my courage and took my first step, all eyes turned towards me. Some of the men shook their bayonets in the direction of the waiting carriage. Lieutenant Mutiez growled something angrily in French that I did not comprehend, then suddenly darted ahead and pulled open the carriage door.

'Procurator Stiffeniis is here,' he announced.

I paused for an instant, then quickly stepped up into the coach.

'What in heaven . . .'

I did not finish. Mutiez pushed me hard in the small of the back. 'Get in, sir. There's no time to lose.' Climbing in behind me, he slammed the door, and sat down on the bench-seat at my side.

'Good morning, *monsieur*. I don't suppose you thought we'd meet so soon?'

Lavedrine's voice was drained of the ironic good humour that had marked him out at the autumn feast. His intense gaze, and the concentrated faces of Count Dittersdorf and Lieutenant Mutiez, suggested something very serious.

Dittersdorf was the first to speak, his face set, avoiding eye contact, as if to suggest that I should keep my own counsel, and listen without interrupting.

'What I have to say is intended for the ears of Colonel Lavedrine as much as for your own, Hanno. You have both been summoned here for a precise purpose. He arrived five minutes ago. Like you, he knows nothing of the circumstances. There is a house at the end of the lane'—Count Dittersdorf pointed quickly over his shoulder with his gloved thumb. 'A crime has been committed there tonight, a most peculiar and, I do not hesitate to call it, a most *horrific* crime. Lieutenant Mutiez was informed of the fact at two o'clock this morning. He hurried here at once, and, seeing the immensity and the gravity of the event, he had the good sense to touch nothing and seal the house. He then notified the French authorities. General Giroux realised at once that the cooperation of the Prussian authorities was essential. At that point, I was advised of the situation, and I sent for Colonel Lavedrine, whose name had been put forward by the French general staff as a suitable person to lead the investigation. Then, appreciating the complexity of the question, Colonel Lavedrine decided that you should be brought in to assist him. He is a criminologist of recognised ability; you are an experienced magistrate with intimate knowledge of the local situation. You will work together to throw light on what has happened. Do I make myself clear?'

I was certain of one thing alone. Dittersdorf found himself in an impossible position. Though District Governor of the North Marches in name, he could do not a thing without the approval of the French. Indeed, it appeared to me, in this instance, he had been told exactly what to do. The needs of Lieutenant Mutiez and Colonel Lavedrine, *criminologist*, were overriding. Count Dittersdorf was authorised to smooth the way for them. Jena had robbed every Prussian of the freedom to decide. He, and I, had orders to follow, and those orders were French.

'Am I to understand that Colonel Lavedrine is in the same position of ignorance as myself?'

'If you wish to see it as a contest,' Lavedrine replied sharply, 'I can hardly stop you. But that was not my intention. I suggested your name as the only magistrate that I know. If a Prussian must be involved, then you are the man.'

He relaxed visibly as I nodded my agreement.

'I could have gone ahead without you,' he continued, 'but it would be neither fitting, nor useful. Four eyes will be more useful than two, two brains better than one. Your experience will counterbalance my own.'

'Excellent!' Dittersdorf enthused, evidently relieved that a tricky situation had been succinctly explained by Lavedrine. 'I will say no more of the political implications, but the need to cooperate is of the first importance. The situation is explosive. And not in Lotingen alone. There are subversive elements on both sides who would only too happily exploit any divisions. They must not be given the opportunity. Now, sirs, if you have any questions, this is the moment. Lieutenant Mutiez and I will answer, if we are able. I urge you to be brief.'

Lavedrine and I regarded each other for an instant, then the Frenchman bowed his head and smiled down at the carriage floor. It was a minor victory, but a significant one. Clearly, sharing an investigation with the Frenchman would not be an easy task. Would our questions come naturally, or must each of us always defer to the other, before daring to open our mouths?

My eyes fixed on Lavedrine, I began: 'May I ask what has happened?'

'I'll answer that,' Mutiez replied. Despite this bold declaration, he stopped and turned to Dittersdorf, waiting for his assent. 'Just after one o'clock, a man was taken into custody by a patrol on the outskirts of town. Obviously, he was in defiance of the curfew. He was brought to my office at a quarter to two. As a rule, anyone breaching the curfew is held in the cells until morning, but this man demanded to see an officer. He had news, he said, which he could reveal to no one of a lower rank. It is a common excuse. All curfew offenders have some 'urgent business' which is more important than staying at home. But rules are rules, I was obliged to see him. He was a most . . . well, a peculiar-looking creature. More beast than man, I would say. His name is Franz Durskeitner. He sells game to the company cook. He reported seeing something out of the ordinary in a house down there—' Mutiez nodded over his shoulder.

'Who is in the house? Frenchmen, or Prussians?' Lavedrine snapped.

Mutiez turned to Dittersdorf again.

I was perplexed by their reticence. Why would neither man say what he had seen until Lavedrine and I had seen the same thing? What was waiting to be discovered that was so unusual?

'That is *not* the problem,' Dittersdorf mumbled.

'Durskeitner passed near the house yesterday afternoon,' Mutiez went on. 'He says that he saw nothing out of the ordinary. But when he returned around midnight . . .'

'So late?' I intervened.

'He sets his traps in the afternoon, and empties them at night. That is his method, though it defies the curfew. Something odd attracted his attention . . .'

'Can you be more exact?' Lavedrine declared with a flurry of exasperation. 'Nothing out of the ordinary? Something odd? Did this witness tell you nothing more factual?'

'It was windy tonight, as you know . . .'

'Is that strictly relevant, Henri?'

Mutiez stared back at Lavedrine. 'It is a matter of some importance, sir. The hunter was perplexed by the noise the wooden shutters made. Loud enough to wake the dead, he said. But no one had troubled to close them. There was a strong wind yesterday afternoon, too, but all had seemed in order then. He crept up to the window and looked inside. When he saw no one in the kitchen, he entered the house, thinking that something was wrong. He was on his way to town to report the news, so he says, when they arrested him.'

'Where is this man being held?'

'Bitternau fortress,' Mutiez replied. 'He was questioned there, but I believe he knows more than he admitted to me.'

'What exactly did he tell you?' I demanded.

Mutiez glanced at me, then back at Lavedrine. 'You must see for yourselves,' he replied. 'Unless you have any other questions.'

Lavedrine did not wait for my reply, but threw open the carriage door.

'I have none,' he said, jumping down to the ground.

As Lieutenant Mutiez followed him out of the vehicle, Count Dittersdorf laid his hand on my sleeve, and held me back.

'Hanno, do not disappoint me!' he hissed.

· 5 ·

THE COTTAGE WAS secluded behind a thicket of trees and bushes. It would have been hard to find even if one came looking for it, address in hand. I had passed along the Pieniezno highway on many occasions, but had never been aware of a dwelling there, nor seen any sign of the inhabitants.

A pathway penetrated the dense vegetation like a tunnel, so narrow that we were obliged to pass in single file, holding up our hands to protect ourselves from the overhanging branches. No attempt had been made to cut back the thorns and bushes, which slashed dangerously at our eyes. Mutiez held up his lantern and led us on. Dittersdorf followed, muffled up in a heavy cloak of dark-green wool. Lavedrine wore the ankle-length leather cape that he had worn to the autumn feast. He had embellished this bizarre black outfit with a woollen shawl of the same colour, wearing it over his head to protect his ears from the cold. I came last, my travelling mantle wrapped twice around my shoulders in the Pomeranian fashion. Had it not been for Mutiez's uniform, we might have been mistaken for a band of thieves.

The dark shape of the house loomed into view.

Mutiez halted in his tracks.

'I thought you left a squad to secure the place?' Dittersdorf whispered, his voice fading away as he spoke. There was no suggestion of criticism in this question. Only fear and apprehension.

'So I did!' Mutiez replied sharply.

In that instant, four soldiers appeared from the side of the house. A groan escaped from the lips of Mutiez. There was something ridiculous in their manner of guarding the place. They were formed up in a tight square. One of the two in front held up a lantern, the other clasping his musket to his chest. The two men behind held muskets also, but they were facing in the opposite direction. All four moved forward awkwardly, back to back, as if they feared an attack from every side, and were prepared to return the enemy fire. As the two in front caught sight of our lantern, a general cry went up and all four men twirled round to face us, lining up their arms, clicking their flintlocks into the firing position, the leader dropping onto one knee, setting his lamp on the ground, sighting along his musket barrel.

'*Fermez!*' Mutiez shouted, stepping forward. 'What are you playing at? Walking back to back like idiots! Whose idea was this?'

The men stood up hastily and shuffled to attention, bringing their muskets up to 'present arms' before the lantern-bearer spoke.

'There were noises in the woods. We, er . . . thought it was the safest way. Best to be careful, sir!'

'Report what you found,' Mutiez snapped.

'A boar rooting for acorns,' the lantern-bearer replied, the red pom-pom quivering on his helmet. 'No one has been here since you left, *Monsieur 'tenant.'*

'Very good,' muttered Mutiez, turning to face us. 'Count Dittersdorf has been inside, and so have I. That's it, with the exception of Franz Durskeitner, the man who discovered the crime, and these fellows . . .'

'Good God, Henri!' Lavedrine exploded. 'Do you mean to say that half the French army has been traipsing through the scene of a crime?'

Before Mutiez could answer, Dittersdorf spoke out.

'I can assure you, sir, we were very careful.'

Lavedrine cursed aloud before the old man could finish. 'Henri, can you find a couple of lanterns for myself and Procurator Stiffeniis? If we are to examine the house properly, we will need plenty of light.' He turned to me. 'I believe I speak for both of us?'

I nodded. 'I have a further request to make.'

'Name it, sir,' Mutiez replied with a sigh of resignation. He must have found himself in a most irregular, embarrassing position, subject to the whims and the wishes of a Prussian with whom he had clashed.

'I will need some paper and something to draw with. I was carried from home with no hint of where I was being taken, or why.'

Bewilderment flashed upon the face of Mutiez, but he turned to his men, and sent one of them running off to obey his orders.

'*Voilà!* Our methods differ before we start, Stiffeniis!' This observation seemed to amuse Lavedrine. 'Am I to suppose that you always make sketches and notes at the scene of a crime?'

I took a deep breath, trying to suppress my irritation, then I stepped closer to the light with what was, I hoped, a dismissive smile on my face. I wanted the Frenchman to understand that I would not be subjected to sarcasm, or to any presumption of superiority on his part. We were equals. I would allow him to make his decisions only on condition that my own were not forced into second place.

'I was privileged to work with Herr Professor Kant,' I said, conscious of the power this statement would have over him. 'He believed in recording the mechanics of a crime. Faithful reproduction of footprints and other physical evidence played a central part in the interpretation of those murders in Königsberg. I sketch what I see. I will be intrigued, sir, to discover at first hand which method you use to analyse the *locus crimini*.'

Lavedrine did not reply immediately, though all eyes turned on him. With a smile on his face, he raised his right hand, the middle fingers folded into his gloved palm, the index and little finger outstretched to form a pair of horns. He pointed these two fingers at his eyes. 'I use these,' he said. Then his little finger closed and he touched the side of his nose with his forefinger: 'And this.' Finally, he closed his fist and thumped gently on his broad brow. 'And when I have gathered together what my senses tell me, this. The brain can cope with more than fragmentary, disconnected details.' His fingers spread wide, hovering over the broad expanse of his forehead, as if to suggest the immensity of the organ contained therein.

This singular display was interrupted by the soldiers bearing lanterns, together with the paper and graphite I had requested. I glanced at Lavedrine.

'When you are ready, *monsieur*,' I said with an exaggerated show of deference.

He turned to Mutiez and Dittersdorf. 'You lead, sirs, we will follow.'

'I'll wait here, if you don't mind,' Dittersdorf declared, stepping aside. 'All the gold of Peru would not tempt me to enter the house again! You'll have no further need of me, I'm certain.'

With a curt nod, Mutiez turned away, and stepped over the threshold.

Lavedrine followed him into the house, and I brought up the rear. I expected to enter the hall, but we found ourselves in a small kitchen. My heart was racing as we huddled by the door. I was excited, nervous, having no exact idea what to expect. What evidence should I record as vital and important? Which elements could I safely ignore? Dittersdorf expected great things of me, and I was determined not to let him down. But my most immediate concern was to impress the Frenchman with my professional expertise.

We raised our lanterns and looked around the room.

The scene had all the appearance of a theatre, the actors having just left the stage. An oil lamp had been suspended from a rusty hook above the kitchen table, providing a dim, gloomy sort of illumination. The wick had burned right down for lack of trimming, thin wisps of smoke curling upwards into the darkness above.

Lavedrine turned to me. 'What are your first impressions?'

Mutiez stood off to the side, as if he had no wish to interfere. I had the feeling that he would have preferred to wait outside with Dittersdorf.

The room was cramped, but everything seemed to be in order. There was little to see, with the exception of a blackwood dresser, a stone sink and a long-handled pump in one corner. A rickety wooden ramp of stairs ranged at a steep angle along the far wall disappeared upwards through a hole in the ceiling. The table in the centre of the room had been set for four persons. The chairs were carelessly arranged, pushed back slightly from the table. Four rough-hewn wooden bowls, spoons, and cups were laid out for dinner. A tall glass jug stood in the middle of the table. Almost empty, it appeared to contain mere dregs of milk. A large wedge of black bread had been broken, then sliced on a cutting-board. A long, bone-handled knife lay among the crusts and crumbs. A few red and black berries were scattered on the table-top. An untouched roundel of cheese sat stoutly on a pewter plate, the meagre remains of a ham bone on another.

'It's the sort of scene that you might find in any cottage in the neighbourhood, *monsieur*,' I said, more nervous about saying too little than too much.

Lavedrine walked twice around the table, holding up his lantern as if it were a compass.

'They sat down to eat,' he confirmed, taking up the dishes, one after the other, raising them to his nose. 'But I'd swear that this bowl was never used.'

Setting down the bowl, he pointed to the nearby cup.

'And neither was this vessel. There is liquid in the others, while this one is empty. Can you see?'

He stood with his lantern tilted above the cup, inviting me to step close and share his discovery. I looked around the room instead, noting a small ramshackle cupboard, an ancient armchair next to the fireplace, a shelf above it, holding cups and plates. It was a country cottage, rough and ready, but well kept in its way.

'The man who reported the discovery,' I said. 'What did you say his name was, Mutiez?'

'Durskeitner, sir,' the lieutenant replied.

'Did he find nothing more than this?'

'Upstairs, sir,' the lieutenant murmured, glancing at the ceiling. 'In the bedroom.'

He made for the staircase in the far corner of the room, which creaked as he placed his weight on it and began to climb.

Lavedrine got there before me, and began to follow him.

Halfway up, he turned and looked down at me. 'You will observe,' he said, 'that there are no unsightly marks, no mud, no scuffs, on these stairs.'

I looked at the wood before my face. Each plane was varnished black at either extreme, well worn, almost white in the centre. Even in the poor light, it was easy to see that the stairs were clean.

Lavedrine reached the top. He stood in silence, as if he were waiting for me before he stepped up into the bedroom. Thinking that it was a gesture of unexpected courtesy, I hurried to reach him. But when I did so, he made no effort to move on, or make space for me. He was standing frozen, as if a large hound had appeared in the upstairs room and threatened to bite his head off. Even so, I heard the creaking of the boards as Mutiez moved around in the room.

'Lavedrine?' I questioned, inciting him to move forward.

Without a word, he edged up to the wall, making way for me.

I stood by his side, and looked into the bedroom.

A broad marriage-bed with a white counterpane dominated the room, the ample carved-oak headboard pushed up against the far wall. Next to the bed, on the right, stood a small bedside table. On the left, a double casement window took up half the wall. The curtains had been left open all night. A single chair was placed at the foot of the bed. Lavedrine had set his lantern on the floor, lighting up the bare wooden boards, and the stains.

The light was of such an unnatural pearly hue that morning that everything seemed unreal. My mind was pulled and torn in every direction. The paper slipped from my hand, the stick of graphite rattled and broke as it fell down the stairs.

Three lifeless bodies had been laid out on the double bed.

Not end to end, as one usually sleeps, with the feet aiming at where we were standing, but side by side across the mattress, the heads aligned along the right-hand edge.

'Dear God!' I gasped. 'Children!'

· 6 ·

LAVEDRINE PICKED HIS way to the bed with infinite care.

'Who are they?' he whispered across the void, as if his voice might wake them up. The *Grande Armée* could have marched in at the casement window and exited down the staircase, trumpets blasting, fifes a-piping, drummer-boys beating their hearts out, without any risk of disturbing those three tiny corpses.

I heard Mutiez rummaging in his satchel, then the crackle of paper being unfolded. Every sound seemed to be abnormally magnified.

'It wasn't easy, sir. Not at this time of night,' he whispered back. 'Count Dittersdorf had to send his men to find the clerk and tip him out of bed. The family name is Gottewald. The victims are registered as Helke, Martin, and the smallest, Ludwig, eleven months old. The children of Bruno Gotte-wald, first major in the Eighth Hussars. The father has been stationed out in Kamenetz, East Prussia, for the past four months. The family has been in Lotingen for five. He was sent here from Eischen-Luslau, but they moved him on again. And there's the name of the mother, Sybille Gottewald.'

'Where is she?' Lavedrine asked, staring intently at Mutiez. 'Is there no other room in the house?'

'Just the kitchen, this bedroom, the closet over there,' he pointed. 'A privy built onto the side of the house, but there's nobody . . . No *body*, I mean to say.'

I dragged my eyes away from the bed and the rust-red spatter marks that had soaked into the pale ochre walls and ceiling, and turned to Mutiez, who continued to scrutinise the information on that paper as if his life depended on it.

'Three dead children, and no adult?' I puzzled.

Mutiez nodded. 'The corpse of the lady . . . It's not in the garden. We've searched out there, sir. My men are spreading their net wider. All the roads out of Lotingen have been blocked.'

I stepped to Lavedrine's side, and looked down on the corpses.

'These children were too young to be left alone. She *must* be here. Or else . . .'

'She's been carried off,' Lavedrine concluded, air popping from his mouth like smoke from a volley of pistols. He stared accusingly at Mutiez, as if the fact that the children were dead and abandoned was the officer's fault. 'Well, Henri? What are our chances of catching him? Of finding her?'

Mutiez raised his hands in a gesture of inadequacy. 'Hard to say, sir. The woodsman reported finding the children, but he didn't say a word about the mother. He'd seen her here in the afternoon, carrying water from the well. He was the last person to see them alive.'

'Do you suspect the man?' Lavedrine asked.

'That's not for me to say.'

'But you do suspect him, don't you?'

Lavedrine leant over the bed, breath rising up above his head like a surging ectoplasm. He bent closer, studying spots of blood that had soaked into the cotton counterpane covering the bodies.

'If you're asking for my impression, sir,' Mutiez began, 'I *do* suspect him. He admits having seen the three children and the woman. He must have known that there was no man in the house. When we searched him, we found an item which could only have come from here. A scent bottle. That man has never smelled *eau de Cologne*. He hardly looks human. A sort of raving wild man, sir.'

'The sort who might commit a crime such as this?' Lavedrine added.

'Would any normal man do such a thing?'

'He entered the house,' I summarised, ignoring this outburst. 'To steal? To rape? In either case, why kill the children? And why carry the body of the woman somewhere else, alive or dead? Above all, why go to town and flaunt the curfew, knowing he'd be stopped by the first soldier he met? It sounds improbable . . .'

'Wait till you see him. One look will change your mind.'

'The mystery remains, lieutenant,' I said. 'Before going into town, he had to dispose of the mother. If he was capable of *this*,' I waved my hand above the massacre, 'he would hardly shrink from murdering her, or carrying her off. But where would he hide her?'

'My men are searching in the forest,' Mutiez replied. 'He has a hut in the woods. She may be there.'

'And if she isn't?'

Mutiez shrugged and looked away.

Lavedrine broke the lingering silence.

'Procurator Stiffeniis is convinced that you are taking the easy way out, Henri, because you have no better suspect.' The Frenchman did not wait for a reply, as he lowered his lamp to examine the severed throats of the children. 'Procurator Stiffeniis is asking himself whether we are interested in this fellow for no better reason than that he is *Prussian.'*

Lavedrine had read my thoughts.

'That isn't true,' Mutiez protested. 'My fear is for the consequences. Things are tense already. When I knew that Prussian children had been slaughtered, I advised the Count to set up a joint investigation.'

He looked at me pointedly.

'I am not seeking a scapegoat. I have simply related my suspicions, as an officer should. That man admits entering the house. He points his finger at no one else. There were no French patrols around last night. No one reported sighting rebels in the area. It's in everyone's interests to clear this matter up. With all the cards laid plainly on the table. Count Dittersdorf shares my view, I assure you.'

'In a nutshell, we must work together to find him guilty,' Lavedrine observed with a wry smile. 'Politics makes our business urgent, but we will need cold hearts and clear minds to make sense of this butchery. Let's start.'

We held up our lanterns, and the shadows slid down the wall like retreating assassins. My shoulder brushed Lavedrine's. The children had been laid out face upwards across the mattress, a white counterpane covering their bodies. The child nearest to me, head and long hair dangling back over the edge of the mattress, was the girl. Her nose was thin and long, her cheeks sucked in by the sudden agony. There was a pale yellowish pallor to her skin. Her eyes stared back to a point where the wall and ceiling met. They seemed to express surprise, rather than fright. That was my impression. It was cold in the room, the fluid surface of her eyeballs flashed brilliantly with every shift of light. Her lips were parted, the tongue protruding from between sparkling white teeth. On the extreme tip was a globule of something that looked like sticky strawberry jam.

I bent closer.

'Congealed blood,' Lavedrine explained, moving his forefinger above the child's face, never once touching her. 'A clot of formidable proportions. It must have curdled almost instantaneously.'

I looked away, reminded of my own children's insatiable desire for strawberry preserve. Manni would stick out his tongue at Süzi, trying to frighten his sister, giggling and spluttering, spitting chunks of jellied fruit onto his chin.

'It came from here,' Lavedrine added. 'The blood surged upwards from the throat. This clot fell short, being heavy.'

His finger traced an arc from the windpipe to the tongue. From the instant we entered the room, I had found it hard to tear my eyes from those massive gashes at the children's throats. The wounds were unsightly. A stroke from right to left, narrow and incisive where the knife had entered, wider, larger, more hideous where it had pulled against the muscles on its way out. Blood had gushed up like wine from a barrel split with a sharp axe, and left a curving trail of spots on the low ceiling, larger at one end, thinning to infinity at the other. The slanting light of early morning tinted the larger droplets a dark blue against the yellow wash of domestic colouring. Was that the last thing the child had seen? Her life's blood spouting in the air like a fountain?

'There's no sign of a weapon,' I said.

'The killer took it away with him,' Lavedrine replied distractedly. 'Or used a knife from the kitchen. We can look, but blades don't speak.'

He turned and looked at me.

'Have you noticed how little blood there is?'

There was too much of everything in that tiny room for my taste.

'I'd have expected more,' he continued. 'On the floor, for example.'

As the first flush of daylight swelled, the traces of blood on the wooden floorboards to the right of the bed, a crazed puzzle of black streaks and slither marks, began to turn a dull shade of brown.

'Do you know how much a body contains?' he enquired calmly. 'A child holds enough to fill several wine bottles.'

'What are you suggesting?'

'It may have soaked into the mattress,' he replied, beginning to peel back the bedspread, lifting the corner nearest to the pillow, pulling it away in a triangle as he moved in front of me towards the foot of the bed.

'Heavens!' I whispered, as the bodies lay exposed and the yellow lamp-light danced on the cold, sallow surface of the flesh.

The nightshirts of the boys had been pulled up to their chests. Their tiny penises had been neatly cut away, and laid out in orderly fashion on a pillow at the bottom end of the bed like two small slugs.

Mutiez's angry hiss broke the shocked silence.

'That damned woodsman . . .'

'Later!' Lavedrine snapped. 'The boys were cut, but the children were dead already. No blood has flowed from those wounds. Only from the throats . . . And yet, even then, there's no great quantity, given that three murders have been committed. The mattress is more or less dry. It is almost as if the blood has been carried away.'

Lavedrine hesitated, considering the immensity of what he had just supposed.

'Like the mother,' I reminded him. 'She has to be found. That must be our immediate concern. She may still be living.'

Lavedrine nodded in agreement.

'My men are combing the woods,' Mutiez reported. 'And the hunter can do no further harm in Bitternau. If she can be found, they'll find her.'

'The house must be sealed off until we can examine it more carefully,' I said to the lieutenant. 'Nothing is to be moved, or taken away. This is most important. The corpses should be stored in a cold, dry place until the father is found. He will decide where he wants to bury them.'

'Follow those instructions to the letter, Henri,' Lavedrine said, as he moved around the room, minutely inspecting everything.

I went downstairs again to retrieve the charcoal and paper that I had dropped coming up. Then I began to make a plan of the room, showing how the furniture was positioned. From different angles, I rapidly sketched the children. I heard Lavedrine opening and closing cupboards and drawers, dropping down on his knees to look under the bed. Grunts of disappointment signalled his findings as he passed into the small adjoining room, where he repeated his search.

Before long, he was at my side again.

'Next to no furniture. Some shoes and gowns,' he muttered. 'Some children's clothes. A cot next door, but very little else.'

He stood by my shoulder, watching as I put into practice the teachings of Immanuel Kant, drawing everything I thought would be of relevance. Meanwhile, his glance darted around the room, a bemused expression on his face. 'There is something odd about this house,' he murmured. 'But I cannot put my finger on it.'

I stopped drawing and looked up.

'Perhaps you Prussians are used to a more simple, spartan way of life than us,' he said. 'A family with three young children. So few things.'

'The father is a soldier,' I replied. 'You ought to know from experience. They never carry much, or stay in one place long.'

'Something is missing, I'm sure of it.'

'I kept a close watch, sir,' Mutiez spoke out. 'None of my men has taken a thing.'

'Don't worry, Henri,' Lavedrine cut him off. 'That is not my meaning. I am struggling to understand what has happened here.'

Suddenly, he dropped to his knees on the far side of the bed, straining to see something, moving his lamp about, angling it beneath the window sill. 'What do you make of this?'

I went across and knelt beside him, straining to see.

'Blood,' I said.

He huffed impatiently. 'Why here, beneath the window? These marks are not spots or drops. They don't appear to be accidental. It's as if they had been made by somebody.'

I looked more closely.

There was nothing natural about the blood on that rough plaster surface, unlike the blood that had dripped to the floor, or spattered in a spray on the walls and ceiling. 'How would such an abundance of blood reach this remote location, so far away from the bodies?'

'It is physically impossible,' he said, his gaze unwavering.

Professor Kant insisted that no detail should ever be ignored, or attributed to chance. I had made a passable series of sketches, but greater accuracy was required in this instance. I could have pressed paper against the blood, hoping to obtain a transfer of the impression, but I was hesitant to do so. The mark might be irreparably damaged in the process.

'We can make a closer examination later on,' I said. 'We'll do it better in the light of day . . .'

Down below, boots crashed loudly on the pavement of the kitchen, interrupting our scrutiny of the bedroom wall. A loud voice called out the name of Mutiez. 'We've found it, sir. A cabin in the woods. A mile from here.'

'What about the woman?' the lieutenant shouted back from the top of the stairs.

But Lavedrine was already rushing past him, clattering down the stair-ramp.

'There is no time to lose!' he urged.

· 7 ·

WE ADVANCED AT a jog-trot in single file.

Spruce trees formed a shallow canopy, blocking out the light. The tangled undergrowth became thicker, wilder, ever more treacherous, thorns and hip-rose bushes catching and pricking at our hands and clothes. A lashing branch had caught Lavedrine in the face, tracing a row of tiny bloody droplets beneath his left eye. The pale winter sun had crested the horizon an hour before, but we were obliged to keep our lanterns lit.

Lavedrine, Mutiez, the troopers who had taken me captive, two more who acted as guides. I brought up the rear, my head a jumble of thoughts. Three hours earlier, I had been sleeping in my own warm bed. Now, I was trudging through the sort of inhospitable wilderness that cropped up so often in the tales that Lotte told the children when it was time for bed. Her forests were full of witches, ogres and hobgoblins, places where magic and trickery abounded. There was something dreamlike about the forest at that hour. Frosted leaves crackled and crunched beneath our boots as we moved over the frozen ground. If a branch snapped, it sounded like the crack of a musket, and raised raucous cries of protest from rooks nesting high in occasional bare oak trees which towered above the evergreen pines. For the rest, apart from the occasional hoot of an owl, or the cooing of a partridge, all was silent and still.

Even the soldiers seemed to have lost their tongues. Mutiez was the first to break the silence. He spoke to the man in the lead, then announced that we had ten minutes' marching ahead of us. No one else had a word to say, nor any wish to say it. The memory of what we had seen in that cottage had seized hold of our minds. But as we pressed on through the all-pervading smell of decaying leaves, bog-moss and deer-musk, a number of questions troubled me. Why would a salaried officer in the Prussian army leave his wife and children in such a godforsaken part of the countryside? Why take himself off so quickly to Kamenetz? Could he find no better refuge for his family? Surely, they would have been safer inside the barracks, or in one of the requisitioned houses set aside for officers in the poorer part of town. What had attracted Gottewald to that cottage? And how would he react to the news? Would he blame himself for what had happened? Had he put the safety of his loved ones at risk for the sake of his career?

'Are you sure we're going in the right direction?'

The voice of Mutiez brought me to earth with a bump. We halted in a glade, surrounded on all sides by skeletal trees which reached up to the leaden sky, shielding us from the biting wind. The smell of decay was stronger there. The man in the lead looked left and right. He seemed unsure of his bearings.

Lavedrine turned to me.

'Is this going to take much longer?' I asked.

'God knows!' he murmured, shaking his head. 'The guide's been sniffing the air for the past ten minutes.'

He raised his nose to the damp air, closed his eyes, and twitched his nostrils.

'There *is* a trace of something, though,' he said. 'Can you smell it?'

I stared into the forest gloom. The atmosphere was dominated by the mouldering damp of the earth and decaying leaves which lay thick on the ground. But beneath it all, there was the merest trace of a stench.

'Sweet and penetrating,' he suggested. 'Something organic left to putrefy above the ground.'

As the breeze shifted quarter, that stench seemed to vanquish every other vegetable essence, like the cloying miasma that issued from the town drains in summer.

Had we stumbled on the corpse of Frau Gottewald?

'Over there, sir,' the lead soldier informed Mutiez, and led the way at a run towards a thicket which seemed to float above a waving sea of pale green nettles and brown decaying ferns.

'The smell of shit drew us here, sir,' the guide announced. With a mirthless laugh, he added, 'Gournier has a nose for it. Heaved his guts all over the place.'

Trooper Gournier, a fat, red-faced man, cursed fiercely beneath his breath, but hung back as we moved around the perimeter looking for the entrance.

'Worse than the camp privy after the battle!' the lead man prattled. 'We were told to bring you gentlemen here, sir. No one said a word about going in again. There's the entrance. Can we take a blow, sir?'

Mutiez hissed something harsh between his teeth, and the men dropped down on their haunches, unscrewing the caps of their tin bottles, pulling out smoke-stained pipes from their leather pouches.

An expression of resigned disgust on his face, Mutiez turned to

Lavedrine and myself, and made a sign to follow as he pushed aside a roughly woven gate of branches and twigs and led the way into the compound. Inside, the smell of rottenness was overwhelming. I raised my scarf, veiling my nose from the vapours, which hung in the air like a plague. Lavedrine reached for the hem of his cloak, while Mutiez held his *képi* to his face like a mask as we advanced on a mound in the centre.

A mass of sticks like an unlit bonfire had been raised in the clearing. It might have been an otter's lodge, but there was no water nearby. And it was six feet tall. Long branches had been raised to form a skeleton, the frame dressed with sticks, mud, leaves, and ferns. There was method in the construction. The pieces of wood diminished in size as the edifice rose to a point, where a mesh of willow canes bound the lot together. I had read that the savages in Canada made shelters of this sort. Signs of the hunter were everywhere. Animal skins in various stages of curing or decomposition, pieces of meat—some fresh, dripping blood, others black and rotten—dangled from nooses thrown into the branches overhead, then tied fast to the trunks lower down.

As we moved around, looking for a way inside, the stench grew overpowering. Severed heads had been impaled on pointed sticks. I recognised the curved tusks of a boar, a black bear, the striped muzzle of a large badger, the rotting head of a lynx, but could not put a name to others. They reminded me of the hideous gargoyles the French used to decorate their Gothic cathedrals. But this blood was real, the eyes glazed, the yellow teeth long and sharp.

'What sort of beast would live in such a manner?' muttered Mutiez, turning to me. 'Will this convince you, sir?'

I did not reply, but forced myself to examine the trophies attentively, noting the worms and maggots that wriggled and squirmed inside the eye sockets and muzzle of the boar.

'He is quite a hunter,' I said.

'A prodigious supplier to the company cook . . .'

The lieutenant's voice faded away, a grimace twisted his face.

'What's up, Henri?' Lavedrine enquired. 'Wondering whether the meat from these things ended up on your plate?'

I could not shake free of the belief that what we had seen in the house, what we were seeing there, were related episodes in the same nightmare. The mutilation of the children and this butchery were the work of the same remorseless hand. My heart sank at the thought of finding Frau Gottewald. Whatever Durskeitner was, his predatory nature seemed no different from that of the beasts he trapped and slaughtered. I shrank with shame to think that he was Prussian.

'Shall we go in?'

Lavedrine narrowed his eyes and glanced at me.

'I am ready,' I said, hiding behind a show of boldness, taking paper and graphite from my satchel, though my hands were shaking.

Mutiez pulled aside the wicket gate and bent low. He seemed to think twice, as if some obstacle prevented him from going further. The creaking of the door had set off a barrage of noise inside, as if a thousand devils were eager to escape from Durskeitner's hell.

He drew his sword and dashed in. Lavedrine and I followed him.

Our lanterns illuminated a scene that I will never forget. The hut was crammed with roughly made wooden cages. On one side, squirrels, moles, ferrets, hedgehogs, rats, and voles. Against the other wall, animals of potentially greater dimensions, though they were all extremely young: a deer, three snarling lynx kittens, a baby bear, three infant badgers, a dozen fox cubs, and many another creature. Along the far wall, cages full of birds were piled precariously one upon another. Twittering sparrows, tits, blackbirds, crows and starlings. A young kestrel or kite, which was nursing a broken wing. Before we finished that morning, I had counted fifty-seven cages in the menagerie. All these creatures began to cry out in fear, showing off sharp teeth and baring their claws, while some began to squabble in their cages, snarling and snapping at one another, as if our arrival had signalled the start of a fight to the death.

Lavedrine ventured into the corner, pointing out a bed of moss, complete with torn and filthy blankets thrown roughly to one side. Above this nest, a French military jacket was hanging from the wall on a peg, together with a collection of ropes and cords of different lengths and thicknesses, and a pair of hats roughly fashioned from fur.

Turning back towards us, Lavedrine raised his hand and gently touched the skeleton of a bird that had been suspended from the roof by a piece of twine. Wings outspread, as if in flight, it began to spin wildly. Above our heads, a flock of dead birds shifted and twisted on the currents of cold air that entered by the door and escaped through gaps in the walls.

Taking care that my mantle did not touch the unsavoury mixture of mud and excrement, I half-knelt on the floor to make a rough sketch of the layout of the place.

'What do we know about this man?' Lavedrine asked above the noise, making a circle of the room, gazing into each cage as he passed, bending low to peer into the least accessible.

'Not much, sir,' the officer replied, looking nervously around him. 'He may have told the guards something since I left him, of course.'

'Let's hope so,' Lavedrine continued, but he did not seem convinced.

He reached above his head and set another skeleton spinning. The bird seemed to come to life, trying desperately to make its escape. 'Corvus nigro,' he added with a thin smile. 'A scavenger and pest. One of the largest birds in Europe. This one died, or was killed, before it grew.' He glared at Mutiez. 'Does the hunter know anything about Frau Gottewald's fate, do you think?'

I gave over attempting to represent the chaos. For the sake of clarity, I had limited my sketching to a rough indication of the general layout of the hut, adding a word here and there—birds, vermin, and so on—to indicate what was contained in the cages, more as a show of methodology than a useful exercise.

'Do you doubt that he's guilty?' I asked.

Lavedrine shrugged. 'What have we got here? Dead animals, but no dead woman.'

His attitude continued to puzzle me. What did he want? A Prussian had been captured, a man that even the most patriotic of his countrymen would judge to be a criminal type. Animal-skinners, bone-merchants, men who handled the carcasses of animals—with the exception of licensed butchers—belonged to the lowest social class. Durskeitner lived from hand to mouth, trapping game, slitting throats, stripping the creatures of their fur, trading their meat for a crust of bread. On the evidence we had seen, he was a reprobate who went further than his sordid trade required. He lopped off heads, and stuck them on poles. A savage. He had admitted entering the house, seeing the corpses. Did Lavedrine see fit to defend a monster who had cut the throats of three children, sexually mutilating two of them into the bargain?

'This hideaway is close to the house,' he continued. 'Durskeitner must have passed there often on his way to town. He sells fresh game to anyone willing to pay, or barter.' He raised his hand and set another skeleton spinning. Looking pointedly at me, he asked: 'Would Frau Stiffeniis swap carrots for a fresh rabbit from a poacher that she knew?'

Mutiez held up the palms of his hands. 'Et voilà! He saw the woman. Some violent passionate impulse possessed him. Then, he eliminated the witnesses.'

'And mutilated them after death,' Lavedrine reminded him.

Mutiez scratched his head.

'Just wait till you see him, sir.'

Lavedrine laughed, clapping his hands sharply, which set the animals off in a frenzy of scuffling and rustling again. 'Is that what you think, Henri? Sex? Let me ask you a question. I'd wager fifty francs on your answer. This renowned slayer of rats and mice is physically impaired, is he not?'

Mutiez stared at him, eyes wide open with surprise.

Lavedrine ploughed roughly on. 'Just look around you. This man is not only a hunter. These animals are a source of income, but that is not the principal use that they serve. He hoards these creatures, holds them captive, lords it over them. He is their king and master! Have you ever eaten a badger, Henri? The meat would kill you. A kestrel, or a rat? These animals are not all edible. There is a non-utilitarian principle at work here,' he added thoughtfully. 'They look well nourished, regularly fed. These beasts have been treated with care, I would say.'

Mutiez closed his right eye and sighted down his nose, as if to say: 'What in God's name are you thinking, sir?' But Lavedrine was looking pointedly at me.

Was he trying to impress me with his investigative skill? Was he telling me to keep to my place and leave the brainwork to him? There was a superior air about his way of thinking out loud that seemed to hint that whatever I had seen in Lotingen (or in Königsberg with Kant, for that matter), it was naught compared to the sights that *he* had seen and the cases he had solved in Paris. If that smile were a provocation, I ignored it. I had no intention of being drawn into a pointless discussion.

Even so, he had made a strong impression on me. Perhaps it showed on my face, for he said: 'Strange, don't you think, Stiffeniis? The man is physically hampered.'

'How did you guess?' Mutiez asked.

'It was not a guess,' Lavedrine replied. 'I simply interpret what I see, Stiffeniis. If you had observed the closeness of the cages to the ground, the small stature of these animals, you would have reached the same conclusion.'

I bridled at the mention of my name. He used it carelessly, the way a teacher calls the name of one to catch the attention of many.

'He only kills the largest specimens,' he continued. 'He skins them, chops them to bits, then impales the useless heads on stakes like so many scarecrows.'

'Is that what he uses them for?' I asked, won over by this clever interpretation of those horrid trophies. As a child, I remembered helping our serfs to plant their men of straw to frighten off the ravaging birds in my father's cornfields.

'Only the larger heads. They tell us that Durskeitner is an able hunter, and proud of his skills. Also, they frighten off scavengers that might feed on the fresh meat. Which brings us back to these cages.' Lavedrine walked along one row, running his fingers against the bars with a loud clicking sound as his nails struck the uprights. 'They contain animals that are small by nature, or in terms of maturity. So, what does he feed them on?' His finger suddenly stopped, pointing into a cage that held three lynx kittens who began to spit and snarl ferociously. These have been fed on meat. Fresh meat, and generously. There's still a good bit left inside the cage. Liver, by the look of it, and from a large deer, like the one hanging up outside. Each one of the carnivores—there are hundreds here—has been rewarded with a piece of meat from a larger animal. He treats them well, but when they outgrow his pleasure, he'll kill them, too. It is an endless chain, and Durskeitner exploits it like the dominator that he is. Can you see one single large animal inside the hut?'

Like children set loose on a treasure hunt, Mutiez and I began peeping into the cages. I would have liked to find the exception that brought his castle tumbling down, though I was disappointed.

'You're right, sir!' Mutiez cried excitedly, darting around the room.

If he were right, I asked myself, did the evidence prove that Durskeitner was the author of the massacre, or was Lavedrine convinced that the man was innocent? Something in the Frenchman's manner made me less than certain of his opinion. And in the course of his detailed disquisition on the arrangement of the animals, he had made no reply to the question that Mutiez had asked.

'What is this physical defect?' I asked.

'Are you asking me, or Mutiez?' Lavedrine replied with a sardonic smile. 'Do you trust my intuition, or must he tell us what he knows for a fact?'

'Before we entered the cottage,' I reminded him, 'you claimed to be able to read the signs at the scene of a crime by means of your senses alone. I should like to see this remarkable talent put to work, sir. Here and now. As you say, Mutiez will confirm the accuracy of your predictions.'

Was it a challenge? I suppose it was, yet I knew that I should have been grateful for his refusal to condemn a vagrant Prussian mole-catcher out of hand. Mutiez had said nothing to deny that he had touched on a remarkable truth. The die was cast against me. But it did not change the fact that I found the Frenchman's ability to deduce physical deformity in Durskeitner so disquieting.

What had he seen in that hut, that I had not?

'Procurator Stiffeniis is surprised by my hypothesis, Mutiez. He asks you to confirm or deny it. Durskeitner is deformed, is he not?'

Mutiez scratched his neck inside his collar, an embarrassed smile on his face.

'I . . .'

'Stop there!' Lavedrine cried out, taking a step towards him. 'Let us say that this man is *not* of normal height. Let's say that he is affected by "nanismus". By which I mean that he is a dwarf.'

Mutiez touched his side below the ribcage with the peak of his *képi*. 'This high, sir. If he'd lived anywhere else, he'd be entertaining kings. But here in Prussia, giants are revered.'

'I am right then. And for no better reason than his diminutive size,' Lavedrine concluded, raising his hands like a lawyer, 'you, Henri Mutiez, consider this Prussian dwarf to be guilty of slitting the throats of children and abducting women. Are you of the same opinion, Stiffeniis?'

Was Lavedrine convinced that I would defend Durskeitner despite the evidence, simply because he was a Prussian, like myself?

'One thing is certain,' I said. 'You do not believe in the thesis that you have just described. Some sixth sense leads you to deduce that Durskeitner is not like other men, but it does not tell you whether he is the murderer. Nor that he has carried off the mother.'

Lavedrine bunched his cheeks and let out a sigh.

'Exactly,' he said. 'I wish this sixth sense were a thousand times sharper. I might have solved a hundred crimes that have puzzled me.'

'If Durskeitner is innocent, I'll be surprised,' Mutiez interrupted.

'Remember what I have told you: there is purpose here,' Lavedrine went on. 'He kills animals for meat and skins. This is not senseless butchery. More to the point, he has not deflowered them afterwards. If Durskeitner, the dwarf, protects and nurtures the young, why in God's name would he murder three children?'

Lavedrine seemed to be engaged in a furious debate with himself, as if he had thought the argument through, but feared he might have reached the wrong conclusion.

'To possess himself of the mother,' I replied. 'To rape and kill her.'

Lavedrine shook his head, and looked around in silence, as if he might have missed some clue that would throw a shining light upon the matter. 'It makes no sense,' he murmured. 'No sense at all. There is something here that does not fit. Something incompatible with what we have seen at the Gottewald house. They are such different places . . .'

'If I may say a word,' Mutiez interposed. 'If she is dead and buried, she's somewhere here. With your permission, I'll have a squad brought up with spades. If we can find any sign of freshly turned soil, or leaves that have been shifted, we'll be well on our way to ending this mystery.'

'It will take time, but something may come of it.' He turned to me. 'What's your opinion, Stiffeniis?'

I nodded, my mind empty of any alternative proposal. 'I'd like to finish sketching,' I said. 'Then we should speak to the prisoner.'

'While you are busy, Mutiez will send for reinforcements, then he and I will make a more complete search of the hut and outlying land. We can send back anything of interest with the soldiers and make a more thorough analysis when we get back to town. Does that suit you?' The memory of Kant's macabre 'laboratory of crime' flashed through my mind: the human heads floating in glass jars, their clothes stored in boxes, a folder of drawings recording the exact position in which the dead bodies had been found. Lavedrine would have loved that harrowing place.

'Very well,' I said.

We divided our tasks, working for little more than an hour. I finished my drawings—seven sketches of the interior and exterior of the hut—while they went through the contents of two tin chests, finding nothing except for bits of clothes, worn-out shoes, and a rusted knife broken off at the hilt. Then, we retraced our path through the forest led by one soldier, while the others remained behind to guard the hut.

A phrase Jean-Jacques Rousseau had written jangled in my head.

He spoke of the 'delicious inebriation' he always felt while wandering in the woods near Paris. That morning, I had felt the violence that Nature can hide. I had had my fill of woods. My only desire was to return to my home, and the comfort of my wife and children.

· 8 ·

Franz Durskeitner was being held in Bitternau Fortress.

I stood with Count Dittersdorf by a window on the first floor, looking out on a courtyard on the northern side of the building. As we spoke, we watched French soldiers down below transporting bloody carcasses on their shoulders from a cart to the kitchen. Another man was pushing a handcart loaded with steaming intestines to a rubbish dump in the corner. The stench of boiled horse-meat and rotten cabbage was nauseating.

'Somebody will have to go to Kamenetz,' I said, my bones still aching from the chill of the woods. Lavedrine had raised the question as we returned to town. 'The father must be told.'

'Make sure the task falls to you, Hanno!' Dittersdorf urged. His voice was a hoarse whisper as he issued this command.

I wanted to speak, but he prevented me, laying his hand on my arm.

'Not now,' he hissed, barely moving his lips. His gaze shifted to Mutiez and Lavedrine, who were talking by the door. He squeezed tightly on my arm. 'For the love of God, they must be kept away from that place!'

I glanced towards the Frenchmen. 'That will not be easy, sir,' I whispered. 'Mutiez may send his own men. Lavedrine might want to go himself.'

Dittersdorf's other fist beat impatiently against my imprisoned arm.

'General Katowice is there,' he growled. '*You* will go, Hanno! Do I make myself clear?'

The Count's ferocity startled me.

'Hasn't he been put out to grass?' I asked. 'Katowice, and others like him?'

'The French are not so stupid,' Dittersdorf replied, *sotto voce*. 'They have left a number of minor fortresses under our jurisdiction for the moment, but only to avoid swelling the ranks of the rebels, or pushing them into the open arms of Russia.'

He shrugged his shoulders. 'Sooner or later, the French will want to extend their dominion to every forgotten corner of the kingdom. General

Katowice hopes that it will be as late as possible. We should humour him, Hanno.'

'I'll do what I can,' I said, though I could not imagine what argument might be used to deflect Lavedrine if he had already made up his mind to go to Kamenetz.

'You must do better. Swear to me on the heads of your children.'

He broke into a sudden fit of coughing as Lavedrine left Mutiez alone and turned in our direction.

'If you've finished telling the Count what we saw in the woods,' the Frenchman said, 'we should interrogate the prisoner.' His gaze shifted to Dittersdorf, then drifted back to me. He half-closed his eyes, and smiled uncertainly. 'Unless you have both been inventing plots to frustrate the French oppressor? Was that the subject of your hushed conversation?'

Fearing that the pallor of Count Aldebrand's face might give the game away, I searched desperately for some distraction. 'We were just talking about Kamenetz, and the dangers of travel,' I said. 'The East is swarming with Prussian rebels. From a diplomatic point of view, it would be most embarrassing if an accident were to happen to a French officer on such a mission, don't you agree?'

A cloud seemed to darken Lavedrine's features.

'How long will the journey take?' he asked.

'Two days, if the roads are clear. Maybe more. Out there in the frozen wastes, *monsieur*, the difficulties are rife,' Count Dittersdorf replied vaguely, waving his hands in a gesture of helplessness to suggest the unseen dangers.

'He must be sent for!' Lavedrine exclaimed.

'*Brought*,' Count Dittersdorf insisted. 'Someone must go and fetch him. You cannot think to entrust such news to a messenger?'

I addressed myself to the Count, affecting an air of thoughtful concern for the Frenchman's benefit. 'If Durskeitner tells us nothing, what option do we have?'

No one spoke for some moments.

'I don't know how you'll take this, Stiffeniis,' Lavedrine began slowly, 'but you are Prussian. You'll be able to move more easily through Prussian-controlled territory than I could ever hope to do.'

Though his voice was flat and toneless, I detected a trace of a smile on his lips. Dittersdorf wanted me to go, and Lavedrine, for reasons of his own, was clearly of the same opinion.

'There may be advantages to the arrangement,' he added smoothly. 'The father will have to pass two days with you in the coach. With nothing else to talk about, he may suggest a motive, or provide a clue which will assist the investigation. If we sent a note, and the man arrived exhausted after riding all the day and half the night, anxious to find his wife and bury his children, we'd have to wait an age before he could be questioned.'

Lavedrine rested his hand very lightly on my arm.

'Would you mind going, Herr Procurator? I'll continue the investigation here, and we may confront our findings when you return. If luck is on my side, I will have found Frau Gottewald before then.'

'An ideal solution!' Dittersdorf exclaimed with a burst of enthusiasm. 'It clearly demonstrates Prussian willingness to cooperate with the French determination to clear the matter up. Stiffeniis, what do you say to that?'

'Whatever I discover in your absence,' Lavedrine assured me, 'will be attributed in the final report to the result of our joint efforts.'

'That's all very well,' I answered, my reluctance both real and pretended.

I was hoping that Durskeitner would tell us what we wanted to know, and that there would be no need for anyone to go to Kamenetz.

But Dittersdorf clapped his hands together.

'Your travel papers will be ready within the hour,' he announced.

'What about my wife and children?' I protested, as the enormity of the proposal sank in. 'A murderer is loose in Lotingen. Until he's taken, no one's safe.'

'I'll set a guard on the house,' Lavedrine suggested swiftly. 'Night and day.'

'Excellent!' the Count declared, his face flushing bright red, as if the blood in his veins had begun to circulate freely again. 'That's settled, then. I'll be waiting for you in my office, Stiffeniis.'

As Dittersdorf hurried away, Lavedrine, Mutiez and I cantered down the stairs to the basement. If everything above the ground was as splendid as a small provincial town hall would allow, the lower floor of Bitternau was a truer reflection of Lotingen after the invasion. Mutiez led us on down a long, narrow corridor which was dimly lit by candles. Though the walls had been whitewashed, they were scuffed and filthy. Six or seven closed doors of rudimentary manufacture on either side were marked with chalk. *Palais Royale, Saint Sulpice, Bastille*, I read. All the finest monuments in Paris. At the far end, a sergeant was sitting on a chair reading a letter. Another man was playing with a bayonet, dropping it from shoulder-height, attempting to hit a small rust-brown spot on the wooden floor. Prussian blood, I had no doubt. Splatter marks on the walls indicated what went on down there. In that small arena every man would hear the cries when a prisoner screamed out in vain for mercy as his interrogation took place.

At the sight of Mutiez, the men drew themselves up smartly.

'At ease,' he said. 'Is he still in there?'

The sergeant nodded to a door marked *Versailles*.

'You lead the questioning, Stiffeniis,' Lavedrine murmured. 'Be stern, un-bending. Cruel, if necessary. Durskeitner is a Prussian, after all. You know the old trick, friend and foe? Hammer him until he breaks.'

This suggestion took me by surprise. 'I'd have thought that *I* was the ob-vious friend,' I said.

He shook his head. 'That's what he'll expect. We must throw him off his guard. If one of his countrymen shows no pity, he'll believe there's no es-caping the responsibility for his crime.'

'If he has committed one,' I countered. 'Our aim is to find the woman.'

'Tell him that you know he has taken her,' Lavedrine insisted. 'Don't ask him, tell him. We want to know whether she is alive or dead, and where he has hidden her. Speak German. If he attempts to answer in dialect, stop him. I want to understand every word he says. Do you wish Mutiez to stay?'

Mutiez was convinced that Durskeitner was guilty. As we examined the hunter's lodge, he had almost persuaded me to share his belief.

'You and I alone,' I said.

'As you prefer, Hanno.'

His voice lingered thoughtfully as he spoke my name. He seemed to im-ply that we were friends, equals. Not invader and invaded, victor and loser. Certainly, not enemies. You and I will question this man together and dis-cover whether he is guilty, he seemed to be saying.

'No one else.' I nodded.

Lavedrine called Mutiez and whispered something in his ear. A vivid ex-pression appeared on the lieutenant's face. 'I'll prepare the *laissez-passer* for Monsieur Stiffeniis at once. Come to my office when you've finished here,' he said, as he turned the key and pushed hard against the prison door with the sole of his boot.

The heavy door crashed back on its hinges, heralding our entry into the cell. A three-legged stool lay on its side in a putrid puddle of liquid, like an island in the middle of a stinking lake. A tiny table had been pushed back against the wall to the left, a glass-stoppered bottle of yellow liquid resting on it. Franz Durskeitner lay on the flagstones, curled up on his left flank, facing the stone wall in the darkest corner of the room. He was naked, the flesh of his back bruised and black, his arms and buttocks streaked with blood. Mutiez and the soldiers had questioned him during the night. The French Revolution had altered nothing, I observed. They still tortured sus-pects. The same fate would be in store for any Prussian who crossed them.

'Get up,' I ordered, standing over the prisoner.

As he rolled away, then raised himself to his full height, I realised that al-though Lavedrine had been correct in general terms, Franz Durskeitner was strictly speaking not a dwarf. His head and upper body were as normal as my own, but his legs were short, his feet as small as those of a child of four or five years old. The man was a *lusus naturae*, one of Nature's cruel tricks. The unequal halves of two different bodies seemed to have been joined together to form him. Durskeitner stood in profile, warily taking us in through half-closed eyes, his hands hanging down to cover his private parts. His face was cruelly handsome, his nose long and straight, though it was encrusted with blood; his eyes as black as coal, piercingly direct, though all around was bruised and puffy. His chest was muscular, his arms thick and powerful.

'Sit on that stool!' I barked, playing the role assigned to me, while the creature shied away, raising his arms to protect his face, fearing another blow. As he dodged and feinted, his virile member swayed and shook between his tiny legs. It was entirely normal both in length and appearance, the pink-brown colour of an earthworm. Indeed, it was somewhat larger than the norm. As he sat down, it lay on his shrunken white thigh like a preposterous snake.

'What is your name?'

Durskeitner did not answer. He stared at me in a surly fashion, then glanced at the bottle on the table. He seemed to expect nothing but pain, and more pain to follow. His broad chest was a mat of sizzled hair, burnt and corrugated skin, open wounds. They had sprinkled him with acid, and a stick or knife had been used to probe the folds of his weeping flesh. In the coming days he would suffer the torments of hell whenever anything, even the slightest current of air, caressed his skin.

'You are suspected of murder,' I said in German. 'You are going to hang from a tree very shortly. But before you die, you are going to confess.'

Durskeitner looked up sharply, but did not say a word.

'Do you understand me?' I said, raising my voice. 'The only way to end your suffering will be to tell the truth. Then, we will put you out of your misery.'

The prisoner looked down at the floor, but he did not flinch.

Suddenly, Lavedrine stepped forward, shrugged off his shawl, and held it out to Durskeitner. 'I do believe the man is as shy as a mouse,' he said to me in French.

At first, the prisoner appeared to think that this unexpected act of humanity was a heartless ruse. Durskeitner turned away and retreated to the corner of the cell, where he hid his face against the wall. Lavedrine followed him like a solicitous lover, muttering reassuring words, gently settling that long woollen wrap on the man's shoulders, helping him to cover his body with the heavy material. And all the while, sounds of distress came from the prisoner's mouth as the rough wool rubbed and caught against his injured flesh. Despite his pain, he turned to the Frenchman and uttered his first words.

'Thank you, sir,' he said.

As he returned to his place, Lavedrine nodded at me to continue the attack.

'Why did you slaughter those children?' I demanded.

Durskeitner hunched forward, and his eyes locked into mine. The veins stood out on his neck like thick ropes. 'I'd never touch the little ones,' he cried.

'You did more than that. You slit their throats. You mutilated two of them. Then you carried off their mother,' I said in a stern, expressionless tone of voice. 'You will die for these crimes.'

Like Mutiez, I dared to hope that this was the beast that we were looking for.

'You have nothing to fear from us, I promise you,' Lavedrine interposed.

Durskeitner raised his eyes as the Frenchman edged closer. He seemed to tower above the suspect, though there was nothing menacing in his stance.

'We are only interested in the truth. Just tell us why you killed those children. And where you've hidden the woman. Then you can go back home to the forest,' he said, a note of complicity in his voice. 'You can go on as you always have, Durskeitner. I promise you that nothing will change.'

The prisoner's mouth sagged open, as if he were unable to believe what Lavedrine had said. Everything would be as before? On condition that he told us what he had done with the woman? Something in his expression altered: I could see that he believed those lies. Weren't the French in charge? If one of them told you that nothing would happen, it might just be so. These thoughts raced madly through my own head, and I saw the effect that they had had on Durskeitner. He believed them. He began to sob, his eyes fixed on Lavedrine.

'Where is she?' Lavedrine asked gently. 'Where have you hidden her?'

Would he tell Lavedrine what he had done, believing himself safe in the hands of the enemy? Immune from the authority that I represented? A wave of anger swept over me. I would give him a better reason to speak.

'We've seen your abode,' I snapped. 'The animals in cages.'

I leaned closer, staring into his face.

'We'll kill them. Every single one of them. We'll cut their heads off, and impale them all on sticks. Or burn them alive. That's what we'll do, Durskeitner. Unless you tell us the truth.'

I saw the horrified stare that appeared on his face.

'Can you imagine that, Franz?' I hissed. 'Can you see them sizzling? Can you hear them? They are babies. They'll scream as their fur catches fire. They'll howl as their flesh begins to shrivel in the roaring flames!'

That was the power I wanted him to feel. Fear of Prussian might, not the ambiguous hope of a French pardon. I heard Lavedrine clear his throat, and realised that he was looking incredulously at me.

Durskeitner opened his mouth and let out a roar. He hugged himself tightly inside the cloak. Every fibre of his body seemed to rebel against my threats. Despite his size, the man's strength was clearly immense.

'I did not touch them!' he shouted. 'I heard the shutters banging in the wind. I went to see, but they were dead. They were all dead.' He began to sob in wrenching cries. 'But I did not kill them!'

'You know how they died,' I insisted. 'You saw the bodies. After slitting their throats, you hacked off the sex of those two boys. That's what you do to animals, is it not?'

Durskeitner's face was a mask of incomprehension. I might have been talking French to him.

'Why did you mutilate the children?' I pressed.

'I did not!'

'We have seen those skeletons hanging in your hut,' I said. 'The meat outside. You can't deny the truth. You *enjoy* cutting flesh.'

The man's brow was a furrowed field. He mumbled incoherently, stuttered helplessly, searching for words that would never come, words that would prove his innocence of every accusation.

I glanced at Lavedrine, but he stood like a marble statue.

'Press him for intimate knowledge of the woman,' he hissed in French from the corner of his mouth.

'Did you sell Frau Gottewald meat?' I asked.

'A rabbit, a hare,' he said. 'But I never asked for money. I left them hanging on the door. As a gift for the children.'

'What was the woman like? Was she tall, or short? Blonde, or dark?'

Sweat and blood trickled off his brow, running down his face and neck in rivulets, but he did not heed my question.

'Well, Durskeitner?' I needled. 'What was she like?'

'Small,' he murmured at last. 'Small and black.'

It seemed to cost him a great deal, for he fell silent again.

'Black?' I echoed sarcastically. 'What do you mean?'

'Are you talking of the woman's hair, or her complexion?' Lavedrine intervened. Just as quickly, he qualified the question. 'Her skin, I mean.'

Durskeitner raised his eyes as if to thank Lavedrine. 'The hair,' he said.

'Describe Frau Gottewald's face,' I pressed on. 'Was she pretty?'

'Pretty?' he echoed, as if the concept was unknown to him.

I groaned with impatience. If the woman had been left alone in the forest, anything might happen to her. But suddenly, without any prompting, the prisoner spoke up.

'She was a good woman, that mother. Good to them babies.'

'What do you mean?' Lavedrine asked quietly. 'Did she keep her little ones safe?'

Durskeitner nodded vigorously.

'Who was she protecting them *from?*' Lavedrine coaxed. 'Was someone trying to hurt them? Can you tell us that? If you help us, we will try to help you.'

There it was again. That wheedling complicity grated on my nerves, as much as the reticence of the only witness we had. A witness, I reminded myself, who might well be the killer.

'That house was empty,' the prisoner said, staring up at Lavedrine with wide, unblinking eyes. 'Then, a family came. A soldier, a woman, three little babies.'

'Did anyone visit them?' I snapped. 'A stranger, or someone that you knew?'

'No one,' he muttered. 'Only them . . .'

He did not look at me. His eyes never shifted from Lavedrine.

'But the man went away, sir,' he continued. 'That mother was alone. There was no one to hunt for her. It isn't easy to feed so many cubs. That's why I left meat on the doorstep. But I never spoke to her. Not once! I'd creep up late at night, or very early in the morning, and leave a quail, or a cut of venison. She kept those babies safe from harm. She was a good mother.'

I let out a loud sigh at this prattling idiocy. The Gottewald family had been living in that cottage for months. The husband, too, until he was posted to Kamenetz. The woman had remained alone with the children after he left. Yet all that Durskeitner could decribe of this domestic scene was a mother feeding her young. She might have been a swallow carrying grubs to the chicks in her nest.

'So, you took it upon yourself to give them food,' I summarised.

'Yes, sir,' he replied, as if it were a fact requiring no explanation.

Silence followed, broken only by the irregular rasps of Durskeitner's breathing.

Throughout the interrogation, he had been seized by fits of shivering. There were pools of blood and water on the floor. Probably the soldiers had stripped him off, then thrown buckets of water on him. To wash him off, perhaps, or stop the bleeding. But also to intensify his suffering. The air was icy cold.

'You have hidden her somewhere, haven't you?' I said sternly.

Durskeitner did not move an inch. He might have turned to stone.

'Where is she?' I insisted.

The man looked back at me like a cornered deer.

'We can consider this interrogation over, I think.' Lavedrine spoke slowly, as if to make his meaning clear. I was not certain whether he was talking to Durskeitner, or to me.

'What do you mean?' I hissed.

I was confused. Was this another French trick?

Lavedrine did not answer. He stepped across to the door, and called for the guards.

'We have finished here,' he told the sergeant, adding that Durskeitner should be kept there in case we needed him again. 'Find him some clothes and a blanket. He has been treated harshly enough. I shouldn't wonder if he's dying of cold.'

Then, he walked out of the room without a backward glance.

I followed him, furious.

'I played the part you gave me,' I snapped at his back. 'That man has seen the woman. He knows what she looks like. Why stop now? He hasn't told us one single useful thing!'

Lavedrine turned to me with a show of amazement.

'That man kills animals,' he said. 'He skins them, cuts off their heads and hangs them up on poles. He may be a savage, but he would never hurt the young. He wouldn't drown a motherless kitten. Why waste time? Durskeitner has told us what he knows. It may not be what we hoped for, but that is it. He knows more about animals. He'd have trouble describing any human being. Frau Gottewald is small and dark, and she protects her children. He has told us quite a lot.'

Lavedrine looked down his nose at me.

'If you think that a cabin in the woods is enough to condemn him,' he continued, 'go ahead, declare the case solved. Similar evidence might be found in your house. Or in mine, if you prefer. Is this how you go about solving crimes in Prussia, Herr Procurator? If so, I thank the Lord that I am French!'

'Facing trumped-up charges from the Committee of Social Health?' I parried, unable to restrain my sarcasm.

Lavedrine stared coldly at me. 'I was tried by just such a parody during the Terror, Herr Procurator. Not even a Prussian should be subjected to a travesty of that sort. I am amazed that you would even suggest it.'

We stood face to face. My fists were bunched angrily at my sides. His arms were stiffly crossed. For the second time, we both came close to issuing a challenge that the other could not have honourably refused. And suddenly, I realised the idiocy of it. He, a Frenchman, was bent on defending a Prussian subject from summary justice, while I, a Prussian magistrate, could see no better way out of the impasse.

'That cabin means little, unless we find the woman,' Lavedrine went on more soberly, letting his arms fall. 'This interrogation alters nothing, Stiffeniis. Our enquiries must go ahead. With you to Kamenetz, while I stay here to search out Frau Gottewald. Or her corpse.'

He said all this without a trace of irony. I had the impression that he was taking my measure, drawing his own conclusions.

'My duty is to charge off like a messenger,' I said, tasting acid on my tongue, 'while you stay here, solve the case, and take the glory for yourself. Is that your plan?'

I felt sure that Dittersdorf had overstated the necessity for me to make the journey alone. What could Kamenetz contain which was unfit for foreign consumption? Would the might of Napoleon be intimidated by a fortress full of defeated Prussians in the middle of nowhere?

'My plan?' he echoed.

'To see me out of Lotingen as rapidly as possible,' I snapped.

'You surprise me, sir,' he said, eyeing me curiously. 'I had the distinct impression that you were scheming with Dittersdorf to get rid of *me*.'

We stood in silence for a moment.

'I did have a plan,' he said with a sudden smile. 'A more innocent one. I meant to take you home. Your wife will have passed a sleepless night. I wouldn't want her to think that you've been brutalised by the occupying army.'

'Do not trouble yourself on Helena's account,' I began to say.

'It is my sacred duty,' he interrupted, his sarcasm as finely grained as the crystals in a slab of porphyry. 'As an officer and a gentleman. Frau Stiffeniis must be told that we cannot get along without your help.'

· 9 ·

As I walked through the town with Lavedrine, one thought weighed on my mind.

How could I shield Helena from the truth?

I did not want to tell her of the murders, then announce that I must set off on a long, dangerous journey to the East. And yet, if she did not hear the truth from my lips, someone else might tell her. I would be away for four or five nights at the most. With Lotte's help, the secret might be kept until I returned. The maid would need to watch her tongue, but she could manage that. The most immediate problem was the Frenchman at my side.

Could I persuade Lavedrine to go along with my scheme?

He was in the best of humours. It was as if the corpses of those children had ceased to exist, as if they had melted away with the morning mist. He seemed disposed to chatter about every single thing that he saw. We stopped to watch a herd of cows pass by on their way to the slaughterhouse. Shopkeepers in white aprons were taking down their shutters, exchanging greetings. Their boys were washing the cobbles, shovelling up the warm droppings of the animals. He was delighted with them all.

'It's just like any other morning,' he said. 'No one knows yet.'

I did not reply.

Once the news got out, Lotingen would never be the same again.

'I love to watch a town wake up,' he declared, dragging me from my leaden thoughts. 'It tells you more about the place than any other time. More than the night, certainly. Darkness is the same wherever you go, but morning has a distinctive character. It's the same with passion. In the light of dawn, you discover who your companion of the night truly is. The 'sacred unmasking' is what I call it. Beneath the veil you may find ugliness or beauty, and sometimes both parts, equally mixed. Take Prussia, Stiffeniis. She is a slow-blooded peasant girl wrapped up in a military greatcoat. Not unlike my native Normandy, if I am honest. Look about you, this is the real Prussia.'

I looked without answering.

The real Prussia was standing on every corner. French dragoons with waxed moustaches, infantrymen with hair tied up in greasy pigtails, all clutching muskets and eyeing the people of Lotingen with suspicion.

'Frenchmen are in a privileged position,' he went on, seemingly oblivious to the fact that I was Prussian. 'We are free to travel, to know men and explore the world. And I am luckier than most. I know those men and see those places from a unique standpoint.'

He halted, as if he were intent on drawing me out of my silence.

'Which point of view is that?' I asked.

'Crime, Stiffeniis!' he enthused. 'We plumb the depths of human depravity, and set the upturned world to rights. We go exploring in a strange and secret terrain.'

In this rapturous mood, I found no opportunity to confide in him.

Shortly afterwards, we stopped at the administrative building next door to the town hall. The French had requisitioned it as their general quarters. Mutiez was comfortably set up in a large, bright office with an immense open fire on the first floor. His windows looked out on the tiny courthouse on the far side of the square, where I worked in the shadow of the oppressor.

The French *laissez-passer* had been prepared for my journey to the East, though Mutiez seemed tense when he handed it to me. 'The city seems quiet for the moment,' he said, a worried smile on his handsome face. 'God knows how long the peace will last. Our troops will be suspected of the massacre, I do not doubt. As you requested, the house is being guarded, the bodies have been removed. When are you leaving, Herr Procurator?'

'Stiffeniis is on his way home, Henri. To say goodbye to his wife, and collect his laundry,' Lavedrine put in, resting his hand on my shoulder as if we were long-standing friends. 'The most tiresome task falls to him. Speaking for myself, I am grateful.'

We left the building, and stopped next at the Old Temple Inn, an ancient and dilapidated edifice which had once been the courthouse of Lotingen. Hidden away in a dark and cluttered cupboard of a room, we found the district governor in all his tattered glory. The room to the left of the derelict entrance hall contained the only stove in the building that was functioning, and Count Dittersdorf had wisely reserved it for his own use. With a pile of logs in one corner, and stacks of papers and files in another, there was hardly room for the three of us. The smell in there was musty and foul, as if dead rats were rotting beneath the ancient floorboards, which was most likely.

Aldebrand Dittersdorf seemed put out when he found me in the presence of Lavedrine. We stayed no more than five minutes, as I took possession of a sum of money for the journey, and a Prussian letter-of-embassy which he had hurriedly prepared, signed, and stamped for me. His hand was shaking slightly, I noticed.

'I sincerely hope that this misfortune will not destroy our good relations, Colonel Lavedrine,' Count Dittersdorf said, choosing his words very carefully. He appeared to be intimidated, though whether on account of being discovered in such squalid surroundings, or the necessity of having to eat humble pie before the Frenchman, I could not tell.

Lavedrine replied with an ironic smile. 'In spite of what has happened . . . Because of it, indeed, all three of us may yet sit down to drink a glass of wine and celebrate the capture of the murderer. And very soon, I hope.'

While Lavedrine played the courtier, I looked quickly through the contents of the envelope that Dittersdorf had handed to me. He had barely said a word, but there was no mistaking his glance. Inside the letter of passport, I found a folded note. *For your eyes only* was scribbled on the paper. With a furtive flick of my forefinger, I read the contents. *May the Lord be your guide! In His infinite wisdom, may He open the gates of Kamenetz to no one but yourself.* He was still more concerned with Kamenetz and its secrets than he was about what had happened to the Gottewald family.

I slid the note back into the envelope as Lavedrine prepared to leave.

As we emerged into the street, he stepped straight up into a coach standing next to the kerb, a familiar coat-of-arms emblazoned on the door. 'This will do,' he declared. 'Give the coachman directions to your house.'

Count Dittersdorf's driver was shocked, but did not dare to challenge the Frenchman's rude requisitioning of his vehicle. He looked at me, clearly hoping that I, a fellow Prussian and the town magistrate, would spring to his defence.

'You know the road, Paulus,' I said. 'Your master will understand.'

Lavedrine settled back comfortably against the leather seat.

'Poor Dittersdorf,' he said. 'How will he bear up? The sky has fallen on his head. All the fine dinners in the world won't save him. He'll have his work cut out to keep the French and the Prussians from each other's throats. All his good offices have disappeared into thin air.'

The persistent good humour of my French colleague began to grate on my nerves.

'Before we arrive,' I began, my tongue as heavy as a stone, 'I must discuss a personal matter with you. I do not want my wife to know the truth. Not yet, I mean. Not while I am forced to travel. She has been through hell in the past year. I'm not sure how she may react to the news of children slaughtered in their beds, and a mother who has disappeared. I'll tell her everything the instant I return.'

For some moments, Lavedrine continued to gaze out of the carriage window.

'Do you think that's wise?' he asked quietly. 'I mean to say, in a town as small as this, it won't be long before the people talk of nothing else. Your wife will hear of it. It is a startlingly brutal crime. I don't see how you can hide the news from her.'

'I would prefer to tell her myself,' I insisted. 'But not today. Not now. She'll have spent a bad night, believing that I've been abducted. And like the Gottewalds, we have three young children. The youngest was born two months ago. It has not been easy. And now, I am obliged to go away.'

He turned to face me. His brows creased into a frown as he brushed the shock of grey curls from his forehead.

'What am I to say?' he asked.

I had thought it through, and I told him exactly what I planned. The tale was plausible enough; it would explain the involvement of the French and the Prussians, and also the need for me to go to Kamenetz. I intended to tell her that a messenger from the fortress had been killed in Lotingen, and that a local magistrate would be obliged to look into the Prussian side of the case.

'Half lies, half truth,' Lavedrine observed caustically. 'I will tell the truthful half, if that is what you want.'

I felt relieved. At least in part.

Lavedrine looked out of the window, but the discussion was not over. With careless ease, he managed to penetrate to the heart of the matter. That is, the part which was still troubling me. 'What will happen if Frau Stiffeniis goes to visit friends?' he asked. 'Or shopping in the market square with her children?'

'Helena will not leave the house. Except with me,' I said. 'Since the invasion, my wife has . . . changed. It is as if she is plagued by all that has happened, by all that may yet occur. She put on a show of bravery last night when she thought that Mutiez had come to arrest me, but God knows what was going through her mind.'

Lavedrine sat back and let out a sort of groaning sigh.

'I am sorry,' he said. 'Times like these are hard on women. War is worse for them, I think, than it is for us. Men skate nimbly over the surface of things; women do not. I have always held that opinion. And if I had not, there was a person who would have brought the matter to my attention. I was married once myself. Though not for long . . .'

I had no desire to trade information from his private life for details of my own. I cared not who Madame Lavedrine might have been, nor what had come between them. Helena was my only concern.

Paulus brought the coach around the final corner, the horses began to canter down the gentle slope towards my house, and I looked anxiously out of the window. The sight that greeted my eyes was a balm to my spirit. Lotte had washed the linen and hung it out to dry in the garden, as she always did on a Tuesday. White sheets and shirts billowed in the wind like bunting to welcome me home.

But as the carriage rattled to a halt on the gravel in front of my gate, the exact spot where Mutiez had parked his vehicle the night before, I was obliged to think again. The door flew open, as if Helena had remained on guard behind the peephole all night long, and she came running madly down the path to meet me. She had replaced her nightgown with the light-grey worsted dress and brown apron that she wore about the house, but she was not herself. Her hair was her ensign. The fact that she had not troubled to tame her wild locks and tie them up tightly at her neck, as she always did, spoke louder than any declaration of her true state of mind. She would never allow herself to be seen by any person, except myself, in such an unkempt manner. That tormented, angry bramble of bouncing chestnut curls flew from side to side as she ran towards me.

'Hanno! Is it really you?' she cried with almighty sobs.

As she pronounced the final word, she threw herself into my open arms, nearly knocking me to the ground. I felt her warm tears on my neck, her lips hot and trembling against my cheek. Murmuring half-finished words of thanks to God, and words of hate for all the French, she kissed me wildly on the nose, the mouth and eyes. The thought that Lavedrine was watching hampered my responses, and I drew up stiffly, catching her wrists, struggling to hold her still, while trying to calm her.

Suddenly, glancing over my shoulder, Helena froze.

'Not alone?' she whispered, her eyes bright with terror.

Before I could reply, Lavedrine stepped down from the coach.

'I hope you will excuse this intrusion, Frau Stiffeniis,' he said. 'Do you remember me, I wonder? We met at Count Dittersdorf's.'

Helena stared at him, catching at her lower lip with her teeth. In the sullen silence, her questioning glare turning into a troubled frown. I knew that look too well. I had seen it often. Since the day when news of Jena had reached town, and we began to prepare for flight, that dour expression had become habitual. Those dark chasms appeared on either side of her mouth again, scarring her cheeks. It must have been clear to any man that she was frightened of him.

'I came to offer my apologies, *madame*,' Lavedrine said quickly. 'I was carried off last night in the same rough manner as your husband. I thought my hour had come. But as you can see, we are both safe and in the best of spirits.'

Helena swelled up.

'I doubt that you were half so frightened,' she answered sharply. 'You are French, sir. You have not suffered what we have been obliged to suffer.'

Lavedrine smiled and spread his arms in apology.

'Could I ever hope to deny that you are right? But here is your husband, Frau Stiffeniis. Living proof of what I say. He is well, as I told you, and stronger than he has ever been before. If he was precious to Prussia alone, he is now worth his weight in gold to France.'

Helena turned her gaze on me, her eyes wide and questioning, and I wondered whether Lavedrine had gone too far. What did such flattery mean, she seemed to ask. I guessed how little disposed she was to talk to any Frenchman after the terror of the night and I knew how dangerous she considered Lavedrine to be after our public wrangle at the Dittersdorf feast. Now, I was obliged to inform her that he and I would be working in close liaison, that there would be many more meetings with the Frenchman, whether she liked it or not.

'What has happened, Hanno?' she asked. Her eyes looked deep into mine. They expressed an intensity of feeling that was wholly absent from her voice. 'Where did they take you? No one seemed to know at the police station.'

Lavedrine cleared his throat, as if to reply, but I spoke first.

'There has been a killing. French and Prussian troopers were involved. Colonel Lavedrine and I have been ordered to look into the matter,' I said, raising my hands to the heavens in a gesture of mock despair. 'No more than that.'

My greatest fear was that she would see through this protective wall of lies. How often in recent times had she caught me out with a penetrating stare, forcing me to tell her everything, no matter how cruel the truth was.

'No more?' she echoed, catching my tone exactly. 'How many men are dead?'

'Three,' I said. My chest felt heavy and strained, as if I had been forced to run. 'Two of them were Prussian,' I clarified. 'There's some confusion about how the fight broke out. I must speak to our men; Colonel Lavedrine will question their soldiers. As the laws of both our nations require. The matter should be settled within a few days.'

I was afraid that Helena would latch on to my embarrassment. I looked up at the sky, down at the ground, then at Lavedrine, as I told my tale. I scanned the far horizon, glanced at my pocket-watch, and straightened my cuffs, rather than look into her eyes. My son was four years old, yet even Manni was better at the business of lying. He would wolf down a piece of cake, then tell you doe-eyed—the crumbs and cream spattered all over his face and mouth—that he had not had *his* slice yet.

'Bien sûr, madame!' Lavedrine came to my aid. 'A few days. I only hope that there will be sufficient time for us all to become good friends,' he said jovially, clapping one hand on my shoulder, the other on my arm. 'I am greatly interested in the working methods of Procurator Stiffeniis. Who knows, your husband may even learn something useful from me in exchange.'

He turned in my direction, a sweet and amicable smile illuminating his face. We might have been two old friends recently reacquainted after a silly dispute, eager to put the past behind us. I glanced at the Frenchman, warning him not to go too far, smiling for Helena's benefit. I knew him well enough to fear his irony and incisive tongue. Even so, I had to appreciate the skill with which he played his part in placating my wife's fears.

Helena's hand reached for mine and gently pressed upon my fingers. It was a natural, assured gesture, apparently free of tension, and this impression was reinforced by the show of charm with which she turned and spoke to Lavedrine.

'Do you intend to step into our house, sir?' she asked.

Though this invitation was intended to be cordial, it sounded like a challenge. As if she were trying to gauge Lavedrine's true intentions. As if to remind me that this Frenchman was a dangerous interloper, capable of overturning our peaceful way of life, if he wished to do so.

'That is most kind,' he replied, narrowing his eyes. 'Another time, perhaps?'

I do not know whether Lavedrine had understood her motives, but his show of reluctance was a palpable flag of truce. It seemed to declare quite openly that he had no further wish to intrude upon our privacy, and was ready to retire from the field.

'In my own defence, I insisted on coming for one reason alone, ma'am. To beg forgiveness for the discomfort to which you have been unreasonably subjected. I take the blame for myself, and'—he smiled ironically again—'for the Emperor Napoleon. I pray you will forgive us both. Now, I take my leave. You'll have had your fill of Frenchmen, I do not doubt.'

Before boarding Dittersdorf's waiting coach, he turned to Helena, swept an imaginary hat from his uncovered head, and made a gallant bow. His eyebrows knitted once more, and he added in a serious tone: 'I am your humble servant, Frau Stiffeniis. Do not hesitate to call me if I can be of any service.'

He jumped up, slammed the door, then spoke to me from the window.

'I will see you shortly, Stiffeniis. With good news, I hope, from one side or the other. I'll have them send a coach the minute I reach the town. That should leave you time . . .'

He said no more, but bunched his lips and widened his eyes in an expression that seemed to suggest that he might have said too much.

I waved my hand. 'Thank you, Colonel Lavedrine. I look forward to seeing you again. And, as you say, with good news.'

As Paulus cracked his whip and the carriage creaked into motion, Lavedrine appeared at the window again, moving his hand in an agitated circle above the crown of his head. 'Forgive me if I sound foolish. I do like your hair, Frau Stiffeniis,' he called back. 'It is *tout le mode*. The finest ladies in Paris favour the free and the wild this year, but your style is truly . . .' He struggled for a moment, searching for the phrase, then cried out with a laugh which was warm and genuine: 'Truly *à la Sturm und Drang!*'

Helena touched her hair thoughtfully, standing close beside me, as we watched the coach carry Lavedrine towards town. The instant the vehicle disappeared from view, she withdrew her hand and turned to me with great seriousness.

'Must I really go to him while you are away, Hanno?' she asked.

She gazed into my eyes. Her tone was dry, acidic. It did not sound like a question that required an answer. It was more of a rebuke.

'And where will *you* be?' she added.

Her voice was soft, suddenly tremulous. She appeared to be concerned for my safety, no longer angry for the trick that had been played upon her.

'I must go East. To Kamenetz fortress. General Katowice is there,' I said, adding detail to detail in the hope of persuading her that the soldiers I had mentioned earlier, the dead soldiers, were Prussians. 'Count Dittersdorf insists. I must bring back an officer who knew the victims.'

Her hand came up to rest on my elbow. 'You'll need to pack, Hanno. All your heaviest clothes. The wind here is raw, but out there, they say, it is the Devil's own work.'

While my bag was being prepared, I went upstairs and spoke privately to Lotte, warning her to take good care of her mistress while I was away.

'Do not let her out of your sight,' I said.

'I'll do my best, sir,' she replied somewhat hesitantly.

'Your *very* best, I beg you,' I urged her. 'Whatever you may hear in town, do not frighten Helena with it. I'll be back as soon as I am able.'

A short time after, the municipal coach arrived for me.

While my leather sack was being stowed away by the driver, I took leave of my family in the biting wind by the garden gate. The cheeks of the children were red and very cold. As I held them in my arms and kissed them, I tried not to think of the pale cheeks of the three small corpses I had examined the night before. In that moment, the notion that Lavedrine would keep a vigilant eye upon my wife and babies was a great comfort to me.

'God keep you safe out there,' Helena whispered, clasping me in her arms as if she never intended to let me free. 'May He lead you home quickly, bringing peace for us, and for all in Lotingen.'

I knew not how to respond, and held my tongue tightly in check. She seemed to sense that something bad had happened in Lotingen, something immense, which went far beyond the small-minded violence of rough soldiers.

'Promise me,' she urged. 'Take care out there.'

It was the third time Helena had used that expression.

I kissed her passionately on the lips, then drew away.

Suddenly, I felt sure that she was right. Kamenetz *was* out there. The coldest, the most forgotten place in Prussia.

·10·

BURAN BLOW! BURAN blow!
Bringing snow! Bringing woe!

I used to sing this rhyme when I was a little child, standing in a circle, holding the hands of my brother and my cousins. At the end of the song, we all fell down dead from the cold.

My father's serfs sang another version as they swung their picks and shovels.

Buran blow! Buran blow!
Bury Russians in the snow!

Sometimes it was the Russians, but they could just as easily be Poles, or Jews, depending on the political mood of the day.

The driving wind from the East began to batter the coach head-on shortly after I left Lotingen, and that song rang obsessively in my head as the afternoon wore on. To make matters worse, approaching Braniewo at dusk the vehicle began suddenly to jolt and jerk violently over the pitted surface of the highway. It was like being tossed about in a coracle adrift on the high seas. The keeper of the toll-bridge over the Mülder Canal informed me that fierce fighting had gone on along that road not many months before. Extensive damage had been caused by French cannon and Prussian mortars, then winter had come along to destroy what was left.

'All's wreck and ruin in the area, sir,' he said.

The inn in Braniewo, an ancient wattle-and-daub hovel, sagged in a state of near-collapse. But the potato soup was thick, the black bread crusty, and I washed it down with ale set sizzling with a poker in the company of my driver. His name was Egon Eis. I had never before seen his cratered moon-like face, though he knew me as the magistrate of Lotingen, he said, and we were forced to share the necessary confidences that plague the lives of travellers thrown together on the road. Coachman Eis told me that he was sixty-five years of age, and added that he had spent the last forty years on the box-seat of the civic coach.

There was nothing for it. I had to ask him how he got the job.

'Honourable conduct in battles, Herr Magistrate, sir,' he mumbled gruffly in reply, though which particular honours he had won, which battles he had fought in, he did not care to mention. Nor did I press him. He must have seen action at Rossbach or Leuthen, and had probably invaded Silesia under the old king. After ten minutes more of gloomy silence, we lay down on our respective benches before the sinking fire and attempted to sleep.

Just after dawn, we set off on the road that would take us to Bartoszyce. Icy draughts nimbly worked their way inside my cloak, and whistled through the holes in the musty carriage blanket with which I tried to shield my legs. I attempted to distract myself by reading a book I had brought along to lighten the journey. It was a new and revised edition of Baruch Spinoza's *Ethica more geometrico demonstrata*. Condemned by Pietists, Papists, and Lutherans alike when published over a century before, in our Enlightened age it had been given a fresh breath of life. But no matter how I tried, the cold was so stultifying that I never got beyond the third page. Alone inside the coach, the landscape rendered flat and featureless beneath an endless coverlet of snow, one tedious league following another, I drifted into a sort of mental stupor.

Four years earlier I had been summoned to investigate a series of murders that had disturbed the peace in Königsberg. The philosopher, Immanuel Kant, had been my guide through the labyrinth of criminal science, which he himself had invented on that very occasion. Above all, Professor Kant advised me, the investigator must attempt to enter the killer's mind if he wished to understand what was passing through it—before, during, and after the crime. 'There is a curious and compelling logic, even in the most perverse of human thought,' he insisted. Like an obedient hound, I now did what Immanuel Kant had taught me to do: I began to sniff.

I closed my eyes.

I was standing in the dark outside the cottage.

There were three children and a woman inside. They would be taken by surprise when I broke in on them. But for how long would shock immobilise them? Before they could be slaughtered, I would have to catch and pinion each of them.

Was the massacre the work of one man alone?

I considered the possibility for quite some time before dismissing the idea. There was no sign of a struggle. Submission had been immediate and it had been total. So, I must have entered the house and taken control of the situation in the company of others. Then, we had unsheathed our knives and used the sharp blades to slit the throats of the three children.

Had we come intending to slay the Gottewald family?

No other murder had been reported that night, or earlier that week in Lotingen, or anywhere else in the province. Therefore, I reasoned, it was more than probable that we had come to that house, armed and ready to perpetrate that murder, and no other.

Was there some cause to explain the choice of that family?

They were not rich, and nothing appeared to have been stolen. If Bruno Gottewald were able to supply an answer, I intended to force it out of him as soon as I arrived in Kamenetz. Then again, I thought, there was at least one other explanation. I placed myself in the dark outside the door of the cottage again, and allowed the thoughts to come. I had not come armed to kill the Gottewalds, or anyone else. Instead, I had found myself by chance in that forsaken place, and a sudden murderous impulse had taken possession of my mind.

Where had I laid my hands upon a suitable weapon?

There were knives in the kitchen of the house, and some were probably sharp. But Lavedrine and I had noted no blood in the kitchen, no stains on the wooden handle of the bread-knife on the table. If I had used one of the other household knives, then I had carried it away with me. Or I had taken the trouble to wash it, then put it back where I had found it.

Why remove, or hide the murder weapon?

Nothing in the kitchen appeared to have been disturbed. No furniture had been overturned, nothing had been broken, all seemed to be in a state of reasonable order. The table had been laid for the evening meal, the food had been consumed. The chairs were pushed back, as if the family had risen tranquilly from the table after eating. As if the time had arrived for the children to be put to bed.

I tried to imagine the exact sequence of events as the killers moved through the house. Domestic peace had been shattered when they burst in at the door. The woman and her children had been quickly taken prisoner. Then, the serious work began. The three children had been massacred, and the boys had been mutilated. There had been blood . . .

I sat up with a start.

Lavedrine had pointed out the anomaly while we were standing in the bedroom two nights before, but we had been distracted by the horror of what we were seeing, and the urgency of the search for the missing woman.

There was blood in the upstairs bedroom only.

There were traces of blood on the ceiling, but there should have been blood all over the house. On the floor, on the stairs, on the walls. There ought to have been oceans of blood in the room where the children had been killed. Blood that gushed from slashed throats. Blood that coagulated in the freezing cold night air. Blood that formed a dark lake on the mattress. Blood should have cascaded onto the floor, running in rivulets under the bed. We had noted those heavy spots on the wall beneath the window, far from the bed, but they did not explain the lack of blood in the rest of the room.

There was not enough!

Had the killer cleaned the weapon, then cleaned the house as well?

Another thought flashed through my mind. A more terrible one.

The children had been stripped of their clothes, then they had been killed. Afterwards, the boys had been mutilated.

Were the boys the true object of the raid?

I sat back, gasping for air.

Was that the reason that the mother had been removed from the house?

Thinking like the perpetrator had become a nightmare. I shuddered with revulsion, my mind swamped with terrible images of gross, vile savagery. We ought to have called for a physician to verify whether the bodies of the children had been abused before they were killed. Or afterwards, when they were dead.

That possibility was more unbearable than any other violation. Worse than murder. The faces of my own dear little ones flashed graphically before my eyes. They seemed to accuse me of having abandoned them in Lotingen, all alone except for their mother and Lotte, undefended.

A sexual attack levelled at the children?

Was that the real reason Franz Durskeitner had been so reticent?

I looked out of the window, my mind a blur.

After climbing very slowly up the face of a steep escarpment, the carriage topped the hill and began to run more quickly over the exposed plateau of Górowo. The horses followed a long line of wooden poles which had been driven into the ground to indicate the way across the barren white plain. The undulating surface offered no shelter that could diminish the driving force of the Buran. The wind raked up a filmy dust of snow like the sweeping train of a bridal gown. My driver, Egon Eis, was sitting on his box exposed to the worst of the weather. If he were to die of exposure, I would know nothing of the matter until the reins slipped from his frozen hands and the horses ran off the road, dragging the heavy coach after them. I prayed that the pint of gin hanging from my driver's neck would keep him alive. I had seen him replenish his flask religiously on every occasion that we stopped at an inn. If the weather doesn't kill him, I thought grimly, he will end his days pickled in spirits.

I called up to ask him how he was.

'Cold, your honour!' he grunted back.

Unable to offer help or succour, I settled down again, wrapping my scarf more tightly around my neck, shivering violently as I huddled deep beneath my blanket.

I closed my eyes, and tried to picture the man towards whom I was travelling.

He was a Prussian officer. If he had been sent to the fortress to work under the command of General Juri Katowice, he must be a soldier of the very first order. He would be a vigilant man, one who was capable of defending himself and his family. Almost certainly, he would have taken the presence of Durskeitner into account. He might even have seen the hunter's cabin. It was close enough to the haven he had chosen for his wife and children in the forest. Would such a man, trained to be aware of encroaching danger, leave his family alone in that isolated place if he truly believed that anyone was a threat to them? If he had even suspected that the hunter might harm his wife and babes, he would have carried them to Kamenetz, or found lodgings for them in Lotingen.

I glanced out of the window. Night was falling fast, and the wind had eased off somewhat as the vehicle passed the ten-mile stone and the first signpost to the settlement of Bartoszyce. Before we arrived at the ninth stone, the coach slewed to a sudden halt.

'Hold fast, there!'

Uncertain whether that shout had come from Egon Eis, I pressed my nose close up against the frosted windowpane and attempted to look out. I could see nothing more than a dark shape in the frame. Suddenly, the door jerked open, and the muzzle of a pistol met the centre of my forehead, the metal as cold as a searing iron on my skin.

'Dismount, sir!'

Five armed men in the tattered remains of regimental greatcoats stood in a half-circle. Prussian soldiers. They had removed the colours to avoid identification, but they were such muddy, dirty, ragged overcoats that recognition would have defied an expert. With one notable exception.

'I am Prussian, like yourselves,' I declared, holding up my hands as the man with the pistol waved me down to the ground. I glanced up at Eis in his sparkling, frost-coated waterproof. He sat snivelling high on his box, wiping tears from his eyes, the perfect picture of a helpless waif.

'What do you want from us?' I asked.

A tall, mustachioed man with rough, red skin and the bearing of an officer stepped forward. He wore a uniform that denoted rank, and a shoulderflap of the 2nd Regiment of the Hussars. A well-cut dark-blue overcoat with an upright collar and broad lapels of a rich, bright red stretched down beneath his knees, a sabre hanging from his broad brown belt. His black eyes held immovably on me. They were cold, humourless, pitiless. In that moment, I wondered whether my journey to Kamenetz had come to a premature end. Our rebel soldiers are ferocious in their treatment of Prussians they believe have bent beneath the foreign yoke.

'Food, money,' he said, looking hard at me. 'And information. What is your business in Bartoszyce?'

'I have no business there,' I answered. 'I am a magistrate on official business. I am bound for Kamenetz fortress . . .'

'Kamenetz?' he interrupted sharply. 'You are going to Kamenetz?'

'That is what I said,' I replied.

'Why, may I ask?'

He was polite enough, though his pistol never shifted from my heart by so much as an inch.

'One of the officers there is involved in a case that I am investigating,' I said. It was the truth, less than the whole truth, but I hoped it would be enough to satisfy his curiosity and let me pass.

'Nothing more?' he queried with a hostile stare.

'Nothing,' I confirmed. 'If you will allow me, sir, I have a pass and other official documents in my pouch. My papers will confirm all that I have said.'

He waved his pistol in the air with a gesture of annoyance. He might have been swatting at a fly. 'I am not interested in papers signed by Prussian puppets who choose to collaborate with the French,' he said.

This declaration of insubordination raised a cackle of wild laughter from his men.

'What I am asking,' he continued, 'is whether you have been sent by those who would like to see the French attack the fortress?'

He closed one eye, cocked his pistol, and pointed it at me.

'Are you a spy?' he asked.

If I hoped to save my own skin, and the wrinkled carcass of Egon Eis, who was wailing like a newborn baby, much to the amusement of the renegades, it was best to confess the truth.

'If you read my orders, you will see that I have been sent to prevent the French from entering Kamenetz,' I said boldly. 'I am conducting an investigation into a murder in Lotingen. Naturally, my enquiry has been authorised by the French. But it has been managed in such a way that they will not be involved directly. That is why I am travelling alone, with no one but my coachman to protect me.'

He waved the pistol impatiently, gesturing to see the documents.

I searched in my shoulder bag, my hand steadier than before, then handed him Count Dittersdorf's letter.

'What is the officer's name?' he snapped, glancing quickly at the contents.

The gang of rebels stood in a threatening semicircle, their eyes flicking between myself and their chief. Once, they must have looked like other men, but the scars and the sacrifices of a hundred skirmishes were savagely carved upon their mangled features. It was hard to look at them with hope. A single word from him, they would shoot us dead.

'I seek a man named Bruno Gottewald,' I replied.

'Not the general?' he asked after some moments, turning his head to one side, peering at me through that half-closed eye again.

'General Katowice?' I said. 'I'll have to speak to him before I can talk to Officer Gottewald. He is in command of Kamenetz garrison.'

My inquisitor said nothing, but he clenched his jaw and nodded his head. The answer seemed to satisfy him. He held Dittersdorf's letter up and let it catch in the driving wind. For a moment I had the impression that he was about to let it blow away.

'Inform the general that you met von Schill along the road. Baptista von Schill,' he said with a hint of pride, stepping forward and handing back the papers. 'Tell him that I let you pass, and say that all is quiet looking westward.'

'Major von Schill,' I repeated slowly, my interest fully awakened. I had always thought he was a phantom, a Prussian scarecrow meant to put the fear of God into the French. After every massacre, the name of Baptista von Schill was on all men's lips. A full major in the Brandenburg Hussars, he had led his men out of the besieged bastion of Kolberg in Pomerania after the disgrace at Auerstädt, transforming his followers into a band of bloodthirsty nationalists, desperate men who refused to contemplate surrender. The *Freikorps* of von Schill were feared as much as they were hated, not only by the emperor's troops, but by Prussian traitors also. The rumours spoke of farms and villages being wiped out after the inhabitants refused to aid or shelter the rebels. One story told of a large copper vat which had been filled with snow. Flames had been lit beneath it, and three men accused of treason by the major had been boiled alive.

Had I just run that fatal risk?

'One thing remains,' he said, nodding to one of his henchmen, who stepped up close to me and drew his knife, a six-inch blade flashing close to my throat. I was not half so frightened of the weapon as I was of the man himself. As he stood beside me, the wind lifted the thin leather mask covering the left side of his face, and his features were caught in the light of the carriage for an instant. One cheek and the side of his nose had been torn away with violence. A mottled flap of glistening scar tissue had been pulled tight by a ham-fisted surgeon and roughly stitched from the cheekbone down to his mouth. I could not tell which was worse: the sight and the stink of this monster, or the thought of what he might do.

'Do you mean to kill me?' I asked von Schill.

'Who knows?' he replied. 'The honour of old Prussia lives on in Kamenetz. If you betray the general, I'll search you out in hell and have that head off your shoulders!'

He nodded to the man beside me.

That grotesque face twisted into a horrid grin, the serrated blade slashed down wildly towards my innards. A gasp blocked my throat, everything was a sudden blur. The world turned white, then slowly faded into smothering black fog. Was this the end? A stab of pain, a blinding flash of light, then darkness? I heard the hammering thud of my heart. When its furious beating stopped, I knew, I would be dead.

Raucous laughter brought me to my senses.

It must have seemed a tremendous jape as my money-pouch crashed to the ground with a loud tinkle of coins. Ninety thalers of the cash that Dittersdorf had handed me for the journey lay sparkling in the snow at my feet.

'Dead men don't carry messages,' said Major von Schill, an evil glint in his eye. 'Now, climb aboard and take this moaning wretch away with you. You'll be in Kamenetz fortress before dark, Herr Magistrate. If anyone stops you on the road, tell them that you've had the pleasure of our company. My name will be your safest passport.'

The deformed man grinned and threatened me with his knife again, edging me towards the coach, prodding me up the steps, closing the door firmly behind me. My coachman jumped up nimbly onto his box, as if to give the lie to his age. He cracked his whip, and a minute later we were travelling down the hill again.

Count Dittersdorf had just been robbed by patriots.

I sat in a cold sweat, thinking of the folded twenty-thaler note that Helena had given me, insisting that I slip it inside my stocking for safe keeping.

The major had been precise in his estimation. It was not yet night as the ancient fortress of Kamenetz loomed up two hours later. I lowered the window sash the better to see it. From a distance, a full moon glinting through dark clouds, accompanied by the insistent whistling of the Buran, the fortress was impressively menacing. It was an ugly brute of a place—not on account of its size, which was not so very grand, but for its shape. Eight tall bastions glistened like polished silver, seeming to support the dark, solid mass of the castellated walls above. The fortress perched on the crown of a barren hillside like a huge, hideous spider, ready to attack its prey. So this was the extreme edge of East Prussia, the fort from which the Teutonic Knights led by Ulrich von Jungingen had launched their murderous onslaught against Ladislao Jagellone and the tribes of Poles and Lithuanians. It was the last remaining Prussian stronghold, which the French invader had never reached, or tried to roust.

Twenty minutes more, and we were called to halt outside the gate, then obliged to await the captain-of-the-watch. He came at once, cutting a smart figure, marching quickly over the snow-sprinkled cobblestones, his heels raising a spark now and then. I watched with interest, and despite my doubts I was impressed. It was rare to see a Prussian soldier with military snap in his step, even rarer to see a Prussian officer so immaculately turned out since the coming of the French. His leather riding boots gleamed like polished ebony.

The words of von Schill sounded in my ears again.

He had spoken of Prussia as it used to be, before the coming of the French. Suddenly, I shared his nostalgia. This was the Prussia that I remembered. The wonder was that it had all been cancelled out so quickly.

'Good evening.' The officer came to attention with a spine-snapping salute. 'What is your business here?'

'I have come from some way off,' I said guardedly, 'with important news for the commanding officer. Can I see him?'

Though stiff and formal, I thought I saw a sardonic smile flit across the young captain's lips and light up his eyes.

'Sir?'

'General Katowice,' I insisted.

'You'll have to wait until morning. Herr General's orders. You can speak with him at eight o'clock.'

'But I have been travelling for two days!' I protested, attempting without success to keep a whining note of exasperation out of my voice. 'Inform him of my arrival at once. I bring important news regarding the French. I have a letter . . .'

'I'll give it to him,' he said, taking it from my hand.

'I am a magistrate on official business. I represent the law in Prussia.'

'There is only one law here,' he replied without a trace of humour. 'General Katowice sits in judgement from eight in the morning, seven days a week. I'll tell him what you said, and put you on his agenda for tomorrow.'

There was something final and forbidding in his manner.

'Where am I to sleep?' I asked, as the reality of the situation dawned on me.

'You've been snug inside that Brandenburger chariot for two days,' the captain rejoined. 'Another night won't do you much harm, I think.'

For a moment I was tempted to sound the name of von Schill in support of my case, but I did not. Could I present myself in Kamenetz as a magistrate, then back up the claim with the name of a murderer, albeit a patriotic one?

'You can drive inside the fortress, if you prefer. But shift your vehicle into that corner over there, and keep it out of the way. The garrison wakes at dawn. Goodnight to you, Herr Magistrate.'

With another perfectly executed salute, he spun on his heels and marched away.

All I could do was admire the fine cut of his coat, the perfectly aligned red folds in the tail, the sparkling silver of his spurs and scabbard.

Then I had to break the news to coachman Eis.

I was under an obligation to invite him to shelter inside the carriage on the leather bench across from my own. As I tried to conquer my shivering, his snoring began. Louder than the 'Military Symphony' of Papa Franz, it would persist throughout the night.

· 11 ·

A SCREECH SPLIT the early morning silence.

I took it for the cry of a bird. One of those large, ugly gulls that seek refuge in Lotingen when the weather on the coast is particularly rough. An instant later, it was followed by torrential rain.

I pushed the carriage blanket from my face and opened my eyes. The light was purple. In an attempt to keep out the cold, I had pulled the plum-coloured curtains of the coach as tight as I could. The lanterns set at intervals around the parade ground of the fortress would hardly have disturbed the sleep of a man as tired as I had been.

That bird squawked out again, and the rain ceased instantly.

As slumber tiptoed from my mind, I heard what I now recognised to be a human voice. It was angrier, sharper, more penetrating than any voice that I had ever heard. It grated on my ears, screaming out a rapid sequence of words—*Left! Right! One! Two! Atten-tion!* And each order immediately prompted the disciplined pounding of feet, which seemed like a heavy downpour of rain.

I drew back the curtains, then struggled to lever up the window sash. A thick coating of ice had formed on the glass, both inside and out. The sky was a sickly leaden grey which promised nothing good. But as I looked out over Kaménetz parade ground, I saw a sight that promised far worse: Crime was marching up and down the parade ground with all the energy that a Prussian drill sergeant could bring to the event.

I quickly looked the other way.

No Prussian could ignore the consequences of Jena. One minute, subjects of our God-given sovereign, obedient to the laws and religion of his land; the next, we'd been swallowed up by an empire of atheists. After Jena, we had no Rights, no God, no King to whom we might appeal for Justice. Our legal system was swept aside, as each man scrambled to save the little that he had. Anarchy prevailed. The Treaty of Tilsit brought hostilities to an end: our king appealed to Paris for immediate implementation of the

Napoleonic Codes. I was a Prussian magistrate; those Codes should have told me what to do if one of my fellow countrymen was accused of a crime. But I had never held a copy in my hand. What was I to do? I did what I had always done. I applied the time-honoured laws of Prussia.

I sat inside the carriage, listening, wondering what to do.

When the sergeant yelled a command—to start marching, to turn left, or wheel right at the double, to present arms, or shoulder them—I heard what I took to be a well-drilled squadron of men obey at an instant.

I realised then what Count Dittersdorf had been so concerned about. No Frenchman must ever enter the fortress and see what was going on. Those troops were, without a doubt, a well-trained body of men.

Men?

With the exception of the sergeant, there was not one soldier on the parade ground who was over fifteen years of age. Marshal Lannes had ordered the Prussian standing army to be reduced in size. Soldiers were being sent home without a pension to beg for their bread, and the economy was in tatters as a result. No more Prussian troops were to be trained, the French had ordained.

But General Juri Katowice was training them.

I drew a deep, thoughtful breath.

Was any law being broken?

No *man* was being drilled in the arts of war.

Nor were these strutting boys a 'body of *men*', in the way that the distinctive uniform and the insignia generally identified the members of a specific regiment. Each one was dressed today as he had been dressed the day before. There must have been two hundred children out on the parade square, some wearing fine boots and well-cut jackets, others in clogs and hand-me-down rags.

Those little boys had been moulded into men-at-arms . . .

Again, the word *men* caused me to pause. Around his neck, each child wore a bright red ribbon. I myself had worn a red ribbon. Every male child in Prussia had worn one. And proudly so. Anyone who wore one was old enough to be trained in the local militia. That ribbon implied that he was ready and willing to fight and die for the Prussian fatherland. Two hundred boys were being put through their 'traditional' paces, and I could not fail to be impressed by the ability they displayed. Especially when the fortress bell rang seven o'clock.

They were called to attention, and formed smartly into ranks which were four rows deep. Then, the double gate at the farthest end of the parade ground swung open. Positioned as I was in the coach, I seemed to be sitting in the grandstand. A trill of shrill notes were blown by a cornet, a drumroll exploded in a thunderous cascade, and a group of officers came trotting into the arena on horseback. There were five animals, a white stallion and four blacks. I caught my breath. This was the military excellence of a past generation, and all for the benefit of an audience of motley-dressed boys with shaven heads and spotty faces!

The officers wore waisted tailcoats of Prussian blue with upturned scarlet collars, matching facings interlaced with white stripes across the chest, and white pantaloons with a scarlet stripe along the seam tucked into black boots which buttoned up above the knee. And if his officers were immaculate, which adjective could hope to capture the essence of General Katowice?

I had met him in Königsberg Castle in 1804. On that occasion, he had warned me of the imminent danger of a French invasion, and I had chosen not to take his prophetic words seriously. Yet, within the course of three short years he had been proved correct. Three years? It might have been three aeons, so much had changed. I sometimes thought the azure sky of Prussia had been transmuted for ever to a leaden weighty grey. Despite his splendid uniform and martial demeanour, General Katowice had been marked by Time. His right hand had gone, chopped off above the wrist in some battle—the defence of Königsberg, perhaps, which had been a long and fierce struggle. His rugged face was an ordnance map of age-lines and deeply sculpted wrinkles, which scarred his brow and carved deep channels in his cheeks from his hooked nose down to his square chin.

But his most characteristic feature—the one I remembered him by, long after the exact memory of his physiognomy had faded from my mind—had been defiled beyond recognition. By which I mean his hair. Like many another senior officer in the Prussian army, the general sported a style that had been popularised in the 1770s by the great King Frederick—a long rope of braided hair tied up at the end with a wide black ribbon. As I recalled, the snow-white tail of General Katowice's dressed mane reached down his back and fell beneath his waist. Every caprice or change of mood of that fiery gentleman could be interpreted by his restless braid. It would dangle on his shoulder, or settle on his broad chest like a serpent lying in wait. With a sudden flick, he would send it flying out around his head; I had personally seen many brave men in Königsberg Castle shaken from their normal composure as they ducked, or stood back quickly, to avoid being lashed by it. That braid had disappeared. Roughly hacked away. Katowice wore his shame upon his person, like a scar that he wished to flaunt.

What could he want from this army of infants?

The general pulled his white charger up before the ranks, dominating the beast with his knees, gazing out earnestly over the sea of upturned infant faces. His hollow cheeks were red and raw that cold morning, his nose a crooked beak as sharp and curved as any screeching seagull's, poised to snap and tear at any creature who dared to outface him.

'Men!' he thundered, and the boys seemed to stretch and grow before my eyes as they strained to match his generous description. 'You have been in Kamenetz fortress for three weeks now. Today you will be leaving. It warms my cold heart to see you.'

Each sentence was an exclamation, short, sharp, essential.

'Our nation has been wounded. The Prussian eagle's wings have been clipped. But the offence is not mortal. Thanks to you! Return to your homes, but sleep with one eye open. The call to arms will come. One day, it will come! When it does, I'll hear you hammering at my door. No Prussian warrior will be left outside. We are subject to a foreign power. How long can *he* hold us in chains? We'll wash our wounds in Gallic blood before too long!'

He thrust his crippled wrist straight up into the air, and a great cry rose from the mouth of every child. The mounted officers swept their gleaming swords from their scabbards and waved them in the air, crying boldly: 'Prussia! Prussia! Sword in hand!'

As the shout resounded all around, General Katowice jerked hard at the reins of his charger and jabbed with his spurs; the massive white stallion whipped smartly around, and the general galloped away through the gate, all eyes following his departure.

It was a fine piece of theatre, I thought.

At a shouted command the parade broke up. Suddenly released from the thrall of military duty, the boys shook each other by the hand, some of them embraced, and they began to make their way off the parade ground arm in arm. I watched in silent awe. I might have been attending a service in a Protestant cathedral: there was such weight, such solemnity in the proceedings.

A knock sounded on the carriage door.

'He'll see you now, sir.'

The stern young captain who had ordered me to sleep in the coach the night before was staring up at me, impressively turned out in full dress uniform. The silver stripes sewn across his chest looked disconcertingly like ribs. I climbed down, and fell into step beside this skeletal officer. He did not say a word as we made our way quickly on foot in the wake of the departing boy soldiers.

Five minutes later, at the end of a long, dank corridor, we entered a room so dark and dingy that it must always have been lit by candlelight, whatever the hour of the day or night. Three desks had been placed along three of the walls, with two tall cupboards and a long set of drawers in between. Two young officers were busily at work with files and documents, though they immediately dropped what they were doing and jumped to attention.

'Wait here,' he said to me brusquely.

Then he turned away and knocked softly on the only other door in the room.

The two junior officers picked up their quills and returned to their paperwork without a word. I took the opportunity to look around me. Some moments passed in silence, broken only by the scratching of nibs and the rustling of papers, when I realised that somebody was watching me. That is, a scraped bony scalp, the tips of two pointed ears, and a pair of small, close-set reddish eyes were glaring in my direction from behind the farthest desk. I took a step forward, and spotted a boy there. He was kneeling on the stone floor with a rag in his hand. A pair of long leather riding boots and a tin of beeswax were set out in front of him. He did not look away, but continued to stare fixedly at me as he raised the boot to his lips and spat.

'Herr General is waiting.'

I followed him into the inner sanctum.

Juri Katowice was seated behind his desk in a large spartan room, hardly better lit than the anteroom, though this lofty cavern was enlivened by a huge fire which roared noisily in the grate, and by large maps draped over every wall, like dusty tapestries in an Italian palazzo. A large engraved silver tray was laid out before him, a relic of some ancient regimental glory, complete with china cup and saucer, and a matching plate of hard-tack biscuits. A rusty field kettle bubbled noisily at his elbow.

The general turned his gaze on me.

'Stiffeniis?' he said, without standing up. 'This name is not new to me.'

'We met, sir,' I reminded him. 'In Königsberg. Four years ago. You may recall that I was ordered . . .'

'To catch a killer!' he snapped with a sudden smile, and a concentrated knitting of his brow. 'Of course. Procurator Stiffeniis! In Königsberg! Was there ever such a fine and glorious place? Prussia was still a nation to be proud of, then!'

'I hardly thought to find you here, sir,' I ventured.

'Nor did I,' he confided with a craggy smile. 'But that is military life. We go where we are called. Or where we're sent. In my own case, they decided to send me as far away from the danger as they possibly could.'

His blue eyes clouded over, and he stared at the wall, where one of the maps showed the most easterly territory of Prussia, and its contiguity to Russia. Kamenetz had been highlighted in large, red letters.

'North-east Poland! Or what remains of it!' he said, stretching out his hand and picking up a different sheet of paper from the table. 'I wouldn't last a month at court. Too much backbiting for my tastes. But what's this all about? I can't make sense of this note of Dittersdorf's. It's full of parlour talk. "The national interest," "questions of vital importance," vague rubbish of that sort. The old sycophant is still making up to the odious Frenchman, I do not doubt. Bureaucrats like him have little choice about the company they're required to keep, but it makes my war-worn flesh quiver!'

'There is a great deal of truth in what Count Dittersdorf says,' I protested. 'We are engaged in a daily tug-o'-war with the French military presence, and the confrontation takes many forms. What seems like a local incident of no importance can have reverberations that threaten to shake the foundations of our nation. Yesterday I was stopped on the road by Major von Schill. Just imagine the consequences if *he* had murdered a Prussian magistrate!'

General Katowice lifted up a hard-tack biscuit, soaked it in his beverage, popped it into his mouth. He did not offer one to me. Nor anything to refresh my thirst after a night spent sleeping rough in the coach.

'But he did not do so,' he observed laconically.

'Fortunately for me,' I replied, taken back by the general's ironical lack of concern for the lawlessness of the region. 'And for you, too, sir. He told me to tell you that all is quiet looking westward.'

Katowice looked fiercely up into my eyes.

'The man's a legend,' he snapped. 'Doesn't exist, except in the broadsheets they sell on the streets in Berlin.'

'But I met him, sir!' I insisted. 'Not a two-hour drive . . .'

'Tell me precisely what brings you here,' he interrupted. 'I'm sure you haven't travelled all this way to catch a ghost.'

I had no intention of letting myself be intimidated. I waited a moment before replying. 'I'll sit down first, if I may?'

The general waved his hand, and the young officer brought a chair for me.

'It is an extremely delicate matter,' I began, without saying more.

General Katowice jerked his head at the junior officer, who clicked his heels, bowed from the waist, and left the room.

'What is this extremely delicate matter of national importance?' he asked sarcastically as soon as the door had closed. Despite the harping tone of his voice, he leant confidentially across the desk, as if expecting news from me, some communication which might hasten the day of national reprisal against the foreign invader he had been haranguing twenty minutes before on the parade ground.

'A crime has been committed in Lotingen,' I said. 'I've been appointed to investigate it. The matter concerns one of your men, sir.'

'One of my men?' he repeated slowly, his eyes widening, his crooked nose rising, nostrils flaring as he spoke.

'Before he came to Kamenetz, this officer was stationed for a very short time in Lotingen,' I replied. 'But when he left that town, his wife and three children remained behind. He . . .'

'I am not surprised,' the general said, sitting back comfortably in his high-backed chair, his left hand reaching for a black cheroot from a large wooden thermidor on the table next to the tray. Again, common politeness did not lead him to offer me one. He lit his cigar from a candle on the table and blew an enormous cloud of aromatic smoke more or less into my face.

'There are no women in the fortress,' the general announced blandly. 'By my orders. We take the monastic approach here, preparing young men for what the future holds. From crack of dawn to last light, they are busy working together for the common cause. If they do have any energy left by the time we finish drilling them—that is, if any man needs a woman, and most of them seem to go exploring—there's the usual tribe of sluts selling their wares outside the gate.'

The unsavoury light of lechery shone in his eyes, and I knew I ought to extinguish it before going any further. 'The children of this particular officer were massacred three nights ago, sir. The throats were slit, the bodies mutilated, and their mother has disappeared. That's why I am here. The gentleman needs to be informed. He will be required—as Count Dittersdorf should have made clear—to accompany me to Lotingen at once. I cannot guess how long he may be absent. Everything will depend on the speed with which we . . . that is, with which I can resolve the question and bring the murderer to justice.'

I had almost let slip the fact that I was cooperating with Lavedrine and the French. It would certainly have been a tactical error. If he were to learn how deeply the French authorities were involved in the investigation, he might assist me even less than he had been doing up to that moment. My only desire was to inform Gottewald of the tragedy, climb into the coach with him, and order Egon Eis to set our sights for home.

'The French would love to blame a Prussian for the crime,' I added, 'which would lead to further repression. They seem to think we're little more than animals.'

He let out a groan.

'French troops may be responsible for the killing,' I added, baiting the hook of national pride. 'I hope to prove their complicity with the help of this officer. Every minute is valuable. Rather than waste more time, I wonder if I might be allowed to speak to the man?'

General Katowice looked intently at the lighted end of his cheroot, blowing hard on the tip until it glowed.

'What is the name of the man?'

'Gottewald, Herr General,' I said. 'Bruno Gottewald.'

General Katowice stared coldly at me, his broad brow a crusty and ferocious barricade. 'You've come too late,' he said suddenly, flicking his head to one side, sending the phantom braid flying.

He stood up without another word, dropped his cheroot on the table, picked up a polished half-cannonball which fitted neatly into his hand, and squashed the thing dead. As he did so, his elbow caught the samovar, which rocked on its base, then rolled onto its side, spilling its yellowish contents onto the table top. The letter from Dittersdorf began to soak up the liquid. It was not an intentional gesture, but he did not attempt to salvage the paper from the mess. Instead, he strode towards the door.

'Herr General,' I called after him, 'I am not sure that I understand you.'

'There is nothing to understand,' he said, half turning, looking back as if he had already forgotten why I was there. 'Bruno Gottewald is dead. Accidentally killed while out on exercises. He can no longer help you, I'm afraid.'

No word of compassion escaped from his lips. No praise for the officer who had served under him. No expression of sympathy for the fate of his family.

'Herr General,' I protested, 'I need your help.'

I started from my seat and took three paces across the room towards him.

Perhaps he interpreted my behaviour as insubordinate. When he spoke, his tone was arrogant, dismissive. 'This is a military outpost, Procurator Stiffeniis,' he replied. 'The man you wish to see is dead. You have no further motive for remaining here.'

'A military exercise?' I interrupted. 'What exactly was he doing, sir?'

The general stared at me for some moments.

'Never been a-soldiering, Stiffeniis?' he asked, a thin challenging smile forming on his lips. 'Never been out manoeuvring in the field? Accidents happen. They happen all the time. There is nothing strange, or incomprehensible in that. Men die as the result of carelessness, or crass stupidity.'

'Quite possibly,' I said, never lowering my eyes from his. 'But circumstances alter cases, General Katowice. I know that an official report must be submitted when a man dies in the service of his king and country. I would remind you, I am a Prussian magistrate, sir. I need to see the file relating to Officer Gottewald. Then, and only then, will I draw my conclusions.'

His smile did not falter, but there was a new, hard, unforgiving glint in his eye as he replied. 'You will see it, Herr Procurator. Then, you will leave this fortress with all possible haste.'

'I am not concerned merely with what happened here,' I fired back. 'I need to know more about Gottewald. The details of his career, who he was, what he was like . . .'

'You are looking in the wrong place,' he snapped. 'This is a border out-post, not a literary salon. The only information we can provide relates to the circumstances in which he met his death. During a banal military exercise. You say the French intend to exploit the massacre of his family for po-litical purposes. Go back to Lotingen then, Herr Magistrate, fight them on their own ground, rather than wasting your energies in Kamenetz. Do not throw suspicion on *true* Prussians!'

The door crashed shut, and I ran to salvage Dittersdorf's letter from the sodden catastrophe on the general's table. Without that document I would have a hard time getting home again.

· 12 ·

I LINGERED IN the smoke-scented room, waiting for the death certificate of Bruno Gottewald to be brought to me. But half an hour passed, and no one came. Did General Katowice intend to leave me there all day? Was this the way that visitors were treated in Kamenetz? My patience evaporated in a flash, and I stormed into the outer office.

'Where is General Katowice?' I asked, my temper up.

One of the scribes looked up. 'Gone, sir,' he mumbled, then his head dropped to his work again.

'Will he be coming back?'

The men exchanged a glance, then spoke in unison. 'No idea, sir.'

I bounced nervously on my heels for a moment.

Should I meekly bow to the general's indifference?

Neither man looked up as my footfalls rang out on the stone flags. Neither man said a word as I approached the door. No voice called out to stop me as I left the room. If Kamenetz had done with me, I had not yet done with Kamenetz. I determined to go exploring.

General Katowice might instruct his men not to talk to me, but how long would it take for every soldier in the fortress to receive that order? If I moved quickly, I might be able to learn something. Even the very lowest of the low would have something to say about the death of a senior officer. It might be barracks talk and nothing more, but I would still know more than General Katowice had been prepared to tell me. Then, if and when I did eventually lay my hands on the official report, I would be in a better position to form an opinion of what had happened.

The official report?

If a death certificate was issued, a doctor had to sign it. That was the law in Prussia. The physician of the garrison would have been required to examine the body. Rather than read what the doctor had been obliged to write, possibly under pressure from his commanding officer to gloss over the details, I would try to search him out and question him about the fatal accident.

I set off down a long, dark corridor, a slender loophole at the far end the only form of illumination. Freezing draughts raced and darted up and down the length of the passage. It was colder than on the Heights of Górowo the day before, but the sound of a voice shouting orders dimly reached my ears, and it seemed to come from the other side of the wall.

Just then, I thought I heard a sound behind me.

I looked back, but there was no sign of any person in the gloom.

At the end of the corridor there was a newel staircase, and I began to spiral down the stairs, edging slowly forward in the dark, stepping off each stair as if a bottomless void stretched out beneath me.

Again, I thought I heard a sound.

'Is anyone there?' I called up into the darkness.

There was no reply, no sound, except for the sibilant wind.

I almost stumbled, reaching for a stair that wasn't there, and came hard up against a wall. Feeling about in the darkness, my fingers touched stone, then wood, then the metallic cold of a large bolt. I slid it back, pushed open the door, and stepped out into the blinding light of the dull, grey day.

'Hit him hard!' a bass voice boomed.

I pulled back hastily as a cloud of blood exploded in the air.

It fell in a drizzle on a mob of urchins, who were wheeling around the yard in a screeching vortex. A loud cracking noise followed on, and cheers went up. A nose had just been broken.

I gaped in awe at the only adult in the yard.

Was he supposed to be keeping order?

Black smuts on his once-white jacket suggested that he might have cleaned a chimney recently. His trousers were baggy, his boots caked with mud. One epaulette hung loose from his shoulder, flapping in the wind. Where were the smart uniforms, splendid horses, and the glorious new Prussia that General Katowice had been ranting on about an hour before?

'Break it up!' the officer shouted, wading through the mob.

He turned to me.

'Just look at them, sir,' he appealed, holding the two fighting-cocks up by their collars for my inspection as if they had just been freshly hung from a gibbet. 'Jesus, be saved!'

The boy on the left could not have reached his thirteenth birthday. The other lad, whose nose and mouth were bleeding copiously, was tiny in comparison.

'Scrapping?' I enquired.

The officer peered at me with bloodshot eyes.

'Who are you, sir?' he asked.

There was no curiosity in the remark. The fact that I was inside the fort could only mean that I had been permitted to enter.

'Magistrate Stiffeniis,' I replied. 'I'm sorry, corporal, I didn't catch your name.'

'Puffendørn, sir. *Lance* corporal,' he corrected me.

'I am here to inform Major Gottewald of a fact that touches him,' I hedged.

Puffendørn's eyes widened with surprise.

'He's dead, sir. Didn't they tell you?'

'That's why I am looking for the medical officer,' I replied airily. 'Do you know where I can find him?'

The corporal pushed the two captives roughly away, aimed his forefinger at two others and snapped, 'Get to it!'

A new scrimmage started up with whoops and shouts. As fists and boots began to fly, Lance Corporal Puffendørn stepped up to me, and added: 'Doctor Korna's out a-harvesting.'

'Harvesting?'

Puffendørn raised his long jaw in the direction of the children. 'He found this lot out in the woods near Padelstewtz. He'll be back with another load soon. We try to turn 'em into soldiers. You'll have to wait till evening, sir. The doctor won't be back before then.'

'Where did you say his office was?'

If Dr Korna was absent, I thought, there might be an orderly who would let me see the medical archive of the fortress.

'Far side of the fortress, sir.' He raised his thick forefinger and pointed to a narrow archway. 'You need to follow the rampart all the way round.'

I hurried away between black granite walls which were incredibly high. They shimmered with damp, and sparkled bright green in places with dripping moss. At last, I spotted a weather-worn wooden plaque on the wall beside a narrow doorway: *Sick Bay & Infirmary*.

I stepped into the passage, relieved to be out of the wind.

'Who goes there?' a voice growled at my back.

I froze like a thief, then slowly turned around.

A bayonet was quivering six inches from my throat, the steel gleaming in the half-light. A boy no more than twelve years of age was holding the weapon, and staring up at me. His eyes were small like a piglet's, the pupils two green islands in an off-white sea, the eyelids red and raw, as if he had just been shaken out of a deep sleep, though I had seen him polishing boots outside General Katowice's office an hour before. He must have followed me every step of the way.

'Who goes there?' he again snarled, with a ferocious scowl that made his scrawny features all the more outrageous.

'You know who I am,' I replied, wondering whether this was the most dangerous, or the most ridiculous situation in which I had ever found my-self. 'I am looking for the doctor's surgery.'

'Sick, are you?' he snapped back.

I stared into that impudent face. There was a ragged slash of a deep scar on the left side of his jaw, like the dry bed of a river. His head had been shaved down to the bone, the skin a flaking crust, as if soap and water were rare commodities in Kamenetz. Only his lips were thick and fleshy with youthful immaturity.

'What do you want him for?' he urged, waving the bayonet closer to my face.

'I'm sure you know already,' I said. 'I am interested in the death of an offi-cer of this garrison.'

'Why stick your nose in that?' he replied, dropping his blade with sur-prising speed to prod at my waistcoat.

'The authorities in Berlin . . .'

A gob of spit shot from between his teeth like a hissing projectile, and went whizzing past my arm. If he did not hit me, it was not because his aim was faulty.

'Oops,' the boy apologised with a vicious grin. 'The word *Berlin* always gets on my tits. And as for the Prussian authorities!'

I stared at him in silence, almost certainly failing to match the nastiness with which he glared at me.

'Take care, my lad,' I said slowly. 'You malign the country that bore you.'

'My name is Rochus Kelding,' he replied flatly. 'I am *not* your lad. Nor anyone else's. My country is Kamenetz, and the only authority I recognise is General Katowice.'

As he spoke the commander's name, Rochus Kelding drew himself up stiffly. He was wearing the field-grey working jacket and trousers of the reg-iment. In a year or two, if he lived so long, he might grow into them.

'Which dead officer?' he asked roughly.

'I'll ask the doctor when I find him,' I replied.

'Wrong, Herr Magistrate.' He grinned. 'The name was Gottewald, right?'

He sucked in his breath, slid his left hand inside his baggy tunic and pulled out a sheaf of papers, which he held up to me. The documents were creased and bent. Not only were they stained, streaked and dirty, they actu-ally smelled of something foul.

'Is this what you're after?' he said, thrusting the bundle into my face, as if to taunt me with that penetrating faecal odour.

I took a pace backwards.

'Don't you want them?' He grinned again, waving the papers under my nose again, taking evident pleasure in the embarrassment he was causing me.

I froze for a moment. How should I react? If the boy felt free to behave in such a manner, he had been put up to it by General Katowice. Should I slap the messenger for trying to make a fool out of me, or snatch the papers from him and storm off indignantly, threatening to report the general to his superiors for failing to assist me in my duty?

'Is this how you treat official documents in Kamenetz?' I asked, stretching out my hand. 'Wiping your arse on the memory of a Prussian officer? You'll not live to see your next birthday!'

'He don't deserve no better,' he answered. 'We don't have time for the likes of him. The report they write on *me* will be as white as snow. You can bet on that!'

I considered this statement for a moment.

'Are you suggesting that Major Gottewald died without honour?'

The boy stared boldly into my face, as if he had just heard something funny.

'Which exercises was he involved in when it happened?' I challenged.

Before the words were out of my mouth, I realised that Rochus Kelding would never tell me.

'Exercises where officers who shit themselves die,' he replied with a conviction that was rough, but syllogistically correct.

'Did you know Major Gottewald?'

'Knew him,' he said with a smirk.

'And you didn't like him?'

The boy hawked and spat again, licking his lips with his tongue as the globule splattered on the flagstones between my feet. 'They lost at Jena, didn't they? That's a fact. Next time, we'll do better.'

'The whole of Prussia lost on that battlefield, Rochus. Thousands of brave men were killed. Would you see them all go to the devil?' I asked.

'What do *you* think?' he sneered, an evil light in his eyes. 'Better read them papers fast, magistrate,' he added. 'You've got ten minutes. There's naught else about him in the files—dead, or alive. It's all there. Black on white, shit on shite.'

He waved his bayonet in front of my face again.

'We don't get many strangers nosing round in Kamenetz,' he hissed, 'and some of them don't go home again.'

The threat was clear and unequivocal. The more dangerous for being so openly declared. I had just been told to watch my step, and the warning had certainly come from General Katowice.

· 13 ·

'WHERE CAN I sit? I need to study these papers.'

Rochus might have turned into a statue.

Then, his eyelids flickered and broke the spell.

He looked about frantically, glancing here and there, stretching on his toes to see beyond my shoulder, searching for some place to put me, some nook of which General Katowice would approve, or at least not disapprove.

'Follow me,' he said with sudden decision.

I trailed behind as he darted past, but any sense of relief I might have felt was not destined to last for long. We walked the length of the short corridor, then Rochus veered to the left beneath an extremely low stone arch, obliging me to duck my head as I followed him. He pulled up sharply by another passage coming from the right.

'Will that do you?' he enquired, pointing.

An iron grating had been let into the wall at shoulder height, a narrow step cut in the stone beneath it on a level with my knee. It was some sort of defensive position, from which an attacker could be easily picked off while trying to find his way to the centre of the fortress. But the step had two advantages, which I was not slow to appreciate. There was ample light, and solid support for my spine, which was aching after the journey and a restless night in the coach.

'I suppose it will have to do,' I said, sitting down.

The air rushing in above my head took the edge off the stinking thing in my hands. There were three soiled sheets written out in a bold copperplate hand, each signed with a flourish by Captain Alexei Korna, physician-surgeon-apothecary of Kamenetz, in the bottom right-hand corner. An additional page in a less accomplished script had been signed by nobody at all.

On this, the 8th day of October, I read, in this, the year of the Lord, 1807, being this, the tenth year of the glorious reign of our Supreme Monarch, King Frederick Wilhelm III, Ruler of all the States of Prussia . . .

Since the so-called Boy King had been reluctantly forced to take his father's place on the throne in 1797, glory and supremacy had been in short supply in Prussia. Though shivering with cold, I smiled at this outrageous *incipit*. As I read on, the smile soon faded from my lips.

> . . . the body of Bruno Gottewald, 1st Major of the Eighth Hussars, was conveyed to the infirmary in the fortress of Kamenetz. Clinical examination of the corpse, conducted by myself, the undersigned medical officer of this garrison, revealed extensive bruising of the right side of the head and the body, with multiple cuts and abrasions of the arms, the hands and the upper half of the trunk, both in front, and behind. In addition, a deep laceration crossing diagonally from the right temple to the left-hand corner of the mouth has almost destroyed the recognisable features of the face. This wound involves widespread crushing of the brow-bone, significant breakage of the nose, and total flattening of the cheek structure, with irreparable damage . . .

Irreparable damage? A nursery rhyme that my children loved to sing with Lotte tinkled through my mind. All the king's horses, and all the king's men had tried, but they couldn't put that broken egg back together again.

> . . . to the retentive muscles around the right eye, and the consequent evacuation of the eye socket. The visual organ, which is crushed and badly bruised, remains suspended only by the optical nerve and one partially severed tendon. There is also clear evidence of multiple fracturing of the osteo-nasal triangle, and the loss, either in whole or in part, of several teeth in the upper jaw. The lower jaw has been crushed and broken in at least three places, although compression of the mandible and shattering of the palate makes exact measurement extremely difficult. The tongue has also been severed from its root, and cleanly bitten through at one-third of its extension.

Good God, I asked myself, what had happened to Gottewald?

> The neck and trunk have also suffered extreme violence. The neck has certainly been broken, though whether before or after the man was dead cannot be ascertained with reasonable security. There is widespread evidence of the collapse of the ribcage all down the right-hand side, many bones having pushed out through the flesh, which is, in turn, black and blue with haematin, and blood-caked. The bones of both the arms and the forearms—that is, of both the left and right upper and lower arms—have been smashed and broken in many places from the shoulder all the way down to the wrist. Tearing of the supporting muscles and rupturing of the internal tissue, despite the fact that the webbing of the skin is relatively intact, means

that the arms are deprived of tonic form. Pressure with the fingers reveals that the underlying structure lacks any sort of solid consistency: it is not dissimilar to gelatine. There is also clear evidence of scarnification of the lower abdomen, the testicles and the virile member. The area is marked by deep cuts, scraping and significant crushing or compression.

In conclusion, when physical pressure is applied to the left-hand side of the thorax, there is a sound of loud cracking, which leads me to suppose that the lungs, and perhaps the heart, have been pierced by fragments of bone, leading to lacerations of these vital organs, with consequent malfunction and collapse.

It is my considered opinion that Major Gottewald died of pulmonary suffocation as a result of his injuries. There is ample congealed blood and mucus in the mouth, nose and breathing passages. No autopsy or examination of the internal organs was deemed necessary, given the evident gravity of the observable exterior damage.

The report ended there. I sat back, raised the soiled document to within an inch of my nose and took a deep breath, juddering with revulsion as that unmistakable organic ordure worked its way down into my lungs. What had Bruno Gottewald done to earn such hatred? Was Rochus expressing his own childish disregard for a high-ranking officer whom he did not respect, or was there some other explanation for the posthumous insult?

'What made Gottewald so popular, Rochus?'

The boy was standing over me like a sentinel.

'Is that what it says?' he frowned. 'It's a plain lie. He was a dark one, all right. The fattest rat in the fortress was more popular.'

I stored up this comment, and turned back to the document.

What sort of accident or physical maltreatment had led to the man's death? The doctor offered no hypothesis. He had simply set down the facts of what was clearly a cut-and-dried case of inevitable decease, listing the terrible injuries one after another, as if they were items on a shopping list.

An additional sheet of rougher, darker paper had been pinned to the doctor's report. This page had not been subjected to defecation, I noted with relief, and I read it over with growing curiosity. It was the report of Lieutenant Konrad Klunger, the duty officer, and it was dated 8 October, like the doctor's note.

No smile graced my lips this time as I read the weary formulaic introduction.

On this, the 8th day of October, in this, the year of the Lord, 1807, being this, the tenth year of the glorious reign of our Supreme Monarch, King Frederick Wilhelm III, Ruler of all the States of Prussia, the corpse of 1st Major Gottewald

Bruno was carried into the fortress by trooper-privates Albrecht Rainer, Zoran Malekevic, Ludwig Karteller and Corporal Rodion Luthant at 4.51 this afternoon. By the sworn statement of the four men, corroborated by the other six men in the unit, and by an entry in the Out-Book, Major Gottewald led his men into the woods to the east of Kamenetz not long after first light this morning for a routine hunt-and-kill exercise, commonly referred to as 'the deer hunt'.

Despite the fact that he was officer in charge, whose duty was simply to observe and supervise, Major Gottewald surprised the men under his command by electing to play the deer . . .

I knew exactly the sort of exercise that was being referred to. It was used in every military barracks and training camp in Prussia. I had played the game myself as a boy in the company of my brother, Stefan, and our friends in the hilly woods surrounding the family mansion in Ruisling. The idea was to run from point A to point B without being seen. This was the role of the deer. The hunters were supposed to hide themselves in the woods or grass along the way, and 'kill' the deer before it reached point B. 'Killing' in this case meant actually touching the deer, and shouting out 'you're dead'. When trained soldiers played out such an exercise, it would be extremely dangerous.

How many times in his career had Gottewald been put to the test?

How often had he elected himself to play the deer?

I rubbed my brow in puzzlement, wondering what had gone wrong.

Rainer and Malekevic swear that Major Gottewald insisted on running in a part of the wood where the men had never been before. Gottewald told them to report back to the fortress in time for lunch. He boasted that his men would find him waiting there when they arrived. At 2.00 p.m., the men were waiting outside the mess, but Major Gottewald did not present himself at the officers' table. Having left the fortress at dawn, he had not signed in again at either of the gates. The obvious conclusion was drawn. He had been lost, possibly injured, while out on field exercises. Despite the fact that it was snowing, General Katowice promptly gave orders for a search to be launched, sending the men who had gone out with Major Gottewald that morning to search the same part of the woods where the game had taken place. By late afternoon, the body had been discovered at the bottom of a narrow gorge. The officer's face was covered with blood. Possibly he had fallen over, or had accidentally struck himself in the face. In a state of temporary blindness, he did not see the insuperable obstacle which blocked his path, a chasm approximately fifteen feet wide, and he fell eighty or ninety feet to his death on the frozen bed of the river at the foot of the cliff. He had suffered extensive injuries, and may have been dead on impact. Jutting rocks were certainly implemental in inflicting the mortal wounds.

If the doctor's report and the memorandum of the duty officer had been read out to me in court, I would have had little doubt in declaring that the man had been murdered. Could so much physical damage be caused by a fall alone? Had he been beaten up first, then thrown off the cliff to simulate an accident? But I could see no sense in it. Those soldiers would be taking an enormous risk, killing their officer in the wood while out on an exercise. If they wanted him dead, the dreary fortress was a better hunting ground. Would any murderer, no matter how bold or stupid, wish his name to appear in an official document relating to the death of his victim?

Could it really have been an accident, then?

Given the snow and the treacherously slippery ground, it was, perhaps, a wonder that only one man had been killed.

The corpse has been interred in the cemetery of Kamenetz, I read.

I sat up stiffly.

Sybille Gottewald must have known that her husband had been killed a week or so before death darkened her own door in Lotingen. I felt a welling-up of compassion mixed with horror. What had caused such tragedies to fall on that family? A father and three children dead. In such different ways, and at such a great distance. All within a matter of days.

My thoughts flew to Lotingen. Had Lavedrine managed to find the mother in my absence, or was her corpse rotting somewhere in the woods, deprived of Christian burial, prey to the ravages of the winter and the ferocity of animals? Was it a matter of blind, cruel Fate, or had some darker design decreed the annihilation of the entire Gottewald family?

It seemed impossible that there was *not* a connection. It was beyond the range of statistical reckoning to imagine that violence had struck the whole family indiscriminately. But the opposite was also true. Numerical computation, as Voltaire has demonstrated, is an incomplete science. Nothing under the sun is wholly impossible; it may simply not have happened yet. It would take only a short conversation with that other cynical French Encyclopaedist in Lotingen to remind me. Lavedrine would chuckle if I insisted that they had all been victims of a plot, unless I could present him with convincing evidence to support the suggestion.

But then, another oddity struck me.

Why had the wife made no attempt to have the body sent to Lotingen for burial, as she had every right to request?

'Have you finished?' Rochus asked gruffly. The boy was standing over me in a defiant mood once more, one hand held out boldly in front of him, the other dangling his bayonet. 'I'm to take them papers back where they came from. Orders of General Katowice. He told me to leave you at the officers' mess. If you want to eat, that is?'

I handed over the report without a word, drew my cloak more tightly around me, and followed the boy. A zigzag course through the highways and byways of the fortress led at last to a very large open space, in the centre of which stood a tall narrow building.

Rochus pointed his finger. 'Over there,' he said. 'I'll be waiting.'

So Rochus, or some other trusted minion of Katowice, was to keep me under strict surveillance until the time for my departure. It was not the thought of being watched like a criminal that irritated me, but the implications of what I had just read. Gottewald had died in Kamenetz, his children had been murdered in Lotingen. Was the killer at large in the fortress? Would I find myself sitting down at the same table as a man whose hands were stained with their blood, unable to investigate as I would have wished, simply because General Katowice had set a veto on my doing so?

I walked away across the courtyard, mounting the stone steps that led to the dining hall. As the door swung closed behind me, I paused, open-mouthed, at the size of the room. The mess was in the central core of the fortress. It was impressive and depressing at the same time. The room was octagonal in shape, as high as a church, but no more than sixty feet at its widest point. A log fire roared and sparked colourfully in a fireplace large enough to stable ten horses, but the atmosphere was as cold as a tomb in February. Three large tables had been laid out in the centre. Two officers sat at one table, two more sat at another, while three of them had taken their places at the table nearest to the fire.

I made my way towards the latter.

'Do you mind if I join you?' I asked.

The men looked up, but no one said a word.

I sat myself down on the wooden bench. 'My name is Hanno Stiffeniis,' I said, increasingly uncomfortable in the strained silence. 'I am a magistrate, here to . . .'

'We know,' one of the officers interjected. He did not look in my direction as he spoke. His eyes remained fixed on his plate. He was a solid bull-like man with mottled red skin, and hair that had been shorn to the scalp, except for a black skullcap which had escaped the barber's blade. The heads of the other men had been tonsured in a similarly brutal fashion. They might have been monks of a holy order sworn to silence. Only their uniforms betrayed their profession.

'In that case,' I said, 'I'll not try to worm anything from you that General Katowice would disapprove of. Carry on as you would normally do.'

They needed no encouragement. The heavy silence endured for the fifteen minutes that it took for a bowl of thin spelt soup and a plate of pale boiled beef to appear before me, carried wordlessly in the hands of a serving-boy. While I spooned down my lukewarm broth, and carved away at my half-cooked meat, the soldiers stood up one by one, pushing their plates away, and left the mess hall. No one said a word to me. There was nothing strange in that, of course. They had been told to have nothing to do with me, and they were following orders. But I had not been prohibited from watching them, and I did so eagerly. They were all most meticulous in their observances. If one man alone had done such a thing, I would probably have dismissed it as an idiosyncrasy. But all seven officers went through the self-same ritual. They made for the central wall on the left-hand side of the hall, stood to attention in stiff silence for thirty seconds or so, then clicked their heels, and strode swiftly to the exit. As I cleared my plate, wiping up the gravy with black bread, I sat alone, wondering what it was all about.

'Have you finished, sir?' a voice sounded at my elbow.

The boy orderly was waiting, anxious to take away my dish and set the hall in order after lunch. He looked even younger than Rochus.

'Yes, I have,' I said, but I held my pewter plate firmly, determined not to let go of it until I had got to the bottom of the mystery. 'What flag is that?' I asked, pointing to the far side of the room.

'Sir?' the child asked, his eyes wide with fright.

He was just a kitchen-boy. Perhaps no one had bothered to tell him that I was not to be spoken to.

'That one,' I said again. 'That banner over there on the wall. What is it?'

'That's Grunfelde, sir. Teutonic order, 1410.'

'Thank you,' I said, letting go of my plate and leaving it on the table.

I walked across and examined the Grunfelde Standard, which had been hanging on the wall, gathering dust for three hundred and ninety-seven years. A once-black Gothic eagle spread its wings over a field of oxidised ochre that had once been blood-red. In 1410 the Teutonic Knights had fought their last battle. Every boy who had ever been to school knew the story. The Grand Master, most of the commanders, and about three hundred knights had been slaughtered by a united force of Poles and Lithuanians. Only Heinrich Reuss von Plauen had survived, and he had taken refuge in a remote fortress: Kamenetz, though it was not called by that name then. Did General Katowice see himself as a modern-day Reuss von Plauen? Did he think of his men, and the boys that he was training, as a new Teutonic Order that would drive the atheistic French invader out of Prussia? On the evidence that I had seen, no doubt remained in my mind. But what would happen if the French decided to pounce before the general's preparations were complete?

Rochus fell into step beside me when I emerged from the dining hall.

I no longer smiled at the notion of this boy playing at soldiers. In Kamenetz they were openly fomenting armed rebellion. At that moment I fully understood the danger that I represented for that outpost. And, as a consequence, the threat hanging over me in that place.

'Before I leave,' I said to Rochus, 'I wish to pay my respects as a loyal Prussian to the brave men who died here four hundred years ago to defend our glorious nation.'

In truth, I was curious to see what they had done with the corpse of a man who had died much more recently.

· 14 ·

IF A MAN is noble, his name may grace a church wall. The names of my own ancestors, stretching back to the eleventh century, adorn the Stiffeniis family chapel in Ruisling.

For all the others, oblivion awaits.

The style of burial used in France was closer to my own ideal. The bones were sealed beneath the stone floor of a church, the spot marked with a cross, and the names were listed in the parish records. One memorial tablet in particular had fixed itself firmly in my mind: a simple slate stone set in the north wall of what is now the Temple of Reason in Paris. When I saw the cathedral in 1793, it was still called Notre Dame. That marker recorded the name of Emilie Daguerre and the dates that spanned the six short years of her existence. Beneath, ornately carved, was a single word. *Loved*. There was nothing more. No hint of who she was, who her family might have been, or what had caused her death. Emilie Daguerre was dead, she had been loved, and that was enough.

Napoleon changed all that in the name of 'public hygiene.' *Décret numero 278, Sur les sépulcres*. No more Emilie Daguerres would be buried in any church. No angel carved in stone would weep over a grave. No oak coffin would be made, except for repeated use, employing a swing-gate to release the body into the void. A plain, cheap, cotton shroud would suffice to cover the corpse before it went naked into the cold ground. No poetic plaque, or fond final word would ever again be chiselled or incised in memory of any man, woman or child who was not the Emperor of France. Henceforth, we would all be nameless bones mixed up haphazardly in a pit, waiting to be sprinkled with quicklime.

But Bruno Gottewald had been *buried* in the cemetery of Kamenetz.

To my way of thinking, this was conclusive evidence that the French had no power in the fortress. And if they could not command the Prussian dead, how could they ever hope to subdue the Prussian living?

Rochus led me through an endless network of grim tunnels and fortified ditches with barely a word. The boy would never warm to me, but he did seem curious to know what strange notions chanced to pass through my skull. We had just entered a narrow redoubt, towering stone walls on either side, with steep steps cut into the right-hand wall leading up to a broad parapet, where the defenders of the fort could fire down upon attackers gathering in siege outside the walls. To my surprise, Rochus skipped onto these steps and began to climb quickly towards the raised walkway.

'This is it,' he announced, turning back, waiting for me to catch up.

I reached the parapet, resting my hand on the wall for fear of being blown away.

'It's not much of a cemetery,' I said dismissively, catching sight of a row of primitive, rough-hewn gryphons—more like crows than eagles—which had been set between the castellations.

'You're looking in the wrong place,' he replied, glancing at my feet.

I was standing on a flagstone which had been roughly etched with the number 79. A blank stone followed that one, while the next stone along was marked with the number 80.

'Are they firing positions?' I asked.

'Dead soldiers,' he replied with a smirk. 'On guard beneath our feet. It's always been the way in Kamenetz. When a good man dies, they bury him standing up, facing east, so his spirit can defend the place from foreign invaders.'

The past commanders of Kamenetz had stolen a march on the Emperor of France. No names, only numbers for the dead.

'A good man?' I queried.

'A brave man, a soldier who dies in the line of duty.'

He wiped his nose on his sleeve and looked out over the battlements.

'What about the bad men?' I asked him. 'Do *they* exist in Kamenetz? Does every man under General Katowice's command die nobly, that is, doing exactly what he has been ordered to do?'

The boy spat straight over the wall, leaning out to watch the progress of his projectile in the wind. There was still something of the child left in him, I was relieved to note. As he turned back to me, he spat on flagstone number 79 as well.

'Good or bad, they have to put 'em somewhere,' he sneered.

'In that case, number 79 could well be Major Gottewald. Would you dare to desecrate his memorial stone?'

Rochus looked at me as if I were deranged.

'Why not?' he said with a heartless laugh. 'He can't do nothing, can he? And anyhow, he's standing on his head.'

'On his head?' I echoed. 'Surely not?'

'That's how we bury a coward,' the boy replied, harking back to our discussion before I ate my lunch.

'But Gottewald chose to run that race,' I insisted. 'He wasn't fleeing from the enemy. He challenged his men to catch him if they could, and he accidentally fell to his death. Surely that was courageous?'

The soldier-boy's face screwed up like a withered apple.

'You've taken part in the deer hunt, have you not?' I asked.

He lowered his eyes and looked away into the distance.

'Come, Rochus. You know what it's like. Only a man who is brave and strong can hope to win.'

The boy would not be drawn.

'It's cold up here,' he said after a moment's silence. 'And anyway, you've seen what you wanted to see.'

But I had not yet finished with him. 'They'll have to dig up Gottewald before they can send him home. His coffin . . .'

'He ain't inside no coffin!' the boy retorted. 'Just a hole beneath the stone. I bet he's scared down there. Still a coward, though dead,' he snapped, his face a mask of fierce disgust. 'You wouldn't catch me being scared,' he added, lifting his chin in a gesture suggesting courage and determination.

'I'm sure you wouldn't,' I agreed.

'D'you know why the general has such a hard time finding boys to train? When the peasants know that the doctor's coming, they dig holes in the snow to hide their sons. Sometimes, they're in such a hurry, they forget to leave a marker. If the snow keeps falling, and the doctor takes his time, they never find them boys again! You can die, murdered by your own parents, just because they don't want you to fight for your country. I've been in holes . . .'

He stared at me and he was quivering with rage.

In villages all around the fortress, I thought, there might be skeletons hidden under the snow, children who had been left to die like so many rats in traps. The notion took away my breath.

'My father wanted me to tend his pigs,' he went on angrily. 'Going for a soldier? He'd rather have me dead! But he don't know what it's like to be buried. You can't breathe. The cold gets worse. It takes away your will to live. But someone heard me shout. Do you know who?'

I could guess, but I wanted him to tell me.

'Who, Rochus?'

The boy's face lit up like a lamp. 'General Katowice. That's who!'

And you will do whatever he asks, I thought, even if it means heaping insults on a man when he is dead and buried.

'Did the general always hate Gottewald?' I asked in an offhanded way.

Rochus shrugged his shoulders. 'Ask him, if you want to know,' he said, but the urge to defend his saviour was too strong. 'General Katowice don't hate no one,' he added hotly. 'Do your duty, you'll be all right. Step out of line, you're looking for it. Either you're in his good books, or you're out of them. It's as simple as that.'

'Gottewald was out of them, I take it?'

'Wrong again, magistrate!' the boy replied. 'The others had to sleep in the officers' dormitory, but *he* had a room to himself.'

'Was that why the other officers were jealous?'

'Who said they were jealous?' he countered. 'The only time Gottewald ever opened his mouth was when they brought in a new harvest. Always complaining about "quality", that was him. Wanted to send half the boys home again. Said they weren't fit for active service.'

'Did he argue with the other officers, then?'

Rochus shook his head slowly. 'He didn't speak with no one. He didn't have a single friend in the place, except for General Katowice . . .'

He looked away, as if he might have said more than was good for him.

The general spoke to Gottewald. He seemed to favour him, giving him a room which he was obliged to share with no one else. And Katowice had known him in the field when the war with France was in full flow. I was perplexed by the news. Would the general invite a coward to follow him? Would he reveal his plans to build a new Prussian army to a traitor?

I walked the battlements 'til dusk came on, and the cold grew more intense. The wind howled as if it meant to tear the fortress up by the roots.

'General Katowice mentioned a room where I can sleep tonight,' I said.

'I thought you'd never ask,' Rochus replied promptly.

Clearly, I had stepped back inside the rules that Katowice had set for me.

· 15 ·

ROCHUS DARTED THROUGH the dark byways of the fortress like a malignant goblin drawing me into the depths of an impenetrable forest. But then we passed beneath an archway, and came unexpectedly into the desolate vastness of the main square. Snow glistened on the cobbles where I had witnessed the parade of boys that morning. On my right was the main gate and the command post from which the captain-of-the-guard had emerged the night before. A phrase from the paper attached to the medical report flashed through my mind.

An entry in the Out-Book . . .

Rochus was ten paces ahead of me. Without a word, I veered away and strode directly into the command post, where a finely dressed officer with braided red hair, trailing mustachioes and bushy side-whiskers had made himself comfortable. Seated behind a desk, riding boots crossed on the edge of the table, silver spurs hanging down into space, he was smoking a massive meerschaum pipe. It dangled like an upturned question mark from the corner of his mouth.

At the sight of me, he pushed his chair back, and raised himself to his full height.

'I am looking for Lieutenant Klunger,' I announced.

'I am he,' he replied.

At that moment, Rochus came bursting in through the door. At the sight of the officer, my guardian angel snapped to attention, his mouth shut tight in a fearful grimace.

'I am Hanno Stiffeniis,' I began to say, but the smug smile on the officer's narrow face revealed that my name was known to him already.

'The magistrate, sir!' Rochus chanted, just in case.

'I wanted to ask a question, Lieutenant Klunger,' I said. 'I know that you have more important things to do than answer idle questions from a civilian.'

I glanced at the pipe smouldering lazily on the table-top.

'Indeed,' he agreed rather stiffly. 'Most considerate.'

'You were on duty the day that Major Gottewald's body was brought back to the fort. I read a facsimile of your note in the duty book,' I added, in case he should make any attempt to deny it.

'Indeed,' he said again, though more forlornly. 'The man was dead on arrival, as you know.'

'Indeed,' I echoed, 'but what of the men who brought his body home?'

I struggled to recall their names. 'One was called Albert Rainer . . .'

'Albrecht,' Lieutenant Klunger corrected me.

'That's right,' I agreed, grateful to him for this unexpected assistance. Then there was a corporal whose name was Luthant. Rodion Luthant? And . . . Malevic?'

'Malekevic,' Lieutenant Klunger corrected me again.

'I'd like to speak to them,' I said.

'Sir!' Rochus cried. In warning, I believe, but the officer turned on him as if he meant to stamp on him like a beetle.

'Hold your tongue!' he snapped.

He turned his attention back to me. 'You should have come a month ago,' he said with a sweep of his hand, and an apologetic smile. 'Malekevic has been drummed out for drunken conduct. They should have done it years ago, the man was a disgrace, rude and violent, totally uncontrollable. He'll be drinking himself to death in some lurid den in the wilds of Poland, his head deep inside a barrel of spirits, I shouldn't doubt.'

'What about the corporal, and the other two men?' I tried again.

Klunger clicked his tongue and shook his head. 'All dead, I'm afraid, sir. Lost in a skirmish with rebels just the other week.'

'Prussian rebels?' I asked, hardly able to believe my ears.

'Are there any other kind?' the officer replied with a sardonic smile.

I strode out onto the parade ground again, charging ahead before Rochus caught up with me.

'You shouldn't have done that, Herr Magistrate,' he said.

'Done what?' I asked, enjoying his displeasure, reflecting at the same time that audacity had got me nowhere.

He led me wordlessly on. The whole fortress seemed colder, blacker, more sinister in the flickering light of pitch-dipped torches. Rochus roamed effortlessly through the place, seeming to know its every trick and turn. We climbed steep staircases which might have been carved from solid ice, ran down others that were as filthy as they were slippery, and all the while the Buran ripped and roared through the building, a turbulent gale from the Steppes of Russia.

At last, he pulled up sharply, took a lantern from the floor, lit it from one of the torches, then pushed open a battered door which had not seen paint in a hundred years.

'This is it,' he announced, 'the best that Kamenetz can offer.'

By flickering candlelight the room was ten or twelve feet wide, twenty feet long, and unfurnished, except for a narrow cot and a three-legged stool. A blanket had been placed on the bed, which stood beneath an iron grating set high in the wall. This fissure would have let in light, if daylight there had been, but it could never keep out the cold.

'Am I supposed to freeze to death?' I asked. 'Is that the general's plan?'

There was an unmistakable glint of amusement in the eyes of Private Rochus as he replied. 'He ordered me to make you comfortable, sir. I'll bring you something to eat and drink.'

Then, like a whippet from a trap, the boy was gone.

I walked up and down the length of that cell a number of times, my temper cooling. I would have to make the best of it. The following morning I would be leaving for home, I reminded myself. Never to return.

I took off my heavy, outdoor mantle. Moving more freely, I positioned the stool beneath the window, climbed upon it and used my cloak to block out the freezing draught which surged in through the open grille. I was standing on the stool when Rochus returned, a plate of food in one hand, a large stein of beer with a metal lid in the other.

I jumped down, and took possession of my viands.

'I know that visitors here are rare,' I said, 'but even the hardiest must occasionally feel the need to relieve his bowels and empty his bladder. I see no pot intended for night-soil in this room. Can you bring me one?'

General Katowice had made no plans for me on that account either. A mottled flush spread slowly over the boy's nose and his cheeks as he tried to come to grips with the thorny question of how to dispose of the solids that might come bursting at any moment from my intestines, the fluids that might gush in torrents from my bladder.

'We . . . we don't use pots,' he stuttered uncertainly.

'I do not intend to foul the room where I am obliged to sleep,' I contended.

'We have latrines . . .'

'You'd better tell me where they are,' I said. 'I'm sure the general has more important matters on his plate. If you wish to check with him, of course, I'd be most grateful. He told you to make me comfortable, did he not?'

Rochus stood there, debating silently what to do. An armed French thug might have been standing over him, demanding to know where the keys to the arsenal were kept.

'The latrines on this side of the fortress are beneath your feet,' he said at last.

'Thank God for that,' I said. 'How am I supposed to go there?'

Getting anything out of the boy was like trying to extract gold from the basest of metals. He frowned, scratched his head, looked this way, then threw an uncertain glance in the other direction.

'All I want to do', I said emphatically, 'is *piss*. Am I asking too much?'

'Turn left out of the door, there's a ramp of wooden stairs. Take the short corridor on the floor below till you reach the stone steps. Go down there, and it's right in front of your nose.'

'Is there any news of Doctor Korna's return?' I ventured.

'I thought you wanted to empty your bowels?' Rochus shot back.

'I will use the latrine when I feel the need,' I replied. 'Unless you intend to lock me in for the night?'

The boy glanced at the door.

'I don't see no lock, do you?' he scowled.

He snapped to attention, saluted, and marched out leaving the door wide open. If I had expected to hear a sliding bolt from the outside to seal my tomb, all I heard were his metal-tipped clogs crashing away down the corridor.

I closed the door, pleased to realise that I was not going to be imprisoned for the night. It was a small consolation. Then I sat down to eat. The cuts of meat were cold, tough to grind and harder to swallow, so I washed them down with the beer, which was flat and stale and certainly more than a quart. Afterwards, I lay down fully dressed on the bed and covered myself with the blanket in a vain attempt to keep warm. More tormenting than the cold was the knowledge that my journey to Kamenetz had been a disaster.

At dawn I would be evicted from the fortress, and I had nothing to show for my pains. I had abandoned my wife and children, leaving them in danger. I had travelled for two days only to discover that Major Bruno Gottewald was dead. Thanks to the single-minded obstinacy of General Katowice, I knew the extent of his wounds, but I had found no proof of foul play, no reason to suspect that there might be a direct connection with the massacre in Lotingen. The medical officer might have been able to add some valuable detail to what I had read, but I had not been allowed to question him. My only source of information had been Rochus. If the boy were any measure of the officers and the doctor, I could hope to learn little more before I set off on my journey home. I felt like an eel-fisherman examining his pots on a bad day. All of them were empty.

Suddenly, the light from the oil lamp guttered in the draught and went out.

No matter how I tried, sleep would not come.

I was tormented by another goad that would not let me rest. What had happened in Lotingen in my absence? And what was I to say to Lavedrine when I returned? There was no telling what the Frenchman might have discovered. Had he found Sybille Gottewald? Had Durskeitner confessed? Rather than the eel-fisher, I felt like the hooked fish, twisting and turning this way and that to free myself of the uncomfortable barb.

I was frozen beyond coherent thought.

My cloak covered the window, keeping out the wind to some extent, but it could do little against the numbing cold. After turning restlessly from one side of the bed to the other for an hour or more, I jumped to my feet in the dark, frantically beating my stiff arms and aching legs with my gloved hands. Then I took off my gloves, the better to rub my hands and agitate my limbs, trying to stimulate more rapid circulation of the blood, as the English doctor, William Harvey, recommends.

As time stretched out, the temperature continued to drop. Sleep was out of the question. And that dreadful beer had begun to swell my stomach painfully. Left with no alternative, I opened the door and glanced warily into the gloomy corridor. To my left, a torch dimly lit the beginning of the staircase of which Rochus had spoken. I darted a look the other way, expecting to find the boy lurking somewhere close by, but all was still. The profound silence was ruffled by the wind and nothing more. Stepping out into the corridor, I made my way down the stairs, smiling to think that even the most dutiful of boy soldiers had to rest.

I could have found the latrines in total darkness, as Rochus suggested, by following my nose. The acrid smell of organic waste was heavy on the cold night air. And there was nobody on patrol. Indeed, I did not recall seeing a single soldier on guard in any of the yards, corridors, or passages that I had traversed that day. And yet, it made sense. If the French decided to take control of the fortress they would not bother doing so under cover of night. They would come marching straight in through the gate. Dittersdorf was right: Kamenetz could only survive so long as the French persisted in ignoring its existence, or the Prussian high command continued to close a benevolent eye on what Katowice was doing there.

On the floor below, a torch illuminated a legend written in chalk on the wall by a door in what seemed to me to be a childish scrawl—*PISSHOUSE*. I dashed into the room, unbuttoning my trousers as I went. The latrine was long, narrow, totally unlit, except for the pale glimmer of the moon which filtered in through an iron grille taking up most of the wall at the far end of the room. This grid had been provided to disperse the oppressive smell, no doubt, but even the driving power of the Buran had little chance of doing that. On the right-hand side, a structure of planks had been set like a long bench with holes cut at intervals. On the left was a tin sink full of water which had frozen solid, the surface glistening, a wooden handle trapped in the ice until spring. There would be a sea-sponge or a bundle of rags attached to the end of the stick for the purposes of cleansing one's body.

In my desperation, that stinking cavern was like an oasis in the desert. I sat down at the first place on the bench-top, the wood warm and smooth to my naked buttocks. The stench that rose from beneath me might have caused a less desperate man to flinch. Where there's filth, I thought with revulsion, there are rats.

I gave myself up to hopelessness, let out a sigh, and unclenched my bowels.

In that instant, a voice spoke out in the gloom.

'Don't move, sir! I will come to you.'

·16·

THE BULK OF a man shifted into silhouette against the moonlit grille, moving swiftly towards me.

I reached for my trousers.

'Do not stand up, Herr Magistrate,' he hissed, his face hidden by darkness. 'If danger threatens, I will leave, and you will remain. You are doing what you have to do, while I have my own sort of immunity.'

I thought I heard a trace of humour in his words.

'Puffendørn said that you'd been asking after me. I expected you to come again, and I waited late in the Infirmary. Finally, I took the onus upon myself. I know too well how things go in Kamenetz. I've been here longer than I deserve. I hope that you will remember that?'

His voice had sunk to a whisper, and he waited for an answer.

'I will,' I said, though I had no notion what I was promising.

'My name is Korna,' he continued. 'Alexei Korna, medical officer of this garrison. I knew I'd find you here if I waited long enough.'

I could not see the smile on his lips, but I was aware of it.

'The human body was not made for a place such as Kamenetz. Rochus told me where they'd put you. I knew the cold would do its work. All you had to do was drink a little water.'

'I drank a large jug of flat beer,' I said, and heard him chuckle in the dark.

'I wanted to see you, sir,' he said suddenly.

'And I wished to see you . . .'

'My need is greater,' he added quickly.

I did not know how to reply.

'This must come to an end,' he continued gravely. 'It will be better for all of us. You can't imagine the risks I had to run to get that message out of here. He is vigilant, I'll say that for him. But I will not be cowed. I have reached an age when . . . how shall I put it? What career can I look forward to here? What future anywhere? My only price is a ticket out of Kamenetz on the post-coach. I speak as a Prussian, and proud to be so. This is not what I call king and country.'

I tried to hush him, but passion had got the upper hand. He would not be silenced.

'I hope you will not take it ill,' he continued, 'if I express my surprise that the authorities have been so slow to wake up. They should have sent a regiment long ago. But why are you alone? No, forgive me, sir,' he ranted on. 'Affairs of State, I can understand. I ought to thank my lucky stars you're here at all.'

Before I had the chance to say a word, he rushed ahead.

'What did Baron Stein make of my note?'

The newly appointed Chancellor was the most powerful man in Prussia, more influential than the king himself, according to almost every voice that I had read in the newspapers.

'I've no idea,' I began, intending to inform the doctor that I had never been privileged to meet that gentleman in my life, but he did not allow me the time.

'How many men does he intend to send?' he insisted.

I was ever less sure where he was leading me. The doctor knew my name. My business in Kamenetz was plain to one and all.

'When will they arrive?' he pressed me. 'A rebellion in the East will have terrible consequences for Prussia. They are bound to fail. Violent repression will follow on.'

'I am sure the fault is mine,' I cut in on him. 'I know nothing of secret notes, nothing of the Chancellor, or of troops being sent to Kamenetz. To be honest, I have not clearly understood what anyone is doing in this place—much less am I calling for more men to be sent here.'

'What?' he cried in a strangled whisper, his hands reaching out to grab the lapels of my jacket. His face caught the moonlight as he twisted to secure me, his eyes wild and flashing, his hair a tangled white forest, chubby mutton-chops of the same colour framing his square jaw. Yet his face was that of a younger man. He was no more than forty years old.

'If you have not been sent by Stein, who the devil are you? They said a magistrate had come on a royal commission. And that Katowice had ordered Rochus not to let you out of his sight. What are you doing here?'

I placed my hands on his, vainly attempting to free myself.

'I am a magistrate,' I replied, 'though not the one that you were expecting. I am investigating the murder of the children of an officer who was stationed in Kamenetz. I am interested in nothing else.'

'Children?' the doctor echoed weakly, releasing his grip on my jacket. 'I thought . . . that is, there's been a mistake. On my part, sir. I beg your pardon.'

'I am glad you've found me,' I said. 'I read your report concerning the death of Major Gottewald.'

'Was he the father?'

I told him briefly of the events that had brought me to Kamenetz.

'What has the death of Gottewald to do with the murder of his children?'

I hesitated for a moment.

'I am not sure,' I whispered. 'General Katowice told me that Gottewald died as the result of an accident, nothing more. As you guessed, my movements have been severely hampered since I arrived. No one will speak to me. I know no more than you reported of his death.'

'What more is there to know?' the doctor murmured.

I had the impression that he wished to cut short the conversation. He had taken a risk in speaking to me, but he had mistaken his man. Now, he feared the consequences.

'That must be obvious, Doctor Korna. It did not sound like an accident to me. You reported what you saw, but I would like to know what was going through your mind as you examined the body. Wouldn't you describe the death of an officer in such dramatic circumstances as being suspect? He was resented for some reason, I gather, though what he might have done I cannot say. Your report had been fouled with excrement, for one thing!'

A strange rumbling sound came from the man.

'Ah, you met Rochus,' he replied, trying to suppress his laughter. 'Didn't the little patriot tell you what it meant?'

'A mark of cowardice,' I said. 'But what was cowardly in such a death? That is what I do not comprehend. I suspect that Gottewald was murdered.'

'Silence, sir!' he hissed. 'This place is dangerous. We might not be alone for long. Pull up your breeches, and follow me.'

He tugged me up roughly from the bench, and waited while I adjusted my clothing. In silence he led me out into the corridor, turning away from the stairs that I had used to descend to the latrines. At the far end, there was another staircase, which we began to climb in the dark without the help of any light.

Up one flight, then another, then a third.

We stopped on a landing, and I heard a key being turned in a lock.

'We are in the highest tower of the north-west bastion,' he whispered. His hand touched my arm, guiding me into a room which was dimly lit by moonlight. I watched attentively as he locked the door behind us. There was a peculiar odour in the room, as if it were a store for meat or butter. If it was a larder, I thought, the meat had turned, the butter had gone off.

'We are safer here,' the doctor said, 'but keep your voice down. We must not be seen together. If I help you, perhaps you can do something for me.'

Again I did not understand what he was hinting at. But the fact that he was willing to speak was enough for me. 'If I can help you, I will,' I promised.

'Fair enough, sir,' he said, as if a bargain had just been driven between us. 'Tell me what you wish to know about Gottewald.'

'You reported severe lacerations to the man's face, crushing blows to the body, damage to his sexual organs,' I replied. 'Were such wounds compatible with a training exercise out in the woods?'

'Do you know anything about the deer hunt?' Korna asked.

'I know enough.'

'They take it very seriously here. I've seen many soldiers who have died while running in the forest, and some of their injuries would surprise you. Gottewald was not the worst, by any means,' he said with a deep sigh. 'If you believe he was killed, Herr Stiffeniis, I can provide no medical evidence to support your claim.'

I was silent for some moments. The physician had put paid to my hopes of ever convincing Lavedrine that my theory was correct.

'What sort of man was he?' I asked.

'A Prussian officer,' he replied quietly. 'One of the best. One of Katowice's own. Wherever the general went, Major Gottewald was sure to follow. They had been together in Königsberg, I believe. Gottewald was carrying important despatches for the general when he got caught up in the battle at Jena. He fought valiantly, by all accounts. When the battle was lost, he made his escape alone by night, and managed to return through the enemy lines all the way to Königsberg castle, where Katowice still held out against them.'

'Quite a deer hunt!' I commented.

'When the Armistice was signed, the men of Königsberg garrison were allowed to march out bearing arms, and Katowice withdrew to Kamenetz. Gottewald followed him here a short time later. Always at the great man's heel. They say he saved Katowice's life when the general's hand was severed during the fighting, making a tourniquet out of his own shirt.' He paused, as if to add weight to what was to come. 'If Katowice is bent on training the next generation of Prussian heroes, Bruno Gottewald shared his ideals, and assisted him to the utmost. I wouldn't be surprised if he were up above the clouds at this very moment, petitioning God to bring an army of angels to the aid of General Katowice and Prussia.'

'The apotheosis of a hero,' I said, astounded at this singular description. 'He had a wife and children, though he did not bring them here.'

'Could not,' Doctor Korna interposed. 'The general won't have them in the fortress.'

'So I heard,' I admitted, 'but didn't Gottewald ever speak of his wife? Did he never talk of his boys? Didn't he want them to follow him into the army?'

'This may surprise you,' the doctor began, 'but I can tell you absolutely *nothing* about Major Gottewald. Nor can anyone else in Kamenetz.' He hesitated for an instant. 'Except for General Katowice . . .'

'What do you mean?'

'Gottewald was a loner,' Korna replied. 'He sought solitude, and the general, for reasons known only to himself, allowed that man to have a private room. I am obliged to retire to my infirmary when I want peace and quiet. Like many others, I asked for similar privileges, but Herr General was his usual, inflexible self. Gottewald was his favourite. I had no idea he even had a wife and family. Isn't that odd? I thought he was wedded to the army. You asked General Katowice, I take it?'

'It didn't get me far,' I said. 'He referred me to your report.'

Doctor Korna let out a long thoughtful sigh.

'Which takes your enquiries nowhere,' he said at last.

We stood in silence, face to face in the stench and the gloom.

In retrospect, it seemed as if both of us were waiting cautiously for the other to make some offer, or suggest some compromise, like hungry men bartering fish for flesh in a meagre market.

'I may be able to point you in the right direction,' he said, but he did not say what he had in mind.

'Which direction is that?' I asked.

'You must help me, sir. You are a magistrate. You've been sent here on an important mission. You must have important friends.'

I thought of Dittersdorf, and even Lavedrine, though I was wise enough to wait before I spoke of the Frenchman.

'What of it?' I said.

'Friends with friends in Berlin, perhaps?'

'Perhaps,' I echoed.

'To be frank,' the doctor said, moving closer, placing his hand on my arm, 'I must get away from this place. I am being slowly poisoned here. The air . . . Can't you smell it? The air in Kamenetz is foul! They can send me east or west, north or south, I do not care. However, Potsdam would be nice . . .'

'If you have any information that can assist my investigation,' I said, 'I will do everything in my power to help you. I can give no guarantees, but I hold a promise to be a serious matter.'

'Well said, Herr Magistrate!' he replied, but he added nothing, waiting for me to state the conditions of our complicity.

'What information can you add to what I know already?' I insisted.

The doctor looked around, as if he feared some spy might be lurking behind the three metal-hooped vats that filled the far end of the room. Even by moonlight I could see that they were large.

'Gottewald was second-in-command to General Katowice. Have you stopped to ask yourself what he was doing, running from the hounds on a cold winter morning? Such an exercise is not meant for an officer, not even the least of them. In the name of God, what was First Major Gottewald *doing*, racing half-naked at dawn over dangerous ground with a pack of trained men chasing at his heels?'

I considered this for a moment. 'Rochus told me that there's nothing difficult or dangerous about it . . .'

'Those men were *not* raw recruits!' he interposed.

'Perhaps not,' I said, 'but the boy said it is a game, and nothing more.'

'Take everything that Rochus tells you with a pinch of salt,' the doctor warned. 'A pinch? A shovelful! The officers at Kamenetz study theory, tactics, logistics, the strategy of warfare. They sit at tables and drink tea. They leave the "deer hunt" to Rochus and the other boys.'

He said no more, but seemed to be listening for any sound that might suggest that we had been discovered. Suddenly, turning back to me with decision, he said, 'Come, sir. For my part of the bargain, I'll show you the treasure of Kamenetz.'

Turning away, he pointed to the vats at the far end of the room.

'We must be careful,' he warned, leading me towards them. 'We'll need light. One minute, no more. An enemy can spot the glimmer of a candle a mile away.'

As he spoke, he dropped on one knee and sparks exploded on the floor, throwing dramatic shadows onto the wall. He stood up clasping a peculiar little device in his hand, shading a tiny, flickering flame.

'Hold it, would you?' he said, offering me the short length of what looked like a shorn-off gun barrel. A flint had been secured to one end with a clamp, and a length of tarred hemp passed inside the metal tube and out at the bottom. It was an ingenious little lamp.

Those vats might have been bathtubs, except for the fact that they were chest-high and covered with metal lids. Doctor Korna prepared to open one by pulling on a hinged lever. But first, he stared at me with great intensity.

'One glance,' he warned as he pulled, 'then douse that flame.'

The lid came up, I looked inside, and my head began to spin.

Suddenly, the light went out. The smell of *aqua vitae* was overwhelmingly strong. Doctor Korna had blown out the flame none too soon. 'The whole place might explode,' he hissed.

Still, I had seen what I had seen.

'Heads?' I breathed.

'The private collection of General Katowice. Frenchmen, for the most part,' he whispered. 'An occasional Prussian traitor. Now you've seen them, let's get out of here.'

I reached for his arm in the dark, and held him back.

'What does this mean, sir?' I asked.

'It means that we are in the hands of maniacs, Herr Procurator. The general pays von Schill a bounty for each French body that he brings in. Then I am required to do the dirty work.'

'Major von Schill comes to Kamenetz?'

The threat that the major had pronounced as he robbed me took on new meaning: 'Betray the general,' he had snarled, 'I'll search you out in hell and have that head off your shoulders!'

'He is an honoured guest whenever he brings a trophy of war. For fear of being branded a traitor, I have been obliged to use my surgical instruments on numerous occasions. I must escape from here!'

'Did Gottewald know?' I asked.

'So close to Katowice? Of course, he knew. And he approved. The Prussia they want will be a fearsome place. A better place, or worse, I do not know. But it will be free of the French and their sympathisers.'

'Is this why you wrote to Berlin? You thought I'd come to investigate?'

'Exactly,' Korna replied. 'But I was wrong. No one will come. Katowice will build a vat that's big enough for all the French in Prussia. And I will probably join them. Help me, sir. For the love of God, help me leave this mad-house. I pray at night that the enemy will come and end this nightmare.'

THE BURAN WAS howling like a dirge the following morning.

Flakes of snow flew like scraps of paper in wild flurries.

Though relieved to be going home, I prepared myself to face the dangers of the road, the risk of meeting Baptista von Schill and his brigands again. I took a final look back, wondering what had happened to the boy. I had expected to find Rochus waiting outside my door that morning, but he was not there. I thought to see him standing in the yard as we boarded the vehicle. There was no sign of him. As Egon Eis cracked his whip and the horses pulled away, I almost hoped that he would run to curse me out of the fortress.

But even there, I was disappointed.

As the coach rolled down the hill and into the woods encircling the fortress, I spotted flames among the trees. I wiped the condensation from the window with my glove, but the rapid motion of the vehicle made it difficult to see what was going on. A group of figures stood in a circle holding torches, with two more in the centre—one very tall, the other short, face to face. A man, and a boy.

I opened the window and leant out, but the scene had already disappeared behind the trees. Suddenly, a strangled cry broke the silence of the woods. It was not unlike the howling of a wolf, but I was certain that the voice was human.

I pulled the window up to avoid hearing more, and felt guilty as I did so.

I could not shake the boy soldier from my thoughts.

Was that the vision I would carry away from Kamenetz?

Rochus being whipped for his failure to watch over me through the long, cold night?

· 17 ·

WE HAD BEEN travelling in a frozen daze since dawn on the second day.

A rose-coloured sky and the pale lemon ghost of a winter sun heralded my approach to Lotingen. But long before the coach entered town, the wind blew up a gale and a mass of dark storm-clouds came charging in from the coast, wiping out the changeling beauty of that brittle winter evening.

The church bells were chiming six o'clock as the carriage pulled up outside the shadow of the Rossbach Gate. Night had fallen like a heavy curtain over Lotingen. As I took off my gloves to lower the window-sash, my fingers seemed to attach themselves to the brass frame. Thrusting my head out of the coach, looking for the guard, eager to be admitted, the cold nipped viciously at my nose and ears. A knot of French soldiers were huddling around a brazier outside the guardroom. The fierce wind toyed and tugged at the raging flames, forcing the men to pull their hands away for fear of being scorched.

I was so relieved to be home, I smiled at the gendarme who grudgingly left the warmth and the firelight and came across to inspect my papers. That Frenchman stared at me with bulging eyes from beneath the visor of his sweat-stained *shako*, growling something that was not intended to be welcoming as he pulled a percussion pistol from his belt and cocked the hammer, snatching the travel documents rudely out of my hand.

'Where are you bound?' he growled.

I wanted to say that I was going home, but decided against this in an instant, and gave him a different address. He nodded sourly, thrust the papers back into my hand, and looked at me with evident mistrust.

'One hour, Herr Magistrate, then get off the streets. You'll find yourself locked up in a cell if you don't.'

Egon Eis cracked his whip at the horses, and the carriage passed noisily beneath the medieval gate and onto the cobbled streets of town. Looking out as the vehicle made its way along Frederikstrasse, I was suddenly struck by the oddness of everything. Not one single shop was open. All the houses were closed and shuttered, too. There was no sign of life, no hint of commerce, though we were passing through the heart of Lotingen. I tried to dampen down my fears: the wind was freezing, the curfew almost upon us, and heavily armed French patrols on every corner were not good for trade. Even so, something was out of kilter.

'Can you go no faster?' I shouted up to Eis.

My wife and children had been left alone in a city where a massacre had taken place. I had abandoned them. *Just like Gottewald . . .* The thought struck home with force. In Kamenetz I had been so busy, I had not had time to think of private concerns. Now, I was anxious to conclude the business and hurry home. In the meantime, I could only pray that Lavedrine had kept his promise to look out for the safety of my family.

As the hooves of the horse clattered loudly, echoing off the dark walls in the tomb-like silence, I realised that the only light in the whole street was our carriage-lamp. None of the lanterns had been lit that night. As I gazed out of the window, mentally urging Eis to go faster and faster, the shadow of my driver rippled along the walls in a broken silhouette. He might have been the only soul left alive in the entire town. Then again, I thought, he might have been the Angel of Death, scurrying from house to house, striking down the first-born.

Had there been another murder? Had another family been massacred?

The carriage skidded violently, turning left, then speeded up again.

After a quarter of a mile, the holly hedge and kitchen garden of my home appeared. All closed, all shuttered, not a single light was shining to welcome me. Then again, they did not expect me, and I was not going home. Not yet. I looked the other way with pangs of regret as the house fell behind.

At last, the carriage wheels crunched along familiar gravel, then drew to a halt.

The building was steeped in darkness. Eight graceful Corinthian columns and a triangular pediment above, a broad flight of shallow stone steps below. As I glanced out of the window, I noticed that not all of the shutters had been closed. There was a glimmer of light in one of the rooms on the ground floor.

'Give me your lamp,' I said as I jumped to the ground.

'Stopping long, sir?' Eis asked wearily.

His voice was hoarse, weak with exhaustion. He had set his sights on a hot meal, strong ale, and a warm bed.

'I won't keep you much further,' I replied.

The iron knocker was cast in the shape of a Prussian eagle. I let it fall three times on the front door. My attention was caught, as it always was, by signs of rude entry which a French axe had left in the oak panels the year before. Like every other inhabitant in the town, I puzzled over why the damage had never been set to rights. The householder was not short of money. Our more malicious neighbours claimed that the damage had been left untouched to remind the world that the victim of this outrage was a Prussian. That scar was meant to prove that he was not a traitor, but was only doing his duty as a public figure.

I knocked again, wondering whether General Katowice would be taken in by Dittersdorf's damaged door.

'What do you want?' a voice cried from beyond the splintered panelling.

There was such a pitiful tone to it, I asked myself once more if something terrible had happened while I had been so far away from home. In a rising panic, I shouted my name and struck the eagle against the door again.

Bolts were drawn and chains rattled. The door opened a trifle, and a pale servant looked out. I raised my lamp to show my face.

'I must speak with the count,' I demanded.

A shadow cut across the rhombus of pale yellow light that fell on the tiled floor of the entrance hall. Someone was watching from the doorway of the reception room.

'Let him in, Hans.'

I recognised the voice, but when I stepped inside, crossed the hall, and found myself face to face with the man himself, I was shocked. He was, in truth, the haggard ghost of the Count Dittersdorf that I had left in Lotingen six nights before. He looked more like a wrinkled bloodhound than ever— his long, jowly face was lined, tense and drawn, his eyes sagging, red-rimmed, as if he had not been able to sleep for one single instant since the day that I set out for Kamenetz.

'I did not expect you so soon,' he said, crossing the hall to meet me. Then, remembering himself and what he was, he retreated into his habitual shell of formal hospitality. 'I am pleased to see you safe and well, Hanno.'

'What has happened, sir?' I demanded, fearful of the reply.

'Shouldn't I be asking you?' he replied, taking my arm, leading me towards the lighted room. Suddenly, he smiled timidly and turned to me. 'I know what you intend, of course. Much has happened while you've been away. None of it is good, but at least no more innocents have been murdered.'

'Thank the Lord for that!'

Those words did not come from my mouth. Nor did the doleful sigh that accompanied them. Count Dittersdorf and I had barely set foot inside a large room illuminated by a single candle in a brass mount. It flickered above the mantelpiece, where a log fire crackled and blazed, throwing up a shower of sparks. A large, winged armchair was set squarely in front of the fire, as if whoever was sitting there was unwilling to share the warmth and light with any other person.

'Indeed, my dear,' Count Dittersdorf replied, bowing in that direction, as his wife peered out from behind the high back of the leather chair. She was wearing a large woollen bed-bonnet, and held a white handkerchief to her eyes, as if she had just been weeping.

'I apologise for disturbing you, ma'am,' I said with a tilt of my head. 'I have just returned to town. I thought it best to inform the count.'

The countess made no answer, but raised the linen square to her eyes again to stifle a sob as she turned back to face the fire.

I glanced at Dittersdorf, hoping that he might offer some explanation for his wife's state, but all I received was a raising of his bushy eyebrows and a sagging of the bags beneath his eyes. Like a bloodhound that had lost the scent. 'There, there,' he cooed, in what was meant to be a soothing manner. 'Why don't you go up to bed, my love? I won't be long, I promise you. Hans will stand outside the door until I come to you. I must speak to Procurator Stiffeniis. It should take, what . . . five minutes, no more.'

Dittersdorf went to the door and called for his servant. I stood watching in respectful silence while the lady was escorted from the room. The instant the door was closed and we were alone, Dittersdorf blew out a loud sigh.

'These are troubled times,' he said. 'Lotingen is a city under siege.'

'Have the French insisted on a blackout, too?' I asked.

'They didn't have to,' he replied with a shake of his head. 'No one wants to give the impression that he's a sitting target. They fear that lighted windows may bring the plague crashing down upon them. There's been nothing like it since the day the French swarmed through the town last year.'

Pushing his lady's armchair to one side, he dragged a straight-backed chair close to the grate. 'Come here and sit by the fire,' he said. 'You've had a terrible journey, I think. Such dreadful weather! 'Tis a foul wind, as the English say.'

He crossed to a magnificent rococo carved side-table with lion's legs and a marble top, and poured two glasses of something from a pewter jug.

'Tell me what has happened, sir.' I was almost reduced to pleading.

'Spiced wine,' Count Dittersdorf announced with a gleam in his eyes as he brought me a crystal goblet containing liquid of a dark mulberry colour. He sat down heavily, and took a sip from his own glass, which carried off half the contents. He had been drinking. 'Mmm, that will take the chill off your bones. Taste the cinnamon! Now, Hanno, I want to know your news. I can hardly wait to hear it.'

I looked at him fixedly, but he sank his nose inside his glass and glanced away.

'Count Dittersdorf,' I said, like a father quizzing his son about where all the sugared almonds had gone, 'I want to know what has happened during my absence.'

'Nothing, Hanno,' he assured me blandly. 'That's just the trouble. The missing woman has not been found. Nor has the murderer been caught. Each day that passes weighs on us like an imminent death sentence. No one knows when the axe will fall. Nobody knows if it is *his* neck that will take the blow. Until the death-stroke comes, we live in fear, afraid of our friends and neighbours.'

'But no one else has died?' I insisted.

He raised his forefinger. 'Not yet,' he replied darkly.

I was tempted to echo Countess Dittersdorf's 'Thank the Lord', but I did not. I told him the little that I had been able to discover in Kamenetz. The sooner it was done, the quicker I would be able to excuse myself and hurry home to Helena and the children. But the fact that Bruno Gottewald was dead occasioned many questions, and even more pressing demands were to follow as I informed the count that General Katowice was training boy soldiers in defiance of the French. The old man appeared to sober up quickly as I complained of the lack of assistance I had faced from the commander of the fortress. I told him of the help I had been given by Doctor Korna, but also of the gruesome contents of those vats that the physician had chosen to show me.

'These things . . . I do not need to tell you. They must never go beyond these walls,' Dittersdorf insisted. 'That's why you had to go alone. The French must never know. I had heard rumours of atrocities, but what you have described . . .'

He stood up, lifted the tails of his jacket, and turned his backside to the warmth of the fire, bracing his knees for some moments.

Suddenly, he looked down at me.

'You believe that the death of Gottewald, the massacre of his children, and the disappearance of his wife are all related facts. That is what you are thinking, isn't it?' he enquired.

'It is difficult to think otherwise, sir.'

He trundled across to the side-dresser and refilled his glass.

'I have serious doubts,' he said as he returned to the fire. 'Let us say, for the sake of supposition, that Gottewald was murdered, and that the killer is still at large in Kamenetz. What motive could drive that same person, or his accomplices, to strike the family of the victim here in Lotingen? To murder three children? I can find no logical justification for your assumptions.'

He had put his finger on a problem which had racked my mind from Kamenetz to Lotingen. This was a trial run for the opposition I would meet from Lavedrine. He walked from the fire to the window, shifted the damask curtains, peered out into the darkness for some moments, then let the heavy material fall back into place.

'You cannot ignore those pieces that do not fit,' he chided me.

'Nor can I ignore what I discovered there,' I replied, sipping my wine, which was stone-cold. Even so, I felt it hit home as it reached my stomach. The little that I had drunk had certainly rescued me from the cold torpor that had worked its way deep into my bones with every frozen mile of the journey. 'If Doctor Korna is a reliable witness, and I have no reason to doubt his veracity, Gottewald was killed in the most unlikely circumstances. But the men who found his body are "conveniently" unavailable, either dead, discharged or absent from the fort. All these inconsistencies, in the unchallengeable opinion of the commanding officer, are "normal". But my instinct tells me that they are suspicious coincidences. Gottewald was the first, but not the last, victim, and I believe that more than one person in Kamenetz is involved.'

'A plot?' he spluttered.

Now that I was safe in Lotingen, distanced from the people and events that had made such a strong impression on my mind, Kamenetz seemed to be a closed and dangerous world. I had barely scraped the surface, but I had felt the strength and unity of purpose that held those men so tightly together. They were clenched in the fist of a single-minded maniac whose only concern was the liberation of his country. General Katowice would allow nobody to stand in his path.

'Lavedrine has not found the woman, then,' I murmured, uncertain whether to be relieved that the Frenchman had not succeeded in my absence, or worried that the investigation had ground to a halt.

'The search goes on,' Dittersdorf said. 'At least, I hope it does. I have not seen him since the day you left, and have no idea where his investigations may have taken him. Rumours are rife: they make them up by day, then take them apart by night, like Penelope's tapestry. If Frau Gottewald had been found, of course, I'd know of it. He is probably questioning Durskeitner . . .' He broke off, and peered at me. 'I mean to say, he is still the prime suspect, isn't he?'

Every time that I attempted to put all the fragments into order and make some sense of the whole, I had managed to weave the deformed hunter into my scheme. Sometimes the presence of Durskeitner reinforced the tale, but just as often it unwove the stitches that I had so carefully bonded together.

'Unless Lavedrine has been able to squeeze something incriminating out of him, he is the man who found the bodies. Nothing more. There is no evidence against him,' I said, rubbing my hands, which were still very cold.

'He may even be the perpetrator of the massacre, but following instructions given by others. The butcher's boy, let's say, given the brutal manner in which the children were murdered, and the crude facility with which he uses his blade on the beasts that he captures.'

'An executioner in Lotingen obeying orders from Kamenetz, is that what you suggest?'

I nodded.

'But what could be the cause?' he asked, a puzzled frown on his careworn face. 'What motive could there be for such hatred of the father?'

'The only opinions I have been able to sound suggest that Gottewald was considered a coward for his inability to carry out a field exercise. But the taint of betrayal and cowardice had already been cast on his character. I heard this rumour from the mouth of a boy. I am plagued by suspicions I cannot prove, or shake off.'

'What do you mean?' he asked cautiously.

'The French have chosen to ignore the existence of Kamenetz,' I replied, 'but the troops in the garrison live as if they expect to be attacked at any moment. They fear betrayal. Katowice warned me off. The doctor told me of the danger. The officers and men refused to speak to me. Baptista von Schill advised me that he would kill me if I did or said anything that would put the fortress at risk.'

'Major von Schill?' Dittersdorf gasped.

'The same,' I nodded. 'Did Gottewald undermine the safety of the garrison? Did his wife share the responsibility? Did someone kill him, then come to Lotingen for her? The murder of the children might be smoke blown in our eyes to throw us off the trail. If one crime provides the key to the others, I believe it is the first in the series.'

Dittersdorf did not reply for some moments. He stroked his chin and seemed to consider the possibilities. Suddenly, he let out a sort of wild groan, and shook his forefinger at me. 'I am worried, Hanno. Extremely worried. If you voice such opinions to Lavedrine or to Mutiez, you may do exactly as Katowice and von Schill have warned you *not* to do. You will paint Kamenetz in the darkest colours, and the consequences may be dire. For the whole of Prussia. Just think, not only do you depict the men as vile, scheming rebels, you also make them out to be cowards of the worst sort, men who lack the nerve to carry out their crimes, delegating the responsibility to that . . . that creature from the woods.'

'I see no other path to follow,' I said. 'Unless Lavedrine can come up with something more promising.'

I set my wine glass down, and sat up straighter in my chair.

'I need to know more about Gottewald's career, sir. Where he enrolled, where he served, and so on. Anything that might be useful. Regiments, battles, barracks, and above all, what he was doing in Lotingen. And why he went so soon to Kamenetz. Anything that Prussian efficiency can reveal.' I took a deep breath, worried that I might be about to offend him. 'My only hope, sir, is to receive more help from you than I received in Kamenetz. Can I depend on you?'

Dittersdorf stiffened, his head pulled back, and two red spots appeared on his cheeks, as if he had just been slapped with a pair of leather gloves and challenged to defend his name and his honour.

'You'll have everything I can obtain,' he replied as civilly as if I had just asked for another glass of mulled wine. 'In exchange, I insist on two inviolable conditions. Will you hear them?'

I made a condescending gesture.

'First,' he continued, 'keep Lavedrine away from any dangerous information until you are certain what to do with it. Once the crime is solved, we will tell the French what we want them to know, and nothing more.'

Not tell Lavedrine? Work on the case in secret? It would be difficult, but not impossible. 'Agreed,' I said, like a man forced to make a hard bargain. 'What is the other thing?'

Count Dittersdorf drained his glass.

'Hit the Jews, Hanno. Hit them hard.'

I was taken by surprise.

'All this talk of babes whose throats have been slashed,' he continued rapidly. 'Ritual mutilation. Christian blood being used to defile the communion host. Rumours that the blood was drunk in the course of a Hebrew orgy. Word is spreading through the province, there's no halting it.' He pulled out his handkerchief and wiped his forehead. 'The scribblers are heaping fuel on the fire. Just yesterday one of them wrote that the Jews are guilty, and he claimed that the French are covering up for them, manipulating Jewish insurgents into murdering their Prussian enemies. Berlin fears a revolt against the foreign troops. I received a despatch this morning. They want to see the matter cleared up without delay. Peaceful coexistence must continue. At *any* price. Do I make myself clear?'

He sat back in his chair, waiting for me. But I did not reply.

'If you have no juicier bone to offer the mob, give them one that they are already chewing on. The French must be kept out of it.'

He stared at me in silence for some moments.

When he spoke again, his voice was low and emphatic. 'The Jews, Hanno. The Jews alone must carry the blame. Speak with Lavedrine about the course of action that you intend to take.'

'I'll speak with him first thing in the morning.'

'Morning?' he spluttered, jumping forward, his face inches away from my own. I felt the spray of spittle settle on my skin, inhaled the strong fumes of the spiced wine that he appeared to have consumed in ample quantities that day. 'Perhaps I have not made the state of affairs in Lotingen clear? We are sitting on a powder keg which could explode at any moment. You must speak to him tonight! He must tell you what he has discovered, the opinion he has formed of this massacre. If no other expedient presents itself, swoop on Judenstrasse. A gate has been erected. The Jews are prisoners, more or less. The bigger the fuss, the better effect it will have on public opinion. The townspeople must see that repressive action is being taken. It must be made clear that *that* is where the blame lies. Convince Lavedrine if necessary, while I . . .' He paused—for breath, but also, I thought, to measure out his promises, thus limiting his own responsibility for the consequences. 'I will provide you with every fact that I can discover about the life of Bruno Gottewald. If you can find a better answer, so be it. Until then, the Jews will take the blame. Have I made myself clear?'

I nodded reluctantly. Instead of going home to my wife, who was probably terrified by the tales circulating in town, I would have to go looking for the elusive Frenchman.

Dittersdorf accompanied me to the door. Standing there in the shadows, he suddenly clasped me to his chest, like an ancient warrior sending a younger one off to battle, knowing that the novice might be slaughtered. I realised that there was nothing affectionate in the gesture.

It was the kiss of Judas, sealing our complicity.

As the bolts closed behind me, and the chains rattled into place, I turned to coachman Eis and informed him that we would not be going immediately to our beds.

An expression of resentful confusion appeared on the coachman's face.

I must have looked at Dittersdorf in a similar fashion when he chose to thwart my own homecoming.

· 18 ·

I CLIMBED ABOARD the coach, but gave no order to the driver.

I had no idea where Lavedrine might be. I had met him only twice. On both occasions he had strutted onto the scene like an actor who has important lines to speak. Having delivered them, he had turned and walked off the lighted stage, disappearing into the dark wings from whence he had come.

I gave a vague order to Egon Eis to set the carriage wheels rolling in the direction of the town centre. We passed achingly close to my home once again, but my thoughts were so fully occupied in trying to work out where Lavedrine might be hiding that the house was gone in a flash. The Frenchman was not a soldier in any true sense of the word. He held the honorary rank of colonel, but he had told me himself that his role was to monitor criminal behaviour by the emperor's troops, while collecting data for his criminological studies. If he had an office, it might be anywhere in town. And as for his private lodging, that was anyone's guess.

As Egon Eis asked me for the second time where I wished to go *exactly*, sir, I came up with a solution so blindingly obvious that it had not occurred to me before: 'Take me to the Old Hotel,' I shouted up.

I was thankful not to see the sour expression on my driver's wrinkled face. Eis was anxious to be home before the curfew, and time was running short. Once the hour struck seven, it would be harder than ever to unearth Lavedrine. Surely, I thought, Mutiez would know where the criminologist could be found.

Called the Hôtel de Ville since the Francophile days of Frederick the Great, the Old Hotel, or 'Old Town—Hall', was a three-storey building on the opposite side of the main square from my own office in Lotingen Court House. The Bonapartists had set up their General Quarters there, and the place was always full of French officers, whether they were on duty, or merely passing the time of day. Proving himself to be the sole exception to a universal rule, Mutiez was nowhere to be found.

As I turned to leave, I almost bumped into Captain Laurent, the requisitioning officer for the town.

'What are you doing here, Herr Stiffeniis?' he exclaimed with surprise.

'I am looking for Colonel Lavedrine.'

'One moment,' he said, and disappeared into the officers' mess. 'No sign of him in there,' he reported when he returned.

He called to a soldier, sitting at a desk.

'Check the address of Lavedrine in the Bible. Make a note of it,' he ordered. He turned to me with a smile. 'That's the name we give to the register where the lodgings of our officers are listed.'

Within a few minutes the man came back with a slip of paper in his hand.

'Chapter and verse, sir,' he joked as he saluted.

'I hear that you and he are investigating the massacre,' Laurent commented, as he handed me Lavedrine's address. 'I wish you all success, and hope you catch the killer quickly, *monsieur*. Lotingen reminds me of my home town during the *grande crainte*. Blois-sur-Loire will never be the same. Nor Lotingen, I fear.'

I knew what he was referring to. Towns and villages in rural France had been engulfed by a tide of hysterical fright as the Reign of Terror unfolded in Paris. People spoke of packs of wolves and covens of witches, blood-hungry thieves and murderers roaming the countryside by night, hideous monsters creeping out of the woods under cover of darkness in search of human prey.

'Many people died as a result of the panic. It was fear that did it. Nothing more. They slaughtered their neighbours indiscriminately, thinking to protect themselves and their loved ones from danger.'

'We must ensure that nothing of the sort happens here.'

'If the local population were to turn on our men,' he said, concern written openly on his sallow face, 'who knows what would come of it?'

Was that what the massacre of those children was intended to foment? I asked myself. The provocation of violence and lawlessness against the foreign invader? If that should prove to be the case, it would be necessary to turn the spotlight back on my fellow countrymen. A raging, angry crowd would be an immensely powerful weapon in the hands of unscrupulous nationalists. Could that be the link with Kamenetz? A scheme devised by General Katowice and his adepts to throw Prussia into a state of ungovernable chaos? It would make things more difficult for the French, and deflect attention away from the rebels.

'I wish you a good night, Captain,' I said, taking my leave, hoping that it really would be an uneventful night for all of us, French and Prussians alike.

Outside, I examined the scrap of paper. Lavedrine had taken up residence within the city walls, I noted, though somewhat off the beaten track, far from the heart of the town.

'Arbeitstrasse,' I called up as I mounted the coach again.

Egon Eis grunted unhappily and flicked his whip at the horses.

I knew the street. A multitude of craftsmen lived and worked in the area. It was busy enough by day, but as we edged slowly through the narrow streets leading down to the wharves of the River Nogat, the area seemed darker, more deserted than the rest of the town. The only signs of life were armed French soldiers on street corners, and patrols of authorised vigilante watchmen bearing cudgels, carrying lanterns on sticks, making sure that everything had been safely locked up for the night. We were stopped and questioned twice by the French. On the second occasion, they pointed out the house that I was bound for, the corporal-in-command mentioning with a grin that one of his superiors had stayed there for a couple of days, then decided to take himself somewhere else.

This wild goose chase was taking longer than I had bargained for. Church bells began to toll, and the nightwatch crier called out the hour of seven. Had it not been for my impeccable documents, Eis and I would have been destined for the cells.

'Sergeant Kakou said the persons in the house were *singulières*,' the corporal said, as he handed back my papers.

'*Bizarres*,' his companion added.

Neither man attempted to clarify what their officer might have meant.

The people living in the house were rag-and-bone merchants named Böll. So said a large wooden signboard hanging above a shop that shared its entrance with the house. ALL YOU NEED, AND MORE, the legend read. A painted profile of a fat man in a tricorn hat, standing in front of that very house, was handing an object to a woman. She, in turn, held out a gold coin in payment for it.

Herr Böll answered my knock some moments later.

He appeared not to have changed his coat or taken off his hat since the day the sign was painted. Glancing beyond his shoulder, I caught a glimpse of the entrance hall. The simplicity of the house surprised me. I had expected to find Lavedrine in exotic and luxurious apartments which would lend lustre to his status as an officer and scholar of renown.

'I am looking for Colonel Lavedrine,' I said, wondering what had induced the Frenchman to choose the place, taking note of the landlord standing before me. He was at least sixty years of age, and even more rotund than the man painted on the sign. His clothes also resembled those in his painted profile: black suit, black shirt, black neckerchief. His leather shoes were black as well, a silver buckle the only point of light in his outfit.

'Herr Lavedrine is abroad this evening,' Herr Böll replied in an unusually high-pitched voice, his eyes protruding like spotted billiard balls of veined yellow ivory.

At his back a tiny woman dressed in white from head to toe, a veil covering her nose and mouth, emerged from behind a black curtain on the right. As she crossed the hallway, her dark eyes peered fearfully into mine. She stopped for an instant, sniffing the air like a wild hare, then, without a word, she lifted the matching curtain on the other side of the hall, and disappeared from view into another room.

'Where has he gone?' I asked. 'It is imperative that I find him.'

Herr Böll did not reply at once. His peculiar eyes rolled up into his head: only the whites were visible. For an instant I feared that he was about to lose his senses. But then his eyes fell back, one after the other, slotting into place like numbers on an abacus. He had been concentrating, I realised, and when he spoke, he was hesitant, perhaps embarrassed.

'I've never been there myself, sir. Colonel Lavedrine seems to . . . well, he seems to go there quite a lot. At the far end of Roederstrasse. *Hunger.* I believe that is the name of the house.'

'Is Colonel Lavedrine working there this evening?' I asked.

Herr Böll peered at me as if I were mad.

'I hardly think so!' he said.

Roederstrasse is in the most run-down quarter of the town, with the exception of the Jewish ghetto, which it flanked on one side. But before I could enquire any further, Herr Böll bowed politely from the waist and shut the door in my face.

I climbed up into the coach again and gave directions to Eis.

'Are you sure, sir?' he shot back. 'At this time of night?'

'You said you were a soldier, Eis,' I snapped. 'Consider yourself on duty again, obeying orders that you don't understand, but know to be useful.'

The coachman saluted like an obedient trooper, and turned his coach in the direction of the lower reaches of town. Five minutes later, we rumbled slowly down Roederstrasse. The houses seemed to be shuffling up the hill to avoid slipping into the river. The roofs stretched out, almost touching one another, like fully grown trees that had unwisely been planted too close together when they were saplings. Barely wide enough for the coach to pass, a sewer ran down the middle which was blocked and overflowing. And yet, one aspect was striking. In contrast with the rest of town, the shutters were thrown back, and light blazed unhindered onto the dirt and refuse that cluttered the way.

The carriage stopped outside a building that was taller than the others.

'Here we are, sir,' Eis announced, pointing to a painted tile on the wall.

HUNGER

The door knocker was gracefully moulded in the shape of a mermaid. No sooner had it dropped than the door swung open, and I found myself staring into a pair of bright green eyes.

Hungry eyes, I remember thinking.

'*Um, ja!*' the girl exclaimed, as if a tasty dish had just been set on the table.

From the glistening sheen on her round cheeks and the rapid rise and fall of the panting breasts beneath her low-cut blouse, I realised that I had disturbed this beautiful creature at her work. My immediate impression—that her work was something less than honest—was tempered by confusion. With shimmering blonde hair which fell loosely to her naked shoulders, she was a most attractive waif, her figure pressed as slender as an hourglass by a whalebone corset. She smiled broadly in welcome, waiting for me to speak, it seemed, and my confusion grew. As we stood on the step, the rich perfume of sweat and something sweeter came washing out of the house and over me like a tidal wave.

'Colonel Lavedrine?' I asked, uncertainly.

The girl turned her head and said something in a breathless, throaty tone to a person inside the room whom I was unable to see. I did not understand a word, but thought I caught the name of Serge Lavedrine somewhere in the middle.

'I must speak with him,' I insisted.

Again, she turned away and spoke. Scandinavian, I thought, though it was beyond my capabilities to recognise the precise language or dialect.

'At once,' I pressed, breaking in on what seemed to me to be an unnecessarily long and probably useless exchange of opinions.

'Serge is busy,' a voice called back from the interior. 'Hilda, ask him if he wants fresh spice on his *Putipù*.'

The girl before me burst out laughing, her breasts heaving and pumping with delight at the joke, then she went away to do as she had been told. A minute later, she was back, flashing a doll-like smile as she slipped her hand beneath my arm and pulled me over the threshold.

I thought for an instant that I had stepped into a bakery. The smell of ovens was strong, the air hot and heavy. My nose twitched with the scent of yeast, but there was also a strong smell of spiced wine in the air. The room was large. At the far end, a fire blazed in the grate. Hanging from the ceiling was a huge chandelier. There were more candles scattered around the place than I could count. And more than one table. Many chairs with spindle backs. And on every wooden surface, a naked man or woman. More women than men, I corrected myself. I counted six, all busily engaged with paintbrushes, which they refreshed from a large cooking-pot in the centre of the room. Honey, I guessed from the colour, smell and consistency. As the door closed at my back, the tongues returned to work. I had broken in upon an orgy.

'Room at the end,' the girl lisped, letting go of my arm, and pointing away down a long corridor.

I went the way the whore's finger pointed.

Before the fourth door, I knocked hesitantly.

'*Entrez, alors!*' came the lively, nasal reply.

Opening the door, I saw the transformation of Lavedrine's face, as debauched good humour gave way to surprise.

'For the love of God, Stiffeniis! I was expecting hot spice, and what do I get? Your pale, starched face. Come in from the cold. Make yourself at home. My friend here will hate you for it, but there you are!'

I stepped uncertainly into the room.

'Sit down,' he said. 'Don't be shy, they don't eat people in Naples as a rule.'

I obeyed, and found myself face to face with a person.

I can find no adequate word to describe the Frenchman's table companion. Nor was I disposed to stare. Naked from the waist up, I would not have dared to imagine what was hidden beneath the table. Slender, with hardly any breasts at all. Olive-skinned, except for the radiant slash of painted lips and glistening nipples, like sliced cherries, the colour of carmine. Above penetrating black eyes, eyebrows arched like the wings of a hawk across a broad and graceful forehead. Those languishing orbs fixed themselves on me, and silently took me in, shining out of two deep, dusky caverns. A finely chiselled nose. Full, pouting lips. A dark-skinned Mediterranean beauty. But the mystery began below the mouth. The line of the jaw was square, the chin pronounced, the shadowy flesh too dark.

'You look frightful, Stiffeniis. Have you just returned?'

'An hour ago,' I said, waking up from dazed embarrassment. 'I had a word with Dittersdorf. Since then, I've been trying to track you down. I went to General Quarters, then to the lodging-house of Herr Böll, the ragman.'

'And the good Böll told you where to find me,' Lavedrine said, evidently amused as he sat back in his seat. 'What did you make of him?'

'I am not here to discuss my opinion of your landlord,' I replied.

'What a pity!' he replied, clearly pleased with himself. 'I take a professional interest in the man. I have never seen any person fall so easily into such a deep and lasting trance.'

I remembered the stout man, the way his eyes had rolled up into his head, my fear that he might be about to faint in front of me.

'Hypnosis is a favourite subject of mine,' Lavedrine explained. 'I was hoping to study this local phenomenon and make the most of my idle hours. It may be of use in my profession, I thought. But you're not here to listen to my prattling tales,' he said, running his hand through his hair, brushing the silvery curls back from his forehead. 'Would you care for a fig preserved in honey?'

He offered a platter from the table, taking one for himself when I refused. He held up another for his companion. Putipù leant forward, mouth open, tongue chasing after the slippery fruit, as Lavedrine pulled it playfully away. Her chestnut-coloured hair shifted lazily to one side, giving off a more tantalisingly sweet perfume than the delicacies on the plate.

'*Bien*, to business! What did Gottewald have to say for himself?' he asked. 'How did he take the news of the massacre?'

'Must we talk here?' I asked, looking towards the silent creature who made up the third member of our party.

Putipù held my gaze. She did not say a word. Only her mouth moved, as she chewed the fig, then swallowed it. She seemed content to sit there, showing off her partial nudity and total ambiguity, as if it was all that she asked of life.

'Putipù will excuse my momentary disattention while we talk. The *gentildonna* comes from Naples, as I mentioned, though *femminiello* is the musical-sounding name they use down there for such entrancing ambiguity. She understands no other tongue,' he said, turning to the object of our discussion with the warmest of smiles.

The girl, if that is what she was, made an impatient grimace, flirting with her eyes in a manner that was almost too feminine to be believed, murmuring words to him in what I took to be an Italian dialect.

Lavedrine blew a kiss to her, then turned to me.

'You must be thoroughly exhausted after hunting Sybille Gottewald all this time.' I said it mildly enough, but I could not suppress a note of accusation.

The smile died on his lips. His large, irregular face, which was, as a rule, lively, animated—fascinating, I supposed, to judge from the greedy way his companion watched him—seemed to crumble and collapse into a mask of tired melancholy. Again, he ran his hand through his hair. Again, the silvery curls fell back as soon as he desisted. He had been drinking heavily, I realised.

He snarled: 'You suppose that I have been on my worst behaviour, while you've been slaving like a dog. Am I correct?'

He threw out his forefinger, which quivered in the warm air.

'I have *not* found Frau Gottewald. Dead, or alive. But not for want of trying. I've searched this town from end to end. It is harder to find a well-hidden corpse than a living, screaming woman, Herr Procurator.'

He sat back, and a deep sigh escaped from his lips.

'I hope you have been more fortunate,' he said, stretching out his hand to take another sweet.

I held my silence.

'Well, damn you,' he said, snatching up another fig, 'aren't you going to tell me what Gottewald had to say while you were travelling together?'

I waited until he had chewed and swallowed.

'Bruno Gottewald is dead,' I announced.

The expression of confusion that flashed across his face might have given me pleasure in other circumstances, but I had more important things on my mind.

'We must hammer out a pact,' I said with fierce determination. 'Just you and I. No one else. The French and Prussian authorities must never know.'

'Coming from a genuine Prussian,' Lavedrine replied, 'that sounds to me like a treasonable offence.'

I nodded two or three times, savouring the words before I said them.

'Exactly,' I said. 'Treason is what I am proposing. In the interests of truth.'

· 19 ·

'I SHOULDN'T BE telling you any of this.'

My throat was sore with cold. It ached with every lie that I told him. Still, I kept my promise to Dittersdorf. As I described it, Kamenetz fortress was a forgotten enclave that could be cancelled out at the drop of the emperor's crown. General Juri Katowice, commander of that lonely outpost, was an ancient relic, a tottering invalid with an amputated hand, content to steer clear of trouble until his pension was granted. His troops were a defeated and demoralised band of melancholy failures. Of boys training for a future war against the French, I said not a thing. Baptista von Schill was another phantom not worth mentioning. And, of course, those French heads pickled in vinegar had ceased to exist.

'They are an innocuous, inoffensive lot in Kamenetz,' I concluded.

'But Gottewald died there,' Lavedrine insisted, pushing a glass of dark red wine across the table, inviting me to drink with them.

'His death was recorded as an accident,' I replied. 'He fell from a cliff while out on a routine training exercise, and broke every bone in his body, including his neck. Herr General Katowice insists that the massacre in Lotingen is nothing but a strange coincidence.'

Lavedrine glanced away with a heavy sigh, while Putipù followed every shift and movement that the Frenchman made. My tale was of no interest to her. Nothing seemed to interest her, except for Serge Lavedrine.

'It happened before the children died. Before Gottewald's wife disappeared.' I took a gulp of wine, and felt a soothing warmth. 'There must be some connection, I am certain. How can there *not* be? I managed to speak with a number of Katowice's officers, and with some of his men. They all believe that Gottewald was a traitor. A coward. That was the impression I got. They hated him for some reason. Which brings me to the point. Why would his colleagues believe that Major Gottewald had betrayed them? He was a career soldier, a typical product of our military cadre. He must have done something extraordinary to jeopardise that position.'

Lavedrine stared back, then pulled an ugly face. 'What do you suspect?'

The nonchalance with which he greeted me had given way to concentration.

'I have no idea yet,' I admitted.

Lavedrine set his glass down on the table-top and refilled it. With a tilt of the bottle, he invited Putipù to join him. The creature smiled. Was there a hint of a shadow under all that paint and powder, the suggestion of closely shaven hair on the upper lip and the jaw? Women from the Mediterranean shore were darker of skin, more careless about their bodies. I had seen hair exposed on the arms and the legs of fisherwomen in Genoa that any decent Nordic woman would have hidden beneath long sleeves and extravagant flounces. Putipù sipped at the wine with a careless grace that was, I thought, exaggerated, stretching forth her chin unnaturally far, pursing her lips to meet the rim.

As her Adam's apple bobbed, over-large, all my doubts returned.

'The situation you have described,' Lavedrine continued, waving his glass in the air, 'may explain the death of Gottewald in the fortress. But does it explain the murder of his children?'

'If we knew why he had been murdered,' I said, 'many things might appear in a clearer light.'

Lavedrine sat up suddenly. His eyes flared into mine. His breath was hot with wine, but his sarcastic temper was more inflamed. 'Are you suggesting that someone came all the way from Kamenetz to Lotingen to kill those children, and carry off the mother?' he challenged. 'The inhuman ferocity of Prussian soldiers does not surprise me. They are renowned for it. On the field of battle they are merciless. But I can make no sense of the notion that a battle-trained soldier would slit the throats of children, then mutilate their corpses. How might this relate to Prussian military honour?'

He sat back heavily, his eyes dull and bleary.

'The final punishment may not have been administered by a soldier,' I replied.

Lavedrine's eyes flashed in the candlelight. 'Who, in that case?'

'Someone who raises no suspicion in Lotingen. Someone who can be discarded, sacrificed, if it comes to that.' I paused for effect. 'Franz Durskeitner, for example. A man who knows the local terrain. A man who possesses skill with a knife. A man who can be easily browbeaten,' I added, remembering the ease with which Lavedrine had insinuated himself into the woodsman's favour. 'The perfect instrument for the perfect murder. Durskeitner will have to be interrogated again.'

Lavedrine held up his hand to stop the flow.

'That man is also dead,' he said, staring deep into his wine glass. 'They found him the day after you left. Inflammation of the lungs was the doctor's diagnosis. You'll recall how cold it was when we questioned him. A prison cell was not the best place for him. Not in that condition.'

A living image of the woodsman flashed before my eyes. The monstrosity of that half-formed body. The knotted muscles in his arms and shoulders, the fragility of all the rest. I recalled the discoloured wounds on his chest which had been doused with acid, then cruelly probed by the French soldiers.

'Surely you spoke to him again?' I quizzed. 'You'd won his confidence. He must have told you more about Frau Gottewald.'

I did not underestimate the Frenchman. He was capable of keeping the best news until the last, if only to confute my theories and exalt his own investigative abilities. But Lavedrine slowly shook his head again.

'The only interrogation he underwent was the one that you conducted,' he said.

I sat in silence absorbing this announcement.

I had gone to Kamenetz to find the father. Lavedrine had stayed in Lotingen to search for the mother. Neither of us had been successful. And now, the last man to see the woman and her children alive was dead.

He raised his eyes and stared at me, drumming on his lower lip with his fingers. 'The morning after your departure,' he murmured, 'I went back to the cottage alone. We were under too much pressure that night. We . . . That is, I was distracted,' he corrected himself. 'Despite my familiarity with murder and violence, I was shocked. The sight of those children . . .'

As he spoke, his expression changed. His gaze was fixed on the surface of the table, though I do not think he saw it. He was in that room again.

'There is something in that house. Some element,' he said, 'that I am unable to put my finger on. I should be able to see it, but I cannot.'

He raised his forefinger and twirled it emptily in the air.

'It is there. I know it. Right before my eyes. But I cannot focus properly.' He shrugged his shoulders. 'I suppose it is because I am a foreigner,' he said. 'It's like the German language. I understand it well enough, but sometimes a particular nuance of meaning escapes me. In a French house, it would be different . . .'

He tapped his fist on his forehead.

'Those stains of blood on the wall beneath the window, for instance,' he mused.

I thought back to those traces. We had puzzled over them together that night. But then, we had been distracted by the horror of the scene in that bedroom, caught up in the frantic search for the missing woman.

'Have you made any sense of them?' I asked.

He raised his eyes and stared at me, again drumming on his lower lip with his fingers.

'They are distant from the bed, where the bodies were found. Yet, they are distinct, thick, dripping with blood. It's almost as if they had been daubed there.'

'What do you mean?' I asked.

Lavedrine did not answer at once. I thought he had not heard me, or that he did not care to answer.

'Let me sum up the situation,' he replied in a monotone, refilling his glass. He turned to Putipù and refilled her glass. Then, he poured more wine for me. It glistened like rubies in the candlelight.

'Durskeitner is dead. If he was hiding Frau Gottewald, she is also dead by now. I failed to find her. She will have starved, or frozen to death in the six days that have passed. The town, coast, and woods have all been searched. There is no sign of her. So, we are investigating four murders. According to you, the solution to this mystery lies within the ranks of the Prussian army in a far-off fortress. But then . . .'—he paused for effect—'you spoke of treason.'

I drained my glass.

'Whatever Bruno Gottewald did,' I said, 'the Prussians will never tell us.'

I paused, looking Lavedrine squarely in the eye before I continued.

'If he were a French spy inside the walls of Kamenetz, the French authorities will know the details. There must be records of his treachery, correspondence, payments made in his name.' My voice was low, my heart was hammering, as I forced on to my conclusion. 'I was not able to breach the Prussian wall of silence,' I said, 'but you may have more luck on the French side. That is the pact.'

'You want me to tell you French military secrets?' he said with a chuckle.

'That is exactly what I want,' I replied. 'For what it's worth, I've told you everything regarding the secrets of a Prussian fortress,' I insisted, fearing that he might see the light of the lie in my eyes. 'Now, you must do the same.'

He stared silently into the depths of his wine glass.

'Bruno Gottewald would not be the first Prussian soldier to change sides,' I pressed him. 'Thousands of Prussians have fled to Russia since the French arrived, and others have thrown in their lot with France.'

'A turncoat?' he queried, looking up. 'Is that what you are thinking? A Prussian who has declared his allegiance to France? And for this, he and his family have all been murdered?'

'This is what I suspect,' I said with a nod.

Lavedrine considered the idea, then stretched out his hand impulsively to touch my sleeve. 'I am a loyal subject of the emperor,' he said. 'But above all else, I am a criminologist. I want to solve this case as much as you do, Stiffeniis.'

I sat back more comfortably in my seat as we drank a silent toast to success.

'Now, I'll tell you what I have been doing in your absence,' he continued in the same confiding fashion. 'I have not been idle, I can assure you.'

'I am all ears,' I replied, raising my glass.

'In the first place,' he began, 'I have discovered the name of the person who rented that cottage to Gottewald.'

'Excellent,' I said, encouraging him to continue. 'Who is he?'

Lavedrine shrugged his shoulders, as if to diminish the importance of the fact. 'A man named Leon Biswanger. I had him brought in to the General Quarters for questioning, of course, but . . .' He hesitated, as if considering how best to express what he wanted to say. 'He is a local man. I think that we ought to speak to him together.'

'Do you believe that he is hiding something?' I asked.

'He doesn't like being seen in the company of Frenchmen,' Lavedrine replied. 'Threats had been scrawled on his wall the last time he was obliged to visit the General Quarters. He has been targeted by Prussian nationalists, he says. He fears them more . . .'

He paused and waved his hand in the air.

'More than the French?' I asked, completing the phrase for him.

Lavedrine smiled and nodded. He rested his elbow on the table, propped up his chin with his hand, and stared at me without saying another word. I was worn out after the rigours of the journey. All I wanted was to go home and sleep. My leaden Prussian humour was no match for the wit that darted like mercury through the Frenchman's veins.

'I planned to visit him tomorrow morning,' he continued. 'At his own home this time. I had no word of your imminent arrival, but I would consider it an honour if you accompanied me. Together we may set Herr Biswanger's anxious mind at rest. What do you say? Is nine o'clock too early for you?'

Before I could do more than nod, he went on: 'I meant to make the most of this short *divertissement* from work this evening. But you, Stiffeniis, have brought the work to me. Which means I'll have some catching up to do when you have gone.' He smiled gallantly in the direction of his companion. Putipù smiled warmly back. 'I'll be late to bed tonight. So, let's say ten o'clock. You've still to see your wife, I imagine. Here's to the sacred duty of the marriage bed!'

He raised his glass to toast this intimate allusion.

'Ten o'clock,' I murmured coldly, wondering how he dared to think of Helena in the same vulgar terms that he applied to his painted harlot. 'Where?'

'The Bull's Eye?' he replied, with unaffected ease. 'They make the most delicious cakes. I do love sweets,' he added, waving his hand in the direction of the platter of figs and Putipù, like a glutton feasting his eyes before sitting down to gorge himself.

'The morning I left you at your home,' he continued, 'I had some posters made and distributed around the town. Nailed to trees, left in shops and taverns. The usual thing. Asking for information about Frau Gottewald. The quickest way to test the waters, I thought. Enlist the help of the local populace.' He slapped his hand on the table-top. 'Too late!' he exclaimed. 'An Arctic blizzard might have swept through Lotingen, carrying the news from house to house. They knew already. Every single person in town knew exactly what had happened.'

He lingered over the last few words, then smiled at me brightly.

I returned it, unaware that I was exposing my flank to the dagger poised beneath the cloak of friendliness.

'A surprising number of people came forward with information,' he said.

This bland statement made me sit up. Had he led me on, inviting me to tell him the little that I had been prepared to tell him about Kamenetz and General Katowice, only to reveal that he had made more important discoveries in my absence?

'Anything useful?' I asked.

'Gossip, hearsay,' he replied with a dismissive shrug. 'Frau Gottewald seems to have been blessed with powers of ubiquity. A number of people report seeing her in various places at one and the same time. Unfortunately, they never described the same person twice!' He pursed his lips, then continued: 'One man said that she was tall and blonde. The next that she was short and stout with a pockmarked face. She was seen on the streets of Lotingen one minute, wandering through the woods ten leagues away the next! Some people swore she had one child alone, others said two, three or even more. An innkeeper reported seeing her drinking gin in the company of soldiers. She drank them under the table, by all accounts. Nothing emerged that might be taken seriously.'

He raised his head and stared at me, that quizzical smile playing at the corners of his mouth. It ought to have put me on my guard, but I failed to see the danger.

'With one exception,' he announced.

A look of contentment appeared on his face, like a cat who had caught a mouse.

'A person who was terribly frightened by the news of the massacre. A person who felt obliged to speak from a pressing sense of duty. A person we should enlist in our enquiry. A most credible and reliable witness, I would say.'

'This is wonderful news,' I exclaimed, surprised by the sudden intensity that had taken possession of Lavedrine. The mirth had gone from his face. He sat back in his chair, his eyes fixed on mine, saying nothing.

'Who is this person?' I asked. 'Shouldn't we speak with him straight away? Even before we speak to Biswanger?'

'There shouldn't really be any problem,' Lavedrine replied. 'Of course, it all depends on you.'

'On me?' I asked with a puzzled smile.

'Oh, yes,' he said, nodding his head thoughtfully. 'The name of the witness is Helena Stiffeniis.'

·20·

I SAID GOODBYE to Egon Eis.

As the coach pulled away, I lingered by the garden gate, wondering how to greet my wife. She had spoken to Lavedrine. She knew what I had tried to hide from her. But Helena left me little time for thinking. Perhaps she had heard the slamming of the door, the pounding of departing hooves. The front door of the house flew open, and there she stood on the step, holding up a lantern.

'Hanno? Is that you?'

Her voice quavered as she called out. Her light made no impression on the dark space of the long garden that divided us.

I froze on the spot.

Helena could not see me, though I saw her well enough by the feeble lantern-light. She seemed more frail and slender than when I left, an impression that was fortified by the heavy shadows and the darkness. Her cotton nightdress clung to her slim figure, her hair a wild, restless halo enclosing that dear, pale, frightened face.

Her hair . . .

Unbound, free, the way it was the day I left home. '*À la Sturm und Drang,*' Lavedrine had said, mixing French and German in an elaborate compliment. The odd expression had taken both of us by surprise, but Helena had been flattered by it. As any woman would. Serge Lavedrine was a Frenchman, he was one of the enemy, but I was no fool. The wit, the charm, and the brash eccentricity of that man would make a favourable impression on any woman who found herself the object of his attentions.

My resentment flared up like a bonfire. Against him. But also against her.

As she took a few hesitant steps towards me, I wondered whether she had let her hair run wild and free ever since the day that I departed. Did she show herself carelessly now to anyone, in that untended and spectacular fashion? Had she gone to visit Lavedrine in that state?

A picture flashed across my mind: Helena sitting close to the Frenchman, speaking with animation, telling him what she knew about the murders, while her hair danced before his gawping eyes with a vitality all its own.

Jealousy stabbed at my heart like a murderous assassin.

'Helena,' I managed to say, stepping forward to meet the light before she could discover me lurking in the dark.

The wind howled in the trees. She did not hear my voice. And yet she came on bravely, holding up her lantern defiantly, as if it warded off wolves.

'Who goes there?' she challenged.

Instinctively, I moved forward to meet her.

'Hanno!' she cried, taking a step backwards. 'Why did you not answer me?'

She did not rush to my arms. Nor did I throw them wide in welcome.

Slowly, the lantern sank to rest at her side. She came towards me, advancing step after step along the path, murmuring all the while like a prayer, 'Thank the Lord! Thank the dear Lord!'

She stood before me, like a child in a trance. Her head fell forward slowly, and came to rest on my shoulder.

'You are home,' she whispered close to my ear.

I set my hand gently upon the crown of her hair, my fingers burrowing down through the thicket until I felt the warmth of her skin. 'Come,' I said. 'Let's go in before the cold puts paid to us both.'

I could find no other words to say.

As we entered the house, Lotte leant over the balcony in front of the children's room.

'Welcome home, Herr Procurator!' she cried in a bright whisper. She was still wearing her apron and day-cap, and must have just finished putting the children to bed. 'Shall I bring the babies down to greet you, sir?'

I waved my hand to prevent her.

'Manni won't forgive you,' Helena said, as we passed into the parlour. 'He said that you would return this night. I promised to bake a strudel if he was correct.'

The apples from our orchard were stored in a barrel in the attic. Helena thought of them as her secret treasure. Every day she would check that all was well, removing fruits that showed any sign of bruising. If fit to eat, they were eaten after lunch. If not, they were used for baking.

'He was correct in his estimations,' I said.

'Then I must sacrifice my precious apples,' she replied.

There was nothing playful in the tone of her speech.

I stood in my parlour in outdoor clothes, like a stranger who had lost his way and come knocking at the first door that he happened to find. The room was warm, though the fire in the grate was almost extinguished for the night.

Already stiff with cold, my fingers trembled with inner tension as I tried without success to unhook the clasp and shrug off my travelling mantle.

Helena's hands settled gently over mine.

'Let me do that,' she said.

Deftly, she undid the fastenings and freed me of the weight. She dropped the cloak over the back of a chair, turned to me, took my hands in hers once more, and led me to the horsehair sofa. Applying gentle pressure, she sat me down, then turned away to tend to the fire. With kindling, some sticks, and a flurry of the bellows, bright flames were roaring up the chimney in a twinkling.

'You'll be warmer in a bit,' she said, glancing back over her shoulder. She employed exactly the same encouraging note when one of the children had a mishap. 'I'll get you a glass of wine in a moment. Just think what a surprise it will be for the children, to find their papa sitting down to breakfast with them in the morning!'

It was not the heat that began to seep from the fire, but the sound of Helena's voice, the selfless goodness of her ministrations, which began to melt the stiffness from my limbs, to break the ice that had encrusted my heart. She brought me a glass of wine seasoned with pepper, carefully wrapping my fingers around the stem of the glass. 'Drink this,' she said, 'it will do you good.'

It was some minutes before I was in any condition to respond.

'I spoke with Lavedrine,' I began.

Helena drew up a chair and sat herself in front of me.

'I thought you had,' she said quietly. 'And you want to know how that meeting came about.'

I had never imagined for one single moment that I would be required to interrogate my own wife. I did so that evening in the hope that she might tell me something, some small, insignificant detail, that she had not already told to Lavedrine. That massacre had fallen from the sky like a meteorite, and it had landed squarely in the middle of my own living room.

'Why did you go to him?' I asked.

'I did not,' Helena replied, her voice as vibrant as catgut on a fiddle. 'I did not go directly to *him*, as such. When I learnt the truth of what had happened, I felt compelled to speak. The truth was not what you had told me, Hanno.'

I did not allow her to finish. 'Who told you?'

'Mother Albers always comes on a Wednesday,' she replied. This matron went from house to house in Lotingen, regardless of the weather, a basket perched upon her head, containing fresh-laid eggs. 'She told me where the family lived, and that they were still looking for Frau Gottewald. She told me what had happened to those children. She showed me a notice saying that the French authorities wished to speak with anyone who might have news of that family.' She was silent for a moment, then she added with decision: 'Lavedrine put out those handbills. It was inevitable, I suppose. Meeting him, I mean.'

I took this information in, evaluating its worth. 'What leads you to believe that you may have known the woman?'

Helena sat stiffly on the wooden chair, looking down at her hands. They rested on her knees, which were pressed closely together. 'I was walking near the wood where the massacre took place. The fact that the victims were three young children. The peculiar state of mind of the woman that I met.'

I said nothing for a moment.

'Isn't that an incredible coincidence, Helena? There is a massacre, a woman disappears, and *you* have met her. By chance. You, and you alone, in the whole of Lotingen.'

Helena's eyes did not flinch from my own. Years seemed to fly by in those few moments. She did not speak, and seemed determined not to do so, as if silence were the only objection she would make to the doubts that I had voiced.

'Why not, Hanno?' she cried suddenly. 'Our whole lives are shaped by chance, by coincidence. Can you believe there is some pattern in our world after everything that we have been through? We are alive, not dead, by chance alone! She was searching for food that day, as many women do to feed their children nowadays in Lotingen. I had never spoken to her before. I'd never even seen her. But I met her, and spoke to her. That day, and no other.'

She looked down, as if to study more attentively the silver wedding band that she wore on her little finger. If I had been the helpless waif a few minutes earlier, as Helena mothered me in from the cold, our roles were now inverted. My wife looked like a very young maid who had been unjustly accused of doing wrong by a stern, unbending father.

But then she rebelled.

'How could you, Hanno?' she murmured. There was pain in the protest, but there was also accusation. 'How could you think to keep the truth from me? Could such a terrible thing be kept a secret? Even for so short a time?'

My thoughts flew back to Lavedrine. He had warned me of the dangers of prevarication. He had read the implications of the situation better than I had done. Then again, I thought bitterly, he has a vast experience with the opposite sex.

'It was cowardly of you. The less I knew, the easier it was for you to go

142

away and leave us here in Lotingen alone. This was unfair,' she concluded, 'not to me alone, but also to your children.'

Was that how she chose to interpret my actions? Not as a conscious desire to spare her the shock and the fright, but as a pretext to spare myself the necessity of worrying about her while I was gone. It took me some moments to regain control of myself.

'When did you see that woman?' I asked in a measured, professional tone of voice. 'I know you have already told Lavedrine. But I want to hear it for myself.'

She looked away.

'Did you enter the house?' I insisted.

'No!' she protested violently. 'I met her walking in the lane. And she spoke to me. I did not ask her name, but it was her, I know it was! It was in that part of the country, near the Wolffert estate. That's why I went to Lavedrine. To tell him what I knew.'

Helena showed no hesitation as she told her tale. She gave no hint that she had understood the real question that taunted me. A question that my lips refused to form.

Why were you there, Helena? What were you doing in that lonely place?

'Was this woman alone when you met her?' I asked.

'She had two children with her. Another child—a little girl—had stayed at home in bed. A head-cold, I think she said.'

'She told you that she had a daughter. But you did not see the child.'

Helena stared at me in silence.

'Why would the woman lie?' she asked sharply.

'That is not the point,' I replied. 'I am trying to establish the facts.' I wondered how Lavedrine had reacted when my wife recounted the tale to him. Was Helena making comparisons between us? Had the Frenchman been a more gentle and persuasive inquisitor?

'How did this meeting come about?' I asked.

Helena began to speak in slow bursts, each sentence followed by a pause. She seemed to be searching for each word, each phrase, before she would let it out of her mouth.

'She had been picking raspberries. She had a basket on each arm. One was almost full to the brim.'

'Raspberries, then. Two baskets. One almost full,' I repeated calmly. But in my mind, I thundered again: *In heaven's name, what were you doing there?*

'I asked what she was going to do with them. The fruits, I mean.'

'And what did she reply?' I prompted.

'She said the children would eat them for dinner. In a bowl. With milk.'

The table laid for the evening meal in the Gottewald house flashed through my mind. The children had eaten fruit that night. And they had drunk milk. Were such tiny details sufficient to suggest that Helena had really spoken to Sybille Gottewald? The abandoned woods on the Wolffert estate must have been a fine hunting ground for wild fruit. How many women from Lotingen might go there every day with a basket on each arm, hand in hand with their children, intent on picking raspberries? Since the coming of the French, whole families had survived on little else.

'Do you remember when it was? The day, I mean? The hour?'

She did not answer, looking away from the fire to the darkest corner of the room.

'Come, Helena,' I encouraged gently, 'surely, you must be able to tell me that?'

Her head drooped, and she stared once more at her motionless hands. 'Early in October, Hanno,' she replied. 'One day is much like any other. It was late in the afternoon. There had been rain. A dull, grey dusk with huge, dark clouds presaging night. A night that promised to last for ever . . .'

I held my breath at this ominous description. Was Helena privately telling me something of her own state of mind that day, something that I, her husband, ought to have realised?

A cold, detached, cynical voice in my head probed at the wound: she had told all this to Lavedrine, he had made no mention of it to me. The Frenchman had left me to draw my own conclusions about my wife's emotional state.

'Before or after Dittersdorf's feast?' I insisted.

'Does it matter?' she said angrily.

'I'm afraid it does,' I replied. 'The missing woman's husband died that month.'

'He died?' she whispered, the colour in her face draining away with her anger.

'That is why I need to know precisely when you met her,' I clarified.

'It was before the Dittersdorf feast,' she said. 'A week, perhaps . . . I remember that it was exceptionally chilly. The first cold day of winter. I recall thinking that the days and nights to follow would be ever colder and more dreary.'

The note of desolation in her voice was harrowing. Helena had always hated the winter season. After Jena and the occupation, her hatred had become more intense. It was as if the French had condemned us to a life of never-ending cold and privation. And yet, I had to admit, there was a hint of something far more ominous, something menacing and even final, in what she had just said.

'In that case,' I pressed on, 'she must have known he was dead, if . . .'

'If she truly *were* his wife.' Helena was staring at me, her eyebrows tightly knit, as if she were in pain. 'They are all dead, then. The husband, wife and children. How did *he* die, Hanno?' she implored.

I told her of my meagre findings in Kamenetz, then turned to her again with questions. 'Did that woman mention that she had recently lost her husband?'

Helena frowned, concentrating hard on her memory of that meeting.

'No,' she said. 'I could see that she was upset . . . No, that is not exact. She was in a state of terror, Hanno. I spoke of this to Lavedrine . . .'

'Terror?' I interposed. 'What was she afraid of? Did she tell you?'

Helena slowly shook her head. Then she glanced up. 'I will never forget that woman's eyes.'

Her own were two dark pools which stared blankly into mine.

I felt as if I were standing on the shore of a fathomless mountain lake—nothing moving on the surface; nothing stirring in the icy depths. All silent, all still. Why was I convinced that she had not told me everything? Or that she had told me less than the unadorned truth would allow?

'Describe her to me, Helena. Those frightened eyes. Her face, her hair . . .'

She protested with a tired shrug. 'I told Lavedrine.'

'Repeat it to *me*,' I replied with a passion that I was unable to suppress. It was, in any case, the first rule of the Prussian magistrature. The witness should be made to tell the story again and again to search out any contradiction or incongruity.

'Very well.' She sighed. The woman was small of stature—*petite*, Helena insisted, employing the French adjective. Her hair was brown, her skin was dark, almost swarthy. Her eyes were sparkling chestnuts—huge, compelling, glistening with fear.

'There,' she said, fright gleaming in her own eyes, 'that's what I told him.'

I do not know at which point her hand had come to rest gently upon my knee. I felt the impulse to place my hand on hers, to reassure her that all was well, but I did not do so. As she finished speaking, her hand slid away. There was no taking it back, I thought with regret.

'And then she said those puzzling words to me. They will always remain impressed upon my mind,' she continued. 'We were talking about the raspberries, and where she'd found them. The baby in her arms had fallen fast asleep. The other little boy was holding onto her skirt. Those children were both dark of skin, and hair, and eye. They seemed to be the image of their mother. Of course, I had never seen their father. I could make no comparison. Two pretty boys in excellent health.'

This description corresponded with the children I had seen laid out across the bed. Healthy and robust, except for the fact that they were dead, the throat of each one gaping like an edible marrow with a slice taken out.

'What did she say?'

Helena started in her seat. 'It was not a question of what she said, but the manner in which she said it.'

When she spoke again, her voice was hardly her own. It was low, piteous, urgent.

'Go home to your little ones. Go home before the long night falls. Before the reaper comes . . .'

'The reaper? What did she mean by that?'

Helena shook her head. 'I cannot say. But she was terrified. I thought for just one moment . . .'

'What?'

'I thought she might be talking of . . . her husband.'

Husband?

I froze. What was passing through her mind?

'Gottewald was dead,' I stated coldly. 'Before his children's throats were slit.'

She sat in silence staring down at her hands.

'Were you alone?' I asked.

I saw her start as the words flew off my tongue. I was not thinking of another man. I was thinking of the children. But those words had been said, there was no recalling them.

'*Our* little ones,' I added quickly.

'Safe and well,' she replied. 'At home with Lotte.'

I was silent, considering this extraordinary admission. My wife had been alone. Wandering unprotected in the country outside the perimeter of the town. Why had she never told me of this outing?

A shiver shook her shoulders beneath her nightgown, despite the flames now roaring in the grate. 'The sky was dark, rain was threatening. Soon it would be night. Perhaps she intended nothing more than that. No more . . . no less . . .'

'But you think otherwise.'

'She was afraid,' Helena repeated, her own eyes wide with fright. 'As a rule, the weather may hamper our plans, but it does not provoke fear.' She shook out her hair, and stared at me intently. 'I may be making more of what that woman said than she intended, but . . . I took it as a warning. A warning to me. Am I a witness, Hanno?'

'Is that what Lavedrine said?'

'I want *you* to tell me,' she replied.

'Lavedrine says, and I quote, that you are a credible witness.'

Then, I know not what took possession of me. My words were rough, but I chose them with care. 'I found him in a bordello this evening,' I said. 'A whorehouse. In the company of a creature of the night.'

She looked at me, her face a mask of troubled incomprehension.

'What were you doing that day?' I asked. 'Alone in the countryside.'

Helena looked down. Her head sank low. I could not see her for the mass of waving dark curls, like seawort in the rolling tide, or the glistening serpents of some mysterious Medusa.

Her words were sharp and clear, though she choked back tears.

'What were *you* doing this night, husband? Roaming the town instead of seeing that your babes were safe. Instead of reassuring me that all was well.'

· 21 ·

As DAWN BROKE, I crept from the house like a thief.

I had no wish to relive the ugly tension of the night before, no desire to add extra fuel to the fire of the interrogation to which I had subjected my wife. Before I saw her again, I would need time to decide how to put the questions that still rankled in my mind.

Under cover of a dense white fog, I closed the kitchen door, and set out along the road to town, making myself and my destination known to the all-too-familiar French soldiers guarding the East Gate. Though preparing myself for a busy day, I had no idea how hectic it would turn out to be. I made my way through the empty town and went directly to my office. I was faced with the tiresome necessity of writing two distinct and different accounts of my voyage to Kamenetz. The first was meant for the eyes of Count Dittersdorf. The other would be added to the mounting pile of documentation regarding the massacre, which would be scrutinised, sooner or later, by the French. If I had hoped that the freezing cold, and the fifteen-minute walk which separated my home from the courthouse, would be sufficient to shake the cobwebs from my head, I was wrong.

I sat by the window for almost three hours with a quill in my hand, an inkpot and sheet of paper laid out before me, looking over the empty square at the vacant gallows where Junior Lance Corporal Braun-Hummel had been executed. As the town began to wake up, I found that I had managed to compose no more than half a dozen lines of the report that was meant for Dittersdorf's consumption. I ought to have repeated word for word what I had told him in person the previous night, but writing it out in fair copy was a more complicated business. Lies that fall with ease from the tongue stand out on the page and scream their falsity.

Indeed, as the hour for my appointment with Lavedrine approached, I left the unfinished report on the table, knowing that I would be obliged to grapple with it again before the day was out.

It was a quarter to ten when I entered The Bull's Eye.

I went there early, hoping to drink a beaker of hot, expensive chocolate in peace while I waited for Lavedrine to appear. But he had arrived before me, no worse the wear for a night of debauchery.

'Would you care to join me?' he asked.

'No, thank you,' I replied stiffly, still smarting from the wedge that he had driven between myself and my wife.

He was in fine fettle, his hair crushed and tousled, as if he had forgotten to brush it, his silver earring notable by its absence. Was it dangling from the ear of Putipù? I asked myself.

'I hope I did not spoil your entertainment last night,' I said, sitting down.

'Not at all.' He smiled. 'Putipù's, perhaps. They are such possessive creatures. They want our attention all for themselves, do they not? Those from the Mediterranean shores are true *divae*,' he said, using the Latin tongue with nonchalant gusto. 'I had to work hard to be forgiven. I hope your return home was equally rewarding?'

I bridled at this familiarity.

Did he not realise the difficulty his intrusion in my personal affairs had caused?

He appeared to be totally unconcerned. He opened his mouth and sank his teeth into a thick slice of shortcake. Despite the war, anything could be had by a man with French coin in his pocket, even in Lotingen, where the price of sugar had trebled in the space of a single year.

'Heavenly!' He sighed, reaching for his coffee. That was another imported luxury which very few Prussians could permit themselves. Then, he bolted down the last of his breakfast, washing the crumbs from his lips with the remains of his coffee. 'Have you seen this?' he asked, pulling a paper from his pocket, throwing it casually on the table-top.

The face was monstrous to behold.

A gaping hole of a mouth, ripping teeth that froze the blood in my veins. The canines were exaggeratedly long, poking from the molars like the tusks of a bloodthirsty walrus. They had pierced the skin of the victim's neck with the ease of surgical knives. Blood spurted in showers to form a dark red pool, the killer's lips drawn wide in a hungry grin, eager to feast on human flesh. The victim howled a wordless protest—eyes clenched shut, a grimace of horrid awareness on his face, ruffled hair dripping blood, drops flying off in all directions, like a hound shaking itself dry after a ducking. A struggle to the death. No doubt which was the predator, which the victim. The nails of the killer were curved, like the raking talons of a dragon. The nose was sharp, hooked, the eyes piercing black, with wild, pitiless lights. Pointed ears, a pointed beard, dark hair flying around the head in greasy tangles and bouncing ringlets. A black skullcap. A crude caricature. A Son of Israel. A large crucifix dangled from a chain at the neck of the victim. A Christian child, a baby boy, awash in a sea of his own red blood. A title formed in the same bright colour:

WHY THEY WANT OUR CHILDREN'S BLOOD

Beneath the drawing, a short explanation, scientific in tone, horrifying in its details. The Jews were creatures of an alien race. They needed blood—the baptised blood of innocent Christian children—to sanctify their pagan rituals. Their rabbis would defile the blessed Host, stolen for the occasion, then eat the sodden mess to perpetuate their own sort in orgies of unthinkable brutality. They were animals, human in appearance only. How long would the Jews go unpunished for their crimes? A list followed on in alphabetical order of towns where similar outrages had taken place, together with the names of Christian children who had been sacrificed to the Jewish lust for untainted blood. The final sentence claimed that the cynical French invader used these heartless monsters to keep the Prussian populace in check.

'Where did you find it?' I murmured.

'Pinned to the door of my house this morning. They could have saved themselves the trouble. Lotingen is papered with them. Very soon after the massacre, they started to appear all over the place. I have twice issued orders for the troops to collect them up and tip them on a bonfire. However, given the nature of the accusation, I wonder whether I have improved the state of things. Any Prussian with a mind to do so will accuse us of trying to cover our tracks. The Jews are in cahoots with the French, whose revolution gave them civil rights. Have you ever heard such nonsense?'

He did not wait for my reply.

'Time to go,' he said, standing up, leaving an inordinate sum of French coin on the table as payment. 'The situation grows more complicated by the day,' he said, sweeping up the handbill and ramming it into his pocket. 'If any other persons were to die . . .'

He did not complete the warning. Nor did he need to. I foresaw only too well the consequences of finding Frau Gottewald. Alive or dead, she would breathe new life into the passions that her disappearance had excited. What she herself might say hardly mattered. The Francophobes, the Prussophobes, the haters and baiters of the Jews would have a field day.

'Let's see if your presence will help to loosen this Prussian tongue,' he said as we walked along the street.

I looked up at the sky. Fog had given way to tumbling steel-grey clouds, one or two with silvery edges. They washed over the town in rapid sequence, carried on the strong breeze, wave upon wave of them, reminiscent of the incoming tide on the nearby Baltic coast.

We were heading for the port.

The house of Leon Biswanger was in the new part of Lotingen, Lavedrine said.

In recent times, King Frederick Wilhelm III had held on stiffly to an uncomfortable position of non-alignment and non-aggression. Before Jena, the economy of the town had prospered as a result. We were only eight miles from the coast, our harbour was deep and frequently dredged, the river wide and gentle enough to take seagoing ships, while the wharf was a solid, respectable crescent of three- and four-storey warehouses. Grain had been imported from Russia through Lithuania, stored for a month, then exported again to Britain at a profit. Until the invasion, the French emperor had not been able to contain us within his rigid 'continental system', as the newspapers called it. But grain was only one of the commodities that fed the growth of Lotingen. Linen, wool, weaving, amber, timber—all of these were valued by the French themselves. They were the local riches, and many men had made a fortune from them. Down by the riverside, a bustling new hamlet had grown up in the service of trade, and it was in this direction that we headed. There was a solid wooden bridge that crossed the river upstream from the dock, and we crossed it, holding on to our hats against the stiffening wind.

If the French bombardment of the old town had caused great loss, there was little sign of it in that district. The damage had been quickly repaired in the pressing interests of business. On the far side of the river, there was not a trace of destruction as we walked the length of the unpaved street. Nor as we stood before Leon Biswanger's freshly polished front door, which was at the farthest end. There were no signs of forced French entry, no split wood, no broken lock hanging uselessly from a twisted nail. If there had been a war, it had not forced its way over that man's doorstep. Indeed, the extensive workshop or storehouse attached to the side of the house gave every appearance of having been newly constructed. Despite its size, there were only two small windows in the wall that ran along the road, and they were tightly shuttered. Whatever Biswanger kept in his storeroom, it needed neither air, nor light.

'What smell is that?' Lavedrine asked, his nostrils quivering.

It was sickly-sweet, like rotting beetroot, something organic that had been left to soak in water. Jute, perhaps, or hemp. Sack and rope were products for which Lotingen was justly famed.

These warehouses are packed to the roof with the riches of the Baltic

Sea, and many another sea besides. Whatever it is,' I added, 'it's pungent stuff.'

'I'm surprised the neighbours haven't complained.'

I smiled to myself, thinking that the Frenchman's flat nose was not the sharp one of a tradesman, as I knocked three times on the door.

The man who opened it was small and robust with large, paw-like hands, a large square face, and grizzled hair turning white, like a dusting of snow, cut close to his scalp. There was a worried, guilty look on his face even before he spotted Lavedrine standing at my side.

'Good morning, Biswanger,' Lavedrine began, with a most un-German emphasis on the final syllable of the man's name.

Biswanger blinked uncomfortably.

'This gentleman is Procurator Stiffeniis,' Lavedrine continued. 'You have heard of him, no doubt. We need to clarify a few details regarding the letting of that cottage to the Gottewalds.'

He left Biswanger to take this information in. The man had not been summoned to appear before us, the Law had come to him. And for the moment, it was wearing carpet slippers and felt gloves. Biswanger took a step forward, glanced quickly up and down the road, then waved us in without a word, shifting his bulk to one side in the cramped hall.

Clearly, he was not happy about this unexpected visit. As he led us into a cold reception room, and invited us to sit down, his face was a rigid mask of deference.

There was a strange, sombre atmosphere about the room. Plain whitewashed walls, a simple floor made of red bricks set in a chevron pattern. Nor was the house furnished in traditional Prussan style. There were no heavy curtains hanging to keep out draughts, no reed matting covering the floor. Unlit logs were piled up neatly in the chimney grate. A single Pietist print in a simple wooden frame hung on one wall—*Christ Beheading Satan with the True Cross*. That chamber was unused, it seemed, except for receiving visitors, then sending them quickly on their way again.

'What can I do for you?' Biswanger asked, his eyes fixed on me, his bass voice brusque, as if he had no time to fritter away. 'I told this French gentleman everything I know about that family of unlucky wretches.'

'Important details sometimes return to the mind on second telling, Biswanger,' Lavedrine interrupted with an acid smile. 'Is that not true, Stiffeniis?'

Lavedrine turned to me with a show of the same perfect understanding we had used while interrogating Franz Durskeitner. But we had not agreed on any strategy, and I wondered which tactics the Frenchman had hidden up his sleeve.

As we sat there, studying each other across the plain pine tabletop, Lavedrine and myself on one side, Biswanger on the other, my attention was attracted by the only piece of ornamentation in the room. It occupied the centre of the table. A brass bowl on three short legs, the lid engraved and pierced with small, round holes. It reminded me of the incense-burner found in churches, though it gave off a strong persistent whiff of camphor, or some other household disinfectant. This was the only evidence of a female presence in the room. There were no embroidered cushions, no linen antimacassars, no decorative tablecloth. No dried flowers in a vase, no sprig of herbs. Nothing perfumed, except for the unmistakable smell contained within that metal casket on the table.

Was Biswanger a widower? I wondered.

'Let us pretend, Herr Biswanger,' Lavedrine went on, 'for the sake of my Prussian colleague here, that our first conversation about the Gottewalds never took place. I would like you to tell him everything that you told me. If you would be so kind?'

Leon Biswanger nodded his head, but he did not speak.

'Begin by telling us how you happened to meet Major Gottewald,' Lavedrine prompted, 'and what you agreed upon between yourselves in the way of business.'

I saw a range of expressions flash across the man's pale face, as though some inner kaleidoscope had been shifted by a hand not his. He seemed to flush, then fade, then plump himself up for what he was about to say, a look of blank determination settling on his mouth.

'I wouldn't want you gentlemen to think that I've been reticent,' he began. 'Nor that I do not wish to help. This investigation of yours must be difficult, I do not doubt.' He looked down at the table and shook his head in sympathy. 'The thought of what has happened in that cottage! Who'd ever have imagined such a thing in Lotingen?'

He looked up suddenly, rubbed his hands together. He darted a glance at the Frenchman, then spoke directly to me, as if Lavedrine had ceased to exist. 'What it was, sir, it was being hauled in to speak to a French official in a French police office like that. Made me nervous, it did. I work with everyone, I do. Frenchmen, Prussians, traders from all over the place that are passing through. I'm not ashamed to admit it,' he hurried on, 'I'll do a deal with any man, if he's honest. Anything to help the nation, know what I mean? Still, it isn't easy. You know better than I do, sir. If a Prussian goes strolling into a French police station bold as a cider barrel, his neighbours are going to think the worst of him. They are bound to say that he's a sneak. Or worse!'

He let out a melancholy sigh, but I said nothing to help him. I found it hard to imagine him telling Lavedrine what he had just told me. He had not looked once in the Frenchman's direction from the moment he opened his mouth. He cleared his throat, as if to shift a fishbone. 'I thought that I had done my best by them, sir. Given them all I had to give, so to speak,' he confided.

'Indeed, Herr Biswanger,' I said. 'By way of business, then, you agreed to rent that house to Bruno Gottewald. You met him, I take it. You spoke to him . . .'

'Very little, Herr Procurator,' he interrupted, shaking his head. 'Half a dozen words, no more. Just the time to finalise the details.'

Lavedrine watched silently. This was a conversation between two Prussian nationals.

'Which "details"?' I asked.

Biswanger nodded his head, and began to speak. His account was short, concise, and plausible. Early in August, he said, a Prussian major named Gottewald came to seek him out. The man had just arrived in Lotingen with his family, and knew that Biswanger had a cottage to rent. The soldier expressed the very greatest urgency in wishing to find suitable accommodation for his wife and children. Out of the town, he said. Somewhere quiet, preferably in the country. Gottewald told Biswanger that he would be leaving soon to join his general in a distant outpost, and wanted to see his loved ones comfortably settled before he set out.

'Why did he come to you?' I queried.

'I did not ask. He did not tell me. I am well known in Lotingen.'

'So Gottewald came looking for a lodging, and you offered to show him that house in the wood.'

'No, sir,' Biswanger countered. 'He asked for *that* cottage, and no other. At the time I was handling a number of other properties. They were larger, more expensive, of course, but that was the one he wanted.' For the first time, he glanced over at Lavedrine, then back at me. 'I told him, sir. I warned him. Out there in the country, all alone, I said, your wife would be happier in town, sir! An' what do you think he said to that?'

I waited without answering.

Biswanger shook his head. 'His wife decided, sir. *She* insisted that she wanted to live off the beaten track. In a quiet place. That cottage was ideal, he said: the fewer the neighbours, the better!'

'It really could not have been any quieter,' Lavedrine murmured, unable to resist the obvious. Something in his tone told me that he was not thinking from the point of view of the victim; he was considering the vulnerability of that isolated house as the murderer must have seen it.

'Did he seem to be afraid for his family? Or for himself?' I asked.

'Not at all, sir,' Biswanger replied promptly. 'As I told Colonel Lavedrine, Major Gottewald was in a hurry—that was the house he wanted.'

'How long had the house been standing empty? Who used to live there?'

I was wondering whether the Gottewalds had been murdered by mistake. After all, the previous occupants might have been the real object of the attack.

'No one has dwelt there for years,' Biswanger answered, promptly stamping on my hypothesis. 'Not since the days of the Wolfferts. Ten years, or more, I'd say. The family living there at that time must have been tied serfs. I've no idea who they may have been, or where they might have gone.'

'The house has been recently refurbished. Did you buy it, Biswanger?'

Lavedrine must have read my thoughts. He had awakened from apparent distraction to fire this question at the man.

Biswanger shifted heavily in his seat, looking from Lavedrine to me, then back again. Then he stared at the back of his pudgy hands, turning them over to examine the palms before he found the answer that he was looking for.

'The house has been set in order in recent times,' he said, looking at neither one of us. 'After Jena, as a matter of fact. It's a bit out of the way if your business lies in town. Then again, it stands on the Danzig highway. Not bad, if your interests point that way.'

'Interests?' queried Lavedrine. 'The French? Is that who you were hoping to rent it to?'

Biswanger rolled his mouth up into a tight grimace. 'Let's say, anyone who might be . . . interested in keeping an eye along that road. The French, of course, sir. But not only them. When politics shift, there's always room for improvisation. An inn, perhaps. Or a hunting lodge for officers . . .'

'A whorehouse for French squaddies,' Lavedrine offered with a wink.

Biswanger smiled uncertainly, and winked back. 'You catch my drift, sir. That house did seem to offer a fair number of commercial possibilities, though it was slow finding an enterprising soul.'

'Until that Prussian officer turned up,' Lavedrine concluded. 'May I enquire how much you paid for it, and how much you charged for the rent?'

'We agreed on ten thalers a month.'

This was more of a murmur from the side of his mouth than a proud proclamation of business acumen, and Lavedrine's eyebrows arched with surprise. 'Not a lot,' he said. A moment later, he added: 'Indeed, the rent is incredibly low.'

Biswanger pulled an uncomfortable face, and looked extremely unhappy, even embarrassed. He had answered our questions, and answered them honestly, I presumed, but still there was a trace of something that I could not put my finger on. He appeared to be telling us what we wanted to hear, but that was not the same as freely telling us everything he knew. Was this the attitude that had puzzled Lavedrine at their first meeting? Did the man have something to hide?

Lavedrine slapped the flat of his hand on the table, and fixed Biswanger with a look of frightful intensity. 'Let us recapitulate,' he said. He raised his hand and held one finger up in the air. 'You set a house in order with the intent to speculate on its commercial use.' He added a second finger to the attack. 'That house was on the Danzig road, and you hoped to make a handsome profit renting it to Frenchmen, or those who make a profit out of them.' The third finger popped accusingly into place. 'But then a desperate Prussian officer arrived on the scene, and you rented it to him for next to nothing. I ask you, Biswanger! In your own words, he was interested in *that* house, and no other. You could have asked for twice as much, but you did not. What miracle of Christian charity took possession of you?'

Biswanger raised his hands in the air as if Lavedrine had pulled a pistol from under his cloak and cocked the hammer. 'You know already, sir, I think.' He looked at me, and made a nodding motion with his head. 'You've laid your hands on the contract, haven't you, Herr Procurator?'

Lavedrine avoided my eye. I nodded my head to hide my incredulity.

'Could we ignore it?' Lavedrine said with a sneer, following it up with a blinding platitude. 'A legal contract is a binding contract, when all is said and done.'

Although he spoke with knowing intelligence, he had made no previous mention of it. The existence of this document was as new to him as it was to me, I realised.

'You know the house does not belong to me, then,' Biswanger declared. 'I should have told you at once, Colonel Lavedrine, but, well . . . there and then, I did not think that it was a matter of any great importance.'

He popped the top button of his bulging waistcoat loose with his finger, and let out a mournful sigh, as if he had been in danger of suffocating.

'In the circumstances,' he went on, his brow red, beaded with droplets of sweat, 'I do believe I'd better make a clean breast of the whole thing.'

'Excellent,' I agreed. 'Rather than make your position worse.'

Biswanger jammed his eyes tightly closed. I thought he was about to cry. 'If you've spoken to lawyer Wittelsbach, you'll know that I am merely the nominee. I do rent other houses, but not that one. It isn't mine to rent.'

'We know that,' I said, stepping quickly into Lavedrine's shoes. 'But before we act on the information, we want to hear from you the name of the owner.'

I hoped my voice would not betray the excitement that I felt.

Biswanger rubbed his chin for what seemed an interminable length of time. 'The trouble with that house, sir . . .' he began. 'The trouble with *any* house . . . You need a respectable name. Isn't that right? If deeds are to be signed, I mean to say, with a lawyer there, you need a man who . . . Well, a person like myself. That house does not belong to me. *That's* why the price was low.'

'Who owns it, then?' I asked.

He jumped to his feet. 'It's not a crime as such, sir,' he said. 'Do you want to see my half of the agreement? It's here in my office, signed by lawyer Wittelsbach, just like the copy you've seen. I can go and get it for you . . .'

'Herr Biswanger,' I said, standing in front of him, 'you are in grave danger of getting yourself into very serious trouble. Who does that house belong to?'

'It belongs to Aaron Jacob, sir,' he said.

Before I could react to this revelation, Biswanger took it upon himself to elucidate.

'Aaron the Jew,' he added.

· 22 ·

So, I thought, this is the new breed of Prussians.

While Leon Biswanger boasted of his schemes for making money, I saw them advancing in legions, rank upon rank, a mighty army, sweeping the whole of Prussia before them. Dirt was ingrained beneath their fingernails, carrying with it the recent memory of an aching back and endless labour in a country gentleman's potato field. For centuries, generations of Biswangers had slaved for privileged men who ruled over them like kings.

Junker lords and their agents watched like hawks while their serfs turned the heavy clods in the snow and pouring rain. *Junker* lords shouted orders at them when the season for compulsory military exercises came around. *Junker* lords with names like Katowice, Dittersdorf, and Stiffeniis led them into battle. My father and his forebears had managed their serfs with un-bending intolerance. Now, fortune's wheel had shifted for men at every level of society. The *Junker* had disgraced themselves in Berlin, defiantly honing their sabres on the doorstep of the French legation the evening before the invasion began. That had been the last straw. The French had con-quered us and brought their revolution with them, instituting the Great Edict in Prussia. They had punished the *Junker* by promising liberation to their serfs. All the Biswangers could be free, if they chose to scrabble for an independent living. The ones who had broken loose would turn a trick with any profiteer who chose to knock at their door. Even the Nation's worst en-emy, by which I meant the French. The country would expand and grow, I had no doubt, as a result of the efforts of Biswanger, and his money-hoarding fellows, but it would not be the Prussia of old.

'Aaron the Jew?' Lavedrine prompted.

Leon Biswanger had met Aaron Jacob three years before, he said. The man had arrived in the small ghetto of Lotingen, a fugitive from Lithuania and the oppression of the Russians.

'He made a fortune,' Biswanger recounted with relish, 'collecting bones from animals and making soap. Aaron's a sharp one, I'll say that for him. He had money, he wanted more, but had no means of investing it locally. It was a lucky encounter for both of us, I have never looked back.'

He stared at Lavedrine as he said all this, avoiding my eye. A Frenchman could understand far better than a Prussian what motives drove him. Aaron Jacob had bought four houses through the agency of Biswanger and lawyer Wittelsbach, two in the centre of the town, two more outside the city walls, including the cottage that the Gottewalds had occupied. Biswanger had signed the contracts and paid the taxes, then he had taken a healthy cut of the profits from the real owner.

'Me and Aaron Jacob get on right as rain,' he said, 'but I would not say I know him well. I only meet him when there's business to be done, or accounts to be settled.'

'Do you meet him in the ghetto?' I asked.

'You wouldn't catch me going there!' he answered quickly. 'Nor bringing him here. We meet "by accident" at Wittelsbach's office. All sorts come and go there, no one gives a toss these days. We had to be more careful before . . .'

His eyes darted at Lavedrine.

'Before what?' I pressed him.

'Well, sir, before Jena.'

His eyes did not waver from mine as he admitted this treachery.

'The coming of the French has made it easier,' he continued. 'No one pays us much attention these days. Business is business.'

'Did Gottewald know that the cottage belonged to a Jewish landlord?' Lavedrine piped up.

Biswanger shook his head. 'He thought the house was mine. Aaron's name and tribe never came into it. Only Wittelsbach knew . . .' He hesitated for a moment, peering hard at Lavedrine. 'May I ask a question, sir?'

The Frenchman waved an encouraging hand.

'Did the lawyer tell you? That man's a viper, I always knew it!'

'You may be surprised to hear this, Biswanger,' I cut in before Lavedrine could reply, 'but no one told us anything. Except yourself, that is.'

Biswanger blew noisily on his lips and sat back heavily. His clothes seemed to collapse in upon him, as if his bulky body had been suddenly spirited away.

'Hmm,' he murmured noisily. 'I had nothing to do with killing them children, sir. Had I known what was going to happen in that house, I'd never have got involved.'

His rumbling voice was reedy and trembling by the time he finished.

'If you have done nothing,' I insisted, 'you will answer our questions.'

Biswanger's eyes opened wide. 'That's what I'm trying to do, Herr Procurator, I assure you.'

'Why did Aaron the Jew want the Gottewalds and their children to take that particular house?' asked Lavedrine.

Did Lavedrine think that the rumours flying around Lotingen had some foundation in truth? Had he been convinced by the revolting caricatures on that Jew-hating broadsheet?

If Lavedrine's question left me breathless, it provoked a quaking spasm on the podgy face of Leon Biswanger. 'Sir, you cannot believe . . . Oh no, sir, not *that*! I did not know there was a motive in it. I was convinced they wanted that house. Why else would Aaron . . . You can't believe what people are saying, sir! I was just the go-between.'

'Yet, in your own words, that house was intended to make a profit,' Lavedrine ploughed on. 'Not ten miserable thalers. What other reason could there be for letting the house go so cheaply?'

'Major Gottewald . . . he *wanted* that house, sir,' Biswanger repeated piteously, as if that frail argument were his one remaining hope of salvation. 'There was no other profit to be made from it, at least in the short run. I told Aaron about the offer, and he instructed me to accept it . . .'

'And in the long run?' Lavedrine challenged.

'Sir?' Biswanger whined, uncertain where he stood, incapable of guessing where Lavedrine's sharp reasoning would take him next.

'You are a businessman, Biswanger,' Lavedrine replied smoothly. 'Surely, you know the current price on the local market of a pint of Christian blood?'

If Biswanger was flabbergasted, I was horrified.

Lavedrine smiled benignly at the pair of us. 'A tiny rent on the house, but a huge profit on a certain rare commodity sold in the right religious circles, don't you think?'

He looked at Biswanger, whose head was in his hands, as he tried in vain to stifle his wailing. Then, Lavedrine looked at me and winked reassuringly.

'But come, Herr Biswanger,' he said, turning his loaded cannons on the man again. 'You are, as I said before, a businessman . . .'

'You'll have to speak to Aaron, sir,' the man protested defiantly. 'I don't know nothing about *that* business.'

'We will speak to him soon,' I interposed. 'You can swear an oath on it.'

But Lavedrine brought the discussion back again to his own chosen path. 'This business with the houses, Biswanger. Tell me, what sort of a profit do you manage to make in that line of work?'

Biswanger studied the Frenchman's face for some moments. 'Thirty per cent,' he said, and for all his discomfort he could not prevent a hollow smile from appearing on his fat lips.

'So,' Lavedrine summed up, 'thirty per cent of ten thalers. That's three, if my sums are correct.'

'Indeed, sir.'

Lavedrine smiled, then chuckled to himself. 'I took you for a mastiff, Biswanger. Instead, I find that you are a puppy. A benefactor, if I am truthful. If Aaron Jacob's other houses yield so little, you can't be doing very well for yourself.'

'That's just a sideline, sir,' the man shot back. 'I have my own business to put the clothes on my back, and *Pfennig* in my coffers.'

'What is your business?'

'If you are hiding something more,' I warned him, 'the next time you speak to us, you will be wearing chains inside a prison cell. What is your trade?'

The man joined his hands and looked at me, as if he were amazed. 'I beg your pardon, sir,' he said. 'I thought you knew. People passing in the street are always going on about the smell. We don't have neighbours living near. We are used to it, and someone has to do the job. The workshop's on the windward side, away from the river. It's open country out back. I have a license from the General Quarters now, and it is of great public utility. Still,' he sighed, 'there's no accounting for ignorance and superstition.'

'*Pour l'amour de Dieu!*' Lavedrine exclaimed. 'What do you do, man?'

'How can I explain it to you, sir?' Biswanger replied, a terrified frown on his face. 'You have a name for the work in France, I do believe . . . *jux crux*,' he mumbled at last, making an execrable attempt to pronounce these words in French. He jumped up, wiping his sweaty hands on his trousers. 'It would be better if I showed you.'

He led us along a brick-tiled corridor, then out into a paved courtyard at the back of the house. Taking a large key from his pocket, he unlocked a narrow door which opened into his workshop. As the man bowed and waited for us to pass inside before him, I threw an eye at Lavedrine, hoping for elucidation, but the expression on his face pitched me into greater confusion. He was smiling in a manner that suggested amusement and lively curiosity, equally mixed. I think he knew what we were about to discover, but decided to leave me in the dark.

One thing alone was indisputable: the smell.

While knocking on Biswanger's front door, we had remarked upon it. But inside that room it was sickening. Daylight entered by means of the same narrow slits we had noticed from the street, the rays cutting through the gloom like stabbing swords. Six lamps were set at intervals along the other wall, each containing a candle. Beneath each lamp was a wooden table covered with a slab of slate. Laid out on five of them was the 'merchandise' of Leon Biswanger.

'You almost hit it, Biswanger. *Jurés crieurs* is what we call them in France,'

Lavedrine said with a laugh. He turned to me and explained. '"Announcers of death",' he said. 'An edict issued by Louis XIV made them into a hereditary guild. Sons follow by right of birth in their fathers' footsteps in every town and city. Their duty is to inform the people of a death, then assist with the interment.'

He turned to Biswanger. 'Well done, sir! A trade in constant expansion, given the times we live in.'

My eyes were riveted on the row of corpses. Two men and three women, all dressed in their Sunday best, as if they might stand up at any moment and decide to take a stroll. The women were artfully displayed, each wearing a headdress of black lace thrown back to expose the face, the trailing veil expertly moulded along the shoulders and down the arms. But as my eyes grew accustomed to the light, I realised that the first impression had been misleading. These people would never stand again. Their cheeks were sunken where bones gave no support, the skin as thin and brittle as parchment. The jaw of one of the women had locked at a lopsided angle, exposing yellow teeth and putrid gums.

Smiling now, confident of having won the approval of Lavedrine, Biswanger led us into the room, stopping beside one of the trestles. The candlelight flickered mercilessly on the dead man's face. Clearly, he had suffered. His body was unnaturally twisted, his aged face aghast with pain. His tongue was steely blue, protruding from between clenched teeth, lolling along the side of his stubbly chin. He had gagged in the moment of decease. Had the agony gone on longer, he would have bitten his tongue off.

'Gunthar Loesse, bellringer in the parish of Allenswerder,' Biswanger recited smoothly. 'Fell from the bell tower. Probably the worse for drink. Broke his back and every rib.' He turned to me. 'Horrible sight, don't you agree, sir? There's not much I can do for him. I'll have to remove that tongue before we lay him in an open coffin. A very popular man with the local Pietist congregation, apparently. The parishioners agreed to pay for my services. They brought him in last night, so he still don't look his best. By the time they bury him on Friday, he'll be as handsome as a bridegroom,' the undertaker explained with joy.

'Do you save the better specimens for medical schools?' I asked. 'Or sell the organs by the pound weight when requested?'

'What do you take me for, sir?' he protested, making the sign of the Cross on his forehead. 'I go to chapel every Sunday. Sell human remains? I'd never dream of doing such a thing. Why, I . . . I'm a . . .'

He was trembling from head to toe. My conviction grew. There was more to his business than he had chosen to show us.

'You are what, sir?' I insisted.

'I was going to say, sir, I am something of an artist,' he replied. 'If the parents, relatives, or friends ask me . . .'

'Pay you,' I corrected him.

'First, they ask. Then, happy with the results, they pay. I . . . well . . . You'd better come with me,' he said, moving towards a jutting wall which enclosed a second room. 'In here, Herr Procurator. And Colonel Lavedrine, sir. Step this way, please.'

We might have entered a different house. The smell of death was dominant out there, but in this sanctum we might have been inside a church with a hundred burning candles. Oil lamps flickered in the room like votive lights, but the persistent smell—a delicate perfume, overwhelming and cushioning the scent of rotting flesh and corrupt innards—was a familiar one.

'Wax?' I asked.

A great quantity was cut into square blocks, piled high on shelves. As Biswanger wound up the wicks of his lamps and light invaded the gloom, a dozen forms laid out on the central worktable were thrown into stark relief. Each piece was milky grey, though the lineaments were different. Each one possessed the same deathly stillness. With blank unseeing eyes, they appeared to float in a world without feeling or emotion. Yet pain and torment were stamped on their faces.

'Death masks. There's no better way to remember the departed. Each is a true original. When a loved one has passed over, the mask remains for the living to cherish. It keeps alive the memory in their fickle minds. This is what I do. Of course, if the death is of an unusual or unnatural sort, I sell copies to the medical profession. Or to scholars who may be interested. As was the case with those three little angels recently massacred . . .'

Lavedrine was hardly listening. He may not have realised what the man had said, but he sprang into action as he saw the difficulty Biswanger had in breathing. My hands had closed in an instant around his fat windpipe. I was trying to squeeze the life out of him, thumbs straining hard against his larynx.

'Leave him, Stiffeniis!' Lavedrine boomed in my ear, his hands on my wrists as he tried to drag me off. 'Let him speak!'

Biswanger began to heave great gulps of air into his lungs as I relaxed my grip. Turning away, I gasped for breath myself.

Lavedrine stepped between us. 'Biswanger, repeat what you said.'

The undertaker's eyes swivelled to meet mine. 'He tried to kill me,' he whimpered, coughing and spluttering, his voice rasping with fright.

'He will not try again,' Lavedrine replied. 'Though I may throttle you myself, unless you tell the truth. *Which* children were you speaking of?'

'The Gottewalds, sir. The ones whose throats were cut. They were brought to me to . . . to put them in decent order before being buried.'

'Who brought them?' I shouted, shaking with rage.

I felt Lavedrine's hand on my arm as he laboured to hold me back.

'Prussian soldiers,' Biswanger murmured, his eyes racing between us, as if to gauge where the next attack might come from. 'Count Dittersdorf sent an order. It was countersigned by a French lieutenant. Requesting me to sew up the gashes, and cancel out the marks of violence on the corpses. Telling me to make them look . . . well, *human*, sir.'

The face of Dittersdorf rose up before me like one of the death masks on the table.

'Has the count buried them in my absence?' I said to Lavedrine. 'Did he tell you about it?'

'Nothing,' he replied. 'Let's hope we do not need to dig them up again.'

'It was not easy,' Biswanger continued. 'The state they were in. Wounds so . . . so . . .' He hesitated, fearing for his safety, perhaps. 'It was a severe test of my skills,' he concluded, unable to restrain his boasting.

He was silent for a moment. 'I would not want you to think that I've been misleading you,' he said. 'You'd hear it from Aaron, anyway.'

Lavedrine repeated the name. 'What has he to do with this?'

Biswanger seemed to swell back into his skin, happier to talk about another man than to be interrogated about himself. 'Aaron knew those children were in my workshop.' He expressed himself carefully. 'He asked me to make some casts in wax for his own use.'

An image flashed through my mind. I saw warm, grey molten wax. I saw the hands of Biswanger moving over the faces of the three tiny victims. The bodies were cold and stiff. As the artist applied himself to the gaping throats, dry blood attached itself to the warm clinging wax. Perhaps the heat had caused the blood to dissolve and flow again.

I reacted instantly. Not driven by anger this time, but riven by curiosity.

'What would any man want with such things?' I asked.

Biswanger's eyes were sparkling with fear.

'Aaron Jacob is a scientist, sir,' he said.

· 23 ·

'BISWANGER HAS COMMITTED no crime.'

Lavedrine broke the silence as we made our way back towards the river.

'No crime?' I snapped, disgust welling up in me. 'It may be legal to tweak at dead flesh like a crow, but the bounds of moral necessity have been stretched beyond the limit. Nor will we know how far, until we speak to the Jew. What studies is this ghoul engaged in?'

Lavedrine turned fiercely on me. 'You can't believe there is any truth in the rumours?'

'Of course I don't,' I replied curtly. 'But blood *was* carried away. And now a Jew is involved. How long before the crowd gets wind of it?'

'That all depends on us,' he warned.

'We must seek him out,' I insisted, as we came to the bridge on the River Nogat, the boards rattling beneath our feet. 'Dittersdorf ordered me to make enquiries within the ghetto. Now, we have no choice.'

Along the wharf, my attention was caught by a noisy gathering in the square where fish were sold, though it was late for the morning market. French soldiers in dark-blue trenchcoats pushed the crowd back, two or three of them with bayonets fixed.

'An ugly-looking mob,' Lavedrine said.

I am well known in Lotingen. In a smallish country town the local magistrate is loved and hated in equal measure. As a rule, I steer my own straight course, stopping to listen neither to flattery, nor recrimination. But those voices could not be ignored.

'What are ye waitin' for, Herr Procurator? They'll be drinkin' the blood of our children next!'

The cry was quickly taken up by others. The crowd turned as one. They spotted me, a Frenchman at my side. They began to surge towards us in a horde, faces ugly with rage. Against a mob, two men could only save themselves if the soldiers chose to intervene, or with the help of weapons. But neither of us was armed, and the soldiers made no move to rescue us. As if they had been ordered not to shift from their stations.

Sticks began to pound the cobblestones. Then a cry of battle was given, a word in the local dialect that I had never heard before. Like the beating of a night-owl's wings as it swoops to snatch its prey. *Wup, wup, wup!* Whatever it meant, repeated gruffly over and over again, it made the violence palpable. Lavedrine and I were at the very centre of a throbbing tempest.

A red-cheeked women pressed close to me.

'Kill the yids!' she screeched in my face, her spittle raining on my skin, her eyes glaring ferociously into mine. 'Kill the yids!'

Before I could react, Lavedrine sprang forward.

His hand shot out, then pulled back. A sheet of blood poured down her cheek below the eye. That woman's scream shut out all other shouts, as if the noise of a band tuning up had been sucked into a bugle that had blown one single, piercing note for silence. A musket was discharged, and the crowd fell back in a tumbling mass. Another followed it, and they whirled away, crushing bags underfoot, making their escape as a wall of blue materialised in front of us.

'*Merci, citoyens!*' Lavedrine encouraged the French soldiers. 'Another minute, we'd have been lynched.'

I had never been so glad to see armed Frenchmen.

The officer in charge, a young infantryman with a smoking pistol in his hand, came running over. 'My apologies, sirs,' he said with a salute. 'We were slow to see what was going on.'

He glanced down at Lavedrine's hand. 'That is a very fine piece of weaponry, sir, if I may say so!'

Lavedrine held up the ring on his middle finger like a proud bridegroom. The brass cylinder was mounted with a curving triangular point, and a drop of blood fell from the metal.

'A trick I learnt from my cat,' he said. '*Lionel est terrible!* A claw is the finest defence under the sun. Speed is the secret. This is a poor copy, though it does the job. It has saved me more times than a loaded pistol.'

'You struck a woman, Lavedrine,' I objected.

'Is that what she was?' he asked sharply. 'She'd have had her teeth into you.'

'Colonel Lavedrine?' the officer interrupted. 'I've been looking for you, sir. For you and Procurator Steffenars'—he mangled my name.

'Here we are. In one piece, thanks to you and your men!'

'Lieutenant Mutiez's compliments,' the man replied. 'A body has been found this morning. The body of a woman, sir.'

Lavedrine turned to me, a peculiar light shining in his eyes.

'Is it her, do you think?'

Mutiez was in a warehouse at the end of the row, the infantryman reported, pointing down the wharf. The weak sun glistened over the windswept waters, rattling the sails and the tackle of a two-master which was making ready for sea. Petrels skipped, skimmed, and dived in the wake of a homecoming fisher-boat. There'll be a storm before the day is out, I thought, but inside the head of my companion, a tempest was already raging.

'I told them!' Lavedrine remonstrated, as we hurried along the sea wall, holding on to our hats against the driving wind. 'Search the town from top to bottom. Enter every barn and outhouse, every shed and derelict building. Did no one look inside these warehouses?'

He was a handsome man, but in a rage his face was dark, brutal, ugly.

'If a killer hides a body,' I replied, as the cobbles gave way to square-cut blocks of worn stone, 'he does not want it to be found. Discovery boils down to luck on our part, or miscalculation on his. Seven days have gone, and each one reduces the probability of finding her alive, I fear.'

Lavedrine was not listening.

'What is their business on this quay?' he asked in an angry burst.

'What do you mean?'

He pointed ahead at a huge wooden winding-drum.

'Whales,' I replied. 'They used to handle whales.'

The Old Windlass warehouse is different from the others. Built from rough red sandstone fifty years ago by Adolphus Gummerstett, it played a greater part in the history of Lotingen than it does at the present. In the last century, a small flotilla of herring boats would take themselves off to the Swedish fishing grounds in spring, passing through the Malmö Straits and into the Kattegat, searching for the whales that mate along the coast from Halmstad to Gotteburg. The vessels were not equipped to handle animals of any great size. They would kill what they could, then sail home, towing the carcasses in their wake. When they arrived in our estuary, the labourers at the Old Windlass would be waiting. Doors all along the quay were thrown open, vast tubs for boiling blubber were set out on the stones. There was a shelving ramp in front, where the whales could be secured. Then, the windlass that had caught Lavedrine's eye was brought into play. 'The Peeling Wench' was the playful name the fishermen gave to this vast wooden engine. A dozen strong men pushed staves to drive the winch around the bole, ripping the blubber from the whale, which rolled in the river, shedding blood as its skin and fat were unwound in strips and dragged to the top of the ramp. There, it was hacked, chopped and boiled. As the operation proceeded, the oil was filtered into barrels and stored in the warehouse, to be sold in chandlers' shops around the town.

'The owner died intestate, leaving a mountain of debts,' I added. 'The Old Windlass has been closed for many years.'

'It is open now,' Lavedrine replied sharply, making for the double doors, one of which hung awkwardly from a broken hinge.

As I followed him into the cavernous warehouse, I saw that Mutiez was talking with a man. That is, Mutiez tried to talk, while the man was shouting.

'I can do nothing,' the lieutenant insisted.

'These goods are mine! By what right . . .'

'By the right of conquest, *monsieur*,' Mutiez answered with a smile. 'Your oil has been requisitioned for the French army. You should be pleased to serve *l'Empereur*. You will be compensated eventually.'

'I very much doubt it,' I muttered to myself.

Lieutenant Mutiez saw Lavedrine and saluted, while Gummerstett turned on me.

I had met him on numerous occasions, and knew his case by heart. Julius Gummerstett still lived in the house that his father had built next door to the warehouse. He must have seen the empty barges arrive, the doors being broken in, the soldiers milling around outside.

'Herr Procurator, I'm being robbed! My property . . .'

'Strictly speaking,' I replied, 'the property is not yours. No decision has yet been handed down from Potsdam . . .'

'There'll be nothing left to inherit by the time they've finished!'

Rather than enter into a legal argument, I turned to Lavedrine. 'This is Colonel Lavedrine of the French . . .' I hesitated, uncertain of the Frenchman's precise military status.

'Thank heavens!' Gummerstett exclaimed, offering his hand to Lavedrine, who did not take it. 'I hope that you can make short work of the tangle of Prussian bureaucracy, sir.'

'The workers found a body, sir,' Mutiez was explaining. 'A woman . . .'

'He won't let me see the damage!' Gummerstett protested again.

Lavedrine turned on him like a fierce dog. 'Did you hear intruders, or see anyone entering in the last few days?' he snapped.

Gummerstett took a step backwards as if to avoid a blow. 'Nothing, no one. As I have already explained to this man . . .'

'Then get out!' Lavedrine barked. 'Before I order your arrest.'

The frustrated heir pulled angrily at his heavy plaid overcoat, then cursed the heavens roundly. But not before he had reached the safety of the door to the quay.

'Where is she?' Lavedrine growled.

'Hard to call that *thing* a she, sir,' Mutiez echoed, as he led us next door into a vast storeroom. 'If it hadn't been for the dress . . .'

He looked around as if the sheer size of the place had robbed him of breath.

'Who found the body, Henri?' Lavedrine pressed him.

'The bargees, sir. They'd been given orders to empty the place. Our soldiers had been sent to safeguard the proceedings. They called for me at once.'

The room was piled high with barrels. There must have been three or four hundred stacked in row upon row along the back wall. Rich takings for an army marching on its stomach. Each barrel was taller than my waist, and there were four or five solid layers. On the face of each was a brand bearing a date. Near the door, 1789. But as we marched down the room, the year progressed to 1794, which was when Adolphus Gummerstett had died, and the Old Windlass had been placed under juridical supervision.

'Why was this place not searched?' Lavedrine demanded, his black eyes glinting.

'It *was* searched,' Mutiez replied. 'Five days ago. Nothing was found.'

'A body within the last week?' Lavedrine looked away, as if digesting the news. 'Did she come of her own volition, or was she brought?' he murmured. Suddenly, he raised his nose in the air: 'What smell is that?'

In Paris, I thought cynically, they recognise the smell of American oil from the South Seas, and pride themselves on dabbing ambergris behind the ears of their ladies. But we in Lotingen know the secrets of the Arctic whale, from the stink of rotting flesh to the odour of the densest spermaceti.

'That is blubber oil, I think.'

Lavedrine looked at me. 'There is a rancid quality to your Prussian oil that I have never met before,' he observed.

The face of Mutiez was set in a grimace. 'A quantity of oil has been spilled,' he said, 'but there are other odours in the air, sir, for a man with a sharp nose.'

'What are you talking of?' I asked as we reached the far end of the room.

A number of barrels had fallen away from the wall, crashing onto the floor and breaking, spilling their precious contents onto the paved flagstones.

'Crushed spleen, spattered brains, a split stomach, the shit and piss of rats,' the lieutenant said, pointing at a blackened mess beneath a creamy lake in the far corner. As we moved nearer, I saw that streams of blood had twisted and interlaced with the congealed oil, standing out like veins in the milky mess. At the source, just below the surface of the oil, was a body, like that of a person who had drowned.

Was this the corpse of Sybille Gottewald?

'. . . ten barrels at least, sir.'

'A crushing weight . . .'

Fragments of conversation seemed to reach me from some other world.

'. . . if she'd been hidden here, against her will . . .'

'There's not a rope in sight, sir.'

'They left the body here, confident that it would not be found. They did not know that the warehouse was about to be emptied.' This was Lavedrine. 'As you said before, Herr Procurator, a matter of chance, or miscalculation. Who would know of this place?'

I tried to drag my eyes from the matted soggy pile and the broken wood. A human hand protruded from the oil, as if the victim had not been quite struck dead on the spot. As if she had made a vain attempt to call for help, to lift and shift herself, perhaps, before the oil flowed into her throat and choked her life away.

'I'm sorry?' I said.

'Who knows about Gummerstett's warehouse?'

'Everyone in Lotingen,' I replied hopelessly. 'Fourteen thousand, eight hundred and thirty-nine adult souls, according to the census taken seven years ago. This place is no secret to anyone. But how did she arrive here?'

'I think we'd better take a closer look,' Lavedrine responded. He began to remove his boots and peel off his stockings, urging me to do the same. 'Are any other Lotingen women known to be missing?' he asked.

I stifled a bitter laugh as I placed one naked foot on the cold stone floor. 'How far do you wish to go back?' I asked. 'If you are asking how many women have disappeared since the French came to Prussia, I can give you a fair idea.'

'They do not interest me,' he said, as we took our first careful steps into the chill, slippery pond. 'Has any woman disappeared in the past few weeks with the exception of Frau Gottewald? That's the period I am concerned about.'

'No one, so far as we know,' I said, struggling to keep my balance and prevent myself from falling. 'Of course, not everything is reported to the police.'

'The clothes may help us identify her.'

Even as he said it, the conviction seemed to die on Lavedrine's lips.

A tun of oil holds 252 gallons. A fair-sized whale will yield 150 barrels, ten or twelve of which had cascaded down from a height of twenty feet and struck the body. A great deal of oil had run away down the guttering which formed a canal down the centre of the long narrow room. It would have trickled out of the building and dribbled into the estuary without anybody noticing. But a huge slick had frozen solid, and in the middle of this milky mess was the flattened form of a black dress, a black bonnet, and a vivid red mash which had once been a human body. That grasping hand protruded from the oil like an isolated tree in a field that had been flooded.

We stood on either side of the body, looking down into the ooze.

'It will not be an easy task,' I said. The face had been crushed and splattered by the falling weight. Fragments of the skull were scattered like a broken moon suspended in aspic, as if the head had shattered beneath the repeated blows of a heavy sledgehammer. A halo of brain fluid and tissue made a pale trace in the dark blood and greenish oil. The body was flattened to a wafer in places, as if some malignant force had chosen to take a flat-iron and impress that woman's form on the ground. Entrails spread like pink tentacles from her stomach and her abdomen. 'Impossible to tell how old she was,' I said. 'Or whether she was dead before the barrels fell on her.'

'The clothes,' Lavedrine repeated stubbornly. 'They can be recovered, Stiffeniis. They can be washed and cleaned. There may be a tailor's mark, a name-tag, or some clue in her pockets. The shoes, too,' he pointed. 'Would you mind? You are closer. Moving is a risky business.'

I steadied myself, bent forward, and stuck my hands into the oily goo, which was cold and dense, but malleable, like soap that has been left in water and forgotten overnight. I felt a sense of sickness and revulsion as I moved my hand down the woman's leg. The bones shifted easily beneath my fingers, not one of them was whole. At last, I touched the foot, and felt the raised surface of leather. I pulled the shoe away from its sticky moorings with a sickening squelch, and held it up.

'The heel has broken off . . .'

I said no more, but vomited where I stood, a shower spurting out from my mouth to compound the oily soup in which I was standing, ankle-deep.

'Impossible to distinguish the colour,' Lavedrine murmured. Then he looked at me with an air of concern. 'Are you all right?'

My hands were slick with oil; blood and blubber slowly trickled from the shoe and ran down my wrists and inside the cuffs of my shirt.

'Well enough,' I replied, gulping air into my lungs, holding on to my hard-won prize, struggling to quell the queasy rhythms of my stomach, and calm the racing of my pulse. 'Her hair,' I said, making an attempt to be as cold and practical as he appeared to be. 'You are nearer. Can you see the colour?'

Lavedrine let out a snort of frustration. 'This damned stuff has impregnated everything. Her hair was long, but more than that I cannot say. Blonde, black, or brown. Who can tell?'

'All we have for the moment,' I said, 'is that hand. The rest will have to be collected.'

'It is not the hand of an old woman,' he said, sitting back on his heels, the tail of his coat soaking up oil, visibly changing colour before my eyes.

'If she had been dead long,' I said, 'it ought to have rotted away to nothing.'

'Have you never . . .' He stopped, turned to me, smiled wanly. 'But no, of course, you haven't. You have no oil of olives here in Prussia. The merchants in the south of France use olive oil to conserve certain delicacies—olives themselves, truffles, and certain precious kinds of mushroom. Oil will preserve anything for an indefinite length of time.'

'There's nothing to preserve,' I said, forgetting the tail of my own coat, sinking down on my haunches close to that clutching hand. 'The nails and the tips of the fingers are black with decomposition . . .'

'Where the oil has run away,' he insisted, 'but the hand is a young hand. There are no age wrinkles. And there is a callus on the knuckle of the thumb. Can you see it?'

With trepidation, I leaned closer. A wave of nausea swept over me in a shudder as I pulled the clutching fingers open, letting the hand flop back lazily onto the oxidised skin of oil. 'There are hard pads on the other fingers,' I said, fighting to hold down another retching lurch of my stomach. 'This woman worked . . .'

'We have no way of knowing what she may have done. Housework, perhaps.'

'Or chopping wood . . . The nails are broken. There is a trace of blood.'

'Her own, or someone else's?'

'She'll never tell us,' I said, standing up, feeling the cold, grasping damp of oily stickiness as my coat attached itself to the calves of my legs. 'We cannot proceed in this manner,' I said. I was thinking of Professor Kant, and the investigation we had undertaken together four years earlier in Königsberg. 'We need to be more scientific in our approach. Everything here must be gathered up, then examined in conditions that are conducive to a more precise analysis.'

'I agree,' he said, raising himself to his full height.

With some difficulty we slithered and waded our way back to where Mutiez was waiting.

'Can you get a gang of men in here?' I asked him. 'Fellows with strong stomachs. Tell them to recover whatever they can lay their hands on. There are four tanks ranged along the wall,' I said, walking across and placing the sodden shoe in one of them. 'They can drop everything in these, and leave them to soak. Water can be heated up in tubs, I suppose.'

The lieutenant saluted and ran off to bring his men.

I tried the handle of a water-pump beside the sinks. Cold water gushed forth, and I began to remove the blood and blubber from my hands and feet. Shivering as I cleaned myself, I glanced at the wreckage in the corner—the smashed wood, the forest of broken laths and twisted metal hoops. A cannon might have scored a direct hit in the warehouse.

'There must be some way of identifying her,' Lavedrine murmured, almost to himself, as he came across to clean himself up.

The clatter of steel-tipped boots coming in through the door distracted me for a moment. 'When her things are clean and dried,' I said forlornly, sitting down to put on my stockings and shoes, 'some person may be able to recognise them.'

'Your wife? Is that what you are thinking? She met the woman.'

Lavedrine was not looking at me as he said it.

'Helena was *not* the person I had in mind,' I insisted. 'There are seamstresses, shoe shops, hatmakers, and the like, who may be able to distinguish their own work. If doubt remains, then, I suppose we may be forced to ask Helena. We can show her a scrap of cloth or leather, for all the good it's likely to do.'

I had no intention of subjecting Helena to the horror.

'Would you care to instruct them in their duties, sir?' Mutiez enquired, as the men formed up in a line. He addressed himself to Lavedrine, though there was a wayward drift in the question, which seemed to include myself.

'Speak to them, Stiffeniis,' Lavedrine urged. 'Your investigation with Professor Kant was motivated by detailed analysis of the minutiae that were found at the scene of each crime. My own experience is limited to the study of criminal behaviour, and the perverted nature of the men who commit such acts.'

I turned to the men.

'A woman has been crushed beyond recognition. Her clothes and other effects are preserved in whale oil. Those objects must all be carefully collected,' I stated mechanically, struggling not to think of the horror of the task. 'Every item, no matter how small, which may have come from that woman's body will be subjected to detailed examination. Do not ignore a hairpin, a clip, or a scrap of paper. Do not cast aside anything. If it is located within a ten-yard radius of the corpse, it probably came into this place with the victim, or with whoever killed her. It may be useful in our attempt to establish her identity.'

I paused for a moment, collecting my thoughts for what I was about to add.

'There is a need for delicacy in what you are about to do,' I continued. 'It will not be pleasant. Many bones have been broken into fragments. I want every piece of the skeleton separated from the rest. Anything that you think is human'—I looked around, then pointed to the tin sink nearest to the open door—'should be placed in that tray over there. If you are not certain, but you think that something may be organic, it should go into that tray, and no other. I will examine the contents and judge what is to be kept, and what is to be discarded. Do you understand me?'

The soldiers were a fair cross-section of the French forces in the town. Some were large, some were smaller, all were battle-hardened, proud of their waxed moustaches and their greasy pigtails. Some nodded, some sighed.

'Are there any questions?' I asked.

A tall fellow with a pair of gleaming black eyes beneath his weatherworn canvas-covered *shako* spoke up at once. 'Jewellery, sir? Personal effects? What d'you want us to do with those?'

'Lieutenant Mutiez will be responsible for handling them,' Lavedrine shot back.

'This is a murder investigation,' Mutiez added. 'Remember that fact. If there is any suggestion of pilfering, you will find yourselves lashed to a gun carriage and dragged in shame before the ranks.'

Lavedrine and I exchanged looks.

'Send a runner to look for us if anything of interest comes to light, Henri,' he said.

'Where will you be, sir?'

'A fair question,' Lavedrine said with a smile. 'Where will we be, Stiffeniis?'

'Judenstrasse,' I replied.

We lingered for five minutes, watching them get down to work. 'The evidence should be moved away from here, I think,' I said to Lavedrine. I was thinking of Professor Kant's laboratory near the castle of Königsberg. 'Somewhere that is clean, dry, and cold. A place which is safe and secret, where you and I may examine the remains without being lynched by another mob.'

Lavedrine nodded. 'I'll speak to Mutiez.'

A few minutes later, still trying to clean the worst of the dirt from our clothes, we moved towards the door.

'Is it her body, do you think?' Lavedrine asked uncertainly.

If he were asking me to confirm or deny the possibility, I refused to help him. He would probably have belittled my reasoning. The total devastation of that corpse, and the cruel death that the woman had died, were enough to convince me. I recognised the same crushing annihilation that had overtaken them all. One by one. Her husband had been hounded to his death. Her children had been mercilessly slaughtered. The mystery of how that woman had died was perplexing, but in the details only. Had she been murdered there, or somewhere else? Had she been raped, then left, stumbling about in the dark, accidentally bringing those barrels cascading down upon her head? Or had her lifeless shell been taken there by someone who knew that the warehouse was deserted, and believed that it would long remain so?

'If it is her corpse, we are no closer to finding the killer,' I replied, stepping out into the daylight. 'He will be accused of four murders, rather than three. But we have to catch him first.'

·24·

DUSK WAS FALLING as we began to climb the hill in the direction of the ghetto.

Our Judenstrasse is a winding, narrow street near the top of Nogatsstrasse which falls away towards the west, trailing out into the flat countryside in the direction of the Berlin road.

If a man needed carpets, kitchen utensils, pots and pans, or knives and forks, someone in Judenstrasse would provide them at a reasonable price. There was nothing, except the name, to distinguish it from any other street in the oldest part of Lotingen, and it was frequented as much by Gentiles (so they called us) as it was by Israelites (as we called them)—in a word, a Gentile was a customer, and a Son of Israel was a trader, and they got on well enough.

Indeed, Gentiles were oftentimes obliged to go there, for services were offered in our Judenstrasse that could be found nowhere else in town. If a man had money to invest, the only place to make contact with an agent who would expedite the movement of money against shares was Judenstrasse. Coffee was a movable commodity, but all of it passed through Holland. Russian hardwoods were equally profitable, but who in Lotingen would know the name, address or language of the man in St Petersburg who happened to administer the trade? And who could invest in English cotton with men who spoke only English, if it were not for Jews who spoke Yiddish between themselves? Of course, Napoleon and his Continental System had severely restricted the possibilities for investment, but the Jews knew ways to get around the prohibition and the English naval blockades. And if you had to go to Vilnius in the East, or Transylvania in the South, and needed coin of those places, who else but a Jewish money-teller would have some ready and waiting in his coffers?

All this was Judenstrasse with its coffee shops and cluttered emporia, its kosher butchers and taverns. But as we turned into the street and walked the first fifty yards, I realised that much had changed with the coming of the

French. I had had no reason to go there in more than a year. Many Jews had been forced to abandon the larger cities in Prussia out of fear, I had heard, and had made their way to smaller, safer towns, such as Lotingen. Our Judenstrasse was neither long nor wide, and it had always been busy, but not uncomfortably so. Now, the street was packed, and it grew increasingly difficult to push our way through the crowd.

All at once, we were forced to pull up short in front of a gate.

A large gate made of iron, which had not been there before.

Armed soldiers were standing guard in front of it. During my absence in Kamenetz, a high wooden paling had been erected across the street, beyond which the milling crowd inside the ghetto seemed suddenly wild and agitated. This mêlée was caused by the fact that the soldiers, who were members of the Lotingen Palisaders, had presented arms with a loud clash, slamming their rifle butts to the ground at the approach of the local magistrate.

'Herr Procurator,' the corporal in charge saluted. 'Do you mean to go inside, sir? We have orders to let no one out.'

'It would be better if we entered alone,' Lavedrine suggested. 'If the people in there intend us any harm, four members of the local militia can do nothing to stop them. If the soldiers come in with us, they may provoke a riot. Word will soon get out that we have entered the ghetto. The town will think that we are taking the accusations very seriously. That was what Dittersdorf intended, was it not? An investigation inside the Jewish quarter.'

Lavedrine had put it in a nutshell. The greatest fear of the authorities, French or Prussian, was not prompted by what the Jews might have done. They were afraid of what the people of Lotingen might still sink to. So long as indiscriminate mud-slinging against the inhabitants of the ghetto continued in the papers without a sign of a visible response, there was a danger of a full-blown attack against the Jews.

'Wait here,' I said to the militia-men.

I was filled with doubts as I gave the order. Entering alone might produce the opposite of the desired effect. The people might think that we had gone inside to arrest the killer of the Gottewald children. If any man came out with us, he would be lynched on the spot.

'Keep your hands in view,' Lavedrine warned me, as one of the soldiers stepped forward and turned a key to let us through. 'They must not think we are armed, or bent on doing them any harm.'

Before the gate was halfway open, a cry went up, many voices shouting out in strange tongues that I did not recognise, and an ululating chorus of high-pitched female voices assaulted our ears. The crowd fell back, scattering this way and that, fanning out before the opening gate, making space like ants that feared being crushed underfoot. As the hubbub swelled, an old man emerged from the crowd. He shouted something in their tongue, and the noise inside the ghetto began to dwindle, then die away.

This man, his face a wrinkled target of concentric rings, stretched out his hands, and placed them on the vertical bars, pressing his forehead hard up against the metal.

'Have you come to murder us?' he asked quietly.

Lavedrine placed his own hands above the old man's. They could have been friends meeting by accident at a garden gate.

'My name is Colonel Lavedrine,' the Frenchman said, in a relaxed, collo-quial manner. 'I am French. You know the laws of France, sir. All men are equal. No man is a slave. No man is better than any other man, except in what he does. The Jews are men with rights, like all the rest in French law. We make no distinctions.' He turned to me. 'This is Procurator Stiffeniis,' he said. 'He is the Magistrate of Lotingen. He can go wherever he wishes. This town belongs to him. He can call for the police if he needs them. He asks no man for permission. But . . .'

He paused for a moment, and the old man nodded, as if encouraging him to continue. 'We do not wish to force our way inside without your consent,' he said. 'We will not enter, if that is what you prefer. But three children have been murdered in town. Their mother has disappeared. Those people out there'—he nodded over his shoulder—'believe that the Jews are responsi-ble. If you have nothing to hide, sir, let us enter.'

I was impressed by his composure. Not a word or a gesture was wasted.

'Nothing will happen,' I promised, trying to sound equally reassuring, but a tumult of voices began to drown out mine.

I glanced over my shoulder. A large crowd was gathering at our backs, pressing forward, edging closer, but never too close to the armed soldiers. The windows of the street outside the ghetto were filled with screaming Prussians, egging on the mob to do its worst. Inside, terror was written on the faces craning out of the windows all along Judenstrasse.

Suddenly, a warning shot rang out.

Silence fell like a blanket on the street. It was smouldering, hate-filled, menacing. One shout, one object thrown on either side of the gate, and the militia would shoot to kill.

'They want Jewish blood,' Lavedrine murmured. 'We must enter, or fight our way back. Tell the guardsmen to hold the gate.'

Some signal might have passed. Lavedrine pushed, the old man pulled. We ran in, the soldiers ran in behind us, and the heavy gate crashed closed.

'It was meant to keep them in,' Lavedrine muttered. 'Now, it will keep their enemies out. What strange times we live in!'

Beyond the gate, the mob began to howl again. I felt as though we had run away from jackals, only to step inside a lion's cage. But the way the Jews retreated before us, *we* might have been the lions.

'Hold your guard here,' I shouted to the corporal.

I looked around, wondering whether this alien place could rightly be called Prussia. The panic we had caused outside the gate was mirrored inside the ghetto. There was a wild babble of voices, a sudden scattering as people ran away. But that old man did not flinch. He might have been turned to basalt.

'We are looking for a man named Aaron Jacob,' I whispered, leaning closer to his ear. 'It is not our intention to arrest him, or to harm anyone else. We are here to protect you all from false accusations.'

The Jewish elder stared at me intently. He must have wondered whether I represented salvation, as I promised, or the levelling arm of Caesar.

'I will take you to him,' he said to me in refined German, slipping his hand protectively under my arm, as if I were a child. 'If you carry Aaron off, it will mean death for the children of our community. Bear that in mind. He is *Baal Shem*. The only man who knows how to cure them.'

Ten or twelve men—each one wearing a skullcap or striped mantle on his head—formed around us like a protective phalanx. We turned as a mass and began to walk down Judenstrasse. The place seemed to grow darker, more forbidding, as if we were entering the tunnel of a mine. I raised my eyes from the damp, muddy cobbles, and looked up. The roofs of the houses, three or four floors high, let in light, but not very much. On the upper floors, grey faces stared down at us, only to pull back quickly as they caught my eye. Not a word was heard, not a shout, or a whisper. Those houses might have been inhabited by ghosts.

'Is Aaron Jacob a *médecin?*' Lavedrine asked.

The leader nodded, turning into a side-street that was narrower than the one we had just left. This cul-de-sac ended in a dark walled-in courtyard. In the centre stood a large rusty anvil, like a forgotten image of the Golden Calf. It was impossible to guess what went on in that place.

We stopped before a worm-eaten door. Our leader raised his hand and knocked. A moment later, he spoke to a woman who opened the door a crack.

'Aaron is waiting for you,' he said. He waved his hand, as if inviting us to enter, but neither he, nor any of the other men, made to follow us.

'After you,' Lavedrine quipped.

I stepped inside the dwelling.

The room was larger than I expected. On one side stood a vast chimney-piece, where two or three logs were smouldering. A large black pot hung from a fire-iron. It was covered with a stiff sheet of grease-stained canvas. Above the fire, on the mantle-shelf were three red-clay jars of a sort we use in Prussia for convenient evacuation of the bladder during the night, more commonly known as piss-pots. Each jar was covered with a lid, but what surprised me more was the fact that each one had been scrupulously marked with a written note in Jewish script, indicating the contents at which I had guessed.

The woman seemed to melt away, leaving us alone with the acrid smell of excrement and urine.

'Why would any man keep piss-pots in his living room?' I murmured.

The labels protruding from the stopper of each jar suggested an attention to detail that was at odds with the notion of slovenliness. I was trying to make some sense of the foreign squiggles when I heard a voice behind me.

'Herr Magistrate, I will not invite you to enter, since you have already done so,' he said. 'My name is Aaron Jacob.'

I had to narrow my eyes in the penumbra to make out the dark face against the dirty plaster. As he moved closer to the candlelight, I judged him to be no taller than my shoulder. He held himself straight and proud beneath a grey shawl that he wore upon his head and shoulders. His nose was large, his black eyes glistened brightly, his cheeks hung like heavy folds on either side of a large mouth with fleshy lips.

'You have spoken to Biswanger, then,' he said, and seemed perfectly at ease.

'Who are you, sir?' I asked. 'Where are you from?'

He replied at once, and spoke earnestly, as if he were willing to answer any question we might care to ask. He must have known that idle curiosity had not led us there. His full name was Aaron Abraham Jacob, he said. Five years earlier, he had been living in Vilnius, a town in Lithuanian Russia. After a disastrous harvest, many people drowned when the river flooded.

'The population concluded, as the population usually does, that it was an act of God, and that the Jews were to blame for all their woes. Our people made the usual mistake of hiding in the synagogue,' he told us with a sad smile. 'And there was the usual massacre. That synagogue was burnt to the ground. Then, the Jewish quarter was set alight. But I had had the good sense to lead my family out of town, so we survived. Some months later, the result of wandering through the snow without adequate food and clothing, my wife was carried off by a fever of the lungs. A short time after that, my only son died . . .'

He said all this with quiet dignity, as if Fate were an undeniable fact. Alone, he had wandered into Prussia, and settled for a short time in the city of Bromberg, but there the situation had been tense, especially before the

French arrived. A friend invited him to come to Lotingen, a small town where nothing much ever seemed to happen. He had been living in Judenstrasse for going on three years without any problems. 'Until this massacre,' he murmured.

'The man who brought us said that you'd been curing children. He claimed that only you could save them,' said Lavedrine. 'He used a particular expression . . .'

'*Baal Shem.*' Aaron Jacob smiled faintly.

Perhaps it was the smile that triggered Lavedrine's fiery reaction.

'If this story of saving children is intended to protect you from accusations that may be made against you, regarding the murder of the Gottewald children, we will not be taken in,' Lavedrine warned him. 'Procurator Stiffeniis and I are interested only in the truth. Leon Biswanger spoke of houses, shrewd investments, business dealings. He made no mention of curing children.'

I studied the face of Aaron Jacob. The man was intelligent. He realised that the only hope for himself and his people was to assist us. Until the murderer was caught, the crowd outside the gates in Judenstrasse would have no time for excuses or stratagems. As his black eyes followed Lavedrine's, his pale face became even paler.

'The man who brought you here was speaking of my most recent studies,' Aaron Jacob said, breaking in upon my thoughts. He hesitated, then moved swiftly across the room. His hooded tunic reached down to his toes. Rather than walk, he seemed to float like a dark phantom.

'Let me explain some facts,' he said, reaching up and taking one of the covered pots from the shelf above the fireplace, 'before I show you the cause of my—how shall I call it—success? A number of people have died in the ghetto, many children among them. The symptoms were, in all cases, similar. Sudden weight loss, accompanied by ravenous hunger. The more the patient ate, the hungrier he felt, and the thinner he became. There were also secondary symptoms: strong pains in the abdomen, stomach, and digestive tract; a nervous trembling; and faeces that were extremely nauseous. It was as if those people were being eaten from inside. Death by consumption followed on in every case. For quite some time, I was a helpless onlooker, but then I had a lucky intuition. I found the culprit.'

He unscrewed the metal cover from the jar.

My hand rose instinctively to my nose and mouth, as the stench uncoiled like a venomous serpent.

'Excuse me.' Aaron Jacob laughed lightly. He bowed his head to us, then raised the chamber pot, and offered it, inviting us to look inside. 'There's no alternative, I'm afraid,' he said, still smiling, 'if you ever hope to put your curiosity to sleep. Science is a dirty business.'

A dark soup of lumpy faeces slopped in the bottom of the pot. And from it, whitish skin made brighter by contrast with the dull brown slime, peered a worm as thick as a baby's little finger, as long as the baby itself, its body twisting and turning upon itself. Again, my stomach lurched. For an instant, I thought I might be about to add a quantity of my own filth to that already gathered in the jar.

'Here is the monster,' Aaron Jacob said. He might have been showing us a pretty little kitten. '*Tenia saginata*, the "solitary worm". This parasite is generally found in the stomachs of domestic animals. Cows, pigs, and sheep. If meat is not properly cooked, the larvae may be ingested by humans. We do not eat pork. *Kashrut* forbids the eating of the meat of unclean animals. But beef and mutton are not so innocent or clean as they seem.' He pointed his finger at one rounded extremity with two pointed horns which wriggled blindly in the mess.

'Those claws are sharp. They attach themselves to the walls of the beast's intestine. But the digestive muscles of a cow are even stronger. Sometimes the worm is expelled in the faeces of the infected animal. Poor little worm! How does he survive all alone in the world?' Aaron Jacob raised his finger and shook it rhetorically. 'Like the Wandering Jew, sirs, he looks for a new home. Our children play in the dirt and mud. In Judenstrasse, there is no lack of filth. The tiny worm enters the human body, and it will not be so easily evicted a second time. It will grow and grow, and the host will eventually die. The smaller the child, the quicker the fatality. I have chosen to fight this parasite, and I seem to be winning. This is the evacuation of . . .' He clapped the lid on the jar, held it up, and glanced at the label. '. . . - Tobias Horowitz, five years of age. I keep the worm to see how long it can live without a source of nourishment. This one was expelled just yesterday.' He tapped the side of the vase proudly. 'The child's mother will be pleased, no doubt.'

Every woman fears the worm, and the mortal danger it represents for her children. Lotte had told Helena the most horrific stories, and would inevitably let out a frightful scream whenever she caught Manni playing in the dirt. What I had seen went further than the maid's worst imagining.

'How did you make it come out?' I asked, curiosity overcoming disgust.

'A pound of garlic boiled in vinegar. Little Tobias has been force-fed with a tube. That vile concoction, and nothing else for seven days. The child hates it, but the worm appears to hate it more.' He replaced the jar on the shelf with the others.

'Detached from the warm tissue of the stomach, deprived of blood, the worm begins to starve to death. Just as the sufferer would have done. It escapes by way of the bowels, and goes in search of a new home. If the Gentiles knew the habits of the worm, they would swear the Jews had created it. It sucks the blood of its victims, and drains them dry. Is that not what the Prussian people say of us, sir? And yet, it is a false analogy. *Tenia saginata* loves Jewish blood as much as any other.'

He looked at me with a mild, amused expression on his face.

'*Baal Shem*,' he added. 'The people here in the ghetto call me the Worker of Miracles. I know the man who brought you here. His granddaughter is being treated at the moment.' He pointed to the jar at the end of the shelf. 'Rachel Pfieffer . . .'

'You have interests outside the ghetto,' I cut him short. 'Biswanger asserts that you possess properties in the town and rent them in his name. Is it true?'

At the mention of Biswanger, the man's face was shaken by a jolt.

'Three of my houses are rented out by him,' he admitted.

'Including the cottage let to the Gottewalds,' Lavedrine intervened. 'Why did you allow it to go to them at such a miserable rent?'

Aaron Jacob was not much older than myself, but there was a fragility about his figure that did not augur a long and healthy life. His head seemed too large and heavy for the slender neck that poked out of his robe. He was short of leg and large of chest, but neither legs nor chest gave any impression of strength.

He turned to face me.

'Do you wish me to tell you that I hired out that house because I wanted the blood of the children?' He was frightened, but not cowed. 'If that is what you believe, sir, you may as well throw me to the mob outside the gate. Let them tear me to pieces, if it suits your purposes. You could not torture such a falsehood from my lips, Herr Procurator.'

Lavedrine came to my rescue.

'It is a simple question. You will do us the justice of replying, Herr Jacob. We are not seeking a scapegoat. We want the truth. We came to Judenstrasse to placate the animosity of Lotingen. Those people are as frightened as the Jews. Tell us what you know about the Gottewalds, and we'll be on our way. By helping us, you help yourself, and your people.'

Aaron Jacob nodded once, then closed his eyes, as if to seal his determination.

'Biswanger told me of the Prussian officer,' he replied. 'He told me that the man was interested in that house, and wanted to settle the question quickly. I did not like the business, that's the truth. I was frightened. If that officer discovers who truly owns the house, I thought, he'll report me to the authorities. Or try to blackmail me. It wouldn't be the first time. But if I charge him next to nothing, I calculated, I will have the upper hand. No man, not even a Prussian major, cuts off his sharp nose to spite his ugly face.

That's what I thought! He won't stay long, he'll find somewhere better. They'll send him to another place. These, and a hundred other expedients, led me reluctantly to agree to the contract. In any case, sir, I knew that Biswanger would make the officer pay more. He always does.'

What would it be like, I asked myself, to live in such a manner, forced to calculate every move and weigh every proposition, with nothing in mind but survival?

'Did Gottewald tell you why he wanted that particular house?' Lavedrine asked.

'I never met the man, or his family,' he said. 'That is, not in person . . .'

He hesitated again, fright evident in his darting, evasive eyes.

'What mystery is this?' I demanded. 'Did you meet Gottewald, his wife, and children? Or did you not?'

'I never saw them,' he replied. 'Not alive.' He gulped noisily at the air, as if a hand had been laid upon his throat. 'But I know what they were like. The children, anyway. I asked Biswanger to make casts of their heads after they were dead . . .'

His voice sank away to a whisper.

'Biswanger told us,' I said gravely. 'Why on earth were you interested in such macabre trophies?'

When he spoke again, his voice was little more than a murmur.

'I can tell you why those children were killed,' he said.

· 25 ·

LAVEDRINE WAS THE first to break the stunned silence.

'You know why they were murdered?'

The man answered as if a simple statement of the obvious were a sufficient explanation of the massacre. 'Those children were victims, sir,' he replied. 'That is one of my classifications.'

I glanced towards Lavedrine. He stared back, and held my gaze.

'You doubt my sanity?' Aaron Jacob observed with dignity. 'I can explain to you how I reached this conclusion. I have no doubt that you are interested.'

'More than interested,' Lavedrine replied. 'But I asked you a question earlier, and you did not answer it. Are you a qualified physician, sir?'

Aaron Jacob seemed to shrink inside his voluminous robes. He stared at Lavedrine with what might have been distaste.

'Put yourself in my place for a moment, *monsieur*. Do you believe that I could ever qualify as a doctor? In Prussia? I am a Jew. An outcast. I make no secret of my creed, or my origins. I can never be anything outside my own community.'

I knew what he was speaking of. In many of our cities, Jews were allowed to enter the town by one gate only—the gate reserved for cattle and other beasts, and they were taxed at the same rate. Jews were not permitted to own a book published in the German language, and they could be expelled from the country for possession alone. Unless they were prepared to forswear their religion, they were banned from our schools and universities. In my own class at the Institute of Halle, a student known as Franz Schmidt had been unmasked as a secret Jew. The university authorities had whipped him through the town for trying to pass himself off as a Prussian in order to study Jurisprudence.

'Even so, you work "miracles",' Lavedrine contended.

'Inside these walls, I do what I can,' the man replied. 'I know more than common ignorance will allow, but everything that I know, I have learnt by private study.'

'Forgive me if I ask, but which German books have you, a Jew, been able to consult?' I queried.

Aaron Jacob smiled at me. He pulled the coverlet from his head and let it fall on his shoulders. His hair was greasy black with tallow wax, parted in the centre, pulled tight behind his ears in a pigtail. On the crown of his head he wore a small white skullcap.

'I was born in Lithuania,' he said, 'but I am not Lithuanian. I live in Prussia, but I am not Prussian. I am a Jew. We have no *nation*—no home—except for the one that we have lost. I have made my way among fellow travellers. I speak German, but I also know Latin and Italian. French is no mystery to me. I read and understand the language. Russian is my second tongue. I admit to owning no German books,' he paused. 'But not all books are German, Herr Procurator. Many of the best come from Scotland in the north, Italy in the south, and other places, too. I have read everything that is relevant to my studies. From the greatest of the Ancients, Paracelsus, to Professor John Brown, who is living in Edinburgh at this very moment. If you wish to know why those children died, I can show you.'

Lavedrine looked questioningly at me.

'Lead on,' I said.

'We are not going far,' Aaron Jacob replied, taking a hooked stick from the wall, turning towards the windows. 'On that wall, there'—he pointed to the darkest corner of the room—'I keep my specimens.'

He reached up, caught the hook in a loop of string suspended from a shutter, and pulled. I blinked as light flooded in. What had seemed in the heavy gloom like a badly made wall full of unsightly lumps was transformed by light into an exhibition of a most curious sort. As the Jew pulled back the other shutter, I was oddly reminded of my own kitchen. Helena had made a habit of hanging bits of old crockery on the wall by way of decoration. But the objects on these walls were not blue-and-white pottery from the Low Countries. They might have been plain clay bowls, rather than pretty plates. Each one was facing the wall, as if to hide the design, the colour, and the glazing.

Aaron Jacob turned to us like a university demonstrator, his long hooked stick in his hand. 'Which of these belonged to the children who were massacred the other week, do you think?'

I was bewildered by this question, my eyes flashing from one to another of the dozens of dull forms that were ranged upon the wall, searching for examples that were smaller.

'What are they?' I asked.

'Cranial imprints,' snapped Lavedrine, before Aaron Jacob could say a word. Then he turned to the Jew. 'Did all of these come from Biswanger?'

'Oh, no, sir.' Aaron Jacob moved closer to the wall, like a *cicerone* in an Italian church, preparing to explain the mysteries of a fresco for a pittance. 'Only four of these were made by him. The rest were in my baggage when I made my escape from Vilnius. I have friends in places where the Jews reside. Knowing of my research, they try to obtain impressions from a corpse whenever anything remarkable occurs. They send me a plaster cast, and a short history of the person who has died. Sometimes, of course, I pay. As you know, I am a man of adequate means. News of the local massacre spread to Judenstrasse. Biswanger mentioned that he had the bodies in his workshop. I knew what he was after. *Geld* is everything to that man.'

'Why did you want them?' I asked, trying to stifle my feelings of revulsion.

The Jew turned to me. 'Have you heard of Gottfried Treviranus, sir?'

'Another gravedigger?' I asked with a shudder.

'Professor Treviranus recently invented the science of Biology,' Aaron Jacob continued without batting an eye. 'By careful observation of the human body, he says, we may make genial intuitions about its nature, and speculate intelligently about how it functions. A simple instance, the spleen. Does any man truly know what it is for?'

'The seat of melancholy,' I murmured automatically, like any man who has read a book of Renaissance poetry in his youth.

'A genial intuition,' the Jewish scholar of the macabre replied, 'but poetry hardly leads to intelligent speculation about what the organ is *for*. That is what the medical researcher is interested in knowing. If one spleen, or a hundred, are left in water, the liquid will always turn black. Chemical analysis of the fluid tells us that various minerals have been deposited there, and nowhere else in the body. From this evidence, we can deduce that the spleen in every human body is a sort of chamber pot, though we still have no clear idea why certain substances gather there.'

'I see that you are a scientist,' Lavedrine praised him. 'But let us limit our talk to heads. The heads of the Gottewald infants.'

The Jew bowed his own head, as if to acquiesce, then raised his stick and pointed to the top row of plaster casts on the wall. 'Science does not consist in merely cataloguing random facts, *monsieur*. It requires the formulation of a hypothesis that will explain them,' he continued. 'I began with these six Gentile casts. They are impressions taken from the skulls of persons who had led unexceptional lives. This one belonged to a boy of ten,' he said, tapping the plate on the left. 'They range in ten-year intervals—step by step—to this one over here, a man of sixty. Each one died of what might be called unexceptional causes, common illnesses: cold, hunger, congestion, fever, and so on. The sutures—the points of joining of the cranial plates, here and here—are quite regular. They are, I repeat, unexceptional in every way. These six became my template,' he explained.

'At that point, for the purposes of comparison, I began to collect the skulls of Jews and Gentiles who had died of exceptional causes. Accidents, acts of God, for the most part. Murder in some cases. Like the Gottewald children. Their heads are remarkable,' he said. His brow creased into deep wrinkles. 'But we must take one small step at a time.'

'A mob is howling for blood,' I urged. 'How many steps will they allow us?'

'As many as we need to understand,' Lavedrine snapped. As if the subject truly interested him. As if he thought that it ought to interest me as well. 'Please, go on, Herr Jacob.'

Aaron Jacob bowed. 'In 1791, Galvani discovered the existence of the neuro-muscular electrical impulse. This is the same *spiritus vitalis*, or "vital force" that Franz Anton Mesmer also describes. Magnetism is both terrestrial, as Newton suggests, and it is animal. That is to say, the human body is a battleground of conflicting electrical charges. I believe that the magnetic tension inside the head, the ebb and flow within the blood-paths of the brain, is the direct result of external stimuli, and I am trying to construct a theory based on the positive–negative poles of magnetic attraction. Some people appear to attract only positive energy. They live a long and a peaceful life. Others attract negative energy, which will eventually destroy them.'

'Where do the Gottewald children fit into your scheme?' Lavedrine enquired.

The Jew tapped his stick against the last three plates on the bottom row. 'I have examined their skulls with care. Biswanger swears that the casts he made were perfect. Yet there is something truly perplexing about them, and I am hesitant to explain it.'

He set aside his stick, removed the three cranial casts from the wall, and laid them on a small table beneath the window.

'You will see them better there,' he said, taking up a candle, lighting three others that were resting on the table. 'I suppose you are asking yourselves why I am so interested in phrenological science?'

'I do not care,' I snapped. 'Just tell us why the children died.'

I might have been alone in the vast Arctic wilderness for all the response I got. Aaron Jacob turned to Lavedrine, as if I had ceased to exist. 'Do you know the history of the Jewish nation, sir?' he asked with extreme gravity.

'Everyone has heard tales from the Bible,' the Frenchman conceded.

'That is a start, I suppose.' The Jew shrugged. 'The Five Books of Moses inform us that the Jewish people have been plagued with misfortune from the dawn of time. We were God's Chosen, but always—invariably, I might say—we made the wrong choice. We ignored the Voice from the Burning Bush. We worshipped graven images. We offended, we were punished, carried into exile, forced to wander forty years in the desert of Sinai. We have been adrift ever since. On our heads the weight of celestial judgement has fallen heavily, and our sufferings are by no means over. If I were to take down one of the Jewish casts, I could show you, trace for trace, the terrible persecutions we have suffered as a consequence of defying the holy words of the Torah.'

'An interesting notion,' Lavedrine said quietly.

'It is not a question of the colour of our skin, or the peculiarity of our language,' the Jew went on. 'There are actual physical mutations! They may be caused by the way in which a people or a nation is forced to live and suffer, though I cannot swear to it. There may be other causes. God may mark out one people in a certain way, and mark all others differently, in a manner only He can see. But I repeatedly noted minute striations and some significant patterns in the way that the bones are knit together in Jewish skulls, and I have drawn certain conclusions from them. I have made comparison with Gentile skulls and never found a trace of these telltale signs. With one exception. The Gottewald children, but they, of course are Prussian . . .'

'Which signs?' I snapped. I believe in Practical Reason. I have no time for men who see the future written in the stars, or women who claim to read the lines of the hand for a *Pfennig*.

'The human skull is a map,' Aaron Jacob answered, his eyes gleaming with passion. 'In Jewish skulls, there is evident fragility in the parietal suturing, a curious rotundity in the *protuberantia occipitalis*, a distinct porosity of the calcium . . .'

'They are different,' I interrupted again. 'According to you.'

'According to science,' he countered, pointing to an almost imperceptible ridge that ran down the centre of the cranium on the left. 'Here, do you see it? And here, again? In the case of the little girl, there seems to be a less dramatic suture, but it does not greatly alter the matter. What does this mean? The answer is as simple as it is inevitable. These three children were marked from birth as victims. Though Gentiles, Divine wrath was irresistibly attracted to them. They had committed no sin, but they have been punished. As certainly as a magnet attracts iron filings. As inevitably as a Jew calls forth Christian hatred. They have been struck down.'

There was a mad light shining in that man's eyes as he raised his forefinger to the heavens.

'A universal law of violence?' I asked incredulously. 'All who die cruelly bear the mark of Cain? That is absurd! Why should God's retribution fall on the blameless heads of three Prussian children?'

Suddenly, I saw the flaw in the man's argument. Aaron Jacob was a Jew. He would tell us that the world was square if it explained the tragic history of his people. He was obsessed, desperate for an explanation. He thought to find it in his treasure trove of horrid objects.

'Are you suggesting that murder is not the action of free will?' I pressed him. 'That it is simply a casual attraction of contrasting energies? I know the works of Mesmer and his followers, but your interpretation is without parallel, sir. You'll be telling us next that all the victims of the guillotine were unlucky souls whose heads just happened to be the wrong shape!'

'I would give my fortune to examine each and every one of them,' Aaron Jacob replied defiantly. 'Those skulls would provide definitive confirmation of my theory.'

'Or reveal its total lunacy,' I counter-attacked.

Aaron Jacob stared at me in silence. I had the feeling he would have loved to run his fingers over the irregularities of my own head. 'Does the idea disturb you, sir? God knows and sees all things. If He knows of injustice, why does He not prevent it? He could have saved those children, yet He did not. I repeat what I said to you before. They were born to die by violence.'

He might have added Bruno Gottewald to his list. Sybille Gottewald, too, if the mangled corpse we had found that morning could be identified. He knew nothing about them, and I was glad of that. Aaron Jacob would only have twisted the information to suit his own ends.

'We are looking for a more logical solution,' I said plainly. 'A solution that is supported by evidence.'

Aaron Jacob took a step towards me. A light was burning in his eyes. His body seemed to quiver with determination. 'Can you offer one single reason that explains the persistent tragedy of my people over the course of thousands of years?'

'We are not here to investigate the vicissitudes of the Jews,' I answered. 'We are interested in three children murdered in Lotingen. We must learn why they died. And why their mother is missing.'

Aaron Jacob considered this for a moment. His face grew dark and brooding.

'When she is found, Herr Procurator, I would consider it a privilege if I might be allowed to examine her skull,' he said. 'If it conforms to the pattern of her children, she will have met a sudden and a terrible death.'

I thought of the mutilated body of a woman we had found in Gummerstett's warehouse, and a cold shiver ran tingling down my spine.

Had this improbable wise man stumbled on a horrid truth?

'The last report we have of Frau Gottewald places her in your rented cottage,' Lavedrine interposed. 'She was alive, then.'

'Where and when a person dies is beyond the realms of scientific study, *monsieur,*' Aaron Jacob replied. 'God knows the answer. I can only examine the evidence after the fact. If the lady is living when she is found, examination of her skull will still . . .'

'Thank you, Herr Jacob,' I cut in sharply, glancing at Lavedrine. 'We have learnt as much as we are ever likely to learn. We can consider this interview over.'

But the Frenchman chose to ignore my signal.

'Earlier you mentioned classifications, sir,' he said. 'As a criminologist this aspect of your studies interests me more than any other. "Victims" was the term that you used, as if some beings are born with no other purpose in life.'

Aaron Jacob preened like a peacock over this unexpected compliment. 'The Twelve Tribes of Israel were God's ordained people. Now, we are obliged to suffer and pay for our sin. In the future we will be redeemed. *Yom Kippur.* This is the name that we give to the Day of Atonement. Is this pre-destination, or is it fate? In Jewish skulls, as I said before, I have seen the message of impending tragedy . . . No, excuse me'—he paused and laid his hand on his heart—'tragedy is not the word I am looking for. Our history as a people is marked by tragedy. It is our birthmark. There is an even greater trial in store. All the signs point to it. A disaster of unimaginable proportions will fall upon us. The Kabbalah, our book of mysticism, indicates that the Devil's time for harvesting is not yet ripe. *Lilith will come, Time will cease . . .* It will happen here in Prussia.'

'We are wasting time,' I said to Lavedrine. 'Herr Jacob promised to tell us why the children were killed. We have our answer. Destiny. The best way to put an end to the unrest in Lotingen is to find the killer. We will not do so standing here.'

Lavedrine seemed pointedly to ignore my urgency once again.

'All is not so gloomy as you paint it,' he said to Aaron Jacob. 'You are no longer an underprivileged outcast. The Napoleonic Codes have granted civil rights to Jews, not just in Prussia, but throughout the continent of Europe. That includes the freedom to study, and improve your lot. We have turned the old world upside-down. Is it not a better place?'

The Jew smiled uncertainly at Lavedrine, but he made no effort to reply.

I could have answered for him. I had seen the fright in the eyes of my wife and children as the French were storming through the town. If his theory was correct, the irregularity of our skulls had brought violence crashing down upon us. If he was right, Napoleon Bonaparte had been given no choice but to hammer us.

I kept this opinion to myself as we left the house.

Outside it was night.

The crowd of men who had brought us there had dispersed like evening mist. We found Judenstrasse equally deserted. It was as if the hand of God had swept down from the heavens and carried everyone off to the better place that Lavedrine had mentioned. When we reached the gate, we found no angry crowd on either side.

The four militiamen were quietly smoking their pipes.

'What happened?' I asked the corporal of the Palisaders.

'They hung around and shouted,' he replied. 'Then one by one they got tired of it, and drifted off.'

'A propitious inversion of negative cosmic influences.' Lavedrine laughed. 'I have a scientific theory of my own.'

'What is that?' I asked.

'It is dinnertime, Herr Procurator.' A strange shy smile played at the corners of his mouth. 'You'll be going home to dine, I suppose.'

'True,' I answered.

'I wonder, Stiffeniis, may I keep you company? I feel the need for warmth and fellowship after such a depressing day. Would your wife object if I asked her to set an extra plate for me at her table?'

I felt a sudden stiffening in my limbs, a tightening of the muscles in my face. What did this Frenchman want from me? What did he expect from my family?

Warmth, he had said.

Like a flea looking for a new host and fresh blood, thought I to myself, resentfully. If he came to dinner, he was bound to see Helena again. And meet my children. He would sit down at my table, and enjoy the fruits of our limited store.

The curfew sounded as we turned into the cathedral square.

I did not wish him to see the uneasiness that he had awakened in my breast.

'You are most welcome,' I said, but there was no enthusiasm in it.

·26·

HELENA COULD NOT have failed to notice our arrival.

She must have told the maid to wait until we rang before opening the door, I decided. As one would do with strangers.

My wife was avoiding me, as I had chosen to avoid her that morning.

'Wait a moment, Stiffeniis.'

Lavedrine laid his hand on my arm, preventing me from pulling the bell cord.

Had he had second thoughts about inviting himself to dinner?

'I do not think we should tell Helena about the body that we found this morning,' he said, instead. 'Not in her own home. What do you say if we leave her in peace for a while?'

Not Frau Stiffeniis. Not your wife. *Helena* . . .

I smiled weakly. 'I have learnt to my cost,' I said, 'how difficult it is to keep anything secret from my wife. You realised the danger before I did. If we don't tell her, somebody else will.'

Lavedrine nodded thoughtfully. 'I am a guest,' he said. 'It would be a sort of sacrilege to bring what we have seen today into your home. Do you not agree?'

Here was another side of the man. He spoke without a trace of sarcasm. As a rule, it dripped from his lips as naturally as water from a spring. Now he wished to shun any mention of facts that might wound a frail female heart, though I had witnessed the speed with which he could cut a woman's face with that spiked ring of his. Now, this genteel Frenchman would do anything to leave crude reality outside my house. As we were examining that crushed body in Gummerstett's warehouse, he himself had proposed that Helena be dragged into the investigation. Now, this sudden change. What was going through his mind?

'Have you no reply to make?' he added, punching me lightly on the arm in a friendly manner. 'I was saying that you are fortunate in having a wife and children to come home to. For an old dog such as myself, an hour spent in the company of another man's family is all that I have to look forward to. How else am I to shake from my head the sights and smells that we have seen? Sometimes I long for normality. There, that's why I thrust my company upon you!'

Out of sorts on account of the things we had seen? I was no less affected, but why did I deny him the right to be perturbed? Why think so insistently of him as my enemy?

'I believe Helena has made a strudel,' I announced dispiritedly.

The door opened suddenly, though I had not pulled the bell. Lotte stood back to let us enter. The warm sweetness of baked apples wafted out to do battle with the cold.

'We did not know what time you'd be back, sir,' Lotte said with a curtsy that I had never seen before. She spoke to me, but her eyes were fixed on Lavedrine, as if she were trying to comprehend what brought him there. We would not be the first Prussians to lose their home to a smiling Frenchman.

'This is Monsieur Lavedrine, Lotte,' I said quickly. 'A guest. I hope that delicious smell of apple, cinnamon, and honey is not the product of my imagination? I've spent all day thinking of it. I am famished!'

'The mistress has finished baking,' Lotte mumbled. 'And the table is set. For five . . .' she added, uncertainly.

'We'll need to make another place,' I replied. 'How is Helena?'

Lotte glanced uncertainly at our dirty clothes. 'The mistress is well, sir. But what have you been up to?'

'A spot of manual work,' said Lavedrine with a smile, fiddling with his hat, the perfect image of the unexpected guest. He was very good at it.

'Helena, we have a guest,' I called.

My wife came dutifully along the passage from the kitchen, candle in hand, showing no sign of surprise. Neither for the state of our clothes, nor for the presence of the Frenchman. She stopped in front of him, and dropped her eyes to the tiled floor.

'Monsieur Lavedrine, you are most welcome.' She did not look in my direction, nor give any sign of noticing me. 'Come in and warm yourself, sir.'

We proceeded into the parlour. Helena sat down on the sofa, pointing Lavedrine to an armchair on the other side of the hob. In that same room the night before, I had lost her confidence, and I was uncomfortably aware of the unresolved state of our differences. She did not invite me to sit, and I made no move to do so.

'I beg your pardon, *madame*,' Lavedrine began, smiling like a pickpocket who has just lifted a heavy wallet. This French invasion was my idea. Your husband had no part in it, I assure you. I pressed myself upon his generosity. He could not say no.'

I stood by the window and watched them in silence.

Lavedrine had left his oil-stained coat in the hall. He was wearing a dark green jacket made of thick woven tweed, and heavy baggy trousers of dark-brown twill with a chevron pattern. A peasant dressed for duck-hunting, I judged malignly. The impression was reinforced by the stains of oil and mess from Gummerstett's warehouse, which still spotted his clothes. I was more formally attired. My black kersey suit showed less evident signs of the labours of the morning. The starched collar of my white shirt pushed its stiff wings against my jaw. Yet, I had to allow, there was a careless elegance in Lavedrine's rough eccentricity that seemed to reinforce the innate charm of his manner. Had we appeared together at a ball in the same clothes, I knew which way the eyes of the women would turn.

'You'll have to make the best of a dull Prussian dinner,' I said from the window.

'Monsieur Lavedrine will excuse our shortcomings,' Helena replied abruptly, without looking in my direction, stretching out her arms to take the baby, which Lotte brought into the room at that moment.

'I cannot do everything in the kitchen, and look after the bairn, ma'am,' the maid explained, clearly put out by this unexpected visit. She pronounced her German very slowly, her eyes fixed on the Frenchman all the while like a Mesmerist's dupe.

I glanced over at Helena, felt a sudden surge of relief, and knew myself for a fool. She had taken a brush to tame her curls, or Lotte had been ordered to do it. Her hair was tied up tightly at the nape of her neck in the old style.

I gave myself up to enormous pride, then.

Helena presented herself exactly as I wished Lavedrine to see her. That is, as I knew her. As a wife and a mother, a polite hostess, a charming and intelligent woman, who was not uncomfortably married to a member of the lower aristocracy; a Prussian woman who would greet a Frenchman civilly.

A moment later, Süzi and Manni shyly entered the room, hand in hand, and plumped themselves down on the rug in front of the fire. They did not say a word. Their eyes were wide, unblinking, and they were fixed on Lavedrine.

'Aren't you going to welcome our visitor?' Helena chided them, but the children who were five and four years old only giggled, exchanged a glance, then stared back at the stranger with open mouths. 'Nor say hello to your father after his journey?'

I moved instinctively across to the sofa, caressed the baby's head with my hand, then touched my lips to Helena's forehead for just one instant. But even in such a short space of time, she seemed to draw back imperceptibly.

I disguised the motion quickly, leaning closer to kiss baby Anders on the cheek. Here, I was better rewarded. The child let out a cooing *ghaahaaa* that was not exactly a 'papa,' but was close enough to ensure my contentment. Then Manni and Süzi jumped to their feet, taking their lead from their baby brother. They wrapped their arms about my legs, letting out cries of welcome and joy. Manni grabbed hold of my coat, pulling me down, begging me to give him a piggyback. As I rode him around the room, Süzi hung on to the tail of my jacket like a barrel organist's monkey. Everyone laughed with glee.

All was as it should have been. With one exception.

Helena.

Her stiff passivity when I kissed her stung me badly. Why had she not returned my kiss? I sulked for some moments, then reproved myself again. The presence of Lavedrine poisoned everything. She had kissed me passionately once before in his presence—the morning after the dead bodies of the Gottewald children were found. She knew how embarrassed I had been. Did she avoid kissing me now to spare me further discomfort? Or was her lack of warmth meant to punish me?

Lotte came bustling in again with an extra chair.

'Thank you, Lotte,' Helena said. 'I'll do it. Seat the children, if you will.'

She turned for an instant, laid the baby in the corner of the sofa, then carefully wedged him in with a pair of cushions. Then she moved across to the dresser, and took up a knife, a fork, and a slender glass beaker. 'I hope you'll enjoy what Lotte has cooked for us, *monsieur*,' she said to Lavedrine. 'Roast potatoes, and a slice of cold ham. With short beer, and the row that children always make.'

'I don't believe I've ever been offered a better menu, *madame*,' he replied gallantly. 'Given the musical tradition in the north of Germany, I am inclined to think that the voices of the children will sound like a chorale by Bach!'

Lavedrine's eye hovered fondly on the long table, where Lotte was putting Süzi into the high-chair Countess Dittersdorf had sent us after hearing that the French dragoons had used our baby-chair for firewood while occupying the house.

'We can take our places,' Helena announced, surveying the table, a finger to her lips, a look of concern on her brow. 'Sit here next to me, Monsieur Lavedrine,' she called. 'You can see the children, without being disturbed by them. Is that all right?'

Helena had arranged the seating as she always did when we had a guest. The plates and covered dishes were laid out so that Serge Lavedrine would have the first choice of everything. The Frenchman sat down with an energetic *'Bien sûr!'* while Lotte tied bibs beneath the children's chins, then ran off to the kitchen.

I sat down at my usual place. Helena was facing me, Lavedrine on my left, the children on the right. Manni simply could not tear his eyes from the visitor. Suddenly, the boy put his hand up to cover his mouth, and whispered something to his mother. Then, he stared at Lavedrine again, and smiled.

The Frenchman noticed, for he smiled back, and said, 'May I ask, Frau Stiffeniis, what the little boy told you? He was speaking of me, I'm sure of it.'

'Certainly, *monsieur*,' Helena replied, and dimples of amusement appeared on her cheeks. 'He asked if you were French, and whether Hanno would be obliged to shoot you after we have finished dining.'

We all laughed, but Lavedrine laughed the loudest and the longest. The fact that he was seated at a Prussian table did not inhibit him. 'After the strudel, dear Manni, I am willing to be shot,' he agreed. 'Not before. Then, I will die a happy man.'

Lotte brought in hot plates and served the food. I poured out a bottle of wine from a crate that Lotte's older brother had sent to us from Pomerania. It was a rich, dark ruby colour, and I felt a warm tingle as I took my first sip. Lavedrine raised his glass to me in a silent toast. With the exception of him, I thought, this is how dinner ought to be. In my own house, with good food, in the company of my wife, my children, and our maid, though Lotte was more like a sister to Helena than the hireling drudge that the word usually suggests. The faces of the children glowed like angels painted by Tiepolo on the ceiling of a Venetian palace. What harm could ever befall them?

My mind shot off at a tangent. I was in the room of Aaron Jacob in Judenstrasse, looking down at the cranial casts of the Gottewald children. Was there, anywhere in the world, a hand so evil that it would strike down my own children in the same heartless fashion? I found myself peering intently at their bobbing heads, and a terrible fright possessed me. Was Manni's head more pointed than his sister's? Was it the difference of their ages, or was there some other reason?

I chewed and swallowed mechanically as the meal progressed, my eyes drawn as irresistibly as Aaron Jacob's iron filings to the magnet of my children's heads. Despite my incredulity, the words of the Jew had made a deep impression upon me. The more I studied the children, the more fretful I felt. I rejected the man's conclusions as nonsense, but wondered whether the pseudo-scientific jargon he spouted contained a grain of truth.

I looked around the table, and tried to shake myself free of these demons.

What was I thinking? I had sat down to dine with my wife and children, eager to savour the food that Lotte had prepared, anxious to taste the strudel Helena had made, convinced that I had put aside the horrors of the day. Lavedrine had expressed the same notion, and he appeared to have succeeded in dispersing those ghosts. He smiled at Helena, and held out his plate. She smiled warmly back and helped the Frenchman to more roasted potatoes. Why could I not enjoy the innocence of the moment? Why was my mind filled with putrefying corpses, the stench of Jewish hovels, the misery of those people, the macabre vision of those casts hanging from the wall? Why did the words of Aaron Jacob continue to ring in my ears?

'Stiffeniis, your wife's strudel is exquisite!'

Lavedrine seemed transported by pleasure, while Helena sat looking intently at me. For the first time, I believe, since I entered the house. She raised her eyebrows questioningly.

'Is something wrong?' she asked. Alarm cancelled out her smile in an instant. Fear shone brightly from her eyes. She turned to Lavedrine. 'Have you made some discovery regarding Frau Gottewald?'

'Nothing new,' he replied, raising his glass, taking a sip of wine. 'Nothing that . . .'

'Monsieur Lavedrine is afraid of shattering the fragile tranquillity of our home,' I interrupted. 'An error that I made myself, as you remember, Helena.'

My voice was calm, but it smashed like a sledgehammer through a sheet of glass. Did he really imagine that we could wash down what we had seen with a glass of wine and a slice of apple strudel?

'We found a body before lunch. There is every reason to believe that it is the corpse of Frau Gottewald,' I said slowly, swinging the hammer again.

Helena's hands rose to her mouth to stifle a cry.

Lavedrine froze in the act of raising his glass to his mouth.

He glared at me as if I had been transformed into something horrid to behold.

'God save us all, sir!' cried Lotte, who was coming in from the kitchen with a pot of tea in her hands. She set it down on the tabletop with a crash, and made the sign of the Cross. 'Come away!' she urged the older children, pulling them down from the table. 'It's time for bed!'

She bustled them out, and we three adults were left alone with the baby in the deadly silence.

Then Anders began to suck noisily on his thumb. As the seconds stretched out, I suddenly realised my folly. I had unplugged a dam, and all the jealousy and resentment that came pouring out now threatened to drown us. Who, I asked myself, despised and resented me the most: Helena, or Lavedrine?

'Where did you find her?' Helena murmured.

Lavedrine gestured vaguely in the air. 'We cannot be certain,' he offered, attempting to reassure my wife. 'We have no precise description of Frau Gottewald. Except for yours, that is . . .'

'What have they done to her?'

I heard the sudden catch in her voice. I had not seen her so frightened since the night that Mutiez had come to carry me off. She had been strong in the face of the enemy then, knowing him for what he was. Now, she seemed to shrink before the unquenchable force that had obliterated the Gottewald family. She was frightened for her children. I felt the same trembling fear in my own heart. In our terror, I realised, we were reunited. Lavedrine was the odd man out.

'Do not alarm yourself,' he said, his voice ripe with concern. 'Nothing is proven. Your husband is exhausted. The journey to Kamenetz was long and hard. Things took a sudden, unexpected turn this morning. And we have been extremely busy this afternoon. Then—I must excuse myself, *madame*— I made the final mistake, forcing my unwanted company upon you both.'

'Tiredness is not the cause,' I interrupted him. 'Helena complained to me last night of cruelty, saying that I had kept her in the dark. She is convinced that only knowledge can defend us. By sharing the danger, and taking adequate precautions, we may hope to save our own, and other children.' I paused, and gathered myself. 'We must act quickly, Lavedrine. We must crush the evil-doer before he crushes us.'

I heard the words as I said them, and did not recognise myself. Another Hanno Stiffeniis had spoken. This Hanno Stiffeniis was a husband and a father, a man who was frightened, too well aware that he could do nothing to protect those that he loved from evil.

Lavedrine drained his glass, then set it down on the table.

'You need rest, Stiffeniis. The restorative company of your family. Without the need to make idle conversation with an interfering Frenchman who really ought to have known better.' He looked at me like a stern father, or a well-meaning physician. 'Sleep is what you need. I insist upon it.'

He rose from the table, pushing back his chair. 'Frau Stiffeniis, thank you for the most delightful evening that I have passed in Lotingen since the day I arrived.'

I made to get up, intending like a good host to see him to the door, but his hand pressed down heavily on my shoulder. 'I know my way out,' he said. 'And if I am to take a pleasant memory away with me, it is this. The two of you seated at the table. That little baby in your wife's arms. As if this unfortunate scene had never taken place. As if I had never come.'

He towered above me for a moment.

'You are right,' he said. 'We have to clear this matter up. I'll be leaving town first thing tomorrow morning to look for information that may be of use to us. The French play bezique with the cards held close to their chest. My masters may be holding kings and queens that we know nothing about. I'll be away for two days. Three, at the most. In the meantime, rest, sir.'

He turned to Helena. She was holding the baby to her shoulder, patting him gently on the back. 'Lotingen is in good hands. The best of hands. Your husband's,' he told her with a reassuring smile.

A moment later, we heard the front door close as he left the house.

I felt as though a storm had blown itself out.

Helena came to me then, bringing the sun along with her. Or rather, my *son*, whom she placed in my arms.

'Rock him gently for me, will you?' she asked, her hand dallying about my cheek and neck as she released the baby into my care. 'I'll clear the table. Lotte will have her hands full with those two upstairs. You know the way they are at bedtime.'

I carried Anders to the sofa, and sat down before the sinking fire in the darkness of the room, my face bent close to his. Gazing silently into his watchful eyes, I was aware of the sounds that Helena made as she put more logs on the hearth and began to set the room in order: cupboards opened and closed as condiments and napkins were put away; plates and dishes were heaped into orderly piles; the tinkle of glass as beakers were collected on a tray; the clash of knives and forks in a convenient basket for carrying through to the kitchen. But all my thoughts were centred on Anders, on the weight of that tiny delicate head resting in my hand.

As his eyes closed in slumber, I looked up.

My wife was watching me across the table.

'I might be able to identify the body,' she whispered. 'I saw her face. Her clothes. I may be able to help you, Hanno.' Her voice faded away to nothing, but I could see that she was determined. 'It would not be the first corpse I've seen. Remember the woods.'

She was thinking back to our period of hiding from the French. We had seen many corpses then. But the body that Lavedrine and I had examined went far beyond anything that she had ever witnessed.

'You'll keep on searching, won't you, Hanno?' she urged, the plates forgotten on the table, as she came towards me. 'That corpse may not be hers. Lavedrine said so. She may be in danger. I could help you both.'

'There isn't much to see,' I whispered, for fear of waking the baby. 'Bones for the most part. I doubt that they can tell us, or *you*, anything at all.'

I believed that the corpse belonged to Sybille Gottewald. But Helena wanted to be certain. I saw the need in her eyes as she sank down beside me on the sofa, nestling her head against my shoulder, pressing her lips against my cheek.

'I have to know,' she moaned, imploring me to take her at her word and put her to the test. 'I must help her, if she can still be saved. By any means.'

I lay back comfortably in her warm embrace.

By any means, my wife had said, setting off a chain of thought, unexpectedly suggesting a course of action to me.

'You *have* helped her,' I breathed, crushing my mouth against her curls.

We sat in silent communion before the crackling fire.

I listened to the baby's breathing. I felt Helena's head on my shoulder. Beyond the window, night lay like a black mantle over the town. It seemed to me as if the house, and all that it contained, was floating in a void. And that the sofa was the last safe place on the face of the earth.

· 27 ·

'WHY DID YOU bury them, sir?'

The question was not intended as an accusation, but that was how Count Dittersdorf took it. He jumped to his feet, red in the face, blocking out the meagre light that filtered in through the tiny window at his back.

'How can you ask me that?' he exploded. 'Those children were Prussian, Hanno. They had no father to care for them. I could not leave the bodies one minute more in the hands of atheists. I knew what I had to do, and I did it.'

'Without consulting me, sir? Without a word to Lavedrine?'

He glared at me angrily. 'What's done is done,' he said dismissively, pointing to the chair. 'Let us waste no more time.'

The French had requisitioned the district governor's palace, but Aldebrand Dittersdorf's sense of his own power was not diminished. All they had left him was a couple of chairs and his magnificent desk, which filled the tiny, dank closet where he had been relocated. Made of solid oak, it sprouted a Prussian eagle at each corner, his coat of arms in the centre. For generations, Dittersdorfs had signed and sealed the lives and the deaths of thousands of mortals who dwelt between the Wista and the Pasteka rivers. If the French really wanted to clip his wings, I thought, they should have burnt that desk.

'Entrusting Biswanger with the task?' I niggled.

His heavy old face was a mask of wrinkled perplexity. 'Of course!' he snapped. 'He is Prussian. He did a fair job, given the state those bodies were in.'

He darted a fiery glance at me.

'Has Lavedrine been complaining? I suppose he wanted the children tipped into a pit in the French fashion.'

I shook my head, and looked disconsolately away.

'Where are they buried, sir?' I asked, unable to let it go.

His eyes lit up. He puffed out his chest. 'I arranged a grave for them in the children's corner of the Pietist chapel-yard. No one else was present,' he said. 'Just myself, Biswanger, and the pastor.'

As he spoke, he pushed a pile of papers across the desk towards me.

'Here you are. Just as I promised. Everything I could find regarding Bruno Gottewald,' he said. His voice had sunk to a hoarse whisper. 'The archive in Berlin is in French hands, of course, but they hold less than they believe. I'll not tell you where this hoard is kept. It is better not to know.' He placed his hand protectively on the wad of papers. 'You'll have to read them here. To-morrow I must return them. Does Lavedrine know that you've come?'

'He left town this morning,' I assured him, holding back the truth. I did not intend to tell him that the Frenchman was investigating an aspect of Bruno Gottewald's career that would never appear in those Prussian papers.

'So much the better!' he exclaimed, standing up, reaching for his over-coat. He squeezed himself awkwardly through the tight gap between the desk and the wall, placing a large key on the table. 'Lock up when you go, then slip the key beneath the door. I have a duplicate.'

'What if someone comes for you?' I asked with surprise.

'For *me*?' He froze by the door, his expression a mixture of pain and amusement. 'No one comes here, if he can avoid it. Mutiez came running the night the children were murdered, but only because his superiors were uncertain what to do. They were concerned for the consequences. They tell me as little as they can get away with. Why do you think they gave me such a tiny room?' he smiled wanly. 'They don't want Prussians congregating. They know we are dangerous in threes and fours.'

The door closed behind him with a click.

I had just discovered a side to Dittersdorf that I had never suspected. I had always thought of him as a puppet in French hands, but clearly I had been mistaken. What secret channels had he tapped to get his hands on those documents? The night I returned from Kamenetz, I had had the sneaking impression that Dittersdorf wished to protect General Katowice from the French. Did he know other dangerous patriots as well? Were there other enclaves such as Kamenetz on Prussian soil?

I moved around the desk, and sat down in his chair.

There were four thick folders in the pile and I spread them out across the broad expanse of the desk. Prussian bureaucracy is not praised for nothing. Immediately, I was able to establish one important detail, and make some as-sumptions on the basis of it. Bruno Gottewald had enlisted in Spandau, then went on to serve in Marienburg, Königsberg, and, more recently, Kamenetz. In a career lasting twenty-six years, he had been solely under the command of General Juri Katowice.

With the exception of the word 'enlisted', there was nothing unusual in this. The strength and vitality of our armed forces since the days of King Frederick II derives from the fact that military service in Prussia is universal, and it is feudal. This was the enduring power of the *Junker* landlord. I read the inscription again. Bruno Gottewald had enlisted. Men who joined the army freely in the last century were a tiny minority. Most of them were mercenaries and foreigners. What, then, was Bruno Gottewald's precise civil status? If not a tied man, the son of a serf, what was he?

I let this question dangle.

The young Gottewald had bitten the king's *Schilling*, and joined the regiment of General Katowice in Spandau fortress. Prussian regiments were known by the name of the commanding officer. Having joined the 'Katow-icers', or any other line-regiment, a man would faithfully follow his commander. It was rare for an enlisted man to change regiment, sacrificing the reputation and privileges he had gained, though it was possible. Rather than leave his family behind, or carry them off to some godforsaken outpost in the East, following in the footsteps of his general, a man might sue for patronage from the incoming commander. But it was not considered a good career step. It revealed a lack of loyalty and *esprit de corps*. Especially for those enlisted men who hoped to win officer status, and progress to positions of authority.

In a word, Gottewald had put his career first.

I opened the Spandau folder, and took out the top sheet.

> In this, the year of God,—1781—, I, the undersigned, Gottewald Bruno, being free of obligation, birth and will, born on the—*date unknown*—, the birth being registered in the roll of the town/city/canton of—*place not known*—, on this day, *July 22nd*, before a recruiting-officer of His Majesty, King of all the Prussias, do solemnly swear, and avow—

It was a copy of Gottewald's signing-on articles. A scribe had filled in the form. The same secretarial hand had made a note beneath the roll of his physical description to confirm that the applicant met the requirements for juvenile enlistment. *Big, strong boy with facial hair,* the crude description read. They had assumed from his size that he must be ten years old, or more. He was *five feet five and one quarter inches of height*—one inch over the regulation minimum for an enlisted soldier. He was *to be engaged in the rank as a junior private for nine years (renewable).* Bruno Gottewald had signed at the foot of the sheet with a symbol in the form of a heavy-handed two-barred cross: ‡.

It was not an auspicious beginning to a military career. I went looking for the renewal contract, which he had signed nine years later at Marienburg. He was now identified as a *second junior captain.* He had been *seconded* to Staff with a particular responsibility for the general's horses and saddles. Katowice had evidently entrusted his personal safety to the young man. I had seen the quality of the magnificient stallion that Katowice rode at Kamenetz. And in the intervening years, Bruno Gottewald had also learned to read. Or at least, to write. He had signed the renewal form for nine more years in a firm, legible hand. *Gottewald Bruno.* The boy had made unusually rapid progress.

I skipped back to his record at Spandau fortress, and there, on the second page, was a note signed in September 1781, by Juri Katowice himself, recommending that the boy should be *given careful instruction in the German tongue.*

I sat back.

What language had the boy spoken when he was signed on? Was it something other than German? And what had he done to win the favour of the general in a few short months? I continued to look through the pages that followed, but I found no clue that might explain his remarkable success story. Rather the opposite. As I darted through the mass of reports, facts began to emerge that seemed to contradict the initial notion that I had formed of him as a young man with evident military talent and an impeccable record. He had been severely punished just one week after joining the regiment, and almost every week afterwards. *Fifteen lashes—Monday.* Gottewald had been whipped again a few days later, and the punishment had been more vicious. On the second occasion, he had been thrashed for gross insubordination to a gunnery officer: *he spat at Corporal Litevski, calling him 'a piece of shit from the arse of a Polish bitch' before the assembled ranks.* Young Bruno had been whipped for fighting with boys older than himself, and often senior in rank. In one instance, in 1782, he had caused serious injury. I read a medical report relating to a sixteen-year-old soldier: *Heinrich Bruger sustained a broken nose and seven broken fingers. Three teeth were also removed, one of which had pierced his cheek.* An appended note recorded that for this act of violence Bruno Gottewald had been given *forty lashes—no pay August—seven days in the black hole—no food—no water.*

But punishment did not stop him. Having won another fight convincingly, he continued to maul and kick the loser into a state of bloody unconsciousness. For this offence he had been given *thirty lashes with the cat on three successive days.* If Gottewald still had a back afterwards, it must have been as scarred as a butcher's chopping block. He had been beaten for every misdemeanour under the sun, but fighting with his barrack-room mates and insubordination were the principal causes.

I sat back again, and rubbed my eyes.

He ought to have been drummed out of the regiment. Dishonourably discharged at the very least. Any other man would have ended up in the salt mines. Instead, Katowice had promoted him twice in the eight years that he spent in Spandau. What had Gottewald done to merit such favour? He had been made up to junior lance corporal in 1782, then to second junior captain just three years later. The citation made for remarkable reading: . . . *a true martinet*, the report read. *Gottewald commands those under him with remorseless rigour. In the past month, no trainee in his platoon has been reprimanded. Shows every sign of making a capable officer. Immediate promotion recommended. Pay increased to 7 thalers per month, plus liquor ration.* The note was signed by General Katowice.

A year later, on 22 July, 1786—again, a question mark was inserted next to his date of birth and land of origin—he had been sworn in as a regular adult member of his regiment. His rank was readjusted to lance corporal, and he was being paid at the rate of *10 thalers per month.* By early 1792, shortly after the regiment moved to the fortress of Marienburg, General Katowice had appointed him staff sergeant. Gottewald could not have been more than twenty-four or twenty-five years old, but he had been taken directly under the wing of his commander. He was flying.

Was this the sort of career Rochus Kelding might expect in Kamenetz? Juri Katowice seemed to have a penchant for young boys who displayed aggression and brutality, and were willing to put those qualities at their commanding officer's disposal. Not a week before, Rochus had menaced my own throat with a bayonet. If I looked attentively in my shaving mirror, I could still see the impression that the blade had left. Yet that boy was still a private. Did this difference suggest that Bruno Gottewald had been a greater terror, a more fearsome boy soldier than Rochus Kelding? Or had he revealed some other talent that the general had admired, and decided to foster?

Gottewald stayed in Marienburg with General Katowice for the next four years. There were a string of dull reports about the routine training of soldiers in that fortress. The 'Katowicers' were being reorganised as a frontline regiment after ten years in the Reserve at Spandau. There were endless listings of men, as the various companies and battalions were shuffled, balancing out their strengths and weaknesses. Gottewald's name appeared regularly in the lists, but I turned a page, and there he was again, mentioned in relation to a specific assignment.

On the 12th October, 1795, I read, *a patrol was sent to the village of Korbern on a night-training exercise. Twenty-five men under the command of Third-Lieutenant Gottewald B., saddled and armed, returning to the fortress before dawn.*

Apart from registering the almost inevitable fact that Gottewald had been promoted yet again, nothing more was said about the composition of this patrol, nor about the aims or the goals that it had been set. The fact that armed men had been sent out of the fortress on horseback at night was something of a surprise, of course, but I knew little of military matters, and I supposed that *that* was what the exercise was all about. Horseriding at night, and bearing arms. Bruno Gottewald was an expert with horses. I moved on, distracted by a cutting from a court despatch which had been attached to the foot of the same page. I read it once, then read it again.

Gottewald was mentioned nowhere in the text.

Had a careless clerk in Marienburg slipped up? Instead of filing that note under some other letter, had it found its way by accident into Gottewald's file? He had led his men on night patrol to a village called Korbern and the court despatch was about something that had happened at around the same time out in the countryside not far from there. Was that the cause of the error?

I read it anyway.

The decomposing bodies of two Jewish persons, a husband and wife, were discovered in the environs of Korbern in the canton of Marienburg on 20th October, I read. The couple appear to have been slain in their beds. The local constable reports that nothing was stolen. Vicious attacks on Jews have been widely reported throughout the length and breadth of the country in recent months . . .

There was nothing new or startling in such news. Only God could know how the Jews managed to survive in the countryside, where thoughtless violence against them by their neighbours was the order of the day. Still, I felt an uncomfortable shiver as I read of the manner in which they had been murdered. Like the Gottewald children, *their throats had been cut from ear to ear.*

I turned over the page, and carried on with my reading.

The next mention of Gottewald was in an undated regimental memo which might well have referred back to the night-training exercise in Korbern. *I am always pleased to hear that my orders have been carried out in every single detail. You will be rewarded.* The note was signed by General Katowice.

Which detail was the general referring to?

Two months later, I read on, Katowice had been despatched, together with his troops, to command the more troublesome fortress of Königsberg. Hardly another quarter passed—we were now in January 1796—before the general sent the following despatch to Berlin:

In view of meritorious services in the line of duty, immediate promotion and increase of pay and pension has been recommended in the following cases:
1. Aloysio Munz—1st company trumpet-major;
2. Oswald Trieschkel—3rd company sergeant-at-arms;
3. Bruno Gottewald—staff, 2nd lieutenant . . .

I sat back and stretched out my arms, easing the cold ache in my shoulders.

Outside, the cathedral clock struck again. It was three o'clock and I was only halfway through the mountain of documents. The winter sky was already growing dark, and I had to turn up the lamp.

Königsberg . . .

I must have seen Bruno Gottewald. I had probably met him! The regiment had moved to Königsberg, and they were still garrisoned there in February 1804, a year and month that I would never be able to forget. I had been called to the city to investigate a series of murders. Obliged to live inside the fortress, I had met General Katowice on a number of occasions. With the expert help of the aged Professor Kant, I had solved the crime, but . . .

My mind flew back.

While waiting for permission to examine a corpse which was being held in the castle, I had spoken to General Katowice. He had been attended by a group of junior officers. One of them must have been Gottewald. But which one? What did the man look like? How did he behave? I racked my brains, but could remember nothing that was useful.

I shook these thoughts from my head, turned back to the folder, and continued to read the reports. The years that Gottewald had spent in Königsberg had been relatively uneventful, as the papers revealed. Still, he had been promoted again—to first lieutenant, that is, fifth or sixth in the order of command under General Katowice. His discourse with the general was established on a daily basis. If Katowice had an order to give, then it would come at first or second hand to Gottewald, and there was little reason to doubt that he would carry out his duties with admirable precision. But no details were available.

What did this long silence mean? Did it mean anything at all?

With the outbreak of war between France and the united forces of Austria and Russia in 1805, and the catastrophic defeat of the unlikely allies at Austerlitz, Prussia found herself in an impossible position. King Frederick William III's much-discussed *Thoughts on the Art of Government* amounted to nothing less than a plea for peace and neutrality for Prussia. But Napoleon had other plans. He struck hard and fast, and every available Prussian soldier had been drawn into the defence of the country. Including Senior First Lieutenant Gottewald; he had fought with remarkable courage at the battle of Jena. While travelling to Berlin carrying despatches for Katowice, he had been swept up in the events, and had discharged his duties with such élan that he had been awarded the King's Own, the gold medal for bravery. As the battle drew to its close, and the French invasion of the country began in earnest, he had made a swift escape and withdrawn to Königsberg, bringing news of the national disaster to the fortress. He had then taken an active part in the defence of the garrison, and had distinguished himself again:

General Katowice took chain-shot to the arm, and lost his hand. 1st Lieutenant Gottewald made a tourniquet with his sash, and carried the general to the company surgeon at great risk to his own life. He had, of course, been rewarded. Within three months, he was made up to second major, to replace *Second Major Hans Krantz, who had died of wounds in the defence of the fortress.*

Gottewald had marched out of Königsberg bearing arms, and led half of the troops to Kamenetz. As the report of the ordered withdrawal stated, *Herr General Katowice was in no condition to do so.*

I did a quick calculation. In the course of twenty-four years of military service, Gottewald had risen to third in command. This amounted to a fairy tale. How many men of uncertain birth had gone so far in such a short measure of time? How many men of noble extraction had gone less than half that distance in twice that number of years? Had he signed articles for another nine years of service, who could say how far he might have risen?

Gottewald was dead—he would make no further progress in the army. But what if he had lived?

If Prussia revolted against France, if Katowice led the revival of national pride from Kamenetz, if Gottewald had been alive and fighting at his general's side, what might the future have held in store for him?

The report of Gottewald's death was too recent to appear in those files, of course, but the details of the report that I had read in Kamenetz were engraved on my mind:

> *. . . extensive bruising of the right side of the head and the body, multiple cuts and abrasions of the arms, hands, and upper half of the trunk. A deep laceration crossing diagonally from the right temple to the left-hand corner of the mouth has destroyed the face . . .*

Seen within the context of all the rest, the behaviour of Bruno Gottewald was both strange and inexplicable, and made his sudden death seem even more striking. What was he doing leading a deer hunt? What excess of zeal had pushed him to take such a risk? If every other recorded act in his military career suggested the calculation of a man who meant to shine, what dim light had drawn him on that day? What was he trying to prove? And who was he trying to prove it to?

I huddled inside my cloak, as these questions rattled inside my brain. I could have added a dozen more. Why was Gottewald held in such low regard by his fellows? Why had his career slowed down before it was brought to an abrupt and bloody halt? Was it true that he had shown leanings towards the French? Could he have been a spy? And what about Sybille Gottewald? There was no mention in those files of a wife or children. Had he failed to ask the general's permission to marry? Was that why they had *both* been punished?

I stacked the files together on the desk, and stood up.

A moment later, I sat down again. I picked up a quill, and chewed on the end for quite some time. Finally, I came to a decision. There *was* one person who could tell me more. The only person who had made an effort to assist me in Kamenetz. A man who was desperate to escape from the fortress. I had met the garrison surgeon, Doctor Korna, in great secrecy, and I had promised to help him. But before doing anything on his behalf, he must help me a great deal more. Though I had found nothing in those documents to support my opinion, I was still convinced that the motive for the massacre lay in Kamenetz.

I penned a brief request to the Minister of Justice, to be sent on my own initiative. Without telling Count Dittersdorf. Without referring to any authority, except my own.

Then, I took up the key that Dittersdorf had left on his way out.

The street was deserted. The hour of curfew was drawing near, and the dismal weight of that long day crushed heavily down upon me. Now, another thankless task awaited me. I would have to speak to Lieutenant Mutiez and tell him what I wanted for the following day. Without Lavedrine at my side, I was not sure how far my power would stretch.

What would I do if he refused?

To bolster my courage, I tried to imagine that things had ended differently on the battlefield of Jena, and that I, a victorious Prussian, was about to impose my will upon one of the defeated Frenchmen.

In this belligerent frame of mind, I marched across the square to face the enemy.

·28·

LIEUTENANT MUTIEZ KEPT his pledge.

A hooded barouche was waiting in the lane outside my door at seven o'clock the following morning. The fields were a crusty carpet of frost, the sky a startling shade of blue, the colour of a robin's egg. I had not seen such a beautiful start to the day in over three months.

I climbed up, and closed the carriage curtains.

No man would see me leaving town in a French vehicle, or ask himself where I might be going.

The driver cracked his whip, and the vehicle rattled along the rutted lane that follows the west bank of the River Nogat in the direction of the sea.

With the town well behind, I threw back the curtains.

The blue sky had vanished. A pale orange glow hung low over the invisible far bank of the estuary. Thick fog rolled in off the dark tidal waters like an invading army, wiping out everything in its path. On the landward side, close beside the carriage, the head-high sandstone levee glistened dull and black with moisture. The light seemed to flicker, as if a total eclipse were pressing darkness down upon the morning. Then, the sun went out altogether. The rippling water faded to opalescent grey beneath the encroaching mist. Every sign of life seemed to dissolve away. All forms lost shape and substance, and were blotted out by the time we reached the coast.

I had not been out along the coast road in the past year. The area was heavily guarded. French troops patrolled the quay and the wooden doors that ranged raggedly along the sandstone cliff-face in all shapes and sizes. I remembered visiting the bay the summer before last with my family, driving slowly, passing these irregular openings in the rock, peering into the deep, dark caverns that lay beyond. Manni was curious to see what went on there. In one vast lock-up, fires burned languorously, damped down with hay and sea-wrack, throwing up huge aromatic clouds of dense smoke that made us cough. Lines of charcoal sparkled dully on the ground. Rows of gutted herring hung from hooks in the roof. The fish were being smoked inside, the useless innards tossed out onto the quay, where petrels and larger solan geese squawked and scrambled, fighting over the pickings.

In another shed we watched them making ropes, winding the different strands into massive cables. I remembered standing hand in hand with Manni, watching the work. The torques let out almighty creaks and terrible groans as the hemp was wound ever tighter. The little boy laughed, then clung to my legs as the noise grew fiercer. It was a glimpse into hell—the black-faced labourers, the thick smoke rising up to facilitate the twisting of the heated cord.

All this had gone.

The basic trade of the place had always been fish. Fresh fish, live fish, fish just caught, their tails slapping and thrashing in shallow tanks of seawater. Dead fish were gutted, then stored in barrels, packed down with salt. Fish of every shape and size laid out in boxes on the stones. This bounty had been sold in the Old Fish Market. But now, it, too, was closed. The fishmongers, ropemakers, coopers, and all the rest had been pushed out by the French. The masters and their labourers had moved to the area closer to the town, the new port, where Leon Biswanger had his workshop. Meanwhile, the estuary had been requisitioned for the use of the invaders.

'I discovered the place myself,' Mutiez confided triumphantly. 'You won't be troubled there, Herr Procurator. When we held the bodies of the children in Bitternau, there was a riot in the square. But there, they'll stop a bullet if they try anything.' He hesitated for a moment. 'I hope you'll find it to your liking, sir.'

Professor Kant was in my thoughts when I spoke to Mutiez. Kant had devised an ingenious method to preserve the body of a murdered man in Königsberg four years before, instructing soldiers to protect the corpse inside a tarpaulin, then cover it with snow. I had asked the lieutenant to find a dry, cold place where I might examine the body that I believed was Sybille Gottewald's. Kant's methods had horrified me at the time, but I found myself in the same position. I did not want that corpse to decompose before I had made every effort to identify it.

Was this the best that Mutiez could do? He had sent me to a place where putrefaction was the order of the day.

The coach stopped suddenly, and the driver announced that we had arrived.

I stepped down before a huge double door which opened into the rock. The wood was ancient, pitted and rotten, grey with caked salt and the spray of the sea. The number '11' had been painted freshly on the door in large white strokes.

The coachman leant down from his box, holding out a large key in his hand. 'For you, monsieur,' he muttered. 'I'll be back with the other gentle-man inside the hour. The fog seems to be lifting.' He whipped the horse, and cantered ahead, looking for a place to turn the vehicle and retrace his route to town, while I stood before the door, jiggling the ancient key in the rusty lock.

The door swung inwards, and cold air swept out to meet the damp of the day.

On the floor lay a storm lantern and a flint. I struck a light, adjusted the wick, then pushed the door closed behind me. As I looked about, I began to wonder whether I ought to revise my unkind opinion of Lieutenant Mutiez.

The air was incredibly dry compared to the fog on the dock. There was a constant whistling current of ventilation, as cold as a mountain breeze. So cold, indeed, that my teeth began to chatter as the bones and muscles grew rigid in my jaw. Holding up the lantern, I made my way deeper into an un-expectedly vast space. The hollow in the rock was twenty yards wide, but three times as long, and surprisingly well lit even by a single lamp. The walls had been covered with shining white ceramic tiles, and on each tile there was a tiny design of a fish, and undulating green lines to represent the shifting sea. I might have been walking under water in the middle of an extraordinary shoal of every imaginable species, each one of an identical size. Crabs, clams, crayfish, flounders, brill, halibut, narwhals, plaice, eels, a thousand other mysteries of the deep. Huge beams had been fixed cross-ways in the roof, and the wrinkled carcasses of larger fish suspended from the tree trunks shifted and swayed in the air currents above my head. I spot-ted a huge stingray, a dolphin, the body of a shark, the corpse of a walrus with curving tusks almost as long as my legs.

Along the walls and down the centre of the room, wooden tabletops had been used to display the catch before it was sold. But my attention was cap-tured by a table at the far end of the hall. In the gloom, I could just make out the uneven contour of the remains of the woman, which had been laid out for my inspection. Moving closer, I had to marvel once again at the fresh-ness of the place. Cold was hardly the word for it, and only the merest hint of the smell of fish remained. As I held up the lamp, and looked down onto that table, I saw that Henri Mutiez had not merely done what I had asked— he had done a great deal more.

The shattered remains of the corpse had been carefully recomposed to form the shape of a body, while the clothes, now washed and dried, had been laid out in perfect order next to the corpse. It was as if a set of twins had been laid out side by side. One was decently dressed, if flat, lacking only a head and hands and legs. The other was a ravaged skeleton: the head, the hands, the legs, the feet, and all the rest were visible, but the skin and the recognisable features of the face were crushed and mangled.

I set the lantern to rest, then turned my attention to the corpse, starting from the top, and working slowly down, as Kant had taught me to do. The skull had been broken into several pieces, most probably crushed under the weight of falling barrels. I counted them. There were six plates of different sizes, which would have formed the casket of the head. Brain tissue, stained dark-grey by oil, traced scrimshaw patterns over the remains. Clumps of straggling hair and wrinkled skin still held the pieces together. Shattered fragments of vertebrae led down to the ribcage which had split apart, like the gaping halves of a huge oyster shell. The bones of the ribs had splintered, but they hung together as if the calciferous fibres refused to be parted. And in the centre of this human oyster, a terrible spectacle of crushed, compounded organs had coagulated as a formless black pearl, the size of a plum cake.

The bones of the upper and lower arms had been fragmented into pieces of varying lengths. The pelvis was cracked and broken, the larger bones of the thighs also. One hand was whole; the other a collection of bones, too many, too fractured, and too small to be reassembled. How many barrels had fallen on the woman? I hoped to God that she had died in an instant, or was already dead. The frail composite bones of the lower legs and feet had been roughly laid out as a primitive and approximate map of human anatomy. It would have foxed the wits of the author of *Exercitatio anatomica* to make sense of that osseous puzzle, but Lieutenant Mutiez, or one of his men, had done a remarkable job of reconstruction.

'Who were you, ma'am?' I murmured helplessly.

I looked from the clothes to the bones, and back again, trying to imagine what that body had once looked like. I struggled to see that woman on her feet, fully clothed, her hair neatly dressed, but I floundered. What had she been in life? A wife, a mother? Who had she loved, and who had reciprocated that affection? Was somebody somewhere still seeking the dear companion that he had lost? Or were they all dead? Helena had told me of the woman she had met. She was dark of skin, small of stature. She had been afraid, as if some imminent danger threatened her. If the body were truly Sybille Gottewald's, my lantern supplied irrefutable proof of the implacable destruction that had fallen like a thunder-clap on every single member of that ill-fated family.

'Herr Procurator?'

I started with fright.

How long had I been staring at those remains, searching for some clue that would confirm the identity of Sybille Gottewald?

The door at the other end of the cavern had opened a crack. The tenuous light of day crept in with a swirling cloud of fog. A solid figure stood silhouetted against the light, starkly framed in the doorway. I stared down at the corpse again, wondering whether I had made a mistake by inviting him there.

'Did anyone see you board the coach?' I asked.

His footsteps halted short of the table. 'I don't think so, sir. Your instructions were precise, the coachman acted with caution. I didn't realise he was French till we were well away from Judenstrasse.'

I felt better for that. 'It was not my intention to bring more trouble on you, or on your people,' I said, turning to look at him.

He was wearing an ancient overcoat which fell far below his knees, blue trousers with ragged cuffs that had seen better days, and an enormous tricorn hat. In his left hand he held a dirty sack of jute. He might have been a man who had fallen on hard times, wearing clothes that he had found by chance, rather than picked by choice. He was certainly not recognisable as a Jew.

'Are they your own garments, Aaron Jacob?'

'A loan from Burckhardt, the ragman,' he murmured.

We stood together in silence, looking down on the body. His clothes gave off a smell of soap and mould, as if they had been washed a long time ago, but never worn until that day.

'Sir?' he asked, a note of uncertainty in his voice.

'This is why I had them bring you here,' I said.

'Whose body is this? A woman, I can see that. But what happened to her?'

'Colonel Lavedrine and I suspect that this is what remains of Sybille Gottewald,' I said, never taking my eyes from the corpse. 'We have no proof to confirm or confound the hypothesis. I have a task for you, if you accept it.'

He replied with such eagerness, I felt the need to block him immediately.

'Is it possible to find some evidence that this woman was the mother of those three murdered children?'

No noise disturbed the silence but the high-pitched whistling of the draught in that large storeroom. I felt it race across the surface of my face like a cold shiver.

Aaron Jacob nodded, set his sack on the table, untied the knot, and carefully extracted the skull casts of the Gottewald children. He laid them out next to one another above the woman's head.

'I was wondering why you wanted to see them again,' he began, his voice trailing away as he spoke.

'I did not know where to start,' I answered brusquely. I did not mention my fear that he would find only what he was looking for. I hoped against hope that this man was as scientific and analytical as he claimed. 'I had a feeling that some sort of comparative physiognomic examination might . . .'

He raised his hand, and I fell silent, uncertain what to add.

'I congratulate you on your intuition, sir,' he murmured. 'Comparison may be possible. But the plates of her skull have been laid out in a very rough approximation. Do you mind if I set them straight?'

'Go ahead,' I encouraged, watching as he shuffled the pieces into a different sequence on the table, like a dealer shifting playing cards.

'We must establish the lines of the *sutura sagittalis* and the *coronalis*, both of which appear to be relatively intact. I'll need to clean these fragments properly first. The bone will have to be separated from the tissue, decomposing skin and compacted hair.'

He turned to me for permission, and I nodded solemnly.

He bent to his sack, took out a scalpel, then leaned on the table, his elbows braced, his eyes inches away from those human remains. Knife in one hand, a fragment of skull in the other, he began to peel away the rags of flesh from the bone, like a cook preparing onions for the pot, moving from one piece of the skull to the next, removing skin here, skeins of knotted hair and blood-spots there, cleaning and polishing each piece attentively with a rag.

Hardly a word was said for twenty minutes.

His blade clicked and scratched against the bone. No other sound penetrated the vault of the Old Fish Market. As each piece was cleaned to his satisfaction, he set it aside, then moved on scrupulously to the next, accumulating a pile of detritus, slowly separating the remains of the head from the clinging remains of the body.

'There,' he murmured, at last. He stood upright, stretched himself, then bent back to examine the fragments on the left-hand side of the table. Having arranged them to his own satisfaction, he looked at me.

'The largest piece is this one,' he said, indicating with the point of the scalpel. 'It is one exact half of the *squama frontalis*, that is, the bone that supports the forehead.'

He picked it up, and held it close to the lamplight. 'The two sutures of the *margo supraorbitalis* are intact, together with a connected part of the *os parietalis*. They will be sufficient for our purposes. The blows to the skull were devastating, sir. Do you know how this woman died?'

'I have no idea,' I murmured. It would not serve my interest if I told him more. I wanted him to tell me. 'This is what was found.'

Aaron Jacob sighed out loud. 'Hmm, just as I thought. The problem, *my* problem, is this. In the present state of damage, it is impossible to trace the patterns of the maternal *suturae* and make a fair comparison with those of the children. The lines are interrupted here, and here,' he pointed. 'Fragmentation of the missing pieces as a result of the impact makes any true comparison invalid.'

He held the pieces of the female skull in his hands, then set them down on the table close to one of the plaster casts. 'There are junctures missing at this point, and this one. Can you see? The child's skull has a squiggly imprint at this meeting-point. These are the telltale signs in an undamaged skull, but in these pieces, they have been obliterated.' He looked up and shook his head uncertainly. 'The remaining pieces of the woman's cranial plates have been even more severely damaged. I am not certain that I can help you. Not on the basis of the skull alone.'

I had dared to hope that I would find definitive proof before Lavedrine returned. I had been silently praying that Aaron Jacob's ability in the handling of skulls would pay dividends. I felt my heart sink. All that remained to convince me that the body belonged to Frau Gottewald was the fragile statistic that no other woman had been reported missing recently.

'Is there no other way?' I asked, impatience welling up inside me.

Aaron Jacob held a piece of the skull in his hands, running his fingers over the surface with a look of intense concentration on his face.

'I might be able to reconstruct the face,' he murmured. 'Not the details, but the general shape and form. Whether it was long or round. Whether the cheekbones were high, or prominent. The jaw is broken into five pieces, but it could be reassembled. We might attempt a general description. Approximate in the extreme, but better than the fragments of the faceless ghost that lie here on this table.'

'Have you attempted it before?'

His words had thrown fresh wood on the dying fire of my hopes.

'Sometimes,' he replied, 'but only as an academic exercise. I have made a face when a skull came my way without accompanying notes, trying to imagine what the person looked like in life, but . . .'

'But what?' I insisted.

The man smiled uneasily. 'There was no way of verifying whether I was right, Herr Procurator. I did not ask for a portrait when I was looking for a skull. That aspect did not form part of my studies.'

I began to search inside my leather shoulder bag. I carried it with me wherever I went. It contained a spirit-case, an assortment of linen handkerchiefs, which Helena always pressed upon me as I left the house, my French and Prussian identification papers, and a hundred other odds and ends.

'Perhaps we can combine our talents, Herr Jacob,' I said, taking out the silver carrying-case with a screw-top where I kept graphite, and my rectangular drawing-album with the stiffened leather back. I had taken the trouble to glue in the loose drawings that I had made at the Gottewald cottage: the corpses of the three children, the sketches of the kitchen and bedroom, and a plan of the cottage and the grounds. On more recent pages, I had inserted the drawings of Durskeitner's lodge, the animals in their cages, skeletons of birds dangling from the ceiling, and the totems he had set up all around the hut. There was also an artistic sketch of the grim outline of the fortress of Kamenetz, as I had seen it the night I arrived, and rough attempts at portraits of Rochus Kelding and General Katowice, as I whiled away the hours on my return to Lotingen.

'You are a fair artist, sir,' Aaron Jacob said, as I flicked through the contents of my sketchbook looking for the next empty page.

'Could you help me to trace out a shape for the face of this woman on the basis of these bones?' I asked, ignoring the compliment.

He glanced down at the table, then back at me. There was a bright, excited gleam in his black eyes. 'An interesting experiment,' he said. 'And we may make it easier for ourselves.'

His hands dived for the sack again and pulled out a thick candle. He lit it from my lantern, then set it down in a pool of its own wax on the edge of the table.

'We may use it to good effect,' he said.

In the flickering light, I watched as he began to handle the bones, selecting and laying them out in an order known only to himself. Taking up a piece of the cranium in one hand and the candle in the other, he allowed wax to drip thickly along the fractured edge of the bone. Before it had dried, he picked up another piece and squeezed them together to form a single, larger plate. He continued in this way for some minutes, laying the shallow bowl on the table, building up the fragile walls with the remaining fragments of the skull. His hands worked quickly and efficiently, as if he knew exactly what he was doing, and had done the same thing many times before.

The smell of hot wax and the smoke of the burning wick lent a rich perfume to the cold air, as it does in a church. If any man had entered in that moment, he might have thought that we were performing some strange pagan funeral rite.

'That's the best I can do, sir,' he said at last, standing back. A moment later, he stepped forward again, gently lifted up the structure, turned it over, and placed it on its base, the right way up.

I gaped at that skull in the gusting light of the candle.

I remembered a gift that a friend of my father's had brought back with him from Venice. This man had been to Italy during the winter carnival, and he presented father with a mask that he had purchased there. *Bauta* was the

Venetian name for it. A spectral facial cast made of *papier mâché*. It was the glowing whiteness of the painted surface that gave the skull-like thing its power. As a child, I had been terrified of it. Then, as children do with things they fear, I managed to smash it 'accidentally'. But the image never left me.

I was speechless. And as pale, perhaps, as the skull resting on the worktop.

'You must imagine this as the base, sir,' Aaron Jacob said, 'with muscle and fat piled on top, contained within a malleable skin. She was no more than thirty, I would guess, so the features would tend to be soft and round. If you design the general outline, I'll venture to suggest how the form might be modified by the jutting of the bones beneath, and the cushioning of the softer tissue. I will tell if something is probable, or not.'

We worked together for an hour or more, in perfect harmony. Sometimes, he praised me for what I had done. At others, he chided me to do more. And when he was happy with the shape I had drawn, he told me so, and warned me not to change a detail.

'All that's missing now is the hair,' he said at last. 'This is the most difficult. We are almost bereft of clues. The strands were dark, I think, unless the hue has been altered by soaking in blood and oil. And long with a slight undulating wave. But how did she comb it? How did she dress it? There are no combs or clips. No ribbon, or band, and Gentile women are noted for being fickle. They wear their hair one way today, and it is altogether different the day after. And then, there is the fashion, which changes year by year, and month by month . . .'

As he was speaking, my mind drifted off. I thought of Helena, and her rich head of dark rebellious curls. Then, I saw them pinned and tamed. She could be two quite distinct and different people. I made a decision then, and drew that woman's hair as I thought it might be, flowing down to her shoulders in a gentle bow.

Aaron Jacob held the sketch in his hand when I had finished.

'Will anybody recognise her?' he asked uncertainly.

I looked at the hazy lines of the cheeks. The eyes were larger than I had intended. The lips and the mouth were more sensuous than a skull ought to have suggested to my mind.

'It is certainly better than scattered bones,' I replied.

After all, there *was* somebody who might be able to identify her.

·29·

'WHERE IS HELENA?' I asked.

Lotte was standing by the hand-pump in the kitchen, peeling potatoes for dinner. The children were seated at the kitchen table, heads down, whispering secretively, slates and chalks in their hands. They glanced up, then quickly looked away. It was a game they often played. The baby was sleeping open-mouthed in his basket, which rested on a chair on the far side of the blazing fire. That scene of domestic bliss ought to have warmed my heart. Instead, I felt the icy grip of fear. Helena was not with them.

Lotte raised her eyes from the potatoes, and looked at me disapprovingly.

'Welcome home, Herr Stiffeniis,' she said archly.

Since Jena, Lotte Havaars had been our anchor. While we were hiding in the woods outside Lotingen, she managed to impose normality on a situation that was desperate in the extreme. She carried on as if nothing had altered, as if the invasion were a child's bad dream to be soothed away. Naturally reserved, if Helena and I had need of privacy, Lotte would curtsy to her mistress and take herself off to look for mushrooms that were edible. Before lying down to sleep, when getting up at the crack of dawn to light a covert fire, whenever she retired to the wood on privy business of her own, or came back again, she was always the same Lotte: treasured nursemaid, the children's second mother, Helena's steadfast friend. We might have been safe at home for all the concessions that Lotte made to dire necessity. 'I'll not let Frenchmen rob us of our decency,' she declared one day. 'They'll harm them babies over my dead body!'

The same defiant spirit shone out of her now, a half-peeled potato in one hand, a sharp knife in the other. She wished me good evening, then stared me down, but she would not rise to my question.

'Your papa is home,' she said to the children. 'Aren't you going to greet him?'

Manni and Süzi lifted their heads, smiling now. They blew me kisses from the palms of their tiny hands, as if they were delicate rose petals. I pretended to try and catch those kisses, and put them safely away in my pocket. But I did not take my eyes off Lotte as the children bent their heads contentedly to their drawing again.

'Mistress is upstairs,' Lotte said, 'putting the stuff in order. Today is *Wednesday*, Herr Procurator.'

I felt my heart lift. At least in part. Mother Albers always came on Wednesday, bringing fresh food to our door. A peasant, not a serf, the widow of a fairly prosperous farmer, she produced eggs and other foodstuffs on her smallholding near Lotte's village, then sold her bounty door to door. She saved the best for Lotte, whom she remembered as a child, and for our children, who belonged to Lotte as much as they belonged to us. Many a time, only the old woman had stood between us and starvation. Helena's fear was always that she would not be able to supply us with enough fresh eggs and other things to last out the week. The French had soon got wind of it, of course, and they were not slow to send requisitioning parties to the Albers farm. Once Sunday had passed, Helena would begin to show signs of an obsessive nervousness that reassurance could not placate. Nothing was to be wasted. Not a thing must be thrown out. Not before Wednesday. Scraps were hoarded in the larder. What if Mother Albers didn't come? That was Helena's terror. Monday and Tuesday were troubled by her frequent visits to the attic. She had to be certain that we had enough to last us till Wednesday. She feared loss, mould, damp, insects, and just about everything else, behaving as if our meagre store might disappear into thin air.

Lotte went back to plucking black eyes from the potatoes.

I stood by the kitchen door, my coat still buttoned up against the winter, unable to ask the question that hampered me.

'Sir?' Lotte was looking at me again, perplexed by my immobility.

I moved close to the sink, not wishing to be overheard by the children. Lotte put down her knife and the potato, and wiped her hands on her apron, inviting confidence.

'In recent months,' I began uncertainly, 'how many times has Helena been out of the house alone? Walking in the country, I mean. Without you or the children, that's what I mean to ask.'

I saw the colour rise to Lotte's round cheeks, I saw the frightened look she threw over her shoulder in the direction of the children.

'How often?' I pressed her.

Lotte wiped her brow with her forearm. 'Twice, sir. No more. You were working. The mistress said she needed to get out of the house. She felt stifled. She wanted to walk . . .' She glanced towards the door, a frown creasing her brow as she was drawn into this confession. 'I offered to go with her, naturally. I would have dressed the children for the cold, or someone could have come to sit with them. But she didn't want no company. She told me not to make a fuss, she'd be quite safe on her own.'

There was a tremor in the maid's voice, as if she feared my reaction to this news.

'Did she tell you where she was going?'

Lotte shook her head, and looked down. 'She was set on going out, I didn't ask.'

'When did this happen?' I insisted.

'Weeks ago. A month, or more,' she replied uncertainly.

It was like squeezing whale oil from a lemon. 'How long was she gone?'

Lotte thought about this. 'The first time she was out all afternoon,' she said at last. 'The second time for two, three hours, no more.'

'Without telling you why she was going?' I asked incredulously.

I would never have believed that I would need to ask such questions of the maid. It felt like a breach of trust with regard to both of them. Especially with regard to my own wife, the woman I thought that I knew, heart and soul.

'She did not say, sir. But I did make a guess.'

'And *what* did you guess, Lotte?'

I did not recognise my own voice. Obliged to whisper on account of the children, I heard the low growl of my mounting anxiety, supplicating and demanding at one and the same time.

'The usual thing, sir,' Lotte replied promptly.

'Food?' I asked.

Lotte nodded, her eyes darting towards the door again, as if she feared that Helena might enter the room at any instant. 'She's terrified—you know yourself, sir—that there won't be enough to go round. Surely you remember when we were in the woods? She'd always been such a happy, chatty thing, but out there, everything changed. One thing on her mind all day, and nothing else. Food, food, food! I'll never forget the day you caught that rabbit with your hands, sir. The look of joy on her face!'

I did not recall the joy, but I remembered the haunted look that took possession of Helena's face while we were forced to rough it in the woods. Terror had gripped her hard. She hardly touched her own ration. And I discovered that she was hoarding food in a bag which she hid beneath her cloak. She was jealous of bread the way another fugitive might guard his coin or jewels. I would never forget the way she used to stare at me as I dared to eat my own portion. As my teeth sank into a stale crust, there was a questioning accusation in her eyes: how can you eat it, Hanno? Manni and Süzi deserve it more than you do.

'When she went out . . . walking,' I asked, 'did she bring things back?'

Lotte nodded. 'Raspberries, sir. We ate them for breakfast. Don't you remember? With Mother Albers' honey. Frau Helena was very pleased with herself. There are things to eat if you go out looking for them, she said. Fruits and nuts, salad grass, radishes, berries. If ever we had to hide in the woods again, she'd know what to look for. That's what she told me, sir.'

Exploring the countryside, looking for food, learning what was good to eat, and what was not. Was that how she had chanced to meet Frau Gottewald? Was that what they had talked about?

'I'll go upstairs and help her,' I said, turning away.

But Lotte called me back. 'Be warned, sir. Mother Albers didn't bring much.'

I understood what Lotte intended. I would have to pick my words with care. I must not harry Helena when her mind was taken up with such important things. I nodded, and left the kitchen.

I climbed the creaking stairway, and began to mount the rickety ladder into the attic. Reaching floor level, I looked inside. Helena was seated on one of the cross-beams of the roof, her back resting against the end wall. A lantern stood on the floor close by. In her lap, was a dull, golden-brown pile of shrivelled russet apples. In her hand she held a cloth. She was polishing them, one by one, until they shone like glass. Fugitive curls peeped out from beneath the white scarf with which she had tied up her hair.

'Husband!' she exclaimed. She seemed surprised, embarrassed. 'Is it so late?'

I looked around, and my heart beat heavily in my chest.

That was *not* an attic, except in name. It was unlike any attic I had ever known. I recalled the happy days I had spent as a child in the rambling garret of my father's house in Ruisling. That place was full of the old, the dusty, the forgotten. There was no order, or organisation in it. Objects fallen out of use, or gone out of fashion, were relegated sooner or later to the attic. A pirate's treasure trove in the imaginative eyes of a child. My brother Stefan and I retrieved those things from chaotic abandon, fantasising about what they were, and whose they had been, as if they were precious relics from another world.

That was not Helena's idea of an attic. Every single thing in her attic was useful. Better kept than any other room in the house, it positively sparkled. It might have been the dispensary in a *lazaretto* where the physician stores his instruments and plies his cures. It had been like this for over seven months. The instant the French moved out, she ordered me to put up shelves. They formed a pyramid at the gable end piled with jars and pots in ordered ranks, like soldiers on parade. In one of the shelves, a rack had been cut—I had drilled the holes to Helena's specification. Eggs were arranged in size: duck eggs in the centre, the others falling off in size to left and right, the colours matching, light at the centre, darker to the side, the very darkest nearest to the sloping roof. Jars were spaced like unexploded shells in a military arsenal. Beneath the shelves were sacks containing flour, corn, potatoes, and what was left of our store of chestnuts. Every single thing had its place, from nutmeg and pepper to samples of rare spices in tiny glass bottles, which she had collected in better times.

I knew the attic well. I knew Helena's attitude towards it. Sometimes, in lighter moments, when she was in a good humour, I would jokingly make reference to the place. *A pound o' hazelnuts for your thoughts, ma'am? Third shelf, left wall? Right you are, then, ma'am!*

I never felt entirely at my ease when I was obliged to enter there.

'I caught him, Hanno,' she announced. 'He'll steal no more from this house!'

Her eyes were glistening with excitement, her voice was a triumphant shout, but I was not happy on either count. Her tone was too sharp, her animation too intense. It was more than just satisfaction. With a nod of her head she indicated the source of her victory. As I strained to see, stepping into the attic, she held up her lantern to aid me.

I juddered with disgust, and had to stop myself from saying so. The spring had sprung as soon as the tiny creature's front paws touched the trap. A little ball of bread-bait lay off to the side. The full force of the spring had caught the mouse across the back, snapping its spine and cutting the corpse into two distinct halves. Blood was still dripping from the separated pieces, soaking into the flakes of sawdust that Helena had laid all around the trap in preparation for this execution. Clearly, she had not wished to contaminate her spick-and-span attic with a single drop of rodent blood. But there was other meatier organic matter on view. It was not a pretty sight.

'I've been after him for a week!' she said, almost squealing at the memory of the campaign. 'He has ruined three apples, and nibbled his way inside a sack of flour. And spoiled it, of course!' She pointed her finger accusingly at the *corpus delicti*. She was better than half the magistrates in East Prussia when it came to handing down a capital judgement. 'There's excrement in the sack! What makes them do such things? Knowing they'll be back tomorrow to eat some more? It is so disgusting.'

'If that mouse were still alive,' I said lightly, 'I'd sentence him to be hanged, drawn, *and* quartered, but you seem to have done the quartering without any help from me . . .'

She cut me off. I think she hardly heard me.

'That's five pounds less for the children!' she exclaimed, her voice agitated and unsteady, as if she were about to burst into tears. Her joy had left her in an instant. 'And Mother Albers told me that the French have been there twice this week. She brought us some potatoes, a few eggs, not much else. No meat, no bacon. Not even a scrawny chicken. What *are* we going to do?'

I moved slowly towards her. She was more upset than she showed. I slid down the wall, and sat myself on the floor, resting my shoulder against her knee, caressing her hand, which still held one of the precious russets.

'I'll speak to Knutzen first thing,' I said to calm her. 'He may be able to lay his hands on something . . .'

'That villain sells his ducks to the French,' she objected. 'The rest goes to feed his own children. I have to be more careful. More attentive. What do you think, Hanno? If I were to wash the woodwork down with vinegar, would the acid keep them away? Mice and rats avoid clean places. Filthy brutes!'

Her voice rose angrily as this monologue proceeded.

I raised her hand to my lips, and held it there, hoping that the storm would pass. I felt helpless. Our supplies were not enough to guarantee tranquillity. Her fears went beyond any simple remedy that I could provide.

'If Knutzen can't help, I'll find someone else,' I promised. 'We could always leave that corpse where it is. At least the other mice will learn to fear the implacable lady who rules over this domain.'

I tried to smile, but Helena drew her hand away from mine. She rested her head against the wall, and closed her eyes. She looked tired, totally worn out by her efforts.

'Do you think that Lavedrine might help us?' she asked after a long silence.

I felt an electrical jolt along my spine.

'Lavedrine?' Her face was an impenetrable mask. 'How could he help us?' I asked, struggling to remain calm.

'He might find us food, if we needed it. He has been here. He has eaten at our table. He has met our children. When he came, I got the impression he would have liked to stay. As a lodger, I mean. Many French officers pay for their food and board. He would do the same. I thought he was going to ask . . .'

'But he did not,' I interrupted her. 'An hour of distraction was all he wanted. He was upset. We had seen such . . . such dismal sights. And Lavedrine already has a lodging. I don't believe he is looking for a new one. There is no immediate need to ask for his help. Or anyone else's,' I said bitterly. 'Should the need arise, I'll make provision, I promise you.'

I took her hand again. 'But now, I must ask something of you. The idea came to me last evening, while we were sitting by the fire. You said that you wanted to help me.'

Helena's eyes flashed into mine.

'What do you want of me?' she asked.

I slipped my leather bag from my shoulder. Pulling out my album of sketches, I turned away as I flicked through the pages looking for the one I wanted. Then, I shifted from the floor, and sat beside her on the cross-beam, my shoulder pressed against hers. I wanted her to feel my warmth beside her. I had asked for her help, but how would she react to the sudden shock of seeing that woman's face?

I raised the lantern and held it up over my drawing. 'This is a tentative portrait of Sybille Gottewald,' I said. 'I want you to tell me where I am right, and where I may have gone wrong. Can you do that for me?'

Helena did not say a word. She took the album from my hands and stared at the charcoal face looking up from the page. She held the picture close, then moved it further away, stretching out her arms, as if to judge the effect at a distance.

'Hardly more than a jotting,' she said uncertainly. 'How did you come by it?'

I told her briefly, without entering into details.

'Indeed, a very rough sketch,' I said. 'Is there anything at all which reminds you of the woman that you met?'

She looked at the drawing again, studying it attentively.

'Frau Gottewald had a more pronounced forehead. A broader brow. More square, angular. Here, you see? At this point. And here.' As she spoke, she traced the lines with the nail of her forefinger. 'Less rounded here . . . and as for the eyes . . .'

I placed my hand on hers.

'I was not able to draw the eyes,' I said carefully.

'Her eyes were chestnut-brown with hazel flecks . . .' A violent spasm shook Helena's shoulders. 'They exist no more?'

'There was very little light,' I answered evasively. 'It is all guesswork, more or less.'

'This sketch confounds my memories,' she said, after another long silent analysis of that drawing. 'Rather than help, it seems to me to suggest different nuances from those that I recall.'

'Tell me what you can remember,' I coaxed. 'You spoke of fear on her face, of the fright in her voice, but I need physical details if this sketch is going to be of any use. If I could get a good likeness, a printer may make woodcuts which I could display around the town.'

Helena handed the sketch back to me. She laid her head on my shoulder, and placed her arm around my neck, looking down as I rested the album on my knee and took out the graphite stick.

'Frau Gottewald's eyebrows were more slender,' she murmured, her breath warm against my ear. 'Like the wings of a gull in flight.'

For the next half-hour we worked, and in all that time she never called that woman by any other name. Frau Gottewald, she said. Sometimes as she spoke, I heard a tremor of compassion in Helena's voice. Frau Gottewald's brow was broader, she whispered, encouraging me to shape and form that brow exactly as she wanted it to be. The eyes of Frau Gottewald were smaller, and more widely spaced. Her nose was slender, longer than I had drawn it under Aaron Jacob's tutelage. The cheekbones were pronounced, and of a rare and delicate beauty. The mouth was a sensuous, delicate bow with worry lines etched at either corner, and the chin was smaller than in my rendition, more pointed and ever so slightly dimpled. As she instructed me, I added detail to the hair, which was dark brown, parted in the centre, pulled back on either side exposing shapely ears. Frau Gottewald tied her curls up behind, said Helena, with a velvet bow.

We sat in silence, looking at that face.

Helena's hand gently took the portrait from me. Taking hold of the graphite, she made a final bold stroke connecting the eyebrows.

'There! Now, it truly *does* resemble Frau Gottewald's face,' she said.

Her voice was calm, and she seemed at peace with herself. All the anxiety and tension that had worried me when I stepped up into the attic had melted away. The dead mouse, the lost apples, the damaged flour, all forgotten. A sort of quiet contentment seemed to hold her in sway as she looked down at the face of the woman that we had drawn together in my album.

'Will this help you?' she asked. 'More than the other one, I mean to say?'

'Oh, yes,' I murmured, unable to drag my eyes away from the portrait.

Helena jumped up in sprightly fashion, walked to the centre of the room, then dropped to her knees beside the mousetrap. She let out a little squeal of renewed delight. 'I'll put these titbits out in the garden,' she said, reaching for a dustpan and a short broom. 'There's a tabby cat that often comes our way. He has to be fed as well, you know.'

My wife was in a bright mood for the rest of the evening. She often smiled in my direction, as if we shared some special, private bond. As, indeed, we did. Together we had drawn the face of Sybille Gottewald, as Helena wanted it to be.

I could think of nothing else all night.

It was as if that portrait were smiling into my eyes, inviting my confidence and complicity. The face that we had drawn was markedly different from the jotting I had made at the prompting of Aaron Jacob. It was more precise, more lifelike. A person, rather than a vague, inaccurate impression of a human face. I had noted the particularity at once, though Helena did not seem to see it. Nor did I dare to mention the similarity. That woman's face tortured me all evening.

As line was added to line, shade to shade, I recognised the face that we had drawn. Apart from the continuous curve of the eyebrows, that portrait might have been of Helena herself.

·30·

KINDERGARTEN—3 *P.M. Something to show you.*

The note was not signed. Nor was it sealed. Brief to the point of rudeness, as if scribbled by someone in a hurry who believed he knew me well enough not to bother with a signature. But I was expecting a note from no one, and could not guess why that person might have chosen the Pietist Church of Christ Arisen for a meeting.

'Who brought the message, Knutzen?'

My clerk shrugged his shoulders. His square peasant face was set in an expression of studied consternation that was habitual.

'Someone pushed it under the door,' he repeated obstinately. 'It was there when I came this morning, sir.'

Gudjøn Knutzen divided his day between sharpening my quills, brushing dust from one corner of the room to another, and showing people into my office, but his heart was with his pigs, ducks, and milking cow. Defending his plot of cabbages from thieves was his only thought. On these resources, his large family eked out their survival. Certainly, they could not have lived on his salary as the Procurator's scrivener. Prussian civil servants, myself included, had seen their salaries sliced by half after the recent war. The other half had gone to France in the form of war reparation, and to the king, who was trying to set the country straight and repair the damage after the invasion. Knutzen had worked in the Procurator's office in Lotingen for thirty years by virtue only of the fact that he could read and write. But necessity had driven him back to the soil. He was more passionate about his livestock than he was interested in my papers, and this attitude showed in his dirty shirt, slop-stained trousers, and mud-coloured boots. Day by day, he looked more like a swineherd.

Four months after Jena, I reopened the Procurator's office, and Knutzen hastened to take up his post again, bombarding me with requests for four months' salary which I was unable to satisfy. As a result, he now presented himself at work only three days a week, 'in lieu of lost pay,' as he quaintly put it. Even then he appeared only briefly, and I could hardly reprimand him for it.

On this particular day, it was almost ten by the time he decided to show his grubby face. I had been there an hour myself when he came, pulling that note from his pocket as he entered the door. He had been there before me, it appeared. Finding the office empty, he had stuffed the note in his pocket and gone about his business.

'One of the pigs is ill,' he said to explain his absence. 'If that sow dies, there'll be hell to pay. The French have put their mark on everything for requisitioning.'

In Knutzen's eyes the health of his pig was of a personal and national importance that far outweighed any criminal investigation I happened to be engaged upon. And his announcement of the French interest put paid to those hopes I had expressed to Helena that Knutzen might be able to make up the shortages in our own food supply.

'Just about anyone could have left that note, Herr Procurator. I can ask . . .' Knutzen began, then decided for himself that it was hardly worth the effort of trying. He shook his head. 'It's useless, sir.'

Five minutes later, I called for him again, but he did not come.

That sick pig had a lot to answer for.

I turned my attention once again to the anonymous note. The cemetery behind the Pietist chapel was little frequented, except by the grieving parents of children who had recently died. If the writer harboured evil intentions, I would be likely to find myself alone and in a difficult position. Unless . . . A name suddenly occurred to me. If Dittersdorf had sent that message, why did he want to meet me there? He had had the Gottewald children interred in that cemetery. Did he want me to see the grave?

I determined to go, but first, a number of things had to be settled.

The judicial life of Lotingen had not been snuffed out by the massacre of the Gottewalds, or the discovery of the female corpse in Gummerstett's warehouse. In lulls between active duty, I had completed my reports to Dittersdorf and the French, regarding my journey to Kamenetz. They were stacked on my desk, together with other reports relating to events in the town. I began at the top of the pile, reading the imprisonment order for the baker's boy, Pincheas Redem, who was guilty of stealing two sacks of corn from his master. As I glanced over the sentence, I pondered for a moment on those sacks of grain. How many pounds of flour would they yield? Despite the statutory six lashes of the cane, and belated promises by his master of forgiveness, the thief still refused to say where he had hidden the goods.

'What a waste!' I thought to myself. Rats or rot would destroy the contents long before he was released. I was tempted to question Pincheas

Redem again, and throttle the information out of him. If the sacks were found, the French would get their hands on them. If I could get to them first, the baker might be persuaded to make the best of a bad job and let *me* have a portion of the flour. That would change the expression on Helena's face. There'd be no more idle talk of appealing to Lavedrine for salvation.

I hesitated one moment, then signed the imprisonment order, and moved on to the remaining documents: petty theft of linen from a washing line, a contested will, a dispute resulting from the fencing of fields after the war. Domestic strife had taken hold of East Prussia again, and I was comforted by the stupidity of it for the best part of the morning and the early afternoon.

I was short of breath by the time I reached the burial ground.

It was bitterly cold in town, but there the temperature seemed to drop another ten degrees. A sensation of leaden desolation took me by the throat every time I was forced to enter the place. This feeling became more intense after the birth of my own children. There is nothing so bleak as a cemetery in winter, except a burial ground for infants. The Church of Christ Arisen had been built in the second half of the seventeenth century, but the cemetery was of a more recent date. The decision to lay out a graveyard for infants in the wooded area behind the church in the summer of 1723 was the brainchild of a pastor by the name of Johannes Huber. An epidemic of choleric fever carried off a quarter of the population of Lotingen that year, and the city fathers had been forced to dig large pits as common graves to accommodate the army of corpses. Shocked by the inhumanity of what he saw, Pastor Huber decided that the children at least should be decently buried, each in an individual grave with a headstone recording the name and age of the victim, together with a brief poetic epigraph. Even now that the epidemic was no more than a memory, the tradition persisted.

Above the gate through which I had passed was a banner worked in metal, badly rusting now, creaking in the wind, which alluded to the tender sentiments that had inspired the creation of that hallowed ground. It was, the parents said, a place where the souls of the dead children would play together for all Eternity, so they had called it the 'Kindergarten'. Dead Babes' Wood was the more sombre name by which the common folk of Lotingen referred to the necropolis where the little ones were laid in fond expectation of their future resurrection.

I closed the gate and looked around. The only sound was the swishing and thrashing of the wind in the trees. Snow lay in that deserted, sheltered place, though it had melted away in the busier parts of town. A shiver ran coursing down my spine. Of a sudden, I realised my foolishness. What was I doing there, alone and unarmed?

'I must say,' I heard the voice as a twig cracked behind my back, 'I do prefer burial in the ground to entombment in a crypt or charnel house beneath the flagstones of a church. Here, you walk among the dead, rather than *over* them. It is more respectful. Don't you agree?'

I spun around to meet that voice. Trees and bushes grew closer in that direction, the shadows more deeply etched. The tiny white headstones stood out starkly, like milk teeth in a baby's gums. Lavedrine's pale face seemed to float in the gloom. But as he stepped out of the dark bower, his black cloak flapped and cracked, whipped about by the wind.

'I am growing tired of corpses,' I said.

'I *never* tire of them,' he snapped back. 'I often find them more stimulating than the living. The dead try to keep their secrets. I try to catch them out. Isn't it a dialogue of a sort?'

The dead do speak to us, Hanno.

The voice of Immanuel Kant rang in my head. He had expressed a similar notion during our investigation in Königsberg. He and Lavedrine would have had a great deal to talk about.

'The way a person dies,' Lavedrine went on. 'The way he faces death. The time. The place. His final words. His will and testament. Those he loved, and those he hated. Those who loved and hated him. It all comes out. Where and how he wishes to be buried. The words his relatives write upon his monument. The death of an individual tells us a great deal about his life, as I am sure you are aware.'

'Wouldn't we be warmer sitting in my office?'

'Certainly,' he agreed, 'but this is the best place for our discussion.'

'The Gottewald children? Is that your drift?'

'Are they here, too?'

'Dittersdorf took the task upon himself,' I said.

Lavedrine shook his head. 'They are one reason for coming, then,' he continued, 'but not the only one. Many other children are buried here, too. Try to imagine it. As the bereaved parents of Lotingen believe,' he murmured with a slight, sardonic smile, 'those children are playing together all around us, Hanno. You and I are surrounded by their ghosts.'

He leant forward and peered at the nearest funeral slab. He took a few paces, then bent to examine another, as if to get close to the truth that might lie beneath the cold earth. 'Look at this one,' he said. 'The poetry is exquisite. *Margaretha von Bisten, born 2nd April, 1800, dead one month later. Here lies the last light of an aged mother's broken heart.* What helpless yearning inspired the expression of such raw sentiment?'

I felt irritation mounting in my breast. There was something theatrical in his manner, desecrating in his smile. His sounding of the words seemed to me like a heartless profanation.

'What have you discovered from the French?' I asked.

'All in good time,' he said, flapping his hand at my impatience. 'I brought you here to see something, as I said.'

'What is there to see, if not for the Gottewald grave?'

'Have you any idea how many children are buried in this cemetery?' he asked, without waiting for an answer. 'Three hundred? Four hundred? And those are just the newer stones. If we were to count them all together, there would be many more. Infant mortality is high in Lotingen, Herr Procurator. Very high. At least as high as in rural France. That is one of the things that I discovered. There are thousands of tiny corpses hidden beneath the ground of this fine cemetery, this *Kindergarten*.'

He began to pace up and down between the stones.

'I heard a nursery rhyme in Italy once,' he went on, stopping close to me. He tapped his forehead, as if to aid his memory. 'The end-verse goes something like this: *Chiccolino, chiccolino, dove sei? Sotto terra, non lo sai? Chicco* is the native word for seed. Peasant mothers sing it to their infants as they sow the ground in autumn. It must seem such a waste to children, don't you agree, throwing the seed onto the soil as the hard winter comes along. The mother tells the children that the seeds will sleep beneath the earth till spring, then they'll sprout and grow into vegetables and fruits. *Chiccolino, dove sei?* Where are you, little seed? I always thought the rhyme extremely sinister. *Sotto terra, non lo sai?* I'm under the ground, the little seed replies.'

He shook his head, then passed his hand through his rebellious curls.

'The little seeds buried in this cemetery will never see the light of day again.'

A different memory cast its shadow over my mind. The tale Rochus had told me in Kamenetz. Children hidden in holes beneath the snow by parents who did not want them to be taken off for soldiers. Children who died, while their parents searched frantically, trying to remember where they had hidden them. All those *chiccolini* buried alive, dead by the time spring came round to yield its bitter harvest of skeletons.

'Why in heaven's name are we here?' I repeated stubbornly.

'While I was away,' he continued, 'I was reading some of those reports that you Prussians love to compile with matchless precision. Can you guess what I discovered?'

He did not give me time to protest the uselessness of the question.

'In the statistics regarding infant mortality,' he raced on, 'East Prussia has an unusually high incidence of child death, even by your own national standards . . .'

'I know the causes,' I interrupted angrily. 'Starvation caused by war. A blighted harvest. Wilful destruction of crops. Heartless French requisitioning of food. Repeated theft and slaughter of precious farm animals. Is that what you're getting at? Is that why so many of our children die?'

His eyes fixed on mine. Slowly, he shook his head. The colour seemed to drain from his face. 'You could not be more wrong,' he said quietly. 'I was looking at the figures for the years from 1725 to 1800. Long before the French set foot in Prussia.'

'Very well, tell me. Why *do* so many of our children die?'

'Look around you, Herr Procurator,' he replied.

The white stones and crosses seemed to populate the ground more densely beneath the darkening sky.

'Sixty per cent of the infants in Prussia die before they reach their tenth birthday, Stiffeniis,' he began. 'Some are not one day old. A day? An hour! All of those children—ninety-nine per cent, let's say—die at home. At least seventy per cent of the deaths were not caused by illness, as one might expect. Babies suffocated in their cots, they fell down stairs, they were crushed by a cow, they drowned in a milk pail, swallowed nails, drank poison. The list is endless. Household accidents? The number of toddlers reduced to a heap of bones by a ravenous pig would astound you. Quite apart from an army of tiny corpses found in shallow graves in the woods, names unknown, deaths unregistered with the authorities.'

His hand fell heavily on my shoulder.

'Take a hard look at this cemetery, Stiffeniis. How many of these children—lights of their mothers' lives, those pious inscriptions say—were victims of culpable lack of care, or something worse? Forty per cent, more, perhaps, did *not* die. They were killed, but no Prussian magistrate appears ever to have investigated these deaths. They are statistics. Nothing more. Can you see this place in a darker light, now?'

His grip relaxed. 'What point are you trying to make?' I asked. 'That note slipped under my door. This lugubrious setting. Tiny seeds sown, but never harvested. Prussian statistics, domestic fatalities. What has any of this to do with the killing of the Gottewald children? *Those* children's throats were slashed open, their bodies were mutilated. Their father died far away in the East, and as for the mother, well . . . They do not enter into your statistics.'

Lavedrine took a step closer. 'Do you remember our pact, Herr Procurator? You and I, no one else?'

'I do, indeed.'

'Very well, then. I brought you here to tell you what I have discovered, and how these statistics relate to the news.'

'I am pleased to hear it,' I said.

In answer, he said not a word. Nothing. His mouth formed that thin ironic smile that was so typical of him, and it persisted for longer than was comfortable.

'I am waiting, Lavedrine,' I hissed. 'What did you find?'

'Nothing,' he replied at last. 'There is no trace of Bruno Gottewald in the French archives. Not a single mention of his name. No one has heard of him. He is not listed as a spy. A French spy, at any rate. If Bruno Gottewald and his children were exterminated for that reason, his fellows in Kamenetz made a huge, tragic mistake.'

As he spoke, an icy coldness closed upon my heart like the clamp of hard frost at the start of the Prussian winter. I might have remained there, stunned and helpless, until the first warm breath of spring, a maelstrom of panic swirling in my mind, sucking my hopes down into black hopelessness.

'Are you certain?' I asked, throwing my last vain hope into the arena.

'Poor Hanno! Your theory is as dead as these poor *chiccolini*.' He chuckled. 'But don't be so downhearted! I did find one scrap of information that might be useful. It's not much, but it is a curious coincidence. You'll never guess who *has* been in touch with the French authorities, and on more than one occasion.'

'Who?' I asked helplessly.

'Our old friend, Leon Biswanger,' he said, and chuckled again. 'Do you recall? So frightened of Prussian nationalists that he did not wish to speak to us? Well, it seems that he has been writing letters to the French general quarters in Königsberg.'

'Is that where you've been?'

He nodded.

'What did he write to them about?'

He began to search about in his pockets. 'I made a rough copy of one of his missives,' he said, pulling out a sheet of paper, shaking it open in the wind, which blew more boldly as darkness fell. 'Here we are. I had to be quick, they would not leave me alone for long, but you'll get the gist of it.'

. . . *in the light of recent political developments,* I read, *in particular, the recent ratification of the Treaty of Tilsit, I wonder whether it may be possible, your Excellency, to name a date at which, I am certain, all men in Prussia will rejoice in being free* . . .

I quickly read the rest, then returned the paper to Lavedrine's waiting hand.

'If you have no more urgent business on your plate,' he said, 'we should speak with the man. Biswanger may be afraid of the power that we wield, but he has told us less than the truth.'

If Lavedrine thought to dazzle me with the light of this discovery, he was mistaken.

'Is there any point?' I asked. 'He will plead personal reasons tied to business, no doubt. He might have written on behalf of Aaron Jacob, or some other Jew.'

'A man like Biswanger?' Lavedrine laughed. 'Strike dead the goose that lays the golden egg? Aaron Jacob is too valuable an asset.' He shook his head. 'I am convinced that this should interest you, Herr Procurator, as much as it puzzles me. Do you have anything better to do in the next half-hour?'

'Yes,' I nodded. 'One thing, since we are here.'

The Gottewald children had been buried in the newest part of the cemetery.

As if to confirm what Lavedrine had said about infant mortality in Prussia, we found two other fresh graves nearby which had been filled in since the massacre, and an open pit with planks around it and a mound of earth, which might have been dug in preparation for a funeral the next day. There was not much to see: three identical white slabs, each one bearing the name of a Gottewald child, the age, and the year, 1807. An identical inscription had been carved on each of the stones, as if the stonemason had been taxed to find sufficient verses for three children, though I suspected that the epitaph had been chosen by Dittersdorf. It had the sort of lofty aristocratic air so typical of him: *Hoc est, sic est, aliud fieri non licet.*

'It is a fact,' I translated. 'It is self-evident. And could not be otherwise.'

'Plain words to cover a mystery,' Lavedrine muttered. 'Now, are you ready to visit our industrious undertaker?'

Outside the cemetery gate, we walked towards the centre of the town. Only then, I forced myself to say, 'So, Lavedrine, you have been to Königsberg.'

'A city you know well,' he replied.

I believed I knew what he was thinking.

'A beautiful town,' he went on with enthusiasm. 'The Venice of the Baltic, they call it. An exaggeration, of course, but it is a fine place. An important administrative centre, too. I wondered whether they might have some general information that would be of use to us. By chance, those ugly statistics about infant mortality that I quoted earlier turned up in the town hall. In a sense, Stiffeniis, I have to admit, I did deceive you there.'

'Really? How?' I asked reluctantly.

'Those figures I cited. The incidence of improbable "accidents" among the infant population in Prussia. They are out of date by now. Indeed, they refer specifically to the years 1760 to 1765.'

'Hardly worth considering,' I said, as we turned into the square and down into Nogatsstrasse, heading for the bridge and Biswanger's dwelling.

'Hardly,' he agreed. 'Except for the question of who compiled them.'

'Who did?' I asked, not in the least interested.

'A private citizen sent those figures to a local magistrate all those years ago. Someone who dared to throw back the curtain on a crime which everyone else chose *not* to see. A man who was convinced that there are many sides to crime. Later on in life, he made a name for himself. A name that you know well. Professor Immanuel Kant. As I thought, he *was* interested in violent death. Very interested, indeed.'

· 31 ·

THE GHOST HAD returned.

Would he never leave me alone?

Immanuel Kant called to me once more from beyond the grave, but I closed my mind to that voice, and talked determinedly of other things. As we crossed the river, I told Lavedrine what I had done in his absence, describing my examination of the human remains in the Old Fish Market the day before, briefly mentioning the help I had received from Aaron Jacob. I was careful to say nothing of the portrait that I had drawn with his assistance. Nor did I tell Lavedrine of the additions I had made at my wife's prompting. What would he say if he were to recognise Helena in that sketch, as I had done?

'It was not wise to bring that man out of the ghetto,' he observed.

'Not wise, but necessary,' I replied. 'I hoped that he might discern a similarity between the skull of that woman, and the heads of the children.'

'Her skull was smashed to pieces!' he remarked with evident surprise.

'Indeed, there was too much damage for any meaningful comparison,' I admitted. 'Otherwise it might have borne fruit.'

'Aaron Jacob is full of the strangest notions.' He shrugged with an indulgent smile. 'What similarity could there possibly be between the skull of a mother and the heads of her children? I have never heard anything so bizarre!'

We were ten yards short of the house when Lavedrine began to sniff the air.

'Not a whiff of rotting flesh,' he observed with a grim smile. 'Has Biswanger no clients today?'

I rang the bell, but it was not Biswanger who answered the door.

The matron looking out at us was stout, middle-aged, her face the colour of pounded beef. Dressed in a stiff white apron and linen house-cap, the sleeves of her black gown rolled up above her elbows, we might have interrupted her preparations for the evening meal.

'Yes?' she said crossly

'Is Herr Biswanger at home?'

'My husband is busy,' she said, folding heavy arms over heavy breasts. She had the same sharp eyes as the undertaker, but a more forbidding manner. 'If it's a burial, I can make the necessary arrangements for you.'

The blood drained from her face as Lavedrine informed her who we were.

Without a word, she turned and clattered off on her wooden pattens. Not a minute passed, but she reappeared and asked us to step inside, carefully closing the door to the street. 'In there, sirs,' she mumbled, pointing to the room where we had met Biswanger on the previous occasion.

We entered without knocking.

Two persons were with Biswanger: a man whose head and shoulders were hidden beneath a large black cloth, and a pale, plump lady of mature years who was sitting very still in a high-backed chair staring straight ahead.

Biswanger turned, a tight-lipped expression on his face.

'One moment, I pray you, sirs,' he called. 'If we can just settle the pose, this gentleman can get on with his job while I attend to you.'

Lavedrine and I exchanged a glance as Biswanger turned away.

'Does it suit you now, Herr Rauch?' Biswanger called out in a loud voice.

Herr Rauch pulled back the black cloth that covered his head and looked up. He bobbed to us by way of welcome, then turned to Biswanger. 'Have a look for yourself, sir,' he invited. 'It will do, I think.'

The young man was tall and thin, with wild, uncombed hair, and spots of paint on his trousers and shoes. Christian Rauch was well known in town as a painter of portraits. He pulled his black cloth further back as he stood up to his full height, revealing a large wooden box which stood on a wooden frame. A camera obscura, fitted up with an adjustable brass lens for focusing; the sort of thing that artists use when preparing a canvas.

Biswanger cleared his throat, then lowered himself to the height of the ground-glass viewing plate. 'Cover me up,' he said, and the artist immediately threw the black cloth over the apparatus and the head and shoulders of the undertaker, whose large backside reared up ludicrously in white duck trousers as he manoeuvred himself into a position to see.

The lens was pointing at the seated lady.

Sounds of a huffing, indeterminate nature came from beneath the cloth. A moment later, Biswanger came thrusting out from beneath the black cloth, as if desperate for air.

'Something's not quite right,' he murmured.

He stood back from the viewing-box, clasped his chin in his hand, and looked intently at the figure of the old lady sitting quietly in the chair.

Her cheeks were chubby, the skin was dewlapped and sagging along the line of her jaw. A dimpled chin, a large nose, and two button-bright black eyes completed the picture.

What was missing, I wondered, in Biswanger's opinion?

The woman was sitting bolt upright, her billowing sleeves resting along the broad arms of the chair, her hands curved over the two turned balls of wood that formed the spindle-ends. She was dressed in a gown of ribbed brown velvet elaborately embroidered with silver thread. A matching bonnet and an old-fashioned ruff completed her ensemble. Large pearls dangled from her ears, the lobes of which were just visible.

Biswanger let out a suppressed cry.

'I won't be a minute,' he said, and left the room, running in his eagerness.

In the mean time, Herr Rauch stepped up to his easel, which stood beside the camera obscura, and began nonchalantly to trace the general outline of the sitter onto his canvas with a large brush dipped in dark paint.

Lavedrine walked across and examined the wooden box.

'Do you mind, Herr Rauch?' he asked.

'Be my guest,' the artist replied. 'You don't need the cloth for an approximate view. But use it, if you wish.'

As Lavedrine bent to look through the viewing-screen, observing that it had a reversing prism, and showed the picture the right way up, Biswanger came running back into the room. He went directly to the lady, and propped a foot-long ebony crucifix with an outstretched ivory figure of Christ squarely in the middle of her chest.

'There!' he said. 'What do you think now, Herr Rauch?'

The old woman did not protest at this rough handling, being dead.

The artist glanced across, then looked back to his canvas. 'If you really think so,' he conceded. 'I prefer the natural unadorned look, as you know. But fashion nowadays is for overt religious symbols. There's no denying fashion.'

I had, of course, seen *post mortem* portraits before—they were a common sight in any well-heeled Prussian household—but I had never seen one being limned, and had sometimes asked myself how it was done. Evidently, it was just another one of the many services that Biswanger offered.

'How did you get her to sit up so naturally?' I asked.

'A dead body may do anything that a living one can, Herr Procurator,' he replied uneasily, humouring me. 'With obvious differences. The state of *rigor mortis* helps. Having evacuated the contents from the stomach, which is done by tilting, allowing all the fluids to drain out of the mouth and into a bucket, the limbs may be moved about and positioned much as you please. An occasional crack of the bones does not disturb the sitter. The face can be washed and cleaned, touches of art and colour added to the cheeks and lips. Herr Rauch will make a reasonable likeness in an hour or two.'

'You are a man of many parts, sir. I admire you for it,' Lavedrine said carelessly.

Leon Biswanger coloured at this compliment, but he did not look happy. He was learning to fear the Frenchman's irony, and did not dare to ask why we had come.

'I discovered a part the other day that I would never have guessed,' Lavedrine continued, smiling brightly at me. He had learnt from his cat how to play with a mouse and frighten it, I supposed.

'Which part would that be?' Biswanger asked with a tremor.

Lavedrine walked to a beadwork chair which stood in the centre of the room. A tapestry of pink roses had been embroidered on the seat. He bent forward and stroked the material with his hand, admiring the quality of the work. Then he sat down, stretched out his legs, and watched the artist at work.

'Have you ever been to Königsberg, Biswanger?' he asked after some moments. 'A pretty town, though freezing cold. We have set up our Eastern operational headquarters there. Under Maréchal Lannes. You've heard of him, I think.'

Lavedrine did not wait for an answer. He plunged ahead, never taking his sharp eyes off the undertaker. 'I was there myself the other day, looking for information. There is a great deal of it to be found in Königsberg. But I expect a man like you knows where to find information. Isn't that true?'

Biswanger seemed to sway.

'I'm not sure what you are getting at, sir,' he mumbled.

'Are you not?' Lavedrine observed, like one of those snakes found in India that freeze in deathly immobility before they strike.

'No, sir, I am not.'

'Let me ask you another question, then. Do you ever wake up in the morning and think to yourself, Heigh-ho, today I shall write a letter?'

'Well, sir . . .' A look of fright crept over Biswanger's face. 'Sometimes, I suppose . . .'

'To whom do you write, when the urge comes over you?'

Biswanger did not reply. Nor did Lavedrine go on. He stretched out his boots comfortably in front of him, as if he found that easy-chair exactly to his liking. He might have been sitting at home in front of his own fire in the company of that cat of his.

'I know my way around, sir,' Biswanger blurted out. 'I know where all the different offices are, and who does what in them. And I can write, sir. A lot of people can't. Sometimes they ask me to pen a letter for them.'

'Ask?' I butted in, unable to restrain myself. 'As a favour, Biswanger?'

'Now, now, Herr Procurator,' Lavedrine warned me playfully, 'our friend here offers services. If there were no takers, he'd strike those services off his list. I think I am right in saying that. If you need to bury a bellringer, or make a portrait of your departed aunt, Herr Biswanger will oblige. But let's talk about these letters. Imagine that I wanted to purchase a castle in, say, Thuringia. Who would I need to get in touch with?'

Biswanger smiled involuntarily as his practical mind turned like a spotlight on the question. 'Well, sir, you'd need . . .'

'Castles do not interest me, Biswanger,' Lavedrine interrupted him. 'Nor do they interest you. You wrote to the Castle of Königsberg for another reason altogether. Would you care to tell us what it was that you wrote to enquire about?'

'I really ought to be seeing how Herr Rauch is getting on,' Biswanger replied, casting a desperate glance in the direction of the artist.

'All in good time,' Lavedrine replied. 'The lady will wait. Königsberg Castle? A letter posted late last August? You don't need to worry, I have already seen it. But I am certain that my friend, Procurator Stiffeniis, would love to hear from your own lips the range and infinite variety of your . . . usefulness.'

I played my part, of course.

'Herr Biswanger,' I said, 'why did you, a Prussian, write a letter to the French?'

Biswanger was sweating, despite the cold in the room. 'I wrote to the office of Maréchal Lannes to ask about the Napoleonic Codes. We've been under military jurisdiction for over a year now, sir. I wrote to enquire when the Codes would be applied here in Prussia.'

'Exactly,' Lavedrine said with relish. 'When will Prussian citizens be given the rights that every Frenchman now considers to be his birthright. And what news were you able to obtain?'

Biswanger appeared to relax. 'Implementation is imminent. A question of weeks, rather than months,' he reported. 'Paris has approved. Our king had signed the plea. The emperor intends to ratify the request.'

'In a word, French law will reign supreme in Prussia,' Lavedrine concluded.

'Yes, sir,' Biswanger agreed.

Lavedrine pulled out his pocket knife and began to clean the dirt from beneath his fingernails. He looked at me, not Biswanger. 'You are going to be busy, Stiffeniis. All these new procedures to read. New laws to be applied. New rights for men who had none before. Hard times for magistrates,' he said. 'Isn't that correct, Herr Biswanger?'

'I suppose it is, sir.'

'And better times for Jews, of course. Aaron Jacob, for example,' Lavedrine prompted, still busy with his knife and his nails.

'Aaron will certainly benefit from the new laws,' Biswanger continued. 'As will all Jews registered in Prussia. They'll be able to go to school, or study at the university, if they wish. They'll be free to practise their religion openly, declare property, buy and sell without deceit. Of course, they'll have to pay taxes, but they paid taxes before . . .'

'They were taxed as cows, or sheep,' Lavedrine said sharply. 'Now they will be taxed as men.'

'That's true,' said Biswanger.

'The end of your business relations,' I said. 'If Aaron Jacob can sign a contract in the presence of lawyer Wittelsbach, what need will he have of you?'

Biswanger looked at me and smiled.

'Business is a shifting sand, Herr Procurator. One opportunity closes down, a hundred others open up. I see the future brightly. A man has every right to know how he stands when the law is changed.'

'True, true,' Lavedrine cooed, like a dove in its nest. 'Especially a Jew,' he went on more earnestly. 'Aaron Jacob, I mean.'

I thought of Judenstrasse, of the people living there, of the Lotingers who had learnt to hate them all of a sudden, as events relating to the massacre of the Gottewald children had thrown a bad light on the Jews.

'Let's hope that life will be better for them, not worse,' I said, having little faith in any change that French justice might bring to Prussia.

Biswanger looked from Lavedrine to me, then back again.

'Amen,' he said in pious confusion.

'Why did Aaron ask you to write that letter for him?' Lavedrine insisted. 'He is a scholar. He could have written it himself, but he did not. Why not, Herr Biswanger?'

Biswanger frowned, his eyes darting from one to the other.

'I did not write that letter on behalf of Aaron, sir,' he protested. 'Someone else paid me to write it.'

'Who paid you?'

'It was Major Gottewald, sir,' he said quietly.

'Bruno Gottewald?' I echoed.

'That's right, sir. I wrote that letter to Königsberg on his instructions. I told you that I'd met him twice. The second time, he commissioned me to make enquiries of the French authorities.'

'Asking when the Napoleonic Codes would be implemented in Prussia?'

'That's right, Herr Procurator.'

'Why did he want to know?'

Biswanger shrugged. 'I have no idea, sir.'

So, in chronological order, I summed up to myself, Gottewald requested information about the Napoleonic Codes, then things precipitated. He 'accidentally' died, his children were 'unfortunately' massacred, and his wife 'mysteriously' disappeared.

'Did he tell you why his name was not to appear?' I asked.

'He did not want to be identified. Not by them . . . the French, I mean,' he said apologetically, glancing at Lavedrine. 'Nor by our lot, I suppose. It is not a good idea for a Prussian soldier to embrace the rule of France so openly.'

'Is that what he said, or is it your interpretation?' I pounced.

'He told me so himself, sir. When I realised how careful he was being . . .'

'You doubled your fee,' concluded Lavedrine.

'That's exactly what I did, sir,' Biswanger remarked, his eyes wide with surprise. 'It was a matter of the most extreme delicacy.'

'Quite right,' Lavedrine agreed with a smile. 'Tell me, did you have any inkling of why he wished to know? Or what he would do if the news turned out as he was hoping?'

Biswanger scratched his head.

'I never thought about it, sir. I sent that letter off to Königsberg, and when the reply came four or five weeks later, I didn't open it, just forwarded it on to Kamenetz.'

I turned to Lavedrine. 'Kamenetz again,' I murmured.

Suddenly, I recalled something Doctor Korna had told me. The surgeon had written to the Chancellor, Baron von Stein, to report on the atrocities taking place inside Kamenetz fortress.

The risks I had to run to get that message out. . . .

'How did you get that letter into Kamenetz?' I asked Biswanger. 'How could Gottewald be sure to lay his hands on it?'

Now that we were down to practicalities, the undertaker smiled. 'Why, Herr Procurator, that was a lark! I addressed it to the inn in Kamenetz village in my own name. All Gottewald had to do was walk in and ask for it, as if he were me. Worked a treat, it did.'

'Thank you, Biswanger,' Lavedrine declared, jumping to his feet.

'Let's hope you have told us everything this time,' I added, pausing by the door.

'Incredible, don't you agree?' Lavedrine enthused as we walked away from the house.

'What is incredible?'

'That man's capacity for business. He'll do anything at a price—handle dead bodies, have them limned, rent Jewish houses, write letters for Prussian officers. It's all the same to him. That man is a genius!'

I walked at his side in silence.

'Of course,' he added, 'you don't approve.'

'It hardly matters what I think of him,' I grumbled. 'He is an emblem of what Prussia will become.'

'Thanks to us? Is that what you are thinking?' He shook his head. 'You should be grateful. You were disappointed when I failed to bring you proof that Gottewald had sold his soul to France. Biswanger has breathed fresh life into your fading hopes.'

I stopped short, and stared at him.

Was it conceivable that a man who had won honours and been promoted, a national hero, might become the target of Prussian nationalists because he requested information from the French? Could that error of judgement explain everything?

'Do you really believe that letter explains the destruction of Gottewald's family, the mutilation of his sons?' I asked.

'Why not?' he replied. 'This news confirms what you have always believed.'

We walked in silence over the wooden bridge, the wind whistling and gusting over the dark, icy waters of the River Nogat.

As he went along the quay, he turned to me.

'Something has been puzzling me all afternoon,' he said. 'I told you earlier that I had been to Königsberg, and seen statistics compiled by Kant relating to the suspicious deaths of children. You have not asked me a single question! You have spoken of anything and everything else. Are you not curious, Stiffeniis? You were not so reserved at Dittersdorf's feast.'

I remembered the claims he had made that night.

'Professor Kant *was* involved in criminal studies,' he prattled on, 'long before events took you to Königsberg. You denied it, but I was right. He was interested in crime forty years *before* those murders. Why are you so secretive, Stiffeniis? Why say nothing then? And why are you so silent now?'

My head was spinning. A kaleidoscope of images flashed through my mind. Königsberg. Immanuel Kant. Dead bodies on the empty streets. I had almost drowned in the turgid sludge of that foul nightmare. Now Lavedrine was dredging it up again.

'A child was murdered many years ago in Königsberg,' he said, veering unexpectedly in a new direction.

'Many children, according to your statistics.' I shrugged.

'According to Professor Kant,' he insisted. 'He must have taken a very special interest in that case if he went to the trouble of compiling statistics to explain it. I looked for more, but all I found were those figures and the judge's sentence.'

His voice was raised against the wind, which drove in off the sea, howling about our ears. But he roared louder in his passion, more interested in Immanuel Kant than any other man that I had ever met.

'What do you want from me?' I said, aware of the fretful anger in my voice.

'What fascinated him about the murder of that child?' He rounded on me. 'That is what intrigues me, Stiffeniis. Kant must have made notes regarding the case. We cannot ignore what he may have discovered. I ought to have looked more carefully. But I have decided. I want to go to Königsberg again and find them,' he said fiercely. 'And next time, we will go there together.'

As we turned into Nogatsstrasse, the wind eased abruptly. But my thoughts were blown and buffeted about like autumn leaves.

'There's another thing, too,' he went on, his drive and energy overwhelming.

'What's that?' I grumbled hopelessly.

'You believe that the murderer is to be found in Kamenetz. I insist that the answer lies where those children were massacred. That house is holding something back, some secret that I've not been able to unveil. We must return there, Stiffeniis. And next time, Helena will come with us.'

· 32 ·

'What will I be required to do?'

Helena's voice cut in on my thoughts, as we sat before the fire that night, and I told her of Lavedrine's plan. There was a passionate intensity in her eyes which disarmed me.

'He has great faith in you,' I said, then quickly added: 'And so have I. He hopes you may be able to clarify our thoughts about the way in which the Gottewalds lived.'

I did not say, *and died.*

'He blames himself,' I continued. 'He thinks that something has escaped his attention because he is French. Perhaps he ought to have blamed me,' I tried to joke, 'for being Prussian has not helped me a whit.'

'What exactly is he looking for?' she pressed me.

'A female insight. He thinks that every person leaves their mark upon a place. The fact that Frau Gottewald was Prussian perplexes him. He'd have no problem if he were in Paris . . .' I said dismissively. 'He is convinced that a Prussian housewife is sure to notice if anything is not where it ought to be.'

'Is that what he does?' she frowned. 'It seems such a strange talent, making connections between objects and actions.'

I reached out to touch her hand. I was thinking of our attic. What would Lavedrine conclude about my wife if he ever got to see it?

'He hopes that you will make some sense of the domestic arrangements,' I said, trying to minimise the gravity of the task.

Next morning, the coach arrived and we climbed up, leaving the children in the hands of Lotte. Just the two of us, as I had requested. If Helena had second thoughts, I would simply order the driver to turn around and take us home.

Lavedrine was sitting alone on a tree trunk in the clearing where Mutiez had brought me on the night of the massacre. A brown saddle-cloak was wrapped more than once around his shoulders, as if he felt the cold intensely, despite the pale sun rippling across the open ground, as it struggled out from behind a ragged ridge of clouds.

As the coach pulled up, he raised himself to his feet.

I jumped down, pulled out the folding step, and helped Helena to the ground. Her hands were cold and slightly trembling. I held them tightly, intending to warm her fingers and lend her courage, but with a quick, furtive gesture, she slipped them beneath her cloak, looking over my shoulder in the direction of the Frenchman.

I felt a stab of jealousy.

Standing beside me, she seemed so very pale and fragile. She had dressed for the expedition in an enormous old black cloak. As she came down the stairs that morning, I had felt an electrical shock run through me. The year before, when we were forced to flee into the woods, I had carried that cloak away with us on account of its size and weight. It was large enough to make a tent to hide the children, warm enough to protect them from the damp and cold. I had never taken it out of the closet since the day we returned home. I assumed that it had been thrown out as a painful reminder of times past. It was too large for me, funereal in style, worn and torn from the rough treatment it had received while we were camping out. Any woman with a smarter mantle would have shunned it. Helena had cloaks enough of her own. But my wife had made her choice, and I was left to puzzle over what it meant.

'I had no idea that garment still existed,' I said.

Helena smiled in a distracted sort of way, and ran her hands gently over the rough, fading material. 'Oh, Hanno! I would never dare to throw it away. I'll never forget or forgive what we were all obliged to suffer. This is my battledress.'

These memories were chased away by Lavedrine's voice.

'Good morning, Helena. I was hoping for a brighter day. Still, despite the cold, we can't complain. You are dressed for the weather, I see.'

I saw a flush of colour suddenly appear in my wife's cheeks. Her hair was tied up tightly behind with a slender velvet ribbon. A bunch of curls at the front and loose tufts on either side had fought themselves free, and the wind blew them crazily about her ears like a nest of anxious adders.

I turned to face him.

'Our Prussian winter cannot be so easily subjected to French hopes,' I said, attempting a witticism, failing dismally.

Lavedrine was white with cold. His eyes gleamed brightly from bruised caverns beneath a corrugated brow, his unkempt silvery hair even more dishevelled than it usually was.

'There's no one else?' I asked, looking around for the carriage and the soldiers who must have accompanied Lavedrine to the cottage.

'No one. As we agreed,' the Frenchman confirmed, nodding to the far side of the clearing, where a grey horse was tied to a tree by the reins. 'I will not impose my company upon you for the ride home.' He smiled as if to reassure me, then he turned to Helena. 'A wise choice, madame,' he said. 'It is cold in the woods, but the house will be colder, I think. Now, while the sun is up, I suggest that we make a start.'

We entered the narrow, overgrown pathway leading to the cottage, Lavedrine leading the way, Helena following, while I brought up the rear. I was relieved to note that my melancholy impressions, gained the night of the massacre, were entirely altered in the light of day. The trees were taller, bare of leaves, the bushes less thick and dense than I remembered them. As we walked through the overgrown tunnel, the sun flashed speckled patterns on the pathway. I did not take my eyes off Helena. She strode after him, head up, following his lead, her foot falling exactly where his had been a moment before, avoiding sharp stones, patches of mud, and pools of water, as he had done. She looked so serious, so silent, as she marched after him, that my heart was moved by infinite tenderness in her regard. She had no idea what she was marching towards, while I had a clear picture in my head, and feared for the effect that it might have upon her. More than once I stretched out my hand, meaning to reassure her, but she did not respond. Her hands remained beneath her cloak, her eyes fixed on Lavedrine's back.

Suddenly, he stopped short.

'This is it,' he said, turning back, looking over Helena's head, speaking to me, a hard glint in his eye. A corner of the house was just visible beyond the end of the hedge. 'Wait here a moment, will you? I'll go ahead and warn the soldiers that we've arrived. Mutiez keeps two men on guard, day and night, to frighten off idle sightseers. It's hard to believe, I know, but the curious know no limits.' A thin smile flashed upon his lips.

'He uses it as a punishment. Our French tearaways are terrified of the place, especially at night. It's almost as if . . .' He stopped in mid-phrase, remembering Helena's presence. I knew he did not wish to frighten her. 'Most of them are city boys. They'd rather fight a battle than camp out in the woods after dark.'

We waited in the shade, while he stepped out and called for the guards. Though he spoke to them in French, I caught a phrase or two—'no one must disturb us,' and 'don't go frightening the lady with your silly tales.' Then he called more loudly: 'Helena, you can come out now.'

Without speaking, or looking at me, Helena walked forward, and I followed. We stood before the house. Nothing appeared to have changed since my previous visit just before dawn almost two weeks before, except that weeds seemed to encroach more thickly around the two shallow steps that led up to the kitchen door.

'I opened the shutters while waiting for you to arrive,' Lavedrine announced from the doorway. 'I hope there will be sufficient light for you, Helena.'

He might have been a charming host, intent on welcoming an unexpected guest. He held out his hand and smiled, encouraging Helena to enter.

She did not hesitate. She skipped up the steps and disappeared inside the house, passing close to Lavedrine who breathed an encouraging word into her ear as she flitted past. I made haste to follow. I intended to keep close and protect her from any residue of horror that the cottage might contain, but Lavedrine caught hold of my arm as I reached him. 'She must not be inhibited by your presence,' he hissed. 'Nor by mine. You and I must pretend, just for a little while, that this house is *her* house.'

'But you can't . . .'

Lavedrine's grip tightened on my arm.

'Leave her alone,' he snarled in a whisper, his lips close to my ear. 'She needs it, can't you see that? She wants to know what happened to the woman and her children. As much as you or I.'

His grip did not relax on my arm as we stepped together into the kitchen, as if he feared to let me loose. Seen from the doorway, the light entering through the narrow windows cast a greyish-blue tinge on everything. We might have been in the wings of a theatre looking onto the stage. The room was just as I remembered it, a kitchen that also served as a dining room. In the centre, the table where Sybille Gottewald and her children had sat down together for the very last time. The room looked larger, more drab and melancholy than it had looked that night. I could understand why the soldiers were afraid. They knew what had happened there, but knowing only a fraction of the truth, the mystery remained, imprisoned in the musty air.

Beneath the window in the far wall stood a sink of heavy, rough-cut stone. On the wooden draining-board, a large cooking pot had been turned upside down, as if someone had washed it out, then left it there to dry.

'My instructions . . .'

'Have been carried out to the letter,' Lavedrine confided quietly. 'The scraps of food were removed, of course. They would have drawn the rats.'

Helena stopped beside the table, her hands still deeply thrust into the folds and pockets of her cloak, her mouth and chin hidden by the upturned collar, her gaze fixed upon the table-top and the plates, as if deciding whether to leave them where they were, or carry them across to the sink. Then, she did something which must have surprised Lavedrine as much as it surprised me. Without lifting her eyes from the table, she unhooked her cloak, catching it up as it slipped from her shoulders. It was cold, but that did not deter her. She looked around the room, as if in a dream, then folded the mantle and laid it over the arm of a chair standing to the right of the chimney-place. Then, she turned again to the table, moving around it, stopping now and then, resting her hand on the back of each chair, considering the perspective as it must have seemed to each of the persons who had eaten their last meal there.

Carefully folding back the sleeves of her gown, she stepped over to the sink and rested both of her hands on the grey stone, leaning forward to look out of the window into the garden. She laid her hand on the upturned cooking pot, then ran her fingers lightly over the other culinary objects laid out on the draining-board. She seemed to caress those things of little worth—a wooden spoon, a colander, and so on—as if each item had a tale to tell. She reminded me of the blind woman who sells fruit and vegetables from a stall in Lotingen market. By touch alone that woman can separate a yellow apple from a red one. Helena seemed to be feeling her way into the house, exploring the objects that had made it a home.

Without any hesitation or prompting, she took a pace to the right and stood before a tall wooden cupboard. Reaching out her hands, she pulled open the drawer. She did not look inside, but felt about with her fingers. A moment or two later, apparently satisfied, she glanced at the contents, and nodded, as if some intuition had been confirmed. She lifted out a breadknife and a cutting-board, turned around and laid them deftly on the edge of the table. Then, she touched the chair on her left.

'This is where *she* sat,' she said quietly.

She turned back and opened the upper half of the cupboard. Crockery and glass were stored in good order on the shelves, but Helena did not close the cupboard door. Instead, her hands ranged along the shelves, moving something here or there, setting it carefully back in its place. Then she ran her hands along the undersides of the shelving, as if she thought to find something hidden or secret. And all the while, her gaze was lost, far away, ranging over the woodland scene beyond the glass of the window. A curtain of trees and juniper bushes enclosed the garden and separated it from the wilderness. In the centre, a clump of saplings, two knee-high oaks, and three smaller evergreen plants, were surrounded by a circle of stones.

Suddenly, a sigh escaped from her lips.

She might have been Sybille Gottewald alone, working in her kitchen.

'She wanted to stay,' she whispered. 'She planted trees . . .'

I glanced out of the window. A cream-coloured deer was standing frozen in the far corner of the enclosure. Helena had seen it. The animal had spotted her.

Lavedrine relaxed his hold on my arm. 'Good. Very good,' he murmured to me. 'She is playing the part exceptionally well.' His eyes followed Helena's every move, gleaming with tender hope, like the eyes of a music master watching his prize pupil perform exactly as he hoped she would.

The sharp blade of jealousy jabbed at my heart, twisting this way and that as it sought out the most painful, vulnerable spot. My wife appeared as a sort of automaton, moving and behaving precisely as her *maestro* indicated. What unseen wires and hidden springs were being worked between the pair of them, I asked myself.

'It did not happen here.'

Helena's voice was low, but it was firm. As she spoke, her eyes ran quickly over the table and the plates again, and ranged once more across the sink and beyond to the view of the garden through the kitchen window. The deer had disappeared as silently as it had materialised.

'Am I right?'

That question was not addressed to me.

'You are,' he answered. 'This is where they ate. Durskeitner, the hunter, often saw them when he passed this way. Earlier that day, he saw the table laid for lunch. And he found the room in this state, the lamp lit, when he entered the house that night and discovered the bodies.'

'Frau Gottewald had just put the cutting-board and breadknife away. But she had not time enough to wash up the plates and put them away again when the killer entered. Were they found upstairs?'

Lavedrine silently nodded.

'I'd like to go up there now,' she said, glancing at the ceiling. 'That ramp leads to the bedroom, I suppose.'

I felt a protest rising to my lips, but Lavedrine spoke out before me.

'It does,' he said.

She turned without a word, placed her hands on the rail, and began to climb.

I made a move to follow, but Lavedrine's restraining hand came up and held me back again. 'Give her time,' he whispered, his eyes on Helena as she climbed upwards, moving slowly, as if fearful that the creaking of the ancient wood might awaken someone sleeping in the bedroom. 'We must leave her alone for some moments,' he added.

I took a deep breath, and let it out slowly.

'What do you expect from her?' I hissed angrily.

'Expect?' he echoed faintly. 'I hope that Helena will see what you and I have *not* been able to see, Herr Procurator. That's what I want! A woman lived in this house for months, alone, except for her children. No man has been present for any extended period of time. Everything is positioned—

organised—in the manner that the housewife left it. This house speaks of Sybille Gottewald. You and I are deaf to that woman's voice, but Helena's hearing is more acute, I'll be bound.'

We remained where we were.

Above our heads, we could hear the footsteps of my wife. She moved across the room, the ancient wooden floorboards creaking and shifting beneath her weight. Each step she took seemed to provoke an echoing thump from my heart. Ever so slowly, she made her way over to the bed. For some moments, no sound was heard. I held my breath for longer than was good for me. Then, her position shifted, back and forth, as if she had moved her weight from one foot to the other, then back again. Was she hesitating? Had fright clasped her in its grip? Even as I made to lunge for the stairs, the wood shifted above my head. She was walking to the window. She stood there for quite some time, looking out, I imagined, at the garden at the rear of the cottage. Suddenly, the boards creaked, and she moved again, following the line of the wall to the tiny adjoining closet-room. I heard the sound of sliding wood, and realised that she was opening a drawer, then silence as she examined the contents. This sequence was repeated three times. Lavedrine and I were standing side by side, our eyes fixed upon the wooden ceiling, as if it were made of glass and we could see what Helena was doing up there. Then, a drawer closed with a rumble, and her footsteps began to move again, crossing the bedroom, skirting around the end of the bed, and coming to rest in the darkest corner of the room, which was the furthest removed from the bed, the window, and the staircase. There, she stopped again.

I cannot say how long we stood in silence. Helena above, Lavedrine and I below.

I prayed that she would stop what she was doing, leave that place at once, and ask me to take her home. Lavedrine, no doubt, was doing the opposite: urging Helena on, hoping that she would manage to see whatever it was that he wished her to see.

'Come up,' she called.

Lavedrine and I sprang forward like unleashed greyhounds after a bolting hare. My hands grasped at the rail leading up to the bedroom, as did his, but I was the first. I edged him back with my shoulder, blocking the way, fixing him with my eye, as if to say that I was ready and able to meet any challenge.

He smiled coldly, lowered his eyes, and stood back.

'This is not a race, Stiffeniis,' he said. 'After you, naturally.'

I did not linger, but scurried to the upper floor. The room was lit by sunlight, a pale-yellow aura, and it was surprisingly warm. I had not expected that, but then again, what was I to expect? Instinctively, I looked towards the bed, as if those three corpses might still be laid out there. The bodies of the children had been buried, of course, but the evidence of their murder had not. Mutiez had done his duty well. The pillows and the sheets were marked with blood, as I remembered them, and they were arranged more or less as I had seen them. In such bright light, however, the effect was weak, pale, like a watercolour painting. The spattered trails of bloodspots, on the wall behind the bed and on the ceiling, had faded to a dullish brown, where I had seen them black, wet, fresh.

'Has the room been cleaned, Hanno?'

I was shocked by the bluntness of the question, and took a deep breath.

'This is how we found it. Only the bodies have been removed,' I said.

'There should be blood . . .' Helena murmured, taking a step closer to the bed. 'Here on the floor,' she said, pointing with her finger. 'There ought to be stains. Though many days have passed, a pool of blood would leave a mark on a wooden floor.'

'They have faded,' I assured her, taking a step forward, then stopping. I did not wish her to imagine the horror that we had seen. 'It may *look* as if someone has made an attempt to clean the place, but . . .'

'You are correct, Helena,' Lavedrine growled from behind my back. He went on in a more determined manner: 'There is very little blood, given what happened here.'

'What reason could there be for anyone to clean it up?'

Helena's hands were tightly clasped together, her knuckles white, as if she were praying for a miracle to happen. I could see that the thought of someone cleaning up the blood perplexed her terribly. Suddenly, her eyes opened wide with fright.

'Is this what those rumours were talking of?' she asked, her gaze shifting from me to Lavedrine.

'Which rumours?' I asked her gently.

'That what the killers wanted was the children's blood. That the Jews might be involved.'

I shook my head. 'We have no . . .'

'The babies were butchered,' Lavedrine spoke out, drowning my voice. 'Two of them were mutilated. And there is, indeed, very little blood. These are facts. Can you tell us nothing new?' he implored her.

I was surprised by the tone of his voice. He had lost all hope of interpreting the mystery of that house. What could he possibly hope to learn from her?

Helena looked around slowly.

She crossed her arms over her breasts and shivered, as if she suddenly felt the cold. She seemed smaller, even more defenceless without her cloak. Suddenly, her head lifted sharply, and her eyes darted towards Lavedrine.

'Frau Gottewald lived here,' she murmured to herself. 'Alone with her children.'

'Does something surprise you?' Lavedrine enquired.

I could see that she was tense. A vein was throbbing visibly in her temple.

'What is here does not surprise me,' she replied. 'I am more surprised by what is *not* here.'

'What do you mean?' I asked.

She looked around as if to convince herself of what she was about to say.

'There is very little sign of a woman in this house,' she said.

· 33 ·

'CLOTHS?'

Our mouths hung open, our eyes gaped wide. We might both have been punched in the stomach, as Helena explained what she meant.

'I have searched all the drawers,' she went on, pressing her lips to the tips of her fingers like a priestess praying. 'Down in the kitchen, up here in the bedroom. In that tiny box-room behind the bed as well. There is a trunk and a small cupboard, containing some clothes. Not many. A few dresses, a worn-out pair of shoes. The children's things . . . They were only here a short time, I know, but, well, there are some things that a woman simply cannot do without.'

Lavedrine darted a look at me.

If he thought that Helena was speaking some strange language that only a married man could comprehend, a common logic of shared domesticity that was wholly alien to him, he was wrong.

'Helena, be more precise,' I urged, equally puzzled.

She stared at me before she spoke. It was a look that I recognised. An expression she adopted when the little ones failed to behave as they ought, or failed to understand something obvious that she had told them more than once. 'Just think of our home. Think of our kitchen. What sort of things do you always find there?'

I shrugged uncertainly. 'Apart from the furniture . . . We have more, of course.'

'Go on,' she urged me.

'Well, there are plates, pots, pans. Shelves where we keep them. The row of cups on hooks. The cupboard, the larder. Onions hanging near the fireplace. Oh, and jars of spices, honey, and preserves,' I blurted out, as if suddenly inspired.

'What else?' she insisted.

I thought for a moment, finding it difficult to recall details, though we had been living in the house for many years, and every day I entered the kitchen frequently. 'The sieves hanging on the wall,' I added, 'for straining flour and making cheese. The flour bin, of course. But . . . what?' I was growing desperate. 'The bread sack dangling from the shelf, so the mice won't get at it. Ah yes, I remember now. Aprons hanging up behind the door. The mop and bucket that Lotte uses when she does the housework . . .' I stopped, but I had not finished. There was more to our kitchen than I had thought. More again that I still had not described. I began to see what Helena was getting at.

'You were in the kitchen just last night,' she coaxed, 'preparing something for today. You told me that it was messy.'

'I was coating writing-paper with silver salts . . .'

She did not let me finish, her brashness grating on my spirits.

'What did you do last of all?' she insisted. 'When you had finished?'

I looked away in embarrassment. What right had she to question me with Lavedrine standing there looking on, a supercilious grin on his face?

'I wiped up the mess,' I said.

'What did you use?'

'Oh, I don't know!' I replied, my patience running out. 'An old shirt, I suppose.'

'Exactly,' she replied with a beatific smile. 'Rags, dusters, cloths for cleaning the house, washing the floors, drying dishes. One for cleaning the windows, a different one for polishing the floors. You can't mix them up. A different one for every separate task.'

As she spoke, I thought of the piece of wool she kept in the attic for polishing fruit. She would use it, wash it, then hang it up to dry, for fear that mould would get into it and ruin the apples that were unblemished.

'Cloths . . .' Lavedrine murmured. 'There are none in the kitchen.'

'Nor here in the bedroom. Or in that box-room,' Helena added. 'But the absence is much more peculiar. It isn't just a question of rags. I have not seen a flannel or a towel for washing and drying the children. Not a single one!'

She said it forcefully, her finger pointing up in the air like a schoolteacher laying down the laws of grammar or arithmetic. 'And that's not all,' she continued. 'I looked inside the drawers and the tallboy. There are three female outfits hanging there, two of light summer material, and a winter dress which is old and worn out. But there's nothing else. Frau Gottewald was the wife of a Prussian officer. She'd have more, much more. And that is not the most glaring omission. Do you recall when we married?' she asked me. 'My trousseau?'

How could I forget it? Two large chests of dark cherrywood had accompanied Helena over the threshold of our house in Lotingen. Her mother had been filling those trunks for years in preparation for her daughter's wedding-day. They contained every piece of cloth or linen that a housewife would ever need; everything to keep her house and person in respectable order. On the night of our wedding, Helena had appeared like a vision from Ancient Greece, a brocaded linen nightdress stretching down to her feet, the cuffs and shoulders adorned with large pink silk bows.

'Every bride banks on her trousseau,' Helena continued self-importantly. 'But what has become of Frau Gottewald's?'

I remembered returning to our house after the dragoons abandoned it. Those Frenchmen had destroyed everything. Only a single cotton sheet was left, and that had been torn into strips and used for bandages.

'Frau Gottewald may have lost her linen in the war,' I said. 'Just as you did.'

'Indeed, it is possible,' she allowed, turning to Lavedrine. 'But we have hardly been back inside the house a year, and I have already made up a good part of the loss. Not the treasures my mother gave me, unfortunately. But the common things. Some from shops and pedlars, others Hanno brought back from Danzig when he went in May. And Lotte is good with a needle. Old things may be made into new. No house can function without rags and cloths of all descriptions, monsieur . . .'

Her hands flew to her cheeks, which flamed with the rush of blood. She turned to me. 'Oh, Hanno,' she whispered, 'I . . . I hardly know how to say it. Unless . . . Unless they are hidden somewhere in the house, I fear to think what may have happened here. Who would carry them away . . .' She hesitated again, covering her mouth as if some thought had shocked her.

'What troubles you?' I said, moving close.

She stared fixedly into my eyes.

'Her towels, Hanno,' she whispered. 'No young woman could ever do without them.'

She glanced at Lavedrine to make certain that he had understood.

'*Bien sûr!*' he exclaimed, slapping his forehead with the palm of his hand. 'How blind men are! A woman of childbearing age. Her menstrual discharge. You are right. How could I fail to think of it?'

In his enthusiasm he did not limit himself to speech, but launched himself across the room like a cat who had spotted a mouse. His hands fell on Helena's shoulders, his face hovered inches away from hers. She looked down quickly, defensively, as if she thought he meant to devour her.

'Your presence has been invaluable, Helena!' he cried. 'Infinitely precious! I knew that you would be our trump card.'

He gazed at her proudly, then suddenly his hand flew up and came to rest on the nape of her neck. His head leant forward, his mouth hovering over her forehead. But with sudden urgency, he dipped his head and kissed her full on the lips.

'Incroyable, ma chérie,' he murmured, pulling back slowly.

I stood transfixed. A wave of rage washed over me. Fire blazed for an instant, then freezing cold took its place. I clenched my teeth, as I had done whenever father thrashed me in my childhood. If I gave in to anger, I would lose face twice over. Cold indifference is a poor defence against violent passions. But there is no other.

Slowly, a curtain seemed to lift before my eyes.

Helena was standing rigidly, her arms dangling helplessly at her sides. The Frenchman's aggression had ruffled her hair and brought more bright colour to her cheeks and forehead, but her eyes flashed here and there, anywhere but at the man before her. I had never seen her so confused.

But Lavedrine was not put out. He held her firmly, his hands resting on her shoulders, and continued to exult. 'How could I miss such an obvious connection? *That* is where the blood went! Taken away, carried off, soaked up, removed by means of the rags and cloths. We did not see them in the house because they are not here. Not one scrap of absorbent material. All gone . . .'

Suddenly, he turned away, and began to pace the room, up and down and back again, from one end of the bed to the other, close beside the window. He ran his hand mechanically through his curls, and muttered to himself in French like a man in a fit.

He stopped in the corner where the ramp of stairs descended to the kitchen below, tapping his forefinger rapidly against his pursed lips. He glanced from the stairs to the bed, then back again, calculating distances, or so it seemed.

'The victims were brought up here, and their throats were cut. Then, the boys were mutilated. . . .' He trailed to a close. 'But why search out the rags in the house? Why carry the blood away?'

'And where was the mother while all this was going on?' I added.

'Perhaps they made *her* clean the mess,' Helena said, aghast with horror. 'Before they took her away with them.'

Lavedrine tapped his temple, as if to awaken a hypothesis in his fuddled brain.

'Where would those blood-soaked rags be taken to?'

'Evidence,' I said. My voice was firm, despite the tension in my jaw, and the bunched fists hidden beneath the folds of my cloak. 'To prove that the massacre had taken place. To demonstrate that the blood of the family had been spilt. Whoever came to do the deed had to take back tangible proof that he, or they, had carried out their orders.'

Helena was quaking visibly, I realised suddenly, her shoulders jerking violently, whether from fright or from the cold. But Lavedrine moved to comfort her more swiftly than I did. He took three paces across the room, unlatching his cloak, draping it tenderly around her shivering frame.

'There is no reason for you to stay here any longer, Helena,' he said with a show of concern. 'You must not fall ill for the sake of a generous heart.'

I did not move, but I watched them: Helena enclosed within the Frenchman's cloak; he, like a solicitous lover, hovering at her side.

'You still hold to your theory, then?' he challenged me. 'That the violence that thundered down upon this house came from Kamenetz. Is that it, Stiffeniis?'

'I have seen nothing to shake my belief. Not even the absence of teatowels can shift me,' I answered coldly. Helena had seen the room, she had drawn her conclusions. While I did not dispute them, I was not convinced of the relevance of her observations.

'You are wrong,' he said, his eyes darting hungrily around the room. 'The answer lies here. Inside this house. In this very room, if you like.'

He strode to the far side of the bed, and raised his finger to the wall.

'The children's heads were aimed in this direction. The pattern of the bloodstains, the spattering of spots on the wall, the size, the colour, the intensity of each spot . . .' He stopped in mid-phrase, and turned to my wife. '*Excusez-moi, Hélène,*' he apologised. 'I say again, you need not stay, you know.'

My wife smiled weakly. 'I must,' she said.

'You are a most courageous woman.' He smiled and bowed, moving close to the bed. 'With your permission, then, I shall press on with my considerations. The children were lying here, their heads resting on the right-hand edge of the bed. Imagine the blade slicing down'—he made a gesture with his hand—'the blood shooting up in this direction. There are blood-marks directly above on the ceiling. That is, almost four feet above the point where the head was positioned. The blood spurted back in this direction towards the wall, falling here on the floor like large raindrops. Can you see the form here, like a flower? Less blood, but a significant amount sprayed up onto the wall beyond. A very fine spray made up of minute droplets.'

He stepped back two paces from the bed, and pointed to the floorboards. 'This is the spot—this area here—where the children bled to death. We ought to find the greatest quantity of blood in this position, but as you see, the staining on the floor is minimal.' He turned to Helena. 'Thanks to you, we now know why. Indeed, I think it might be possible to make out wipe-marks in the bloodstains which do exist. But this is not all that we can say,' he continued, walking towards the foot of the bed, speaking all the while. 'As we move away in this direction, those spots on the wall become smaller and smaller, then, finally, they disappear in this pale spray. Let us say, this point marks off the extreme perimeter of the area within which the actual murder took place. Mutilation after death would cause loss of blood, but without a living heart to pump it . . .' Suddenly, he looked self-consciously at Helena. 'Forgive me,' he said.

'Please, go on,' she implored with a shudder.

'Any sign of blood outside this circle,' he continued, tracing an imaginary ring with his finger over the bed and the wall behind us, 'is not consistent with what we are able to observe of the *modus operandi* of the slaughter. Do you concur, Herr Procurator?'

'Go on,' I echoed, gritting my teeth.

'At this point, something changes. It is significant, I believe.'

He walked to the end of the bed, and crossed to the window. Outside, the sun disappeared behind the massive white clouds. He dropped down on one knee, and stared at the wall beneath the window ledge. I knew what he was leading up to. Mutiez had noticed the marks the night that we had first entered the house. Traces of blood on the far side of the bed, a long way from any other bloodstains.

'Come and look,' he said, turning his head, looking at Helena.

I stepped back, allowing Helena to pass, then I followed her around the room.

'I have been back twice to study them, but I can make no sense of these marks at all,' he murmured. He had told me as much when I returned from Kamenetz, and had mentioned the fact again the day before. It was becoming something of an obsession.

Helena bowed down low, close to Lavedrine's shoulder. I did not need to exert myself. From where I was standing, beyond the mass of the Frenchman's untidy curls, I could just make out those puzzling marks on the wall. They were not random splashes, being larger even than the largest spots on the opposite wall, which were close to the radius of action that Lavedrine had traced out with his finger. It was difficult not to believe that those marks had been left there on purpose.

But why?

Why kill the children on one side of the room, then transport a quantity of blood to the other side of the room? And how had it been done? By dipping a rag in the blood, as Helena suggested, then daubing the wall with the cloth?

'There is something distinct about them,' Helena murmured. Her voice was low, but steady. 'Certainly, these marks are of a different type. Am I correct in saying that? They are quite unlike any other bloodstain in the room.'

Lavedrine nodded vigorously. 'The problem is the rough, porous surface of the wall. The blood has soaked into the plaster, which is already ruined by the damp. And there is mould to compound the mixture. It is all but impossible to read. What's your opinion, Stiffeniis?' he asked, half turning to me.

I did not reply. Instead, I set my shoulder bag down on the floor, opened the flap, and began to take out the materials that I would need to conduct my experiment. I had prepared everything the night before in the dark of the unlit kitchen at home.

'Those marks remained fixed in my mind, too. I thought there must be a way to make sense of their diversity. Science may help us,' I said with more confidence than I felt. I had tried the experiment once or twice in an effort to entertain the children, but it was an evanescent sort of thing, and they soon grew tired of the game. Indeed, Manni complained that it was not much of a game at all.

'What do you have in mind?' asked Lavedrine, standing over me, peering down with interest. 'Another drawing of the *locus crimini*? You've made a hundred . . .'

'This is different,' I replied in my own defence. 'It will be true to Nature.'

'Now I *am* interested,' he growled ironically. 'I heard a magician promise as much at the bear gardens when I was passing through Berlin. They pelted him with rubbish!'

'My son calls this my "magic paper" trick, but there is English science behind it,' I announced, 'and I will need you both to help me.'

As I prepared them for the performance—Helena standing before the window, holding a mirror, angling it down to cast light on the dark wall and its cryptic figures; Lavedrine with a square of black card in his hand, kneeling on the floor to one side—I told them briefly what we were going to do. I had read of Thomas Wedgewood and his silver chloride experiments a year or two before, when Sir Humphrey Davy of London first described them in the *Journal of the Royal Institution*. Our own Institute of Science in Berlin had translated the article into German, and a number of eminent scientists (and a host of frustrated artists, such as myself) had tried it out to see what would happen.

'The great problem,' I said, remembering the poor results that had failed to amuse the children, 'is that we must be extremely quick in our operations. Each of us must do his bit, and in the exact sequence. Then, we'll have no more than a minute. Oh, I forgot to mention my own role,' I added. 'I will see to the curtains.'

'Let's get on with it,' Lavedrine urged from the cold floor. 'My knees are beginning to ache.'

Helena looked at me and smiled conspiratorially.

I drew the curtains tightly closed. As I bent and took a piece of paper from the envelope in my bag, I warned both of my assistants to be at the ready. Using a metal pin, I hung the paper on the wall over the mark that interested us. 'Cover it up, please,' I said, and Lavedrine placed his square of black card exactly over the paper hanging on the wall.

I stood up, pulled back the curtains, and let light into the room.

'One moment,' I warned them, waiting as the sun began to slide from behind the clouds that covered it. 'Helena, hold up that mirror. Its reflection must shine precisely on that square of black card that Lavedrine is holding. One more second . . . Another . . . And a third . . . Lavedrine!'

At the sound of his name, Lavedrine pulled back the black card, exposing the paper hanging on the wall to the sunlight reflected brightly in the mirror. Then, I began to count slowly: 'One . . . two . . . three . . . four . . .'

As I reached ten, I closed the curtains as tightly as I could manage. 'Lavedrine, cover the paper again with your card, please. Helena, put down that mirror, and light the candle on the dresser.'

She was nimble, striking the flint I had brought, lighting the stub of candle I had provided for the purpose. As she stood beside me in the gloom, the candle cupped in her hands, the flickering flame lent a waxy orange glow to her smooth rosy cheeks.

'You can remove the paper from the pin, Lavedrine,' I said. 'Now, we must be very quick. The instant candlelight shines on the paper, the picture will begin to turn entirely black. Are we all ready? Good, let's see what we have obtained.'

I took the paper from Lavedrine, and held it close to the candlelight while they crowded at my shoulders. There, inscribed on the darkening paper, were two indistinct grey letters and some other formless stuff. The coating of silver chloride was less uniform than it ought to have been, but a vague image had formed.

'I can just make out a large *H*,' Lavedrine read. 'A second capital *H* is repeated here, perhaps, in the middle of the sequence. But I can't make sense of the rest.'

Before he had finished, the ciphers disappeared, eaten up by the unstoppable chemical reaction of silver chloride when exposed to light. I held the blackened piece of paper in my hands. Nothing was visible.

'Do you think the murderer left his signature?' Helena suggested.

I remained quiet, fearing that my experiment had been more ridiculous than useful.

'Why leave a signature?' Lavedrine quizzed. 'What could this double *H* mean? If it means anything at all . . .'

'I hoped for something sharper,' I mumbled.

Having seen the letters form, I had been praying they would tell us something. Anything, which might have linked them to Kamenetz.

'Don't take it so hard,' he comforted me. 'You tried. Two *H*s are better than none. Is it your fault if English science is not so perfect as the English claim?'

Half an hour afterwards, Helena and I were riding back to town in the coach. The pale winter sun was swallowed by black rain-clouds which came rushing in from the coast. I ought to have been grateful for the few rays of sunlight that had allowed me to attempt the experiment, but I was sorely disappointed by its failure.

The coach pulled up in town, and I helped Helena down onto the cobbles.

Lavedrine dismounted, tied up his horse, and came to join us.

'You made some interesting discoveries,' he complimented Helena.

'But what do they tell us?' she replied, tucking a stray curl behind her ear. 'She might have been preparing to move. To another house. Or another town. When we leave a house, we burn or throw out all the rags and rubbish. Only one thing makes me doubt it.'

'What's that?' he asked.

'Those saplings freshly planted in the garden. When we want to put down roots, we Prussians often plant a tree,' she said thoughtfully. 'It is almost as if she wanted to stay there for ever, but could not . . .'

Lavedrine turned to me. 'Well, Herr Procurator. Do you still think death came calling from Kamenetz?'

I held his gaze. 'You still believe that the answer lies in that house.'

'Perhaps we have *both* been looking in the wrong direction,' he conceded.

I felt my heart lurch. I knew what he was about to suggest. He did not speak to me, however. He turned to my wife. 'I must carry your husband off with me for a day or two, Helena,' he announced.

Could I object to what he was about to propose?

'Where are you taking him?' she enquired, her eyes wide with surprise.

'Königsberg,' he said, his eyes flashing into mine.

·34·

I HAD READ reports of Kant's last will and testament in the newspapers.

Apart from the dubious pleasure of picking over the bones of a famous person who had recently died, there was not very much that was of interest to anyone, including myself, who had known him better than any man alive at the end. His material possessions had been sufficient to ensure his comfort. He had his plate, his silver, his household linen—he even had a deal of money held as savings in a local bank. But what concerned him most, it seemed, was the question of his papers.

From his youth onwards, Kant had been a voracious reader and hoarder of books and pamphlets. As his own ideas began to gain credence throughout Prussia, then greater authority in the wider world, he wrote on almost every subject that ever interested man, as well as covering many arcane topics that no man before himself had even known existed. And in every case, he had published his findings, or assembled the material for a publication which, for one reason or another, had not materialised.

What would become of it all when he was dead?

This dilemma had assumed vast dimensions in the final decade of his life, the newspapers revealed. Of course, his three greatest works, the *Critiques* of Pure and Practical Reason, and of Judgment, had all been published, not only in German, but in various other languages as well. Lesser essays, written when he was a young professor still struggling to make his way, had appeared in studious journals and in more ephemeral magazines, and he had jealously conserved one or more copies of them, depending how widely the article had been taken up and reported—at second, third, or fourth hand, both at home and abroad. 'A man cannot stop others stealing his ideas,' Kant was recorded as saying, 'but he can keep a jealous eye on the fruits of his labour.'

There was a mountain of books, manuscripts and papers; if they were not to end up on a bonfire, a home must be found for them. The obituary notice in the *Königsbergische Monatsschrift* mentioned that Kant had left a sum of money to pay for a 'suitable person to oversee the classification, and draw up a catalogue of the philosopher's papers and published works'. A qualified archivist had been found in the person of Arnold Abel Ludvigssen. The name was not entirely new to me, though I knew it only in connection with Professor Kant, who had never been short of acolytes. Many students had progressed from one side of the teacher's lectern to the other under his tutelage, and I felt certain that Ludvigssen must be one of them, a bright fellow who had attracted Kant's attention by his diligence, a scholar who had been rewarded for his lesser talent with a few crumbs from the great man's table.

More to the point, I thought I knew where Ludvigssen might be located.

It was almost seven o'clock when we arrived in town.

'The curfew hour,' as I reminded Lavedrine.

'Don't worry about it,' he replied. 'I have my papers with me.'

'And I have mine,' I confirmed. 'But will a letter from Mutiez, or a passport signed by Dittersdorf, hold any power in Königsberg?'

'Do not trouble yourself,' he assured me. 'I will be the Dante to your Virgil. Just tell me which part of this *Inferno* you intend taking me to visit next.'

We were stopped almost immediately by a squad of French soldiers as we made our way through the dark, deserted city, heading in the direction of the university. Lavedrine had predicted correctly. His impeccable passport and high rank were more than sufficient to guarantee our freedom of movement. The soldiers apologised, saluted, and wished us good night without asking to see my humbler papers. Ten minutes more, and we stood before the university library, a tall building in the perpendicular Gothic style with high pointed windows, stained-glass tracery, flying buttresses, and horrid gargoyles. It was deathly silent, and seemed a fitting place for learned tomes to sleep while waiting for a reader.

Lavedrine thumped heavily on the door with the iron knocker.

When nothing happened, he hammered even more determinedly.

Above our heads, a window on the first floor rattled, then swung open.

The dark shadow of a head looked down.

'Closed for the night,' a grumbling sort of voice called out. 'Open at six in the morning. You lads should be abed. Only a cat can read in the dark.'

'We are looking for Herr Ludvigssen,' Lavedrine shouted up. 'Do you know where we can find him?'

A grumbling sort of laugh echoed off the walls. 'He'll be where he is always to be found.'

'Where's that?'

'The Old Goat,' the voice cried, then the window crashed shut again.

Lavedrine turned to me. 'An inn, do you reckon?'

'I have no idea,' I said. 'I think it would be wise if we retraced our steps towards the town centre.'

While doing so, we were stopped by patrolling French troops once more. Again, Lavedrine's papers passed muster. Again, mine were of no interest to them. The corporal saluted and began to beg pardon for stopping and questioning us, but Lavedrine cut him short.

'Do you know a place called The Old Goat?'

It was a two-minute walk.

When we pushed open the door and strode into the bar-room of the inn, it was getting on for half past seven. With the exception of four young men dining at a table in the far corner close to the fire—student lodgers, in all probability—the place was empty. Our entrance did not go unnoticed, however. Any man who walks the streets after curfew with impunity is a man to be feared. There are only three alternatives. He is a soldier, he is French, or else he is a criminal caught out in an act of wrongdoing. As the door swung closed, all eyes turned quickly. The young men looked away just as quickly, but the landlord standing behind the bar was a braver sort. He bent down and came up holding a cudgel, which he slapped three times in the palm of his hand.

'Good evening, gentlemen,' he called. 'What can I do for you?'

Lavedrine walked across the room, set his foot on the bar-rail, rested his elbow on the counter. 'Two steins of frothing beer would make a good start,' he said.

The landlord, a big strong fellow with muscles bulging through his shirt, stared at him for a moment. Then, laying the cudgel down on the nearby bar-top, he placed two beer jugs under the tap of a barrel, and gave a twist to the stopper, glancing at the rising level of the ale, then back to us again in quick succession. He did not say a word until the steins were full.

'Here you are,' he said, placing one beer on the bar, then the other, using his left hand only. His right hand hovered close to the cudgel, a solid black stick with a number of splinters missing, as if it had been used, and recently, for smashing pates. 'You know that there's a law at night in Königsberg, do you not?' he asked.

'In Königsberg alone?' Lavedrine replied, lifting up the jug and drinking through the grey froth that hid the liquid. 'In the whole of Prussia, surely.'

As he pronounced the last two words, he did so with a marked rolling of the 'r'.

'Frenchmen, are you, sirs?'

I set down the beer. 'Colonel Lavedrine is French, but I am Prussian,' I said. 'I am looking for one of my countrymen. And I'm a magistrate, at that.'

'Those lads are staying here,' the landlord said, glancing towards the fire. 'There's no one else in the house, my wife apart, and a couple of other lodgers upstairs sleeping.'

'Unless they go by the name of Ludvigssen, they are safe,' I said.

'Ludvigssen?' the landlord murmured, darting a wary glance towards the far end of the room.

I followed the line of his eye, and smiled. In that shadowy corner was a table with two wooden settles on either flank of it. Just visible, hanging over the end of the far bench, were a dirty pair of boots.

'Go easy on him, sir,' the tavern-keeper warned. 'He's been drinking all the afternoon.'

'Ludvigssen?' I hissed.

He nodded grimly, as if he did not care for the man.

'We do not mean him any harm,' I said, reflecting as I crossed the room that it is easier to drink a landlord dry and pay for it, than to win his affection. 'Herr Ludvigssen, wake up. I need to speak to you.'

Lavedrine helped by kicking the settle and making it shudder.

The sleeping man was wide awake, if bleary, in the twinkling of an eye. He backed along the bench and huddled in the corner by the wall. I sat down alongside him, while Lavedrine slid onto the seat on the other side of the table. We had him cornered.

'What will you drink?' Lavedrine asked, pulling out his purse, waving it in the air to the landlord, who watched all this as if it were a daily, nay, an hourly occurrence in his tavern.

Arnold Abel Ludvigssen was older than I expected—certainly not a student, forty years of age, or even older. His face was long and very thin, and his greasy black hair hung straight down, lank from a central parting, covering his ears and cheeks like two shining curtains. His long, pointed chin and hollow jaw had not seen a razor that day, nor the day before. He looked to all appearances like a man who habitually drank a great deal more than was good for the liver or the soul.

'A glass of porter,' he murmured, his tongue swishing over dry, cracked lips.

'I read of you in the newspapers, Herr Ludvigssen,' I said.

He stared at me dully, but did not open his mouth.

'In connection with Professor Kant,' I added.

'The *Kantstudiensaal*,' he said with a sigh.

'Is that what you call the place where his manuscripts and papers are kept?' asked Lavedrine.

The man looked tiredly across the table. 'That is what *they* call it,' he said. 'I would call it dusty. Very dusty. But the work keeps me in food and drink, and pays for my bed. What more can a man ask of Life?'

The landlord came striding across the room and slammed a pewter tankard of dark-brown beer on the table-top so forcefully that it slopped. He picked up the coins that Lavedrine pushed towards him, weighing them in the palm of his hand, then turned away, growling something to the effect that at least *that* pint wasn't going on the slate like all the others.

'The bursary pays out at the end of the university term,' Ludvigssen confided, but the mug of beer was in his mouth before he had finished speaking. An instant later, blowing beer-froth off his lips, he called loudly after the landlord, 'You'll get what's coming to you, Sigismund!'

It was hard to say whether it was a promise to pay his debts, or a threat.

'Come, sir,' Lavedrine urged him. 'We have serious business in Königsberg. You can help us expedite it.'

Ludvigssen looked at him, then laughed in that bleary provocative manner that serious and regular application to alcoholic drink induces. 'At this hour?' he challenged. 'I'm going nowhere, sir.'

'We'll see about that,' Lavedrine replied. 'Drink up, and tell us about Professor Kant's archive. That's why we've come. Surely, you know more about it than any other man living.'

For some reason, this sentence caused Ludvigssen to laugh all the more, or rather to gurgle, as he continued drinking while he laughed.

'Is there a man living who *is* interested in Kant?' he asked at last. 'I am paid to be, but that does not mean I am. But what is your specific interest, sir? Are you a Parisian philosopher? I thought that they had all said goodnight to Madame Guillotine by now?'

He was a strange surly creature. Not stupid certainly, but his humour was fired by alcohol. If he had hoped to make some progress in the academic world by accepting the bursary left by Immanuel Kant, evidently he had made none, for he was, somehow, marked by failure and an air of dissolution.

'And you, sir?' he enquired, rocking slowly in my direction. 'Are you a Prussian thinker, then? The last of a short line . . .'

'I am a magistrate,' I replied sharply. 'I could lock you up for the night for indecorous speech and conduct, if it pleased me. Just answer as you are requested.'

'I cannot . . . recall the question,' he murmured, burping in the middle of his response.

'The archive,' Lavedrine reminded him. 'Kant's papers. This *Kantstudiensaal*. Where is it?'

'At the university,' the man slurred.

'But you have the key in your pocket?'

He nodded as Lavedrine grabbed him by the lapels and pulled him to his feet, upsetting the little that remained of Ludvigssen's ale.

'Take us there. Now.'

Five or ten minutes later, having pushed and prodded the drink-sodden archivist across the cobbled cathedral square, where snow was gusting in again from the Baltic Sea on the wings of a furious wind, and through the narrow cobbled streets, where the snow fell in gentler flurries, we stood once more outside the doors of the university library.

Ludvigssen fumbled in his pockets, and eventually produced a keyring. The largest key of all turned noisily in the lock. The lychgate door fell back with a resounding creak, and we stepped inside, relieved to be out of the wind.

'Who goes there?' cried an anxious voice.

Footsteps sounded, a hollow echoing in the dark, then a stocky night-watchman appeared in the hallway a moment later, a lantern in his hand, a nightcap on his head. This was the man who had greeted us so curtly from the upstairs window half an hour before.

'Herr Ludvigssen! What are you doing here, sir? Two gentlemen . . .'

'We are scholars,' Lavedrine replied swiftly, stepping forward. 'Come to examine the archive of Professor Kant.'

'Professor who?' the man replied, turning away, probably going back to some warm corner where he had made his nest. There was nothing re-motely aggressive, or even challenging in his manner. The fact that we were with Ludvigssen was enough to reassure him, though I had my suspicions that Ludvigssen's presence would tranquillise any man alive. Indeed, I won-dered how he had managed to stay sober for long enough to impress the University authorities of his competence as a scholar.

'We'll be in my room,' Ludvigssen added, but the nightwatchman and his lantern were already receding into the distant gloom. The archivist turned to us. 'Follow me, sirs.'

Nightlights had been placed along the staircase that spiralled down to the basement. It was not well lit, but bright enough to avoid a tumble. At the bottom of the stairs, we turned to the left and followed a corridor that be-came darker and murkier the further we progressed along it. At the very last door at the end of a corridor which seemed to run the length of the library above our heads, Ludvigssen stopped, and began to feel about on his keyring again. The wrong key went into the lock, then the right one, and the door swung open. A smell of mildew and mice wafted out into the passage.

'One moment, sirs, I have a lamp in the corner here.'

He went into the room ahead of us, while Lavedrine and I stood waiting in the darkness. The sound of a flint being struck was rewarded a moment later by the glint of a flame, and a lantern swinging, as the archivist held it up.

'Come in, sirs,' he invited. 'I can light another, if you wish.'

As he bent over a table, lighting a larger lamp from the one that he held in his hand, he turned to us, the left side of his face glowing like a peach in the candlelight. 'What do you want to see?' he asked.

Before he spoke, I thought I felt the delight of Lavedrine vibrating in the cold air.

'Everything,' the Frenchman said. 'Every single scrap of paper that Professor Kant conserved.'

As we were entering, I had looked around curiously, realising for the first time what a daunting task we had set for ourselves.

Ludvigssen did not speak, he merely gestured with his hand. That room was as large as my own dining room; that is, it was very large by Prussian domestic standards. With the exception of a desk piled with papers in the centre of the room, and a single chair, the rest of the space was taken up with towering piles of manuscripts, folder upon folder of them, each one filled with sheaves of paper, propped up and tottering against the walls to shoulder height. Books and pamphlets filled a cabinet at the far end of the room. That bookshelf was six feet high, and three times as wide. I caught a glimpse of fading gold-tooled letters stamped on vellum spines in many languages: German, of course, but also English, French, Italian, Spanish, some more of Russian, Estonian, and Lithuanian origin, the titles in Cyrillic lettering, and even a group of books that bore what looked to me like curlicues from the Greek and the Arabian alphabets.

'The lot, sir?' Ludvigssen sounded amused. 'You'll be here a good while, then.'

Lavedrine moved quickly around the room, trying to take it all in— attempting, I imagined, to make some sense of what seemed like a disorganised panoply, a huge and disorienting collection of books and random papers.

'How long have you been working here?' he asked.

Ludvigssen sat himself down in his chair. 'Going on two years now, sir.'

'And what have you done in all that time?'

The archivist pointed to the shelves. 'I started with the published works,' he said dispiritedly. 'They are catalogued from A to Z, together with a brief abstract relating to the contents of each book, or publication. I took particular interest in those that were sent to the printer by Kant himself, and those foreign translations that were sent on to him by respectful publishers. Thank God, most of them didn't bother! If I'd had to trace all the robberies as well, I wouldn't have finished in my own lifetime. Can a man write so much, and be so soon unread and out of fashion?'

I walked across and scanned the spines of the books. The three *Critiques* alone took up three shelves, including unrevised loose-leaf proofs cut roughly into book form and held in shape with metal clips, first and subsequent editions, then all the foreign editions as well. One *Critique*—the fourth and final volume, the *Critique of Criminal Reason*—was missing, and the greedy brown waters of the River Pregel would never yield that up again. I would never forget the sight of page after page disappearing beneath the waves. I tore them up and threw them into the river the night of Kant's funeral. That book would certainly *not* have been forgotten. Ever . . .

'What about these papers, Ludvigssen?' Lavedrine asked, with a wave of his hand. 'How far have you got in the sorting?'

Again, the archivist sighed, and seemed amused in the lonely, self-interested way that only a scholar working in his ivory tower can know. 'I have managed to build them into piles,' he said. 'A more Herculean task than you might think, sir. Filthier than the Augean stables. At the time when Professor Kant's house was sold, I had still not been employed to organise his material. Everything went willy-nilly into a hundred boxes, none of which was marked. There was no order in it.'

I remembered the painstaking precision that Kant had brought to his assembly of evidence in the Königsberg case on which we had worked together. Despite his age and frailty, the methodical approach he employed gave sense to material that would have had no apparent meaning whatsoever, thrown haphazardly into a box.

'As each sheet of paper was taken out, I attempted to put it where it belonged.'

'Each sheet?' I queried.

Ludvigssen ran his thin hand through his lank hair. 'It sounds like hyperbole, I know, but I am not exaggerating. Of course, many of his manuscripts came to me more or less intact, a sheaf of pages tied up with a ribbon, or held in a folder, or a cover, identifying the nature of the work, but many thousands of pages—letters from his publisher, his copies of his letters to them, correspondence with readers and critics, notes and footnotes, addenda, and so on—had just been tipped straight into the boxes. Whoever bought Kant's house was in a hurry to make space, and I've been trying to make sense of the chaos ever since.'

'But you have made a start?'

This was Lavedrine, whose impatience knew no bounds. Ludvigssen realised, for he turned to the Frenchman with a mincing smile, and asked: 'Have you ever tried to shift a mountain with a teaspoon, sir? I have grouped everything roughly into related blocks, but that's about it. If you tell me where your interest lies, I may be able to point you in the right direction. Mind, I promise nothing.'

'We are searching for notes or documents written in the 1760s,' Lavedrine replied, giving nothing away. 'Now where would those be?'

Ludvigssen turned and nodded in the direction of the farthest corner. 'Juvenilia and ephemera,' he said dismissively.

I looked where he had indicated, and my heart sank. Imagine a library after it had taken a full hit from a twelve-pounder cannon! Papers lay in a crushed, crowded, knee-deep, yellow pile. It would take a week just to rifle through it, a year or two to read every word.

If I was daunted, Lavedrine was not.

'Let's get started, Stiffeniis,' he said.

'If you don't need me,' Ludvigssen remarked, 'I'll rest my head on the table and sleep until you've had enough.'

Without waiting for a word of encouragement, he did just that.

Lavedrine pulled a loose sheet from the top of the heap. 'A letter dated 1746,' he read. 'From his father's family in Tilsit, expressing regret for the father's death. That's no use to us. We are digging through the dunghill of a great man's life, Stiffeniis. God knows what we shall find!'

I knelt down and began to imitate the Frenchman, picking up a paper, glancing at the contents, setting it aside. One unpublished essay dated 1756 referred to the earthquake that had destroyed the city of Lisbon the year before. Kant noted that an acquaintance of his had felt the seismic shock, though escaping with his life and a few minor scratches. I felt a shudder of relief as I read it. The name of the friend was indicated only by the man's initials, P.D. If Professor Kant had ever mentioned me in his writings, I prayed that he had employed a cipher known only to himself.

As we moved the mound inch by inch and foot by foot from one spot to another, the night wore on. Lavedrine remained fortified by boundless enthusiasm. He did not seem to doubt for a moment that somewhere in that mound of papers he would find some clue to throw a shining light on the case of the Gottewald children. My hands grew cold as I sifted through the life and thoughts of Professor Kant, but a colder sweat drenched my body, and my terror increased as the work continued without result. Somewhere, I was certain, there would be a reference to me. I quaked at the prospect of finding it. *Let it fall to me, or not be found at all*, I prayed. My only hope was that my name, or my initials, were buried as deeply in that sea of documents as one of those rare monsters that marine biologists tell us never leaves the dark ocean bed in search of light.

'How I envy you, Stiffeniis, working so closely with this remarkable man,' Lavedrine said at one point. 'No expert's knowledge or opinion was equal to his own. Just think of it, a fledgling scholar, a promising student of philosophy, still unknown and unrecognised at home, who dared to question

Isaac Newton. There's a letter here from a Swedish astronomer. Kant had written to him, wondering whether the Englishman had got his mathematics right!'

I smiled, as I must, then continued burrowing into the pile, casting aside whatever was irrelevant as soon as I had caught the gist of it. That phrase of Ludvigssen's had me in a state of nervous alarm: *ephemera*, he had called it. Was my own collision with the meteor Kant nothing more than an ephemeral incident, at least in the eyes of an archivist? Each time I picked up and read another sheet of paper written out in Kant's neat, small handwriting, I half expected to find myself the subject of the thesis. His mind had ranged over almost every subject in the academic universe, from German poetry to Lithuanian folklore, from European politics to the most elegant form of wig that might be worn by a gentleman in the aftermath of the Russian occupation of Königsberg in January 1758. My nervous anxiety never ceased. One page seemed to have been written in the early 1740s, the next in the late 1750s, then I jumped ahead to a letter explaining how he had come to publish 'Concerning the Ultimate Ground of the Differentiation of Directions in Space' two decades later. Anything might emerge from that mound of forgotten controversies.

As it soon did.

'Unbelievable!' Lavedrine announced, holding up a letter dated 1750. 'Just look at this. Voltaire thanking Kant for praise of his *Treatise Concerning the Metaphysics*. It makes you wonder whether the young Immanuel had already worked out the whole thing!'

By midnight, Ludvigssen was snoring loudly. I had dusty grit in my mouth and would have given the world for a glass of fresh water. I was on the point of suggesting that we call a halt, when Lavedrine said suddenly, echoing my thoughts, 'Let's stop for the night. These papers will still be here tomorrow.' He glanced in the direction of the sleeping librarian. 'And for many years to come, I believe.'

I stood up, brushing dirt from my hands and cobwebs from my clothes, looking around for my hat which I had laid aside hours before. But there is something obsessive and bewitching about the hunt. *La chasse*, as the French call it with that lilting-nostalgic urge to find and catch and keep at any price. The fisherman's heart is always in his mouth for one last pike to grace his table, the hunter's for one last shot at a rabbit for his cooking-pot. Policemen and magistrates are not so different. If there is one last chance to find a thing, to settle a question, they will take it, in the hope that this may be the key to what they seek. Had I not done just that with Aaron Jacob and the dead woman's bones? With Helena's sketch of Sybille Gottewald?

Standing up, Lavedrine brushed off his hands and shook the dust from his hair.

'I'm ready to leave when you are,' he said, then dropped immediately to his knees again, sweeping up one last bundle of paper, and glancing at the swathe of rag-cloth with which it had been bound.

'*Quelle chance!*' he said quietly, walking across to me, thrusting the manuscript into my hands with the grin of a schoolboy stamped on his face.

The label was peeling from the cover, the ancient glue having lost much of its efficacy:

Concerning the Death of an Infant, 1765

· 35 ·

THE MANUSCRIPT BUNDLE was made up of a number of sections.

To Lavedrine and myself, as we examined the document that night, it revealed the young Immanuel Kant to be an acute observer of social minutiae. Those papers were a vivid testimony to the passion with which he embraced the question of one life cut short by murder, and another cut short by the offices of the public executioner.

Like two climbers who have reached the summit of a high peak, we sank to the floor exhausted. Lavedrine was exhilarated, having found what he was looking for. I felt relief. He had not found what I most feared.

He read the first page, then passed it to me. And so we continued to the end.

PAGE 1: TITLE

Concerning the Death of an Infant in the Year of the Lord, 1765
by Immanuel Kant of Königsberg

All across this title page, from the bottom left-hand corner to the top right corner, the following declaration had been written out in massive capital copperplate letters: PLEA REJECTED. It bore the blue seal of the Central Police Bureau in Berlin, and the scrawled signature of the Magistrate General.

PAGE 2: PREMISE

To His Excellency, the Magistrate General,
Baron Erlich von Bülow, Berlin.

Most noble sir,

I, Immanuel Kant, a private gentleman and loyal citizen of His Royal Majesty, King Frederick II of the house of Hohenzollern, do hereby solemnly swear that every statement and description which follows in these pages is, to the very best of my knowledge, and in the soundness of my judgement, true and indisputable.

It is my intention to examine the following questions:

a. the death of Georg-Albert von Mandel, son and heir to Humbert-Arthur von Mandel, 6th Duke of Albemarle and Svetloye, in the canton of Königsberg;

b. the accusation of murder brought against Karlus Wettig, footman to the house of Albemarle, and serf to the 6th Duke;

c. my relations with the Albemarle household in Svetloye and in Königsberg, and my observations of what I know of both those houses;

d. my conclusions relating to the sentence which is due to be pronounced by Procurator Helmut-Philip Reimarus, magistrate, in the city of Königsberg on 24th October next, in the year of God, 1766.

In faith and loyalty,

Immanuel Kant, philosopher, this day, 1st October, 1766

Page 3 ff.: The event

Death of Georg-Albert von Mandel, heir to Duke Albemarle of Svetloye.

At half past six on the morning of 2nd December, 1765, a nursemaid, Edith Peckenthaal, was present in the bedroom where the eight-month-old son, and only heir, to the Duke of Albemarle was found dead. The infant had been put to bed by his mother, Dorothea-Ann Lundstadt, Duchess of Albemarle, and the nurse, at the usual hour of seven o'clock the previous evening. Nurse Edith sat with Georg-Albert, knitting a shawl for him until 10:30 p.m., when she extinguished the candles in the room, leaving only one nightlight burning next to the child's cot. By her own account, Fraulein Peckenthaal sat by Georg-Albert for another half-hour, or more—the boy's sleep had been disturbed for a week by teething pains. Certain that her charge was comfortably settled for the night, Edith removed herself from the room for fifteen minutes, as she was permitted to do, going down to the kitchen, where she drank a glass of milk and ate several biscuits in the company of the cook, Frau Angela Schmidt.

Frau Schmidt records that nothing appeared to be out of the ordinary. Edith was her usual self. The nurse is renowned within the family for her good sense. Having eaten a late supper, and taken leave of the cook, she returned upstairs to the nursery. She at once took stock of the child, and swears that he was sleeping soundly. At that point, Nurse Edith undressed and washed herself. Having donned her nightgown and said her prayers, she put herself to bed in the same room. The child, she remembers, was gurgling lightly as he slept.

During the night, Edith was disturbed on two occasions:

a. On the first occasion, the nurse was able to say precisely what time the intrusion occurred. Having woken up shortly before for no reason that she could give, Edith says that she heard the estate clock strike two. That clock is situated directly above her head. Its chiming can be heard at distances of up to one mile, depending on the strength and the direction of the wind, as I verified on the morning following the event to establish the veracity of contradictory reports by diverse witnesses.

Lady Dorothea-Ann entered the room shortly afterwards. She had dreamt, she told Edith, that the child was crying for his mother. The nurse reports, however, that the child had been sweetly sleeping, and did not wake up until his mother came in and made a fuss, lifting him up from his cot, and walking him round and round the room—rather quickly, according to the nurse—for almost an hour. Later, the Duchess of Albemarle left the nurse and the child alone again. The servant swears that the clock struck three within a brief space of time.

b. On the second occasion, a footman came to the room. The man in question was Karlus Wettig, occasional second valet to the Duke. That night, as was always the custom in the Albermarle household, one of the menservants was required to sit up from dusk to dawn, patrolling the house to ensure against thieves, fire, or any other accident which might endanger the lives of the family and the Albemarle retinue. As personal tutor to the Duchess—counted, therefore, as one of the servants—I have myself kept the night watch on several occasions. The duty is not onerous and is rewarded by a free day and a half-day holiday the Saturday following. The guardian is required to sit on a comfortable chair in the entrance hall. He may read by candle-light, if he wishes, and I took advantage of the opportunity. Every half-hour, at the striking of the hour, or the half, by the English grandfather clock in the reception room, the nightguard must walk the length and breadth of the house, including the nursery where Georg-Albert sleeps with Edith Pecken-thaal, checking that all doors are closed. In all, the survey of the house takes at least twelve minutes. On my nocturnal wanderings, I have rarely met any person with the exception of the Duke himself, who keeps late hours, and occasionally milady, Dorothea-Ann, who is a notoriously light sleeper.

On the night in question, I was sleeping in my room, though I believe I may have heard Karlus Wettig passing in the corridor outside my room on two separate occasions, some ten or twelve minutes after the hour of eleven; some time later that night, I observed the flicker of candlelight beneath my door. My room is situated at the end of the servants' corridor. Karlus Wettig had been in service with the family for almost twenty years, and was considered to be a trustworthy nightwatchman.

At half past six o'clock on the morning of 2nd December, 1765, I was roused by a piercing scream from somewhere in the house, followed by a flurry of activity, most of the servants already being at their posts and engaged, preparing the house for the family ablutions and the breakfast, which was generally served in the dining room at 7.45. As I was informed in passing by Lucinda Boehmer, one of the lady's maids, the child, Georg-Albert von Mandel, had been found dead in his cot.

Later that day, I spoke to Edith Peckenthaal, who had been seen by the physician, Herr Doctor Fenikker. After verifying that the child was dead, he had been asked to give a reviving potion to the nurse who was in a state of swooning brought on by emotional hysteria. Though unusually drowsy—drugged, perhaps?—the young lady, a dependable unmarried person aged twenty-seven, told me that she had heard nothing during the night which might alarm her, and that the shock of finding the infant dead had 'broken her heart'.

I also managed to speak with the doctor.

He reported that the child appeared to have been violently beaten to death. He counted as many as sixteen or seventeen blows with a heavy, blunt object—a murder weapon which has been neither identified, nor found. The violence of the attack and of the child's reflex physiological response to it is indicated by the pattern of blood which was found in the room. The cot was soaked with blood, as were the two walls in the corner where the baby slept. Paths of bloodstains on the wall suggested that the first blow occasioned massive loss of blood, and that each subsequent blow lifted and sprayed blood over the surrounding area.

Question: Why repeat the attack so often and with such ferocity when the first blow certainly provoked sufficient damage to silence the child and ensure his death?

As the murder weapon was used again and again, the tracks of blood on the walls and the ceiling suggest that the angle of attack was modified with every single blow. In addition, a shower of minute bloodspots, probably caused by violent haemorrhaging of the child's lungs, produced a finer cloud of minute blood-spots on the wall to the left of the cot. Doctor Fenikker, a general practitioner, a graduate of the medical school in Potsdam, and a veteran seagoing surgeon in the Prussian Navy, hypothesised, noting dilation of the pupils and the fact that the eyes were bloodshot, that the child may have struggled in panic before his demise—a matter of no more than one or two minutes. From the relative ease with which he was able to move and examine the tiny corpse, the doctor deduces that the infant had been dead no more than four hours when his lifeless body was discovered.

Georg-Albert von Mandel was buried three days later, on 5th December in the churchyard of Svetloye, the country estate of the Duke of Albermarle, where the body had been removed the day before.

My suggestion, made to the Duke himself, shortly after the physician left the house, that a post mortem examination be carried out by a qualified pathologist—I offered the name of an acquaintance, Doctor Ernst Plucker, ordinary of the Royal University of Königsberg—was rejected out of hand. Indeed, the violent terms in which my advice was rejected led me to proffer my immediate resignation, which the Duke of Albermarle accepted.

NB: There was no acrimony involved in my retirement from my contract of service. The Duke settled the full account due to me, and apologised, [a] for the violence of his reaction, and [b] for the family tragedy in which I had been unwittingly caught up.

Page 8 ff.: The Accused

Accusation of child murder brought against Karlus Wettig—
footman to the house of Albemarle, serf to the Duke of Albemarle

Karlus Wettig asserts that he had 'no motive whatsoever to murder the son of his master'.

We will examine this statement, and draw our conclusions.

Karlus Wettig, born in Königsberg in 1736, is the son of Marta Wettig, seamstress, father unknown. He was taken into service by the house of Albemarle, in the person of the father of the present Duke, in 1747, and was employed initially as a junior boot-boy. He showed 'talent, respect, and restraint', and for these qualities the present Duke decided to promote him on two separate occasions. From footservant he became under-valet ten years ago, then under-butler, a position conferred upon him three years before the events related above.

Karlus Wettig is a reserved, taciturn man, who makes no secret of his misogyny. He is held in fear and respect, especially by the female servants, but also by the men under him. No previous spot has ever tarred his reputation or brought his good character into question. In the words of nurse Edith Peckenthaal: 'Wettig keeps himself to himself,' and is only known to show anger when lesser servants play upon the relaxed and good-natured manner of his master. He has never been accused of any crime, no matter how slight or inconsequential. He is known to be a devout Pietist, and a regular church-goer, whenever his duties permit him to attend religious services. His pastor, the Reverend Astor-Johann Rosavic, commends him for his religious fer-vour, and the generosity of his charitable donations 'within his limited means'. He also states that Karlus Wettig has a 'sound knowledge of the Bible, and a deep and enduring sense of morals.'

I myself have spoken to Wettig on numerous occasions, and I would rec-ommend him to any man. Indeed, I have undertaken to write a character ref-erence on his behalf when the mystery is revealed and the truth shines forth. If he is ever released, he will be sorely in need of friends and employment.

The accusation is supported by no other evidence than the fact that he was on guard duty that night, and that he was observed to enter the room of Nurse Peckenthaal in pursuance of that duty. He states that he was passing along the corridor on the first floor where the family bedrooms are located, shortly after three o'clock [that is, within the time span which Doctor Fenikker posits as the likely moment of the child's decease]. He says that he 'heard a noise and saw a shadow moving away from him down the hall, going in the direction of the adjoining master-bedrooms of the Duke and Her La-dyship'. Though unable to identify the person he believes that he saw, he 'thinks it may have been the mistress, for she was wearing a flowing night-gown.' The door to the nursery was 'ajar', he says, and he entered the room af-ter knocking lightly, to 'ensure that everything was in its place'. Challenged by Edith Peckenthaal, who called out from her bed, Karlus Wettig identified himself, then checked the windows which were secure, and 'peeped into the crib, where the child appeared to be soundly sleeping'. He then continued on his rounds, returning some minutes later to the entrance hall and his chair, where he smoked his pipe, waiting for the clock to strike again. Before the awful discovery at 6.30 a.m., he toured the house six more times, and reports seeing no one, and hearing nothing which might have provoked his suspi-cions. When the nurse began to scream, he was the third person to enter the nursery, following hard upon the heels of the Duke and Lady Albemarle. No accusations were made against him at that time, though later in the day, when Procurator Reimarus of the Königsberg Inspectorate was called, Lady Dorothea-Ann Lundstadt, the Duchess of Albemarle, remarked to the inves-tigator that she 'had never trusted that man'.

On the basis of her doubts alone, notwithstanding the faith expressed in his regard by his master, the Duke of Albemarle, in the absence of any other suspect, Karlus Wettig was arrested the very next day and held without trial for eight months in the dungeon of the Castle of Königsberg.

Throughout the trial, Karlus Wettig always protested his innocence. No material evidence suggesting the contrary was ever brought to the attention of the judge, and all references to the good character and the reputable standing of the accused were struck from the register.

Sentence is expected within the month, and all opinion seems to be—in the light of the man's inability to demonstrate his innocence—that he will be executed.

Conclusions:

a. There is not one objective scrap of proof that Karlus Wettig murdered the infant, Georg-Albert von Mandel, son and heir to the Duke of Albemarle, during the night or the early hours of the morning of 2nd December, 1765.

b. In faith, I believe that legal judgement must be suspended until a better candidate for the hangman can be identified.

PAGE II FF.: OBSERVATIONS

The Albemarle households in Svetloye and in Königsberg,
and what I know of both those houses

The Albermarle family, originally from Svetloye in the canton of Königsberg, owns the Albemarle estate in Svetloye, and a town house located in the Strandstrasse suburb of Königsberg. I was employed in late August, 1765, for a six-month period, starting on 1st September, to instruct Her Ladyship, Duchess Dorothea-Ann, with whom I would be required to spend a minimum of three hours per day.

On numerous occasions, especially on the Svetloye estate, the whole of my day was spent in the company of Her Ladyship and the Duke of Albemarle, both of whom were kind and considerate in their attentions to me.

My employment began in the country house in Svetloye. Every morning from Monday to Friday, I would attend upon my mistress, Dorothea-Ann Lundstadt, Duchess of Albemarle, in the Library between the hours of nine and twelve o'clock. My specific duties were didactic in nature, but in such intimate circumstances, I believe I am correct in asserting that I grew to know

the mistress as well as her own maid. Her Ladyship is gifted in music—
proficient in the flute and the harpsichord—and in sewing, both of which
formed the greater parts of her youthful education, but her knowledge is
more defective in questions relating to geography, economy, politics, and the
sciences, particularly mathematics. My task was to pursue a general course of
education within these blank areas, and I found my Lady to be a diligent, if
distracted, student.

The great problem from my point of view was concentration on her
studies.

Lady Dorothea-Ann, a recent mother, and the mistress to a large estate,
is beset by a number of preoccupations which are not conducive to prolonged
study. There was not a single morning, according to my register-book, in
which she was not called away to attend to some urgent business, relating either to the minding of the young child, or the general administration of the
household. On every one of those occasions, I could not help but notice that
her mood on returning to the Library had taken a turn for the worse. My
concerns, I soon realised, were secondary to her own. On one occasion in
particular, I recall that it was necessary to suspend the lesson. Her Ladyship
was greatly upset by the loss of a blue bonnet. This cap had been knitted by
hand for the infant Georg-Albert by his maternal grandmother, who was expected that afternoon on a week's visit. Lady Dorothea-Ann was so upset by
the loss that she fainted, and had to be revived with smelling salt. The local
doctor, a man of no great science, was called, then sent away again, his further attendance being judged unnecessary. Shortly after lunch, the bonnet
was found in the box where it had always been kept, and the crisis was re-
solved. The mother was always overly concerned that the child's head should
be protected from chills and the cold, even on the warmest day.

On other occasions, from a more strictly scholastic perspective, I discovered the attention of the Duchess to be strongly emotive and even sentimen-
tal in nature. In the matter of geography, she would happily follow my
exposition of the physical nature of the major European countries, but with
two distinct exceptions, any mention of which made her exceedingly testy,
viz. volcanic explosions, and anything which concerned the Czardom of Russia. On one occasion, when I happened to speak in passing of the ancient
civilisation of Pompeii, and its reduction to nothing by the volcanic eruption
of Mount Vesuvius, she broke feverishly into tears and was clearly upset.
'How can something solid just explode?' she asked. I attempted to explain the
nature of explosions, but soon gave it up. The more she learnt, the more dis-
traught she became. Inadvertent mention of the black sands of the shores of
the volcanic Mediterranean island of Stromboli some days later produced a
similar hysterical outbreak. 'Did they come bursting out, too?' she cried.

Russia, in any of its forms, whether political, social, geographical, or historical, provoked angry insolent silence. The only explanation Lady Dorothea-Ann could offer for her aversion to the Russians was the manner in which they treat imbeciles, drenching them in cold water and tying them up, but I was unable and unwilling to explore this vein of thought to any real extent. It was too distressing.

As a private tutor of some experience, I was induced to avoid certain subjects of interest and conversation, and ignore their implications, to the detriment of my general plan of instruction, for the sake of tranquillity in the classroom.

On 1st October, the household moved to Königsberg for the winter season, and I went with them to the Albemarle house in Strandstrasse, where the murder took place. By 15th November, I must report unwillingly that my lessons had deteriorated to a sort of one-sided conversation. That is, I introduced the topic for the morning, then talked to myself about it until lunchtime. Lady Dorothea-Ann, while still protesting her interest, and expressing her great desire to learn, was sinking into a fit of depression. I mention that date, because I asked for an interview with the Duke, and confessed my misgivings to him about the method of instruction which I had chosen and the Socratic means that I had used to implement it. Corrective conversation between master and pupil was clearly not paying dividends. I informed the Duke of an incident that had marred the lesson that very morning. While speaking of mathematics and geometrical forms, I happened to mention the differences between a perfect circle and an oblate spheroid. While circles were much to my Lady's taste, compressed spheres appeared to terrify the life out of her and she began to weep. I had to suspend teaching for half an hour, while my pupil went to see that the baby was quite well. The Duke thanked me for my concerns, and prayed me to continue, suggesting that the heavier obligations on his Lady's time, provoked by the growing child and the busy social programme which their elevated position in local society obligated them to maintain, were the probable causes of the negligence. He would be, he said, most grateful if I would keep to my side of the contracted bargain. He would look out for an opportunity to mention my misgivings to his wife. He also suggested that less conversation, no mathematics, and more reading of literature and, perhaps, some poetry-writing would probably yield greater benefits for his Lady's health. This I undertook to do in the following weeks. However, I noticed with increasing frequency that while I was reading, the Duchess was looking out of the window, and that my requests for poems describing clouds and other 'nebulous' objects which caught her attention were met with an endless string of excuses. In every case, as the Duke had hinted to me, the well-being of their son, or the necessity for dressing and hairdressing in preparation for some unavoidable social gathering that afternoon or evening was the invariable, and probably justifiable excuse which Lady Dorothea-Ann offered for work not done.

I will conclude this section only by expressing my concern for the health of the Lady in the present circumstances. The death of her child, and the fact that death was occasioned by murder, would be a trial for any woman. For Lady Dorothea-Ann, I fear, the consequences may be grave. I have had no opportunity to speak with Her Ladyship, given that I resigned from the Duke's employ the morning after the murder, and I can only hope that she has not taken it too ill. I strongly advise that the Lady should be visited, comforted, and advised by a qualified person with wide experience in the moral and the religious disciplines. A suitable person might be my acquaintance, Christian Jacob Kraus, who is a moral philosopher of the first order, a gentleman destined for an important academic career.

Page 16 ff.: Plea

Conclusions relating to the sentence due to be pronounced by Procurator Helmut-Philip Reimarus, magistrate, in the city of Königsberg on 26th October, in the year of God, 1766.

The conclusion of the trial of Karlus Wettig, footman, accused of the murder of the infant, Georg-Albert von Mandel, in accordance with the Law of all the Prussias, is as inevitable as it is unjust. There can only be one sentence, and that sentence is final and irrevocable. That is the Law regarding punishment of wilful murder. And the Law will prevail. As it must.

But I appeal to you, Excellency, Magistrate General, Baron von Bülow, at the very least for clemency. There is a Moral Order in the necessity for Justice which cannot be overlooked or ignored.

Is this man guilty beyond all reasonable doubt?

If any doubt remains, in what does it consist?

It must consist in the following: Karlus Wettig proclaims his innocence, and no evidence has been provided to negate that claim. He is of sound mind, and of a proven good character. Does this count for nothing? In the face of a capital sentence and the inevitable punishment, even the most depraved of men will recognise that it is better to be known for what he is, to admit his guilt, explain the motives which have led to his crime, and proffer weakness of character as his excuse. Better even this humiliation, than to be thought a coward—so ashamed of what he has done in the face of undeniable evidence, that he will deny it to the very end. Only a fool will rob himself of the flimsy moral justification which a clear motive may provide. Karlus Wettig is neither a fool, nor a coward. What possible reason could there be for this man to murder a child in his cot, and deny it to the end? There is neither monetary profit, nor blustering pride in his own evil to justify it.

Conclusion: If this man is hanged, an innocent will go to the gallows, and the guilty will escape scot-free.

Question: Is Karlus Wettig attempting to shield the name and the identity of the murderer?

There are innumerable reasons which suggest that this may be the case:

1. He may not know the name of the person, but believe [as I have been told by his pastor that he does] that somebody must pay for the crime, or the innocent child will not be permitted a Christian burial in a consecrated church. That is, Karlus Wettig may see himself as a scapegoat, morally obliged to pay for the expiation of a crime committed by an unknown killer, thinking that his own death will redeem the unblemished soul of the victim, and put further crushing weight on the uneasy conscience of the true perpetrator, inducing him or her to eventually confess to the murder of Georg-Albert von Mandel.

2. Karlus Wettig may know the actual name of the person who committed the crime, and may have decided, for reasons unknown to anyone [except himself and that other guilty person], to take the burden of punishment on his own head.

3. Karlus Wettig may not have known the name of the perpetrator, but he may have wished for some unspeakable reason that the child were dead. That is, he may feel that he has somehow invoked the boy's death, and that some heartless demon god had acted upon his unrealised inclination.

How many times have you, Sir, wished that somebody were dead? It is a wish more commonly expressed than is generally realised. Indeed, if a man is so bold as to wish death upon another, he is under a moral obligation to commit the deed. This is, I know, a philosophical paradox, but it is true. And the converse is equally true. If Karlus Wettig has never publicly announced his desire for the death of the infant, Georg-Albert Mandel, if he has never admitted committing such a murder, and if there is no demonstrable evidence to the contrary, then we are morally obliged to believe that he has not committed the crime.

In conclusion, I believe that hate or malice are not the cause, but love and tenderness of a most particular nature, which need to be unravelled before the true motivation for the crime can be satisfactorily posited. Equally, I believe that I may, in part, have touched upon some elements of the mysterious nature of this passion. Naturally, I am unable to demonstrate my thesis, but such incontrovertible evidence might still be obtained if you, Sir, would admit the necessity to open the tomb and examine the corpse of the victim.

Love, Duty, or both, perhaps, may have condemned Karlus Wettig to pay for a crime which he did not commit.

In faith and loyalty,

Immanuel Kant, philosopher, this day, 1st October, 1766.

· 36 ·

WE CLIMBED ABOARD the Danzig post-coach at half-past five that morning.

The same vehicle, or one very like it, would have taken us back to Lotin-gen, but Lavedrine and I were not going there directly. We had discussed the plan as we walked back through the streets from the university library to the post-inn. It was four o'clock, the night sky over Königsberg a black velvet curtain pinpricked with a thousand stars.

Lavedrine pulled on the hostelry bell and we waited for a yawning ostler to draw back the bolts and let us enter. 'I see no reason to stay here any longer,' he said. 'Kant's request for clemency was submitted. And it was re-jected. No post-mortem examination was ever carried out by a qualified pathologist. If Kant was correct, the solution awaits us in Svetloye, ancestral home of the von Mandel family. The philosopher was helpless in the cir-cumstances, but we are not.'

I was too tired to disagree.

Lavedrine was a colonel in the French army, I was a Prussian magistrate. Our investigative powers were endorsed by the executive authorities of both countries. We represented a force that no local interest could lightly oppose—not even the descendants of an aristocratic family who ruled their estates and tenants with all the power of wealth and feudal law at their dis-posal.

'We can catch a nap in the coach,' Lavedrine went on, ordering the ostler to set about preparing a breakfast of boiled eggs. We went upstairs, but only to collect our bags. 'If I were to close my eyes now,' the Frenchman said, 'I would never open them again. I suggest that we pay our bill, then catch the first coach.'

An hour later, as the post-coach trundled out of town and began to climb the glistening snow-covered hills, the rising sun broke bravely through the massive clouds, its rays flashing like multiple rainbows. It was the first time I had ever seen Königsberg by sunlight. Looking back, I thought instinctively of Immanuel Kant. The city he loved lay shimmering beneath us, untroubled by the threat of rain or further snow.

If I was thinking of Kant, so was Lavedrine.

'I wonder whether we have come away too soon,' he said, cutting in upon my meditations.

'What do you mean?'

Lavedrine rubbed his chin, and sniffed. 'That case we read about last night. I've been puzzling over it. It occurred in 1765 . . . Forgive me if I say again that I was correct. Kant was drawn to criminal investigation long before he wrote to me in late 1793, shortly after I had published my thesis.'

'*L'assassix rural*,' I murmured dutifully.

He beamed with delight. 'You remember, Stiffeniis. Good for you! My point is this. What reawakened his interest in crime so many years later? Did something specific occur in 1793, which caused Kant to get in touch with me?'

'Your book was published,' I answered, almost too quickly. 'He must have read it, and found the ideas stimulating.'

'I am not so presumptuous,' he said with a smile and a shake of the head. 'He contacted me because of something specific in my book. I will never forget the words that he used. "I have recently been studying the springs of criminal motivation",' he recited, as if holding that letter of Kant's in his hand, reading it out to me verbatim.

He leant forward in his seat—there were no other passengers—and fixed me with a questioning stare. 'You met him in '93. Did he mention being involved in any criminal investigation at that date?'

He reclined comfortably back against the leather upholstery, inviting me to entertain him with an account of my relationship with Professor Kant.

But I stared out of the window, and refused to say a word.

I had passed the night in a state of nervous anxiety as we sifted the mass of papers in Kant's archive, fearing that my name would appear at any moment in an incriminating note. Somewhere amongst those papers, Kant had written a full account of the day that I went to visit him in Königsberg. I was sure of it. I had found the courage to confess my obsession with violent death, and Professor Kant had offered advice that had radically altered my life. 'Restore order where crime has brought chaos.' That day, I chose to be a magistrate, though I might as easily have become a murderer.

'I attended one of his lectures in 1793,' I answered, shaking off my reluctance to speak of it. 'I was extremely surprised when he remembered my name a decade later.'

'But he did *not* forget you,' Lavedrine replied swiftly. 'And I wonder why he thought of you in connection with such a troublesome investigation when his own life was so close to its end. I mean to say, you were only . . . what? Twenty-six, twenty-seven? And without any experience in such a demanding field.'

'I was twenty-eight,' I corrected him. 'He believed that a young magistrate, a person like myself, would be more willing to follow his suggestions than a seasoned investigator.'

Lavedrine stared thoughtfully out of the window.

A moment later, he turned to me again. 'Let me tell you how I see it,' he said. 'You, a young man from an aristocratic family—lively, intelligent, interested in philosophy—meet Immanuel Kant one day. The greatest Prussian thinker, a metaphysician of extraordinary capability. Does he invite you to study moral philosophy in Königsberg under his tutelage? No, he does not. He sends you off to study Law. And ten years later, still lacking any real investigative experience, Herr Professor Kant calls *you* to Königsberg to help him solve a murder case.'

He shook his head, as if the life that he had just related were beyond belief. That familiar, ironic smile lit up his face and set his eyes a-glistening.

'At pretty much the same time,' he continued, 'I receive a letter from Professor Kant, relating to murder and its causes. I do not mean to draw any facile conclusions, but, well, I mean to say! It's hard to avoid them. Kant, murder, you. You, Kant, and a murder to be solved? These elements are so closely linked, they are almost a syllogism.'

'Syllogisms are often false,' I observed neutrally.

'True,' he agreed. 'But I recall how angry you were at Dittersdorf's feast. I do believe you would have planted your knife and fork in my heart with a little more goading. Thank God Helena was present! We might have ended at each other's throats. And all because I insisted that Kant was interested in murder long before he sent for you. Now, we have conclusive proof. I was right, and you were wrong, Stiffeniis. But you already knew the truth, I'm convinced of it. That was why you were in such a rage. And for the same reason, that is why you are so reluctant to talk *now*.'

'But we are talking,' I replied.

'*I* am talking,' he said. 'You are not.'

He stared at me in silence, as if challenging me to react to the provocation.

Again, I avoided his scrutiny, looking out of the window at the distant hills, the bare trees, the endless snow.

'You would make a most intriguing subject for my studies,' he probed again.

'Really?' I laughed without humour, never shifting my eyes from the scene beyond the window-glass. 'You are a criminologist,' I said. 'I have committed no crime.'

Lavedrine laughed in his turn, but his laughter was genuine.

'Now, you are making connections that are mechanistic,' he said. 'That thin smile of yours gives nothing away. Those dark-brown eyes never betray what is passing through your mind. Did Kant see something there that no one else had seen? Not even you, perhaps? There is a strange ambivalence between the hunter and the hunted, the criminal and the magistrate. They share a set of common values, they move in the same shadowy world.' He looked thoughtfully at me. 'Is that what Helena finds so fascinating? You are a man of dark secrets and violent passions, I think, though you hide them deep beneath a glacial outer crust. I'd love to know what attracts you to crime. I'll ferret it out, I promise you. Sooner or later. The enigma is enthralling, Stiffeniis.'

I did not rise to the fly. He will talk himself out, I thought.

To my immense relief, the coach lurched to a halt twenty minutes later.

We had passed through Svetloye the previous day. I had taken little notice of the place then, but I looked around me more carefully as we jumped down into the road. It was eight o'clock. Not much more. Snow lay thick on the frozen earth, giving the small straggling hamlet an aspect of gleaming purity that it would not have had in more muddy circumstances. The houses along the road were mean straw-thatched cottages, though they were picturesque enough beneath a blanket of snow. On a hill to the north stood a larger house, the von Mandel mansion, as we were told by a group of boys throwing snowballs at each other and at the departing post-coach, much to the anger of the driver cracking his whip on his box, and the red-faced postillion riding the lead-horse.

'There isn't anyone up there now, sir.'

'But there is a church, I believe?'

The boys pointed us in the direction of a pine wood on the western slope of the hill, and Lavedrine tossed them a *Pfennig* or two.

'Are you in the mood for walking?' he asked.

'We have little choice,' I replied.

I slipped and fell down once, but otherwise we proceeded without mishap, emerging from a thick stand of trees to find the small stone chapel and silent churchyard bordering the von Mandel estate. The church was small and squat, little more than a large single room or prayer-hall, with a stone bell tower, but there was a twirl of smoke rising from the chimney of a clapperboard barn that had been built onto the side of the building.

'The priest is at home,' said Lavedrine, stepping up to knock.

But the old man who answered the door was not a priest. He was dressed in the clothes of a countryman, his ancient overcoat tied tight with string at the waist, his legs clad with canvas leggings secured above the knee. He was the estate guardian—'living in the pastor's cottage', he explained, 'for it is warmer and drier than the house up there on the hill'.

'Where is the owner of the estate?' I asked.

The man ran his gnarled hand through the straggling grey hairs of his long beard.

'Over there, sir,' he said, pointing to a funeral monument shaped like a pyramid that stood out from the snow like a soaring Alpine peak. 'Died last year, he did. Them lawyers do take their time to settle things. An' gets paid for doing so. I am a-waiting on them. They'll get shut of me, no doubt. One of these days. Till then, I just keeps the place tidy, and safe from tinkering thieves.'

That word seemed to strike a violent discord in his head.

'What can I do for you gentlemen?' he asked warily.

Lavedrine told him who we were and why we had come. Not in detail, of course, but in a general sort of way. 'Who is buried beneath the pyramid?' he asked.

'Henry Ffinch, sir, a retired, English seafaring gentleman what bought up the old property many years ago.'

'What about the von Mandels?'

'Over there, sir,' the man said, shading his eyes against the harsh glare of light reflecting off the snow, pointing to another part of the cemetery.

'Is there a sexton or a gravedigger?' Lavedrine asked the man.

'There's Pieter Sweiten, sir,' the man replied quickly enough.

'Who is he, and where might he be found?' I asked.

A crack appeared in the old man's funeral slab of a face.

'Why, sir, right here,' he said, tapping his forefinger on his chest. 'I am he.'

Lavedrine pulled out his purse and shook it, noisily rattling the coins. 'We need you to do a little job for us, Herr Sweiten.'

'What's that, Herr Magistrate?' he said, turning back to me, apparently more impressed by my title than that of a colonel in an occupying army, even if the foreigner was the one with the clinking purse in his hand.

'Where lies the grave of Georg-Albert von Mandel?'

'There ain't no grave,' he said.

'No grave?' I echoed.

'No, sir,' the old man replied, his voice a vibrating country burr. 'Not for family. That babe was laid to rest in the von Mandel vault. 'Tain't a grave, if you see what I mean.'

'Can you open it?' I asked, the words out of my mouth before I realised the enormity of the proposal and how it must have sounded to Pieter Sweiten.

The man did not so much as blink. 'That's done easy, sir. Digging would have been a bit of a job with this hard frost,' he said with a smile that seemed to light up his face. He chewed on the proposition for a moment, before adding: 'I have the key, sir.'

Lavedrine pulled out some of the coins and thrust them at the man. 'Well?' he said. 'What are you waiting for?'

Five minutes later, we stood watching while Pieter Sweiten fumbled with the keys on a large keyring, looking for the one that would unlock the perforated metal grating that gave access to the von Mandel family tomb. In comparison with the more recent and fashionable pyramid, it was an unimpressive block of weathered stonemasonry, laid over the interred chamber of the burial crypt, which was reached by means of a short flight of five or six steps. Covered with snow, the pediment dripping icicles, the broad rim of the capstone of the funeral chamber bore a carved legend: *Eccoci, mortali. Qui riposiamo per sempre. Lasciateci dormie in pace.*

'It is Italian,' Lavedrine said with a dismissive shrug. 'Leave us alone is what it says. More or less.'

'There!' the estate caretaker exclaimed. Having found the key, he had released the lock and given the iron grating a resounding kick with his boot which set the air clanging. 'All that rust and ice,' he said by way of exclamation.

'Do you have a lamp in the house?' Lavedrine asked him.

'I do, sir,' the man replied, though he did not move.

'Would you mind getting it?'

'Not at all,' he said, carefully climbing the steps, which were treacherously slippery on account of the snow that had gathered down there in the stairwell.

'We may be home in time for dinner,' Lavedrine murmured in the interval of loitering, though it was clear that dinner was the furthest thing from his mind. 'If Kant was right, the question may be quickly settled.'

The old man returned, his oil-lamp already lit, and we made our way down into the tomb: Pieter Sweiten going first, Lavedrine following, while I came last.

'No one's been down here since the old Duke died. That's twenty-odd year ago, as I do recall it.'

The chamber was cold, dark, damp, musty. The four walls were dressed unevenly in stones of the same material as the exterior, but these were stained brown and green with mildew and rot. Tangled black weeds, which had flourished in the summer, were lank and odorous. The air was heavy, unclean, lacking in phlogiston, and it caused the lantern flame to gutter and fade.

'Here we are, now,' said Pieter Sweiten, dropping down on one knee, rubbing at the stone with the elbow of his coat, spitting and trying again when his first attempt to clean the stone failed. 'This here's the resting-place of Humbert-Arthur von Mandel, 6th Duke of Albemarle and Svetloye. That were my master. I helped to carry him down. It took six of us.'

'Which stone covers the tomb of the child, Georg-Albert?' Lavedrine cut him off, his hand falling heavily on the shoulder of the kneeling man.

Pieter Sweiten looked up, his face as dark and grey as his beard in the poor light. 'Now, that I don't know, sir. He died afore I came here, that child, I mean. You can probably read them things better than me,' he added, which meant, not surprisingly, that our guide was unable to read for himself.

'Give me the lamp,' I said, and almost snatched it from his hand. Apart from the freezing cold, a numbness had begun to creep into my bones at the thought of what we were about to do. I wanted to get it over with. Moving close to the wall, I held up the lantern, and peered at the next stone.

'*Dorothea-Ann Lundstadt, Duchess & Wife, 1741–1770,*' I read, bringing the lamp nearer to the stone as I struggled to read the rough, old-fashioned lettering. 'And here is the little one. *Georg-Albert von Mandel, Aged 8 months, Stolen in his Sleep. Slain by a Foul Hand, 2nd December, 1765.*'

'Sweiten, can you pull that stone out from the wall?' asked Lavedrine, as if it were the most natural thing to do when entering a funeral crypt.

'I can do it, sir,' the man replied, 'but I ain't so sure I want to.'

'This is a criminal investigation,' I reminded him. 'When we have finished our work, I will write you a note in the cemetery register, in case it is ever needed.'

With a great deal of hesitation, and no lack of grumbling, Sweiten put his shoulder to the work, wedging an iron spike with a flattened end between the stones, then pushing and twisting and grunting until the slab came suddenly free with a sickening wrench of stone on grating stone.

'Are you sure about this, Herr Magistrate?' he said, his eyes holding on to mine in the earthy gloom. 'I would not want to get myself in trouble, now.'

'This gentleman is a French investigator, I am a Prussian magistrate. This child was murdered forty-three years ago and we have found new evidence which may reveal who killed him. And why.'

Pieter Sweiten stared from one to the other. 'Who killed him, sir? They hanged the murderer forty years ago. And knowing won't do *him* no good,' he objected. 'Will looking at his coffin tell you who murdered him?'

'No, it won't,' said Lavedrine. 'But looking *in* his coffin may.'

'Oh, Lord help us!' the old man cried, jumping to his feet, pulling back from the violated tomb, the dark shape of the coffin still inside the hole, the faint odour of organic decay, a life corrupted by worms and damp, creeping out.

'You can wait outside if you wish,' Lavedrine added, putting himself between the man and the open tomb, edging him towards the door, the steps, the fresh air, and the daylight. 'We won't be long.'

Pieter Sweiten seemed to suck air into his lungs as he turned and fled. He slipped and fell on the steps going up, but no cry escaped from his lips. Pain told him that he was living, while the child down in the burial chamber was not.

'Give me a hand,' said Lavedrine, throwing off his cloak.

With some misgivings, I bent forward to help him.

Together we reached into the damp, cold niche, and dragged out the coffin. Then, we laid it flat on the frozen earth. The wood was soft in places. It seemed to give like flesh, to yield and fold itself around my fingers. But Lavedrine was immune to any shuddering sensation of revulsion. He picked up the iron spike, then looked at me.

'Shall I do it?' he asked. 'Or will you? You are the magistrate, after all.'

'This was your idea,' I replied. 'Get on with it'.

He wedged the thin edge between the wooden top and the deeper basin of the small black funeral casket, then suddenly he stopped. 'These are winged nuts, I think. The box may be easier to open than I thought.'

He dropped down on his knees and began to exert pressure. His body seemed to quiver, the veins standing out like snakes on his temples, as he twisted hard against the incrustation and the rust of so many years in the corrosive ground.

He let out a grunt as the first nut gave. The second came away more easily. And the third, with no more than reasonable pressure. 'This one won't budge,' he said, labouring hard to no avail on the fourth and final nut. He reached for the iron spike again, wedged it into the gap, edged the point as close to the nut as he could force it to go, then dropped all his weight on the lever. 'Archimedes has a lot to be thanked for,' he said, as the wood gave with a loud snap, and the lid of the coffin flew up and fell away, exposing the contents of the casket.

'Are ye all right, sirs?' Pieter Sweiten called from above.

'Aye,' answered Lavedrine, muttering to me, 'as right as we'll ever be.'

'*As I am now,*' I whispered, looking into the coffin, remembering something I had read on a gravestone, '*So shall ye be.*'

'But you will take up a lot more room,' Lavedrine warned darkly. Clearly, the situation itself did not amuse him, but something in my hesitation did.

Inside the rotten wooden box, the body of Georg-Albert von Mandel had been reduced, but not to dust, as is commonly supposed. The skeleton had fallen in upon itself, or perhaps it had exploded, then settled back in a disorganised stark blackened shell, the remains of the blood a fine brown powder beneath the tangle of the bones. Rags, which might once have been a white burial gown or a winding-cloth, had faded to grey, stained green and brown, slick with snail and worm trails. The material had split and stretched, then rotted like a stark spidery web.

'The skull,' said Lavedrine, recalling me to my duty. 'That is all that concerns us, Stiffeniis. Don't let your imagination run away with your faculties.'

I made no move to touch those sad remains, watching in petrified silence as the Frenchman stretched his hands inside the coffin, reaching for the head. Two lifeless holes in that tiny mask of death seemed to stare up at us, the jaw hanging loose, held by a sinew on one side only, as if the ghost of the child, disturbed after so many years, were amazed at such temerity, and wished to scream, but could not.

'He's still wearing his bonnet, you see.' Lavedrine caressed the grey crusted cap with the tips of his fingers. 'Is it the same bonnet that Kant mentioned in his report, do you think?'

I tried to speak, but no words came. I thought of my own children, and I was horrified. What would Helena say if she could see me? The fright of it registered like a voltaic shock. Lavedrine had taken the head in his hands like a baby marrow, and he was attempting to separate it from the body. Like the roots of the vegetable, some obstinate muscle, nerve, or sinew refused to yield, and he was obliged to apply more pressure than was strictly decent or respectful. Then, there was a crack. Whatever it was gave up the fight, and he held the head of the baby couched in his hands. Some crawling creature fell from the cavity onto his right hand, and he shook it rapidly, holding the skull in his left hand only. The forehead was fragmented at various points. As if some object with a small dull point had tried to penetrate the skull and failed. A web of fine cracks like tracery had damaged the frontal plate of bone.

The Frenchman pulled off the bonnet and held out the head to me in the palm of his hand. 'This is what Kant would have done,' he said, 'but he was prevented. What do you make of it, Stiffeniis?'

'It is a disturbing sight,' I murmured. 'Horrible . . .'

'You miss my point,' he snapped. Despite the macabre circumstances, he was vibrant with curiosity. His eyebrows arched, his head inclined towards his shoulder, he looked at me with a sort of cunning, irrepressible smile on his lips. 'I am not interested in what you think,' he went on. 'I am interested in what you see.'

For an instant, I slipped back in time. I was standing in Kant's secret laboratory, examining the decapitated head of a man, which had been preserved inside a jar in wine. Kant had also been amused by my timidity in the face of mortality. He, too, had insisted that I should use my eyes, suppress my sentiments, and describe only what I was able to observe.

'The skull is misshapen by Nature,' I said, coughing to clear the emotion from my throat. 'It appears to be much larger on the left side than it is on the right.'

'Precisely,' he said, the similarity with Kant ever greater. 'Science is a peculiar trick; it requires an honest eye, and a blunt soul. And what do you . . . Rather, what would our friend, Aaron Jacob, make of such a serious malformation?'

'I have no idea,' I said. 'He might see the coming of Lilith, or some such nonsense in it.'

'But we do not,' Lavedrine went on. It was as if he had discovered the invisible matter that every natural scientist seeks, but cannot find. 'We stick to facts. The child was not normal. Georg-Albert von Mandel was eight months old, but the bulging of his skull was already evident. The mother certainly knew about it. Why else was she so troubled when the child's bonnet went missing the day before he died? Why insist on covering the baby's head? Even in death. Did she hope that no one would notice, but herself? Kant appears to have spotted something, after all.' There was measureless admiration in his voice. 'Just think what effects such a malformation, with subsequent compression of the brain, would have had on the child's existence? Imbecility, at the least. This child was facing a difficult future, despite the immense fortune of his birth. But someone decided—mercifully, perhaps—to spare him the suffering.'

'Kant guessed,' I countered. 'He did not know for sure. He was not allowed to examine the corpse. The child was not struck down by hatred, he said. Love was the cause. But we will never know the truth. In any case, it is not relevant to the Gottewald massacre. What has this expedition taught us that will solve that mystery? Nothing, I am tempted to . . .'

'This case is as clear as day,' Lavedrine declared.

'Is it?' I questioned. 'All the actors are dead. You may hypothesise all you like, but you will never know for certain.'

'We know enough, I believe,' he said, as he replaced the skull gently inside the coffin and reached for the lid and the bolts. 'Kant dared to hypothesise the unthinkable. Little Georg-Albert was put to sleep for all eternity, and love *was* the cause.'

'A sleep that we have disturbed,' I objected.

'Let's get it done, then. And quickly.'

I helped him, twisting and tightening the bolts on one side of the coffin, while he applied himself to the fastenings on the other flank.

As we walked back down the lane to Svetloye, the snow began to fall again. I had written and signed an official note in the graveyard register, concerning the examination of the corpse, and Pieter Sweiten had been rewarded for his help.

We sat down at a table in the post-house, eating bread and cheese while we waited for the coach, talking over what we had discovered.

'Karlus Wettig was innocent,' Lavedrine concluded. 'Do you remember the question that Kant posed? What reason could there be for the footman to murder the child in his cot? And deny it to the very end? Wetting was *not* the killer. He tried to defend the actions of another, and Kant knew it. Only the murderer knew of the flaw in the child's skull, realising the pain and torment that the growing boy would have to face. That person loved him then, and wished to spare his suffering afterwards.'

Lavedrine shivered as he spoke. His face grew pale. His eyes retreated deeper into their sockets. I cannot say what expression appeared on my own face. I felt as if a venomous asp had nipped me, paralysing all my vital functions.

The coach pulled in shortly afterwards.

There were three other passengers aboard.

Thank God, I thought. There will be no more discussion of what we have seen until we reach Lotingen.

· 37 ·

THE NEXT DAY, I did not see Lavedrine at all. Nor did I hear from him.

At first, I was content to be left in solitude. I had no desire to talk about the matters swirling around like a vortex inside my brain. Kant's carefully worded report to the judge protesting the innocence of Karlus Wettig, the evidence Lavedrine and I had uncovered in Svetloye, which seemed to support his thesis. No matter how I tried, I could find no connection between the cases. Nothing in the murder of Georg-Albert von Mandel promised to clarify the mystery of the annihilation of the Gottewald children.

Nevertheless, Lavedrine's absence alarmed me.

Had Kant made everything clear to him, while I was fumbling in darkness and obscurity? Was the Frenchman trying to solve the case alone?

I had sent a letter to Berlin a week before. The reply was due at any moment. *Kamenetz* was where the answer lay, according to me. When the case was solved, I would tell him. He would be furious, but I would be beyond caring as I carried off the laurels. I visited my office twice that morning, but the place was colder than the funeral crypt in Svetloye. No Knutzen, no letter from Berlin, no news from Lavedrine.

Helena was in a state of distraction equal to mine. How many times did I see her glance out of the window that day, as if searching for someone in the lane? As if she, too, were expecting a visitor.

'Lotte's cousin brought a hen while you were away,' she announced. She was silent for a moment. 'Shall I cook it, Hanno?'

'I am expecting no one, Helena,' I replied flatly. In my own mind, I was certain that Serge Lavedrine was the guest that she was yearning to see.

The previous night I had told her of our business in Königsberg. More or less. I tried to give her the impression that I was hiding nothing that related to the murder, and that she was a party to the investigation. Just as Lavedrine would have done, at least in her fond imagination.

'Professor Kant *was* interested in crime, then!' she exclaimed.

In the four years that had passed since murder drew me back to Immanuel

Kant and Königsberg, the philosopher's name was rarely ever mentioned in our house. When it did come up, I made every effort to set it aside quickly, dismissing the subject in the blandest terms: the anniversary of his death, a commemorative article in one of the papers, a new edition of some work or other. All of these would draw some comment from Helena. And I would respond with an apposite exclamation: 'How long ago it all seems!'

Now, the ghost of Kant had been raised once more, and Lavedrine was the necromancer.

'Did he find what he was looking for?'

I answered offhandedly. 'Nothing that will help us, I'm afraid.'

The next morning, I left the house early and made my way into town.

More uncertainty awaited me at the office.

Knutzen ought to have been at his post, but my door was locked.

Had his pig taken a turn for the worse? If so, his duties to me, and, more generally, to the Prussian state, would certainly take second place. And yet, as I entered my room, I realised that he had been there some time earlier in the morning. The day's despatches and other court papers had been laid out neatly on my desk, along with my pens, and the inkwell had been filled.

I rifled quickly through the documents. Not a word from Berlin.

I sat down behind my desk. Without that letter I had no idea where to turn, what to do next. Lavedrine must have found some way out of the impasse. I would have to brace myself to face defeat. While I was blundering about in the darkness, he had chanced upon the light. Immanuel Kant had set him on the right track . . .

I raised my head.

A belated knock came at the door, which I had forgotten to close.

Wolfgang Beck, the flighty young clerk to the civic notary, Osvald Menckeren, whose offices were situated on the floor above my own, was watching me. The youth was an arrogant dandy, much given to embroidered waistcoats and brightly coloured neckties. He was hanging on to the doorpost, holding up a letter which he waved at me.

'This arrived an hour ago, sir. Knutzen had just gone out.'

'Come in,' I said, holding out my hand for the letter.

'There's no name on it,' the poppycock remarked, advancing across the room, waving the envelope tantalisingly just beyond my reach. 'The man who brought it said that he was looking for you. "To be delivered by hand," he insisted. Took an age to decide whether I could be trusted,' he added with a smirk. 'Obviously, he didn't want to hang about. Too many Frenchmen in Lotingen.' He winked. 'He didn't want to take this letter back. In the end my master signed for it'.

He leant closer, letting me grip the letter with my fingertips.

'Herr Menckeren swore on his honour that it wouldn't fall into French hands. Now, isn't that a turn-up?'

He handed me the note, then snapped to salute. 'It's a pleasure to serve the nation, sir, even in such a small matter. We Prussians have to stick together.'

As the door closed gently on his complicit smile, I opened the envelope.

Request granted. The person that you wish to examine regarding the Gottewald case will present himself at your office within the week.

The missive had been dated the previous Friday. A red seal of smudged wax obscured the signature. I dropped the paper onto my desk and felt a thrill of exultation. All I had to do was wait. As for Lavedrine . . . Now, I *had* to know where he was, and what he was doing. My heart lighter than it had been for a week, I rushed across to the general quarters, hoping that I would find him there, or that someone would tell me where to look for him.

The guard was slack that day. The general quarters building was a bustling hive of activity. Officers and their subordinates raced up and down the corridors, waving sheets of papers in their hands, eloquently cursing. I asked to be received by Lieutenant Mutiez, but he himself came striding down the corridor to meet me a minute later. '*Monsieur le Procureur,*' he greeted me, his eyes wide with surprise 'What are you doing here? You have come too late, sir.'

He did not register my confusion.

'I'm not surprised,' he went on. 'Colonel Lavedrine decided on the spur of the moment. We are in a bit of a muddle, as you can see. The Ministry of Defence has issued orders for joint manoeuvres. You just missed the colonel. Or he missed you. In a word, you missed each other. If you will just be patient, Herr Stiffeniis, I'll see if I can find you some means of transportation. These blasted manoeuvres!' He held up his hands and let out a sigh. 'Of course, I realise the urgency of your investigations. The sooner the matter is cleared up, the better for us all, French and Prussians alike. If I can manage to get you there, Colonel Lavedrine will bring you back with him.' He shook his head and laughed as he led me out of the door. 'That coach will take you,' he said. Still smiling broadly, he added: 'You and Lavedrine do mix with such strange company, *monsieur!*'

Still he did not see the confusion which possessed me. Perhaps he put it down to mortification at missing an appointment with Lavedrine. In any case, he made nothing of my silence. He rapped his baton against the coach door.

'Take His Excellency to join Colonel Lavedrine,' he called to the driver. 'You know where the Gottewald house is, don't you?'

'Who doesn't, sir?' the man grumbled.

Despite the amount of traffic on the road, cannon and other engines of war being moved into position, more troops than I had even seen amassed in Lotingen, infantry and cavalry and teams of sappers and artillerymen, the journey was over almost as soon as it began. I took little note of the busy military world through which we passed. My head was spinning with questions.

Why had Lavedrine gone back to the house?

And what strange company was Mutiez referring to?

The cabriolet lurched to a halt, leather brakes screeching against the iron wheels.

Another carriage stood in the clearing. A soldier was asleep on the box. Lavedrine was there, then. And he had been there for quite some time, it appeared. He was alone in the cottage with his chosen guest.

I leapt to the ground and charged along the leafy tunnel leading to the house.

At the end, I drew up short.

In a calm, ordered, commanding voice, Lavedrine was giving orders.

'Slowly. More slowly!' he exhorted. 'Take your time. No one is hounding us.'

I listened for a reply, but there was none.

I moved to the shelter of a tree and took stock of the place.

The Frenchman was standing in the garden at the corner of the house. He was wrapped up in his leather overcoat, his arms outstretched, watching, or directing, something that I was not able to see. He looked taller, more imperious, than when I had seen him last. His hair was tied up at the nape of his neck with a gleaming white ring, the vertebra of a bull, or something equally bizarre. As he glanced left and right, loose silver curls danced in the stiff breeze. His profile was fixed on someone that I could not see. Someone hiding behind the impenetrable screen of his leather mantle.

I took a step forward, holding my breath.

I craned my neck to see.

A small man was gripping the arm of a tiny woman. Wrapped up in vast cloaks and serpentine scarves, they might have been preparing to set off across the Siberian wastes with only Lavedrine to lead them.

But what was he doing there with his landlord and that man's wife?

·38·

I DID NOT shift from my vantage point behind the tree.

Landlord Böll was dressed in a bulging brown ball of an oversized top-coat. The rough-cut fur was shaggy and bristling. He might have been a captive bear at a country fair. All that was lacking was a dark-skinned urchin to blow a fife and make him dance. His round bulk and diminutive size were not improved by a tall black stove-pipe hat that sat uneasily on his head. It was festooned from the crown down to the brim—long white ribbons pinned up with silvery buttons. His wife was holding tightly on to his arm, as if in danger of collapsing. She might have been going to a summer wedding. Her tightly bodiced gown was sky-blue, unseasonable satin, which shimmered and shifted in the stiff breeze. As she turned this way and that, her dress billowed out and trailed lazily behind her, like a deflating hot-air balloon. Frau Böll's air-filled gown seemed to drag her fitfully in one direction, while her legs struggled to take her the opposite way. Her eyes were clenched and closed, as if she were concentrating. Clearly, she was in a trance.

This state of other-worldliness was not the only strange thing about the scene.

Lavedrine stepped aside, then quickly chased behind them, as the husband and wife swirled and floundered around in a never-ceasing dance that twirled the length and the breadth of the garden. In their interlacing hands they held long silver sticks, like rapiers. The couple appeared to be acting out a furious, silent duel against an invisible enemy.

Suddenly, they froze.

'It's stronger here, sir. Isn't it so, Rumeliah?'

Böll's voice was thin and nasal, oddly feminine. His tone was timorous, as if he feared to say what he ought. He watched his wife like a man feeding a hawk, ready at any moment to pull back his finger before it was bitten off. Without any warning, his eyes rolled up into his skull, showing off the whites. He looked like a man who had been blinded by cataracts. He lurched, began to stumble, then righted himself, as if that stick pointing at the earth were welded to the spot, holding him in place.

'Don't move, sir!' he snapped. Lavedrine had launched himself forward, either to support the man, or to help the lady. 'You'll ruin everything. She's far stronger than me, Herr Lavedrine. Her powers are pure celestial.'

Lavedrine stopped in his tracks, his gaze fixed on the points of the silver sticks that hovered over the surface of the ground. Böll held one in his right hand, his wife gripped the other in her left. Whenever their rods happened to touch, the couple recoiled as if a painful electrical shock had passed between them. The tips twitched and quivered like the antennae of sounding insects, vibrating, wavering, separating, coming together again with the attendant shock. Suddenly, the couple's twin sticks rose in unison into the air, and hovered for a moment, before plunging down to the ground again.

'Notable turbulence,' rasped Böll. 'She passed this way for certain . . .'

A shriek cut him short.

'It's pulling her hand off,' Böll confided, glancing with concern at his tortured wife. 'That woman passed here, she did. And she were . . . yes, sir, she were *alive!*'

The landlord's diminutive companion began to scream and screech again. Her mouth gaped open frantically, saliva dribbling in a white froth from her pale lips.

'What can you tell me?' Lavedrine demanded. 'What's happening?'

'I was asking myself the very same question.'

I might have waved a magic wand and cast a spell on all three of them.

The penetrating eyes of Böll fixed unblinkingly on me as I stepped out from the greenery. His wife was in a fright. For some unimaginable reason, their divining rods seemed to have lost all their gravitational pull. They might have been a pair of truffle-hounds that had lost the scent. As I stepped into the garden, the landlord and his wife took a step backwards.

'What strange goings-on are these?' I asked.

Lavedrine passed his hand through his unruly locks. He did not seem pleased to see me. 'I knew it would not be to your taste, Stiffeniis,' he murmured. 'I'd have told you, if anything had come of it. Otherwise . . . well, what would there be to tell?' He shrugged his shoulders. 'I would have put it down to experience. An experiment, let's say. I requested these people to come and use their powers for me. You've met Herr Böll, the sensitive, and his wife, I believe?'

The lady and gentleman bowed together, perfectly synchronised, their eyes and dowsing sticks fixed modestly upon the ground, like performing illusionists in a theatre. Lavedrine, the master of ceremonies, had introduced them as if they were a famous stage act.

'I was under the impression that they kept a lodging house,' I remarked. I did not look at the pair, my eyes still fixed on Lavedrine. Even so, I perceived that Böll and his wife relaxed and breathed more easily, as if some necessary clarification had been made, which released them from all responsibility.

'Very well. You know what we are doing.' Lavedrine stepped in front of the pair, as if to hide them from my sight. 'Those missing rags and cloths that Helena pointed out must be hidden somewhere near the house, Stiffeniis. They were *not* carried away. There is no reason to believe such a thing.'

'Your folly amazes me,' I said.

His face grew ugly. Lines bit deeply into his brow, his eyes narrowed. 'Your lack of faith shocks me,' he replied. 'Are you suggesting that your wife invented everything?'

I shook my head. 'Helena pointed out what was obvious to any woman,' I replied. 'There could be more than one explanation for the lack of rags. Helena herself provided one. The family may have been preparing to abandon the cottage. A tidy woman would destroy everything she was not intending to carry off. Sybille Gottewald did not know that her children were about to be butchered. Or that she herself . . .'

'Oh, that's excellent, sir!' Lavedrine exclaimed haughtily.

He stumped up the garden, then back again. 'If we find nothing, I will publicly admit that I am wrong. I've been pondering on this experiment for quite some time. If paranormal sensibility can help us resolve the matter, why deprive ourselves of such aid? It may be a valuable resource. And how much more intriguing, if such persons may lead us to the heart of an impenetrable criminal mystery? This was too good an opportunity to miss. Humour me for once, I pray you.'

He might have been a father chiding a wayward child. He had the gift of finding the chinks in my armour. It was true, I was too harsh, too dismissive to trust such unscientific claims. I would rather avoid the risk of being taken for a dupe than fall into such a trap. He saw the breach, and thrust through it.

'Herr Böll, would you be so kind as to answer his question?'

Böll looked at me, then rolled his eyes. I stared into the blanks. A moment later, the pupils slotted back into place. 'It's all a question of flux, Herr Procurator. Electrical flux, I mean to say. Energy passes from Rumeliah to me, and back again, by way of these batons.' He raised his silver wand for me to inspect. 'They are copper sticks wrapped around with finest silver wire. Voltaic coils, they call 'em. Copper is dull, but it picks up the smallest trace of any charge. Then the twists of coiled silver accelerate it up to human sensibility.'

'How interesting!' I said. I had never heard such babble in my life.

'The energy increases as me an' Rumeliah make the triangle with our points. The perfect form. The all-seeing Eye. Eye-sosceles triangle. It's not called that for nothing!'

He smiled to his wife.

'Rumeliah's more the practical sort,' he declared. 'I dabble in the theory. Then again, sir, she's Turkish. Doesn't speak or read a word of German. Just feels. I am something of a dab hand myself, but she's the true phenomenon. If there's a tremor, the slightest tickle, she'll feel it coursing through her rod. She's good at fluids and fluxes, but Material Emanation is not beyond her skills . . .'

'What's that?' I asked.

Böll glanced at Lavedrine, who nodded encouragingly. While he looked at the Frenchman with his left eye, his right remained fixed immovably on me. He might have been gifted with independent vision, as certain species of reptile—lizards from Tierra del Fuego, in particular—are thought to be.

'*Effluvia*, sir. Manifestations. Ectoplasms. Spirits . . . There's words and words for it. I only knew of dowsing myself, sir. But then I met Rumeliah.'

'Water dowsing? Divining springs and sinking wells?' I interupted him. 'My father had a man who used to do it with a willow branch.'

'Indeed, sir?'

My father never trusted that dowser, and cursed when he had to pay. He swore that the cunning fellow knew exactly where to look for water before he started searching with his twitching stick.

'Not just liquids, sir. Objects, too. Buried things, things that careless persons have lost. Things that give off a strong magnetic signal. Objects that were living once . . .'

'Could you be more precise?'

'Blood, Herr Procurator. Fresh is easy. Old blood has a different ring to it. It's all a question of the throbbing energy it gives off. Dry blood, now, *that* has a very distinct sort of quivering feel . . .'

'We retraced this path from the house, Stiffeniis,' Lavedrine added brusquely.

'I was watching,' I told him with a smile.

'The vibrations are strong at this point,' he continued unflustered. 'Perhaps they stopped here. Frau Gottewald and the killers. She was definitely alive as she made her way across the garden.'

'Alive,' Frau Böll echoed the foreign word with a shudder.

I shuddered myself at the outrageousness of the suggestion.

'Let me explain, Herr Procurator,' Böll intervened. 'Our rods vibrated all the way along the path from the house, but here the energy really is *tremendous*. That woman was breathing, sir, palpitating with emotion.'

'You and I have passed this way, Lavedrine,' I commented. 'So have the soldiers. If there is any truth in what they assert, it may be misleading.'

Böll hurried to reassure me with a sickly smile. 'You are correct, sir. But let me ask you this, sir. Were *you* afraid for your life? Were *you* trembling with terror? In any case, my wife insists that the presence was female.'

Helena had passed that way.

The thought sent a cold ripple down my back. What passionate emotions had *she* experienced?

'The quivering is powerful here,' Lavedrine seconded, 'but it is even more pronounced on other parts of the property. We must return towards the house—by the garden path, I think—we have not been that way. We will let Herr Stiffeniis see for himself. Frau Böll, will you take my arm?'

Lavedrine bowed and offered his arm with a show of French gallantry that would have stolen any Prussian woman's heart away. Frau Böll looked at the arm, looked at her husband, then deigned to accept, carrying herself as if the benefits were all on the French pretender's side.

'You will be devastated, *madame*,' Lavedrine confided, 'but this will be the last time, I promise you.'

The woman frowned and pursed her lips in confusion, but she allowed herself to be led. I fell into step behind that ill-assorted couple, with Herr Böll at my side. Which pair made the more ridiculous sight, I did not like to think.

'Poor Rumeliah almost fainted just now,' Böll confided in a whisper. 'The force was so strong, as if it meant to rip the sounding-rods from our hands. There are powerful demons present in the earth hereabouts.'

We followed Frau Böll and Lavedrine along the path and began to approach the front of the house. I knew where we were heading. Lavedrine would open the cottage door, lead us all up the stairs, then set those damned divining-rods twitching at the sight of the blood-stained walls in the room where the massacre had taken place. In front of those mysterious letters inscribed on the wall in blood.

But as we were passing through the kitchen garden, before we reached the door, Rumeliah Böll began to perform without any prompting. She let out a bloodcurdling shriek, and broke away from Lavedrine. She gripped her wand and tugged with both of her hands, as if some unseen person were trying to pull it away from her. She staggered across the garden, trying vainly to dig her heels in the frozen ground. Then, all of a sudden, the rod struck the ground and began to quiver violently like a plucked viola string.

She was applying the pressure, making the baton vibrate, I was convinced of it, but I did not say a word. Let them act out their little charade, I thought, steeling myself to suffer the play without comment. I would save my ironic remarks for Lavedrine, when we were left alone. My triumph, and his come-uppance, were drawing nearer with every moment.

But the woman did not stop screaming, as I half expected.

Her nutbrown face was a mask of pain. Her physical posture was quite unnatural. She seemed to curve further and further backwards, towards a point at which she must inevitably fall, or turn a somersault. Lavedrine sprang forward to assist her, but Böll got there before him.

'Stand back, sir,' he warned, waving Lavedrine away. 'We don't want to lose the contact, do we?'

He bent close to his wife, whispering, 'Easy, my dear. Hold on, hold on. I'll take as much of it as I can, I promise you.'

His rod stretched out, touched the point of his wife's stick, and suddenly the pair of them began to spin and spin, chasing after one another, circling around that spot on the ground, going faster and faster with every turn. Frau Böll screamed like a frightened child on a garden swing, but Böll began to shout as he ran, his eyes popping, twirling, twisting his head as he tried to catch sight of Lavedrine.

'This is it, sir!' he called. 'I think we've found something!'

I stood transfixed. I could find no explanation for what I saw. Their divining rods seemed to turn to liquid silver, entwining and running one into the other, as the Bölls circled and chased each other round and round that fixed point on the ground. The laws of Natural Science were cancelled out. I saw their two sticks blend into one.

'This is the place,' a voice breathed warmly into my ear.

Lavedrine's eyes were afire with excitement, his hair caught wildly in the wind.

'We should have guessed,' he hissed. 'Your wife pointed out that spot. Helena has greater gifts then these two put together.'

We were not in the bedroom. We were not *inside* the house at all. Not even close to the door. He and I were standing on the edge of the kitchen garden, while the Bölls were running round and round the tiny enclosed circle of stones in which someone had planted two oak stems and three smaller sprigs of holly.

Without another word, Lavedrine stepped forward, caught Böll by his collar, and his wife by her arm, and yanked them away from the spot. Their sticks seemed to twirl of their own accord before they fell to the ground. He stood like a rock in the centre, holding them apart, waiting for the fit to ease. When he did let them go, Böll staggered off in one direction, his wife spun away in another. They came to rest like spinning tops when they hit something. Böll bounced off the wall of the house, and sat down in a large rosemary bush. His wife was more fortunate, running into a tree, which she had the good sense to hold on to.

'There, sir. What do you think now?' Böll called weakly to me. 'That's the second time it's happened. I ain't never seen Rumeliah like this before. Never have I known such a compelling force.' He sank back exhausted against the wall. 'Right in the middle of them plants. Ain't that correct, Rumeliah?'

Frau Böll had recovered her senses more quickly, and had swayed across the garden to his side. She knelt on the ground and ran her dark hand gently over his red face.

'And there we will begin,' announced Lavedrine, shrugging off his cloak.

'What are you intending to do?' I asked.

He did not reply, but strode away to the end of the garden. He returned with a spade in his hand.

'That's simple, Stiffeniis. I am going to dig!'

'Helena pointed out those plants the other day,' I said. 'Naturally, you mentioned them to your guests.'

Lavedrine shook his head and rested his weight on the handle of the spade.

'I like to experiment,' he declared. 'But I do not bend the rules. Of course I didn't tell them! If we find anything at all, we'll have Helena to thank for it. We ought to have taken her a good deal more seriously.' He picked up the spade as if it were a broadsword. He might have been the Archangel Michael getting ready to do battle with Satan and his horde of fiends. Such was the look of grim determination on his pale face. 'And now, a little healthy *travail*, as we call it.'

He bent and swept away the dead leaves with his hand, using the point of the spade to lever out the encircling stones. Then he set his foot on the spade and attempted to dig in earnest. I almost laughed as the metal blade of the implement struck in vain and bounced up with a sharp ring off the permafrost. *He was deluding himself.* There was nothing to find. That ground had been frozen solid ever since the beginning of October. There had been a hard frost every night for the past two months. It would take a pick and a couple of hours' work to make a hole. *He would find nothing buried in the garden.* The proposal was preposterous anyway. Why would any person who had just committed a murder bother to dig a hole in the garden? With each unsuccessful jab at the ground, I rejoiced in the futility of it. *He was wrong. Wrong!* The answer lay in Kamenetz. Within a day or two, I would be able to prove it . . .

My exultation froze as hard as the ground.

I heard the dull sound of the spade slicing into soil, rather than a clanging rebound.

I watched in awe as he pushed that blade deep into the ground. His foot pressed hard, but not so very hard. The earth had yielded. It had given in more easily than it ought.

Lavedrine looked up at me.

The signs of disappointment on his face had grown more marked with each failed attempt to breach the earth. Suddenly, Janus changed his mask. His eyes gleamed, his features seemed to stretch with amazement, his mouth wide with shock. With a rapid thrust, he bent his body to the spade again, and heaved. His silver hair shook and sparkled in the cold air, beads of sweat glistened on his brow, as he tossed a quantity of loose soil to one side.

He repeated the gesture twice more. My heart was in my mouth.

Frau Böll, standing close by his side, let out a piercing cry, pointing at something dragging on the point of the spade, half in, half out of the hole.

I took three or four steps towards them. Lavedrine laid the spade flat on the ground, then lifted it quickly again at the bottom of the shaft, the handle resting on the ground, the blade rising into the air.

'In heaven's name,' he murmured.

A piece of meat, I thought—black, old, rotten, the buried carcass of a dog or cat.

The tense expression on Lavedrine's face warned me to be careful. He brought his nose close to the spade, and breathed in deeply. His eyes flashed wide open, and I knew that I had lost. Helena had guessed. The Bölls had pointed it out. But *he* had found it.

He raised his hand and touched the heavy object with reverence.

'They are here,' he murmured.

There was no note of triumph in the declaration.

Instead, I thought I heard a fearful tremor.

I fell down on my knees—he sank down beside me—and together we began to dig with our hands, pulling out the heavy pieces of frozen cloth, one after the other, laying them one on top of the other beside the hole in the ground. Each piece was the same dull red-brown tint. The colour of blood.

'Try to lift, rather than pull,' he warned.

Indeed, each piece—there were more than a dozen—had been carefully folded into a neat square before it had been put into the ground, as if they had been put there by some tidy maid.

'A most peculiar domesticity, Stiffeniis,' he murmured as the last of the

Gottewald rags was placed on top of the pile. They are here. Just as Helena suspected.'

Lavedrine ran his hand gently over the topmost cloth, almost as if he could not believe in the physical nature of the find, as if his fingers must tell him what his eyes would otherwise have doubted, as if they might have been conjured up by Böll and his wife. Then, he stretched down into the hole.

'There's something more,' he grunted.

He held up a piece of paper which had been buried at the very bottom of the pit. He handed it to me.

'Read it out, would you mind?' he asked.

I unfolded the paper, which was soiled, barely legible in places, where blood and damp had fouled the ink. The calligraphy was childlike. One line rose up, the next sank down, as if it had been written by someone in a hurry, the paper resting on the writer's knee for want of any better surface.

My darling Sylvie
You have to know though I would rather not

'I cannot make it out,' I said, holding the letter close to my eyes. 'The paper is badly stained, the ink has run.'

'Do your best,' Lavedrine replied quickly. 'We have this, and nothing else.'

'I am Job's brother,' I went on carefully.

Why me. O Lord? Why me? That's what I thought when ...He told me. HE! I followed him ...e was my ...anything for him. Now, I know the truth. God help me!

That's my torment. Sylvie. The Gubermanns. That name is my damnation...

'Gubermann?' Lavedrine interjected. 'That sounds like a Jewish name.'

I remembered what I had read regarding two Jews who had been killed in Korbern, when Gottewald led a night patrol on the village. Might these Gubermanns be the same people? No name had been mentioned in that report. I hesitated, wondering whether to tell Lavedrine. It would mean breaking my word to Dittersdorf. More to the point, I did not know if there was any connection between the murdered Jews, and the name Gubermann. Nor could I guess what that name might have meant to Bruno Gottewald.

'The tests were always hard,' I read on quickly.

You know ████ I never shirked, my love, I have always done my duty. That night ████████ It has cost me my soul. The monster, Moloch, took me to the abyss, made me ████ I am going mad my love! What will ████████ next time?

'What did he have in mind?' Lavedrine murmured.
I did not answer. The line that followed seemed to say it all.

'I am a soldier,' I continued reading.

I'll have no choice. It must be done! If not ████ The future looks as black ████ Storm clouds are gathering. I hear that cry in the night, voices chanting, echoing from ████ I hope that you'll never hear that dreadful sound! They scare the ████ I ████ warned! ████ before the long night falls, and days of atonement follow on.
My aching heart is ever
Your husband Bruno   6/10

Helena had told me of the terror of the woman she had met. That letter was an expression of the selfsame fear. The husband had passed it on to his wife like a disease. But fear of what? Of whom?
'Two days later, Gottewald was dead,' I whispered.
'A week later, they were dead as well.' I felt the warmth of Lavedrine's breath upon my cheek. 'Kant suggested the unthinkable. This letter provides the evidence. Now we know who killed the children,' he murmured close to my ear.
'We still do not know why,' I reminded him.

'She killed the infants, then buried the rags and the letter,' Lavedrine replied. 'Somehow, she ended up in Gummerstett's warehouse. And there she died as the result of an accident, or by her own hand. That is all we need to know.'

He shrugged his shoulders, as I folded up Gottewald's letter.

I glanced down at the pile of rags. They were so stained with dirt, it hardly looked like blood at all. 'When he speaks of storm clouds gathering, what does he mean?' I asked. 'And *which* abyss did Moloch lead him to? The long night, days of atonement . . .'

'The man was mad,' Lavedrine replied. 'And he drove her to the same folly. The ghosts that had terrorised him were transported to Lotingen by means of this letter. The evidence is overwhelming. Helena set us on the track. Kant helped us along it. Now, the Bölls have brought *me* successfully to the conclusion.'

He stared at me and a hollow smile scarred his lips.

'You are ignoring Kamenetz,' I objected.

He turned on me sharply. 'Something *did* come from Kamenetz,' he answered, 'but it was not a killer. It was this!' He tore Gottewald's letter from my hands. His eyes were as bright and challenging as they had been that night at Dittersdorf's feast. 'A letter. Nothing more . . .'

'That letter caused a mother to murder her own children!' I objected. 'We still don't know why she did it.'

'That is for you to find out,' he snapped back. 'You've always been obsessed with Kamenetz as the cause of everything. Just as this house has fascinated me.'

He turned and began to round up the Bölls, preparing to leave.

'I intend to write my report this evening. If you come by Mutiez's office tomorrow morning, you can add your own remarks. I will explain what happened—who the murderer was, and how the thing was done. That is the easiest part, I admit. The hardest part I'll leave to you. You may say what you will about *why* it might have happened.'

'What about this evidence?' I said, pointing to the hole and the rags.

'The soldiers will collect them together and send them back to town,' he said, folding up the letter, putting it away in his pocket. 'Do you wish to ride back with us?'

'I am going to stay here for a while,' I replied stubbornly, pointing at the pile of bloodstained rags. 'Don't concern yourself, I'll take care of those. I mean to bury them again. Sybille Gottewald marked this spot as some sort of family shrine, if Helena is correct. I think we can allow her that, don't you?'

Lavedrine was silent. As if he meant to raise some objection. Then, he shrugged his shoulders. 'You may be right,' he said. 'Beneath the earth is where they belong.'

I watched them go.

Then, I buried those blood-soaked towels exactly where we had found them.

The day was drawing on by the time I replaced the saplings and the holly shrubs, pressing down the circle of stones with my heel. I had no transport to take me back to Lotingen. Mutiez had ordered my driver to return to town at once. But I did not care. I set off along the road in the hope of tiring myself out.

I walked in search of peace, but I did not find a trace of it.

· 39 ·

LAVEDRINE HAD WON.

At every stage of the investigation, he had turned instinctively in the right direction, while I had stubbornly opposed him. If I laid an obstacle in his way, he struggled all the more to prove me wrong. I had been secretive, unhelpful, and all in defence of a hypothesis that I was unable to demonstrate.

As I returned alone on foot to Lotingen, as the daylight began to fade, one question pounded in my head like the remorseless piston of a steam engine.

Was there no connection between the father's death in Kamenetz and the massacre of his children in Lotingen?

I could find no answer as I trudged along the empty road.

Had I not seen Gottewald's death certificate, I might have believed that he had come to wipe his family off the face of the earth. Full of strange forebodings, that letter had been written by a man who feared for his life. Had he still been living, I might have read it as the feverish announcement of an incomprehensible deed.

But Gottewald had died before the children.

And Lavedrine had found the evidence that the mother had killed them.

What was I to ask Doctor Korna now?

A cold wind blew strongly in my face as I entered town by the southern gate, and it began to snow. Occasional dancing flakes settled on my mouth and eyelashes. I could be home within ten minutes. The fire would be burning brightly in the kitchen. Lotte would be preparing dinner. Helena might be darning by the hearth, telling stories to the children as she plied her needle. They would all be waiting for me.

But I had no heart for home.

I turned towards my office, cursing the permission I had received that morning from Berlin. The authorities wished to see the murder solved. The Minister of Justice had given me a free hand to summon Doctor Korna from Kamenetz. How I wished that the reply had been negative! If only the Minister had denied my request!

I climbed the stairs with lead in my heart.

Knutzen started nervously as the door creaked open. He was alone, a broom in his hand.

'Herr Procurator, I did not expect you so late.'

'Did any stranger come today?'

Knutzen shook his head. 'The clerk from general quarters brought some sentences to be countersigned, sir. They are waiting on your desk. A signature, he said, no more. Five minutes' work, I'd say.'

Relief washed over me. It was after six o'clock. Doctor Korna would not be coming. We would see no more post-coaches in Lotingen that night. Still, I had no wish to sit at my desk, pick up a quill, endorse sentences for minor infractions against the French. I was in no mood for it. I was in no mood for anything. I was stinging from the drubbing Lavedrine had given me.

'Don't you have a pig to nurse?' I asked him.

'Oh no, sir,' Knutzen smiled contentedly. 'They'll have slit her throat by now. They took her off my hands yesterday.'

In my mind's eye, I saw that pig, basted with honey, scented with chives, an apple in its gaping mouth, lying in state on some French dining table. I could almost smell the aroma. Among the diners, Lavedrine, perhaps, boasting of his cleverness, laughing at the blind stupidity of the dull Prussian magistrate they had forced him to work with.

'It will soon be curfew, Knutzen,' I advised him. 'Go home while you can.'

Shortly after, I was on the point of leaving myself. My hand raised to pull open the door, when it was pushed violently inward and a large man bundled up in black—a huge cloak, large hat, a scarf wrapped about his face—came rushing in. He surged past, barging me aside with his shoulder. He strode across the room as if he were the only creature left on earth, threw off his cloak and hat, and sat himself down behind my desk.

'My men are answerable to me!' he thundered like a cannon. 'Before you speak to my surgeon, you must tell me what you want with him. I'll instruct him in his answers. Every soul in Kamenetz belongs to *me!*'

My legs gave way, and I collapsed in the chair reserved for visitors.

It was worse than a nightmare. I had sent for the doctor, his superior had come. And I had questions for neither of them. The case was closed, Lavedrine had seen to that.

Yet, there was General Juri Katowice, sitting in my chair.

'Well, Magistrate? What have you to say?'

Blood pounded painfully at my temples.

'You summoned my surgeon,' he accused again, his voice hoarse with anger. 'What did you want with him?' he insisted,

'I wrote to Berlin . . .' I stuttered and stopped.

He closed one eye, sighted at me as if he held a pistol in his fist.

'You won't find anyone to listen,' he roared. 'They know me there. They won't admit it, but they know me. They won't stop *me*. They do not dare. The king must bend to Bonaparte, but that doesn't mean he likes being shafted.' He laughed at this barrack-room metaphor. 'He will need an army, and I'll be ready for him. Our time will come. Tomorrow, or the next day, true Prussians will stand up, and they will be counted!'

He nodded to himself, as if his rhetoric pleased him. 'Harm me, or mine, and I will murder you, and yours, Herr Stiffeniis. I speak the truth. You've been to Kamenetz. You know what we are doing there. You kept your mouth shut then, I'll give you that. In future you will keep it shut. Do I speak plain enough?'

He sat back, waiting for me to answer.

'You do, Herr General.'

He rested his head against the stump of his hand, as if to remind me what he had lost in the name of Prussia. 'Now, what did you want with Korna?' He opened his arms wide in an extravagant theatrical gesture. 'I am here in his place *en route* to Berlin. Go on. Don't be shy. Ask *me*.'

He seemed to take pleasure in my perplexity.

'I want to know about Gottewald,' I said at last.

'Gottewald again,' he muttered angrily. The name might have been a curse. 'Haven't you found the man who killed his brats yet?'

'You did not help when I was in Kamenetz. You avoided me, Herr General,' I said sullenly. Then, I made a decision. After all, what did I have left to lose? 'Since you have come, sir, tell me why you abandoned Bruno Gottewald. He was your favourite once.'

Katowice stared at me, and a smile played upon his lips.

'Have you ever been deceived, Herr Procurator? Have you ever suspected that your wife was attracted to another man?'

The intimacy of his question disturbed me. Lavedrine loomed large in my thinking. Should I tell the truth, and spite myself, or lie to spite the general?

'I have suffered disappointment,' I replied at last.

'There,' Katowice snapped, sitting forward, resting his arms upon my desk as if he owned it. 'Then you know what I am talking about.'

I was lost by this unexpected appeal to shared experience.

'You talk in riddles, sir. What do I know?'

He was silent for some moments. 'Soldiers are the scum of the earth. They protest their wrongs from dawn till dusk. They fail to see the road ahead of them. They are blind to the greater truth, blind to their sworn duty. But in the end, they obey.'

A light dawned.

'And Gottewald did not?' I quizzed him. 'Are you suggesting that he was not what he seemed?'

'What he seemed?' he mimicked. 'What do you know? I raised that boy as my right arm!' He held up the mutilated stump, and waved it in my face. 'Bruno was the perfect officer. He followed my orders to the letter. He was merciless. Do you understand me? As deadly cruel as a soldier must be. As so few really are. He was born without a heart. If Prussia had a thousand like him, I used to think, we'd conquer the world. But there was betrayal in him . . .'

I tried to absorb the enormity of what I had just been told.

'Did he dare to betray you, sir?' I asked flatly.

He laughed, a throaty grumble of a laugh. 'You won't catch me so easily,' he growled.

'Did he seduce your soldiers, then? Did he try to steal their love away?'

'No man gets the best of Juri Katowice!' he barked in reply.

'Gottewald did,' I said. 'Though he thought of you as a god . . .'

He laughed so hard that he began to cough. 'God? Which god are you talking about? Not mine, or yours. The man was Jewish. Jewish! A man who will serve two gods, will serve two masters. I should have realised. He'll turn to the one who promises the most.'

My heart began to race.

'Jewish?' I echoed in astonishment. 'Gottewald was born a Jew?'

'A circumcised Jew,' he replied with fierce satisfaction. 'I knew it from the start. And I didn't give a damn. He was a natural. Born to be a soldier. At the age of ten he was fierce, violent, trusted no one. I let him sleep on the rug before my fire. I treated him like a son. No man is born a general, Stiffeniis. They are nurtured. I coached Bruno for high office. He knew how a general thinks, how a general acts, the hundred strategies passing through his mind in the instant that he makes a decision. Gottewald could have been my heir. Instead, he deceived me.'

Go on, go on, I encouraged silently.

'The French are famed as *tombeurs des femmes.* Women fall to them like flies to honey,' he leered. 'They used to promise pleasure. Now, they promise freedom. Their revolution has done more than kill a king. Republics are made of men who are equal. The colour of their skin is nothing. The colour of their souls means less where religion counts for nothing. The Jews are free men in France. Did you know that? Emancipation, they call it! A Jew may sit in the Assembly. A Jew may wear a judge's toga. A Jew may call himself a Jew, yet aspire to be a general,' he ranted.

'Is that what Gottewald wanted?'

'He wanted everything. He wanted to be Prussian. He wanted a career in the army. He wanted to raise his litter of Jewlets, and call himself by his real name.'

I sat as rigid as a rock.

'Is Gottewald not his true name, then?'

Katowice smiled as if some private joke had tickled his fancy.

'I gave it to him,' he confided. 'With his Hebrew name, he could never be an officer. *Unsuitable*, I wrote on his discharge. But one week later, as I had instructed him to do, he shaved off his curls and came back again, calling himself Bruno Gottewald. A boy is a boy in the Prussian army. No officer looks at them twice. They are cannon fodder. They have no face, no name. But Bruno was special. I kept him away from the others, I gave him a room to himself. No one would know the truth. No one would see the Jewish slash of his sex. No man would ever dare to question him. His violence was extraordinary. For twenty-odd years he followed me, and I promoted him. Then France invaded Prussia. Before Jena there was no other world for him: the army, his commander. But the national defeat destroyed all that. And Tilsit made it worse. He was a changed man. It grew like a worm in his guts. It poisoned his brain. If Napoleon's laws took root in Prussia, he could proclaim his religion, and still be what he was. God in Heaven, he was my second-in-command!'

And so you had him murdered.

Katowice's face contorted in a spasm of disgust. The flickering flame of the oil lamp made him monstrous to behold. A pitiless bigot, the last representative of a dying breed. His white hair, his wrinkles, his severed hand provoked no sympathy. He seemed to me to be hideously old, without dignity or grace.

'The deer hunt,' I prompted. 'Why would an officer submit himself to such an exercise? A test for raw recruits . . .'

He seemed to swell with evil pride.

'A simple matter, Magistrate,' he sneered. 'I ordered it. Gottewald was the prey. I sent four able men to catch him. They were younger, fitter. Bruno Gottewald was no longer the beast he used to be. He could not escape them. They led him where they wanted him to go.'

My blood froze at the calculating coldness of it. They had sent him running off the cliff, falling to his death. My silence seemed to unbutton General Katowice.

'His letters were intercepted,' Katowice clarified. 'I made sure that word got out. Gottewald had been trafficking with France. He was a Jew. I let it be known that he had lost my trust, and had to be eliminated.'

Was this the link between Kamenetz and the massacre in Lotingen? Had the death of her husband guided Frau Gottewald's hand?

'Did you menace his family, Herr General? Did Gottewald believe that you would punish them because he was a traitor?'

He looked up and laughed humourlessly. 'I did not know that he was married until you came to Kamenetz. He never told me about them. Of course, I understand what lies behind your question, Magistrate. The answer is *no*. I did not kill his children. Nor did I have them killed.'

Had I not been present at the Gottewald cottage that afternoon, had I not read the letter which Sybille Gottewald had buried in the garden, I would not have believed him. But I had no option.

'Very well,' I said, pressing on, determined to settle all the unresolved questions that the investigation had raised. 'Two Jews were murdered years ago in Korbern. Is there any connection between them and Bruno Gottewald?'

General Katowice did not reply. He let out a spluttering sigh, as if that question did not merit an answer.

'Does the name Gubermann mean anything to you? That name . . .'

He didn't let me finish. 'Why ask me about Jews? The only one who ever crossed my path was Gottewald.'

He shrugged, a malignant smile on his lips.

'When you promoted him in Marienburg fortress,' I continued, 'you specifically mentioned that he had executed an order *in every single detail*. What was that order, Herr General?'

He leaned forward and fixed me with his gaze. Like a wizened tomcat, he stared me out, as if to demonstrate that he was stronger, more resilient than I would ever be. I am the master here, he seemed to say. Decades of unquestioning command, of instant obedience to his every whim, glared out at me. Any man who disobeys me dies. That was his message. Play with me, and you will suffer. It was the powerful bluff of an old man. How many officers had bent beneath that stern, unwavering front? Had I been able to look into my father's eyes, I would have seen the same implacable malice.

'It was a test,' he replied calmly. 'I wished to see how far he would go. How deeply rooted was his ambition, how absolute his obedience, how pure and remorseless his cruelty. Before I sent him out to die, before I set the hounds on him, I revealed to him how diabolical a creature he had become. Gottewald's hell began on earth.'

He stared at me in silence for some moments.

'He betrayed me. He betrayed Kamenetz. He betrayed every single thing that he had become.'

The air whistled out of my lungs. I felt weak and faint. I tried to speak, but words would not come.

'I saw a handbill in a tavern over the way,' he went on, heedlessly. 'It accused the Jews of the Gottewald murder.' He laughed, and shook his head. 'Now, wouldn't that be ironical? The Jews killing those children, thinking they were Christians, drinking Jewish blood in error?'

He stood up with some effort, using his mutilated wrist to help himself.

I watched, but I made no effort to assist him.

'This interview is at an end,' he said, coming around the desk. He stopped before me, towering over me, his right arm raised, as if to strike. 'Now, you know everything. Take my advice. Forget Kamenetz. Forget me. Forget Bruno Gottewald.'

He walked past me, stiff and mechanical in his movements, stopping only to retrieve his scarf, hat, and cloak. As he dressed himself to face the cold, he turned and looked back at me.

'Doctor Korna couldn't come,' he said. 'My surgeon wanted to escape. And he did attempt it, soon after you left us. But he didn't get very far. There is no safe refuge for a traitor in *my* world.'

'You killed him, too,' I murmured.

He laughed again, but shook his head.

'How little you understand of Prussia!' he sneered. 'The peasants hate us. We steal their children, and try to turn them into soldiers. A pitchfork is as lethal as a sword, Herr Procurator. They knew who he was. They got to him before we did. They silenced him for me. He was found near the fort, half buried in the snow. Dead, of course.'

He stared at me for some moments.

'Kamenetz keeps its secrets, Magistrate,' he hissed. 'The French know nothing, they leave us well alone. Thanks to the interest of true Prussians, our work goes on. But you will hear of us soon, I think. The minute Bonaparte makes the mistake of trying to invade Russia, we will tear his rear end to shreds. Remember that!'

He did not close the door.

I heard the thunder of his boots upon the stairs as he marched off into the night.

I cannot say how long I sat staring at the empty chair on the far side of my desk.

General Katowice had gone, but his malign spirit lingered on, clogging the air.

At last, I rose and closed the door. The room seemed immense and empty, but a burst of new determination took hold of me. I returned to my desk, sat down in my own chair, took paper from my drawer, primed my quill with ink, and began to write the section of the report that Lavedrine had left to me.

To His Excellency, Gottfried von Schultze, Magistrate General, Berlin

Duplicate copy to:
His Excellency, Field Marshal Lannes, French Commander in the canton of Königsberg

Sir,
   As the Prussian magistrate entrusted with the investigation of the massacre of three children in Lotingen, I hereby present my conclusions.
   By way of preamble, it should be stated clearly that I was obliged to look far beyond the immediate family circle in Lotingen for the true cause and motive behind the killing. The father of the murdered children, Bruno Gottewald, was born a Jew . . .

I wrote with rapidity and conviction.

Knutzen had found the time to sharpen my pens, and replenish the ink. I took it as a good omen. The words came with surprising ease. It would take an hour to finish. Then I would make a copy, which I would leave at the general quarters. The Procurator's office in Lotingen was functioning with an efficiency it had not displayed since the dark night on which Lieutenant Mutiez came knocking on my door, and Serge Lavedrine walked into my life. As I signed my name, and set my seal in red wax on the original and the faithful copy, I felt a grim satisfaction.

The case was closed.

At last, I could, I *must*, go home.

I knew that the curfew would slow me down. I would be obliged to stop and show my papers to every Frenchman that I met. But I would be there soon. I prayed that Helena was in the front room, sitting comfortably before the fire, busily engaged in pleasant conversation with Lotte. The children would be safe and sound upstairs, sleeping sweetly in their cots. Lotte's bread would be rising fast, spreading its warm perfume through the house. I wanted to find the house in a perfect state of order and tranquillity. I yearned for a warm hearth and a bright welcome when I arrived.

The peace would soon be shattered.

I knew what I would have to do the instant I took off my cloak, and sat down beside Helena in front of the fire. I would have to tell her what had been discovered that day. The blood-soaked rags in the cottage garden. The bloodstained letter. The death of Gottewald in Kamenetz. Then, I must tell her what his wife had done to their children.

Every word would bring horror smashing down upon our heads.

But Helena would feel it the most.

·40·

THE DOORBELL TINKLED once.

Someone had pulled on the rope, then decided against it.

Helena grasped at my arm, but I was already on my feet. I threw back the curtains. The sky was a translucent creamy yellow laced with wisps of purple cloud. Frosted patterns like embroidered lace had traced themselves on the window-glass. A clinging ground-fog smothered every plant and bush in the rear garden, the trees solid black against the pale light.

'Who can it be?' Helena whispered, half out of bed.

I strained my ears, but heard no sound of movement on the loose gravel path at the front of the house, nothing but the predawn warbling and chattering of birds in the black pit of the garden.

'Stay here,' I hissed, reaching for my pistol.

I had learnt my lesson the night that Mutiez came to carry me off.

I set off quickly down the stairs. In the hall, the doorbell glistened in the dark like a grenade that might explode at any instant. Edging closer, I rested my ear against the cold oak.

A low, raucous gurgle sounded.

I drew back the bolt, removed the bar, and threw open the door, expecting to find a wounded Prussian fugitive on the mat.

Instead, I found a wooden cage.

Bright eyes stared out at me. An imprisoned cat. A magnificent specimen with a long silvery coat, and pointed ears. More like a lynx than a mouser. As we gazed into each other's eyes, that low moan became a fearsome howl, and the cat showed his teeth.

'I did not mean to wake you, Stiffeniis.'

Lavedrine was sitting on the rustic bench in the garden, wrapped up in a military cloak. He was wearing trousers with a regimental stripe and leather riding boots. His silver curls were covered by a forage-cap with flaps that hid his ears.

'I was just about to write you a note,' he added.

'A note?' I asked, uncertainly.

He raised his hand in a nonchalant wave. 'Do not concern yourself, Herr Procurator! There've been no more massacres in Lotingen. I was about to ring the bell, then reproached myself for having contemplated it. I'll wait a while, I thought. But the Prussian cold is too penetrating even for Lionel's fine fur coat. Will you invite us in for a second?'

I stepped aside without speaking, trying to comprehend what had brought him to my door at such an hour, and in such unexpected company.

The Frenchman pulled off his hat, and shook out his hair as I led him into the hall. He dripped humidity all over the place in much the same way that his strange long-haired friend in the cage might have done. They were of the same colour, more or less, the luxuriant fur of the cat, the silvery curls of the master.

'You won't judge me bold if I ask for a drop of something strong to drink. Another five minutes out there, you'd have found two rigid corpses on your doorstep.' His smile was open, winning, his voice low. His glance darted nervously to the door, as if in search of something. Or someone.

'All sleeping, I suppose?'

'They were asleep,' I corrected him. 'Come into the kitchen. I can offer you cider, or *aqua vitae*.'

'Cider, please.'

While I threw a log on the ashes, and lit the lamp hanging above the table with a spill, he sat himself down at the table, raised the wooden cage, and placed it on his knees. 'I have spoken to you of Lionel, I think? Do you mind if I set him free?'

What could I say? Even in my own house, Lavedrine seemed to be the master of the situation. He set the cage down on the floor, pulled out the peg, and raised the door. A head appeared, then a body followed circumspectly. Like a man long imprisoned in a dungeon, the cat emerged from the confines of the cell, sniffing at the air, wary of the dangers of the place and its inhabitants.

I poured two glasses of cider. My eyes were on the door, my ear on the ceiling above my head. Had Helena gone back to bed? Had she heard the Frenchman's voice? Was that the reason she had not come down?

'Take heart, Stiffeniis! I see the question hanging from your lips. What is this damned Frenchman doing at my door at dawn? And what is he doing in the company of a cat? I received my marching orders last night,' he announced with a smile. 'A coach will call for me here as soon as they have finished loading it. Military accoutrements only, I'm afraid. The rest I shall have to jettison,' he said, offering his fingers to the cat, which purred loudly, and licked his hand as if it were a bit of beef. 'I've been ordered East. I hope to make a decent start, and sleep tonight in a comfortable inn somewhere along the way. I mean to take no risks, seeing as I will not be travelling alone.'

I thought he was referring to his cat.

I offered the flagon, and refilled his glass. I drank some more, relieved at the news. The cat made its way about the room, looking curiously into every corner, its bushy silver tail raised like the sail of a fishing boat that was being driven forward by a gentle wind.

'He is a most handsome creature,' I offered, holding out my hand as the animal came close, expecting to be rebuffed. But the cat deigned to stop for a moment and sniff at my fingers, licking them with a rough, dry tongue, before proceeding with its minute inspection of the kitchen. 'Where are you bound?'

'In the same direction I was heading when we met at Dittersdorf's feast,' he replied. 'I said goodbye to you and your wife that night, you may re-member, never dreaming that events would throw us into such close and continuous proximity. I must attend upon the army, which is gathering close to the Russian border. Our engagement in the coming Spring will probably be with the Czar. Unless the emperor changes his mind, as he often does. I will have much to occupy me in Bialystok, no doubt.'

I drained my cider in a single draught. The light-headed inebriation that I felt was not caused by the acidic warmth of the alcohol alone.

'I read the papers you left last night with Mutiez,' he went on, his eyes never shifting from his beloved cat, which had completed its inspection of the room, and settled itself comfortably on the kitchen mat close to the warmth of the fireplace. 'What a tale of terror and persecution! I hope the new emancipation law will save others in the future. I countersigned your report, of course.'

'I am pleased,' I said. 'But Dittersdorf will *not* be.'

'I admire your honesty and courage,' he added quietly. 'A French contin-gent will set out for Kamenetz within the week. Given the importance of the expedition, a detachment of your Prussian forces has been requested to assist our men. Dittersdorf will have no choice but to authorise the attack. You won't be eating roast pork at his table for quite some time, I fear.' He shrugged carelessly. 'All sensible Prussians will be glad to rid themselves of such a danger. Kamenetz is a sword of Damocles hanging over their heads. If Katowice rebelled, and failed, the consequences for Prussia . . . Well, you know what they would be.'

I recalled the ritual solemnity with which the officers in Kamenetz saluted the Grunfelde Standard, the fierceness of Rochus Kelding, his bayo-net pointing at my throat, the raging nationalism of General Katowice, his belief in the ultimate survival of Prussia's finest.

'They will fight,' I said, my heart battering painfully in my chest.

'Not while their general is away,' he countered. 'He will be detained in Berlin. There could be no better moment to attack.'

I closed my eyes and said a silent *Amen*. Whatever happened in Kamenetz, I would have to live with the consequences.

'I gave orders to Mutiez to bury Frau Gottewald. He will tell you where, in case you decide to make some better arrangement.' He drained his glass, and set it down on the table.

'It is a shame,' he continued, 'that your attempt to reconstruct her appearance yielded nothing. I would have liked to include a portrait in the paper I intend to publish in Paris. It will make good reading. No names, of course, but Helena will be given the credit she deserves, together with the remarkable Frau Böll. I'll post you a copy. In the future, I mean to study the utility of physiognomy in criminal identification. In all this time I have never ceased to wonder what she looked like.' He shrugged. 'Frau Gottewald, I mean.'

I thought he was going to demand to see the drawing that I had begun with Aaron Jacob and completed to Helena's specifications, but he skipped nervously from subject to subject, his eyes never far from the door.

'I have also given orders for the soldiers to keep a closer watch on your house,' he went on. 'Until Kamenetz has been secured, you may be targeted.'

The cat stood up suddenly, and began to stretch, raising himself up on the points of his paws, arching his back, yawning hugely. Then, he settled down again and began to clean his coat with his tongue.

Lavedrine laughed quietly. 'Our chatter does not interest Lionel. A warm hearth, a rug, a hand to feed and stroke him, and all his needs are met. The Stoics learnt a lot from cats, don't you agree?'

The cat came across at the sound of his name and began to rub his shoulder gently against the Frenchman's leg, purring as loudly as a bumblebee. Lavedrine stroked the animal for quite some time without saying a word.

'One thing torments me,' he murmured.

'What's that?'

'I hope it torments you as well,' he reproached me. 'The Gottewalds— each one buried in a place where he or she does not belong. Isn't that, somehow, wrong?'

His eyes followed the cat, as it returned to the fireplace, and slowly sank down on the rug again. 'You have acted correctly throughout this affair, and I commend you for it. I begin to see what Professor Kant saw in you. You do your duty without any compromise, disregarding all dangers. I realise that it has not been easy. After all, Prussia is your country, your hands were severely tied. I may sometimes have been over-hasty, and I apologise for not always taking you into my confidence. I gave less credit to your intuitions than was fair.'

I had been thinking similar thoughts as I walked home from the cottage the previous evening. I had hampered him at every twist and turn, refusing to see what was obvious to him.

He ran his hand nervously through his hair. 'I was wondering,' he said. 'Might I say a word to Helena? There is something that I wish to ask her. If you don't mind, of course.'

'What do you wish to ask me?'

We turned as one towards the kitchen door. Lavedrine shot up from his chair as if a trumpet had sounded the charge. He held the empty cider glass in his hand, looking more sheepish than I had ever seen him.

Helena stepped into the light. She had thrown a heavy shawl of red wool over her nightdress, and was wearing the leather riding boots that I kept in the bedroom. They were large and heavy on me. On her they looked like wrinkled tree trunks; I marvelled that she had managed to come down the stairs without giving herself away. Her hair was a tangle of unruly curls which fell about her cheeks, and cascaded to her shoulders.

'You glow like a sunflower, Helena!' he exclaimed, his eyes bewitched.

He made no attempt to hide his admiration.

'I don't believe I've seen one of those,' she observed, a trace of colour in her cheeks. 'In Prussia, there aren't any sunflowers.'

'In that case, you are the first, and the finest,' he parried gallantly.

The scene was more like a farce at the theatre than real life. A Frenchman was in my house, gazing fervently at my wife, paying her extravagant compliments, while I, the husband, stood speechless, looking helplessly on. Helena, dressed up in a gigantic pair of boots, smiled back at the interloper.

'I really came to speak to you,' he said again.

He turned to me, then looked away, but not in Helena's direction. His glance darted here and there around the kitchen. 'Where in heaven's name is he?' he asked.

Helena skipped three paces to her right, as if those boots were ballet pumps. She bent beneath a chair, and came up holding a bundle of fur. 'This, I take it, is Lionel,' she said, hugging the cat to her breast.

'I found him here in Lotingen,' Lavedrine said. 'I must always have a cat about me, and I always call him Lionel. In memory of the first kitten that I ever had. Cats do not like travelling, and I must journey far and wide. I did not know who else to ask. Helena, might you take care of him for me?'

My wife cuddled the cat. Lionel responded by licking the tip of her nose.

'The children will be delighted,' she said. Suddenly, she frowned. 'There are mice in my attic. Is he a good hunter?'

Lavedrine laid one hand over his heart, and raised the other.

'The best,' he declared. 'I solemnly swear in the presence of this magistrate.'

'I hereby witness this solemn oath,' I replied in mock seriousness.

A heavy weight seemed to fall away from our hearts and spirits, a sense of oppression that I could neither describe, nor name. We laughed and crowded close together, fussing over the cat as the children would, the instant they saw him.

A coach and horses pulled up outside the gate.

'Time to go,' Lavedrine announced with a farewell stroke of Lionel's warm coat.

He offered me his hand, and his eyes fixed on mine. He held my gaze, and I felt a warmth which appeared to be genuine.

'Thank you, Hanno,' he said. 'You have helped me more than you know.'

Then, he turned to Helena. He did not try to embrace her, as I thought he might. Instead, with a quick gesture, he raised his hand to the back of his head and unclipped the white bone ring which held his long hair in place. I had noticed it the day before at the Gottewald house.

'With your permission, *madame*,' he said, placing one steadying hand on her shoulder. His other hand caught the wild tresses of her hair between his thumb and forefinger. 'This useful object', he said, as he fastened the clip at the nape of her neck, 'came back from Polynesia with a friend of mine. It is carved from a real whale's tooth, and bears a native symbol signifying Love and Fortune.'

His hands fell away and came to rest on Helena's shoulders.

'I hope that you will long enjoy those gifts.' He looked at me. 'Both of you. Now, sir, with your permission, may I chastely kiss your wife?'

There was nothing sensual in his kiss. It was the fond salute of a dear friend, taking his leave, as if for ever. I made no protest, though Lionel did. Crushed between Lavedrine and Helena, the cat miaowed loudly and raised a paw, his claws snagging in the fabric of the Frenchman's cloak. As Lavedrine drew back, the cat leapt lightly from Helena's arms to the floor, then walked calmly across to the fireplace. He sat down on his haunches, watching us from the mat, as if the kitchen belonged to him, and we had intruded upon his domain.

'Bravo, Lionel!' laughed Lavedrine. 'You are no longer master and mistress in your own house, my friends. His claws are sharp. Remember, Stiffeniis,' he said, lightly tapping the pocket of his coat.

I recalled the strange ring with a sharp short blade which had probably saved our lives the day that we were surrounded by the mob on the quay. 'I sincerely hope that you will not need to use it where you are going,' I said, as we made our way into the garden. That ring would hardly be a match for the bayonets, sabres, and muskets of the desperate Prussian rebels out in the East.

Pale day had come, a cold wind was getting up.

A compact two-wheeled carriage was waiting in the road, a young soldier sitting up in the driver's seat. At his back, the roof was stacked high with an incredible array of trunks and boxes.

Inside the darkness of the carriage, behind the glass, the profile of a person was barely visible.

'You have a mountain of luggage,' Helena noted wryly, her eyes narrowing as she took careful stock of the heavily laden vehicle, and especially of the human cargo carefully stowed away inside.

Lavedrine shrugged helplessly.

'Books and scientific instruments for the most part. The other bits and pieces'—he glanced my way, smiled apologetically, then turned back to my wife—'do not belong to me. I don't know when we will meet again, Helena, but I want you to keep a watchful eye on this fellow you have chosen as your companion.' He waved a finger at me. 'I have still not got the measure of him. Indeed, I am tempted to be poetic. Hanno's soul is as vast, as dark, and as truly impenetrable as the night sky over East Prussia. Take good care of him!'

'I shall,' she promised, paying no attention to his poor poeticising or his fine sentiments. Her eye was fatally attracted by the presence in the coach. The pallid rays of the early morning sun were just sufficiently strong to reveal the outline of a large yellow bonnet and a high black collar.

Lavedrine stepped up and opened the carriage door.

We stood by the gate, shoulder to shoulder, watching him go. He might have been a relative or friend who was setting out on a long journey. But he was neither one, nor the other. Until very recently, I had thought of him as an enemy and a rival, an upstart Frenchman who had conquered my country, but not my affection.

Lavedrine was halfway into the coach, when he suddenly spun round. 'I almost forgot,' he called back. 'Mutiez will give orders to satisfy those particular requests you made in your report. He will respond to me if they are not carried out to the letter. He'll be in touch the instant there is any news.'

'If there *is* any news,' I said.

He waved his hand in the air. 'There will be, I promise you.'

I did not reply.

I had been distracted by a hand catching hold of Lavedrine's as he disappeared inside the coach. White, manicured, gloveless. Too long, too large to be feminine. I recognised those eyes that flashed in my direction from beneath that strange yellow, turban-like hat. As Lavedrine sat down on the far side of the vehicle, the white hand came up again, playing nervously with the long dark curls that fell shimmering to the shoulder and beyond.

'A woman?' Helena whispered, slipping her arm through mine.

Her eyes were glued to the coach as the driver cracked his whip and the vehicle slowly pulled away.

'A person,' I replied. 'To make the journey less tedious, I imagine.'

·41·

CHRISTMAS CAME, CHRISTMAS went.

The most joyless Christmas ever known in Lotingen. The curfew was still in force, house-to-house visiting was restricted to the hours of daylight. The weather was unbearably cold. The Buran brought snow in the morning, freezing winds in the afternoon, more snow that night. Children were glum for Yuletide stockings hanging empty at the foot of their beds. Adults were grumpy for the lack of decent food on the festive table. Everything worth the eating had been carried off by the French quartermaster. But we fared better than most. Manni and Süzi had Lavedrine's cat to distract them from the lack of treats, and Lotte had, somehow, managed to lay her hands on a pheasant.

'Somehow?' Helena echoed.

'There's a poacher in my village,' the maid reported shyly.

'Are we going to lose you, Lotte?'

Lotte blushed, rolling out pastry for a pie that was large enough for ten, and lasted all the way through till New Year's Eve.

I heard the banter, and played my part in it, but the holiday washed over me, and left me untouched. My thoughts were in a far-off, distant place.

It was Tuesday, 7 January, the day after the Epiphany, when I reopened the Procurator's office. There was nothing of interest in the official despatches on my desk. As usual, Knutzen was nowhere to be found. I was making up the fire when Lieutenant Mutiez appeared.

'Bonne année, monsieur,' he greeted me, waving a sheet of paper in his hand, smiling as if he had brought me a belated Christmas present. 'The morning he left, Colonel Lavedrine informed me of your requests, instructing me to let you know what went on in Kamenetz. All seems to have gone according to plan.'

He excused himself in the name of urgent duties, and I made no attempt to detain him, knowing that he would be able to tell me nothing more than the report contained. I sat down the instant that he left me alone. My hand was shaking, the paper trembled. Whatever had happened out there, I had caused it to happen.

The battle in Kamenetz had raged for three days and nights before the rebels finally surrendered, throwing open the gate, allowing the combined force of French and Prussian besiegers to march in. It had taken another two weeks to decide what ought to be done with the men of the garrison. Most of them had been sent to 'work under supervision' (which meant forced labour) in French military installations scattered along the Baltic coast, though fourteen had died in the fighting.

I found the news that I was looking for towards the bottom of the page.

Until the end, Rochus Kelding had defended the fortress valiantly against the assault. Then, as night fell, he had led a group of boys out of the garrison by way of an underground tunnel known only to themselves. They had entered the nearby wood, and burrowed into the snow. Their plan was to surprise and slaughter the French troops and the Prussian 'traitors' as they attempted to withdraw from Kamenetz. But the Buran had brought an unexpected storm that night. Freezing winds and deep snow had trapped the French inside the fort for two days. When they did emerge, they found one of the boy soldiers wandering all alone. Wounded, black with frostbite. He recounted disobeying their leader, Rochus Kelding, digging himself out from beneath the icy crust with his bare hands. That boy had survived. The others had not. Including Rochus.

Chiccolino dove sei?

Lavedrine's Italian rhyme rattled through my head. He was right about it sounding sinister. They would be looking for skeletons in the spring.

The final paragraph mentioned Bruno Gottewald. I had asked for his corpse to be exhumed from its tomb of shame in Kamenetz, requesting that the remains be sent back to Lotingen. The despatch noted that I had been appointed executor. I would decide, and Mutiez would follow my instructions, regarding where the corpse should finally be laid to rest for eternity.

There was only one person who could tell me *which* earth should cover that body. As darkness began to fall, not wishing to be recognised by the Prussians living close to the ghetto, I directed my steps towards Judenstrasse. The sentinel on the gate urged me to go quietly about my business. 'Anything could spark another outbreak of violence, sir,' he warned.

News had been put about in Lotingen before the holiday that the Gottewald case was closed. The official explanation was that the children had been murdered by thieves, who had carried off the mother as they made their escape, using her for their pleasure in Gummerstett's warehouse, then killing her as well. The rioting had rumbled on for a while, but like all such protests against the body politic, it had finally suffocated in its own inertia.

Judenstrasse was dark and silent. Occasionally, a window opened, a head poked out, then the window quickly closed again. The ringing sound of my footsteps in the street was enough to provoke a sudden blackout in many houses. I had no need to ask directions to the house of Aaron Jacob, of course, and his door opened the instant that I knocked.

He was wearing the same dark-brown, hooded tunic he had worn the day that Lavedrine and I went to visit him, but he was not the same proud man. It was not merely the pale expression on his face that told me, but a stark jagged scar that marked his forehead like a streak of lightning.

'What is this?' I asked, tracing a similar mark on my own brow.

Aaron Jacob touched the wound. 'I was attacked, Herr Procurator,' he stated plainly. 'That night, coming home from the Old Fish Market. Some- one recognised me, despite the Gentile disguise I was wearing. Perhaps they saw me walking towards the gate. The French guards had been advised of my coming, but a mob fell on me before I reached them.' He trembled at the memory. 'Thanks to the soldiers, my life was saved. But I took a beating first.'

He shrugged his shoulders as if he had nothing more to add.

'I blame myself,' I apologised. 'I should not have asked you to help me.'

He raised his hand to hush my protests. 'It was an improbable disguise,' he said with a sad smile. 'The Gentiles knew me. With or without a Prussian hat and coat. But please come in, sir.'

It might have been hours, rather than months, since the last time I en- tered his rooms. The same melancholy gloom, the same sweet odour of pu- trefaction, disinfectant, and conserving fluid clogged the air. The plaster casts still decorated the wall. But only one night-vase was standing covered on the mantle-shelf. Another child, I supposed, that Aaron Jacob was trying to save from the ravages of the worm.

I pointed, and smiled. 'Things are looking up, then?'

He nodded. 'My garlic potion does the job,' he said. 'Which does not mean that the cause has been removed. Our children still succumb to it. Filth and squalor have become the principal materials from which Juden- strasse is made.'

He looked up, an unspoken interrogative in his gaze.

'You have not come on that account, I think.'

'The Gottewalds were Jewish,' I told him, as flatly as I might have an- nounced that night follows day.

He raised his hand to his mouth to suppress a cry.

Then I told him what had been the cause of their deaths.

His eyes widened with horror. 'Thieves . . . they said,' he stuttered. 'And the mother carried off . . .'

'That story of a robbery was spread to pacify the hatred in the city.'

'Will you tell me now, sir, that my theory is foolish superstition? I ought to have recognised the signs. The heads of those children. Destruction was written there. Not theirs alone. *Yom kippur*. They were marked by death . . .'

He trembled visibly.

'We live in a terrible world, Herr Jacob,' I replied. 'I would not attempt to deny it. Judenstrasse is an adequate demonstration. The fate of the Gottewalds is further proof. But so is the crushing presence of the French. Every man, woman, child in Prussia is forced every day to face a thousand perils. Not the Jews alone. There is nothing in you, in me, or in *any* person, which inevitably attracts Divine punishment. God had nothing to do with it.'

We stood silently, face to face.

I would have liked to find some words to counter that man's anguish, but no words of comfort came. 'The Gottewalds deserve a decent burial,' I said at last, as if that simple formula could cure all ills.

The darker side of the question occurred to him at once.

'What about the mother? What will become of their . . .'

He did not pronounce the word, but it hung between us in the air. *Executioner.*

'She is buried for the moment in the cemetery behind the building that the French have turned into a field hospital,' I said. 'The children are lying in the *Kindergarten*, but I think they ought to be moved to a more suitable place. Gottewald intended to raise his children in the Jewish faith.'

'He wanted to be a Prussian *and* a Jew,' Aaron Jacob reminded me. 'And he wanted the same for them.' He tried to smile, but managed only a grimace. 'It seems impossible, doesn't it? And yet, it is such a simple wish.'

Suddenly, he placed his hand on my arm. He drew it back quickly, as if he had presumed too far. Even so, he smiled. A warm, luminous, genuine smile. 'The *Kindergarten* is where they should remain, Herr Procurator. Safe with all the Prussian children. And the parents should also be buried as *Prussians*. In a Prussian cemetery.'

'But Gottewald died because he wished them to be known as Jews.'

He stared at me, a burning light in his black eyes. 'God knows and sees all things,' he replied. 'He knows that they belonged to the Chosen People. There is a way to honour his wish in death, Herr Procurator. A shallow dish placed inconspicuously beside the grave.'

'For flowers?'

Aaron Jacob grinned conspiratorially. 'For stones,' he replied. 'It will be a sign. Every time you visit the place, sir, leave a stone or a pebble in the dish. It is an ancient tradition of ours. In memory of the dead. They will be Jewish tombs. And Prussian ones, too. Wasn't that what he wanted?'

'So easy?' I said with astonishment. 'A dish and a stone? The dead are more easily contented than the living.'

'They'll have what Jews have never had,' he erupted with passion. 'Peace! They would find none in a Jewish cemetery.' He narrowed his eyes. 'Surely you've heard of the regular vandalising of our burial grounds, Herr Procurator? I have been to the East, to Insterberg, on four occasions to visit my own wife's grave . . .' He raised his hand and hid his eyes. 'On each occasion, I had to rebuild it.' He choked on the words, then struggled to continue. 'Bruno Gottewald has had his portion of violence. In a Prussian cemetery, they will not be subjected to humiliation *after* death as well. His ears, and the ears of his children, will not be forced to hear that shameful cry. *Hep! Hep!* will never sound again for them.'

I listened in stunned silence. I had seen, and failed to recognise, those words scrawled in blood on the bedroom wall. I had held them in my hand for an instant, before they vanished from the blackened paper.

His eyes gaped wide, as I grabbed his arm and held him fast.

'What does it mean?' I asked.

'It is ancient Latin, sir. *Hierosolima est perdita*,' he intoned. 'Jerusalem is lost. No hope for the Jews. *That's* what it means. It means many things, none of them good. Those words are shouted out to rouse other Jew-haters. Bring your clubs. *Hierosolima est perdita. Hep! Hep!* Slay the Jews!'

As he uttered the words in a rough, urgent voice, like a swineherd rounding up his pigs, I recognised the sound. I had heard it the day that Lavedrine and I ran close to being lynched by the mob on the quayside. My heart felt deathly cold. Was that the 'dreadful sound' that Bruno Gottewald had warned his wife about? The 'chanting voice' that haunted his dreams and hounded his steps in Kamenetz?

'She wrote those words on the wall,' I whispered. '*Hep! Hep!* Written with her children's blood. She'd been frightened by a letter that her husband wrote. What else could drive a mother to such an act? I am convinced that she heard the cry *Hep! Hep!* inside her fuddled head. As if some frightful nemesis were coming.'

He shuddered, then he looked up.

'Describe that room to me,' he said. 'Tell me what you saw there, sir.'

Lavedrine had discovered the murderer. I had found the cause. Was Aaron Jacob now going to pull the threads together and tell me *how* the crime had been committed?

'I can do more than that,' I said, opening my shoulder bag, taking out my sketchbook. 'I can show you.'

I sat on the edge of the unlit fireplace, ignoring the dirt and ashes, and spread the album open on my knees. Aaron Jacob sat down at my side. As

Immanuel Kant might have done, I had inscribed a title on the cover: *Drawings Relating to the Gottewald Murders.*

'This is the first,' I said. 'A sketch of the children's bodies laid out on the bed. As you can see, they were covered with a sheet. Only the heads were exposed, hanging over the edge of the bed.' I turned the page, my fingers trembling as I did so. 'In this one, the sheet had been pulled away. The bodies are exposed to view. On a pillow at the foot of the bed, we found the sexual organs of the two boys, which had been sliced off . . .'

'Rough work,' he murmured quietly. 'I wonder why she didn't call a rabbi.'

'To bury them?'

'To assist her. She prepared her children for the sacrifice, I think. But please, turn to the next page. If I am right, the other drawings will confirm it.'

I ran my finger over the next drawing. 'This is a simple plan of the furniture in the bedroom,' I said. 'As you can see, there wasn't very much. The bed, of course. A small table by the bed, and this chair here.'

He laid his hand on mine, preventing me from turning to the next sketch. He tapped his nail against the paper. 'One chair only in the room? In this position at the foot of the bed?'

I nodded. 'I remember thinking that it was an odd place to leave a chair.'

'Like a humble throne, is that what you mean?'

I nodded again. 'I would not have used those words exactly. But that was the impression that I had.'

'And where was the writing?'

'Just here,' I said, pointing to the wall nearest to the children's feet. 'Beneath the window sill. An awkward and improbable place to write. I can show you exactly what I mean.'

I turned the album leaf. 'There was very little to see. But such thick blood as this, so far from the bodies. There was nothing casual in it. She had tried to write on the rough plaster.'

Aaron Jacob bent down close to examine the marks that I had tried to draw.

'I can tell you precisely what happened in the room,' he said. 'If the children were going to die as Jews, then a sign was needed.'

'A sign?'

'The Jews are renowned for their humour, Herr Stiffeniis. On the Day of Atonement, we say, the Lord will ask each man to stand up. And He will recognise his own.'

He laughed in a hollow, empty manner.

'What do you mean?'

'*Berit milah,*' he answered. 'A rite carried out on the eighth day of a male child's existence. Or any time after, if he has not already been admitted to the community. In this case, there are obvious irregularities. The rite is never performed in the presence of a woman. And never *by* a woman. Normally, a *Mohel* is present. But this woman was alone and terrified. She had no rabbi to turn to. She was not known as a Jew in Lotingen. She cut roughly, but she did her best in the circumstances.'

I knew in a blinding flash what he was speaking about.

The plan of the Gottewald bedroom seemed to seethe with frantic life as he described the scene. The crazed desperation of Sybille Gottewald was given direction and purpose.

'Turn back to your plan of the room, sir. We can see what happened that night. Perhaps she gave them some medicinal substance to make them sleep. She laid them crosswise on the bed for her own ease. They would not have chosen to sleep in such a position, their heads dangling uncomfortably back over the edge of the bed. But their throats were exposed, and she slit them. Once they were dead, she thoroughly cleaned the room. She did not lack respect. She buried the blood, but not the corpses, and when order had been restored, she attempted to circumcise the boys. But every action is marred by fear, by panic, by inadequate preparation. Her knife was long, and not sufficiently sharp. Even so, she eviscerated the boys as best she could, laying their sacrificed flesh on the pillow for the Prophet to witness . . .'

'Was somebody watching while she did it?' I gasped with horror.

The Jew turned to me, and nodded. 'This chair, Herr Procurator, was *not* empty. Elijah the Prophet was sitting there. He may not have approved, but he was there in spirit. He saw it happen. In the *berit milah* ritual, his throne is placed next to the altar as witness to the saving of another soul. A foreskin placed on a pillow is an offering to God. In return for the sacrifice, the circumcised child will enter the kingdom of heaven.'

The album slipped from my fingers and fell to the floor.

Aaron Jacob picked it up and opened it. The book fell open at the page where I had tried to sketch the face of the mother.

'I gave you an outline of her face,' he murmured, 'but this is more exact. Is it the fruit of your imagination, sir?'

'A witness helped me,' I replied cautiously. 'That person may have spoken to Sybille Gottewald.'

'Such unusual eyebrows,' he commented. 'I would never have guessed. Only a witness could describe them so precisely.'

He closed the album, and handed it to me. 'Bury them all, Herr Stiffeniis. In a Prussian cemetery with a Jewish symbol on the grave. Satisfy the desire of Gottewald, the Jew. Have you not discovered their real name?'

'Not yet,' I said. 'But I will, I promise you.'

A knot in my throat inhibited the expression of my sentiments. I did not say how fortunate I had been in meeting him—a Prussian upbringing has its faults. But I hoped that he would comprehend my gratitude.

I walked away from Judenstrasse in a sort of trance. A dense sea fog had smothered the town. All was silent, all was still. I went to my office and penned a note to the effect that I intended to bury the remains of Bruno Gottewald in the Pietist cemetery as soon as the body could be discharged from French hands, telling Knutzen to carry the announcement over to the general quarters, with a copy to the office of Dittersdorf. I was counting on the proven efficiency of Mutiez, and the incapacity of Dittersdorf, to oppose any scheme that had been approved by the French. More so after the debacle of Kamenetz, and the subsequent placing of General Katowice under house arrest.

The fog was gone by the time I left the office, and the temperature had dropped some degrees. I was walking quickly, shivering with cold, when I came in sight of the house. As I looked eagerly towards my door, a wild black spot appeared in the moonlight. Helena was running to meet me without a shawl, her hair flying wildly about her, a piece of paper in her hand.

I saw the strained look on her face as I charged towards her.

'Bialystok,' she gasped, pushing the paper at me, begging: 'Open it.'

'Do you want to die of cold?' I snapped, perplexed by the urgency in her voice, taking her arm, leading her towards the garden gate.

No sooner had I shut the door than she turned to me.

'Read it, Hanno. Please.'

She moved to my elbow, watching as I broke the sealing wax, stretching to see what was written there. One hand flew to her mouth, the other to my sleeve.

'This is madness, Hanno! He wants us both to go. What he says *cannot* be true!'

I read again what Lavedrine had written.

'He believes that the case is still not over.'

Helena had never been parted from the children, but our bag was ready within the hour.

·42·

THE DRIVER RAPPED hard on the roof.

'Next stop, the new Jerusalem!' he announced with a whoop.

We had been voyaging continuously for two days and nights.

The coach trundled across the River Biala by means of an ancient wooden bridge, and pulled up ten minutes later in the crowded market square of Bialystok. As I helped Helena down, I kept a watchful eye on our bag. We might have been in a foreign country. It was more than a matter of geography, the closeness of the Russian border. People swirled around us in the square. The men wore tight black jackets reaching beneath their knees. The women wore smocks of grey wool. The children were tinier versions of their parents. But it was the hair that gave the game away. Long, tangled beards which had never known a barber's blade. Each man wore a black hat, skullcap, or a black-and-white striped blanket over his head, wild curls and ringlets dancing about their cheeks. Those people spoke a tongue that I recognised, but did not understand.

'You were lucky to fall upon me, sir,' the coaching-master boasted, as we hired a trap. 'Not many here in Bialystok know German. Half speak Yiddish. The rest speak Hebrew. This town's pitch-full of Jews.'

'Not entirely full,' I murmured to myself.

French troopers armed with muskets, their long bayonets fixed, stood in tight knots around the square, but they were vastly outnumbered, and would have stood no chance of survival had a rebellion broken out against them. I was still looking around when the trap arrived.

'Where are you going, sir?'

'Doctor Schubert's,' I replied.

The coaching-master looked attentively at Helena for some reason as he handed me the reins. 'It stands over yonder. On top of the hill,' he pointed.

I loaded our bag, took Helena's hand, and helped her up. She sat trembling by my side, as I cracked the whip. Whether moved by fear, or excitement, I could not say. Unused to handling a horse-drawn vehicle, all my attention was concentrated on the busy streets. A huge fellow, wearing a skullcap and a leather apron, the carcass of a sheep slung over his shoulders, cut across my path, causing me to brake violently. I cursed and waved my whip at him. The butcher smiled, nodded thoughtfully, then went about his business.

Afterwards, we made better progress, following a high, winding wall to the top of the hill. A sign was fixed beside the main entrance. *Dr Schubert's Mesmeric Institute for the Insane*. Did the coaching-master believe that I had come to commit my wife? As the trap pulled up, a little man in a slouch hat and rags ran out of the door, and grabbed onto the reins, steadying the horse, holding out his other hand. I gave him one of the Russian kopecks which I had received as change when I paid for the hire of the vehicle. The man nodded towards the entrance, making a gesture of pulling a bell-rope. While helping Helena down, I heard the sound of bolts being drawn and the door opening.

Lavedrine came bounding towards us.

Despite the cold, he was wearing no jacket, only a white shirt, dark trousers, and a long green apron stretching down beneath his knees. His hair had been shaved away to a silvery stubble. He looked like a field after harvesting. The absence made his eyes, ears, nose, and lips seem larger, more pronounced and sensual.

'Frau Stiffeniis,' he cried warmly, reaching for Helena's gloved hand, raising it to his lips. Then he turned to me. 'Hanno, thank you both for coming so soon.'

I shook the hand that he offered. With the other, I pulled his letter from my pocket, and waved it in the air.

'Bring Helena to Bialystok,' I recited, not needing to read. 'Frau Gotte-wald is here.'

Lavedrine's warm smile faded. 'I will explain as we are making our way,' he announced. Then, he took Helena's arm and led us into the building.

A woman large enough to be a wrestler closed the door and turned the key in the lock. Putting her key away in a belt hidden beneath an enormous stomach, she eyed us from beneath her black cowl, as if we were newly arrived patients, eager to run away. Lavedrine had left us standing in the hall, mumbling something about a pass-key and a report.

I took both of Helena's hands in mine, and pressed them gently.

'It does not seem such a horrid place,' she murmured.

The walls were tiled up to the ceiling in sparkling white. The floor was tiled in dark green, like the sea. At waist height, a row of blue tiles had been set into the wall.

'As institutions go, it is paradise,' I replied.

I had been expecting worse. Asylums for the insane in Prussia are often places of extreme squalor and total abandon, where murder among the warders is as common as madness among the patients. But everything here seemed to be functional and clean.

'This way, ma'am,' Lavedrine called, emerging from the room, a large key in his hand, offering Helena his arm again. He might have been bent on coaxing her to go along with him, though she was more than willing to be led. Even so, her anxiety was plain to see.

'Is Lionel the master of the house yet?' Lavedrine asked conversationally.

Helena tried to report on the cat's success with the children, but wild howls and lurid screams assaulted our ears as we proceeded down the corridor. She stopped, her eyes darting around with terror.

'Do not be afraid,' Lavedrine said, increasing his pace as he led her on.

The tall windows on the left were barred. The cell doors on the right were bolted. Now and again, he used his pass-key to open an iron gate which blocked the corridor, locking it carefully once we were through. There was a sort of round, glass porthole in each cell door, such as one might find on a sailing ship. Large enough to see through, small enough to prevent escape. At the sound of our voices and footsteps echoing off the tiled walls and floor, appeals for help and shrieks of abuse followed our progress. Being watched was not a pleasant experience. Howling mouths, fearsome bleeding teeth, hostile glaring eyes.

We stopped in a high domed hall, which must have been the heart of the building, four corridors shooting off, as it were, to the points of the compass. In the centre was a long wooden table covered in beakers, glass jars, and other containers turned upside down, which had been laid on cloths to dry.

'I was invited to see this hospital by the German physician who runs it,' he said, his attention carefully directed at Helena. 'He thought that I might be interested to study the methods they are using here. Magnetism is employed to cure just about everything, from epilepsy to . . .'

'Sybille Gottewald,' Helena snapped, as if she had run out of patience.

Lavedrine pulled out a chair from the table, and invited Helena to sit.

'Very well, this is the story,' he began. 'Doctor Schubert admitted a woman a couple of weeks ago. She had been discovered in a nearby village by the serfs. They woke up one morning, and there she was, resting her back against the wall of one of the cottages, staring up at the sky. They thought she had run away from her master. She was a bundle of rags, starving and terrified. They brought bread and water, but she would not eat or drink while they were watching. Her face and arms were covered in cuts and sores. Her legs were horribly swollen. She must have been in pain, though she seemed to feel nothing. She was wearing a pair of broken boots she had probably stolen from a soldier's corpse, but she'd been walking in the snow without shoes, the doctor says. Her feet are black with frostbite. She has lost a couple of toes. The peasants who found her were frightened. The punishment for hiding a runaway serf is a public whipping. So someone told the estate manager, who called the *gendarmes*, and they, in turn, sent for Doctor Schubert.'

'Did she tell them her name?' Helena interrupted.

Lavedrine shook his head.

'Has she spoken about what happened in that house?'

'They have tried all the languages commonly employed in Bialystok. Russian, Lithuanian, Czech, Slovak, German. Hebrew, of course. But she would answer to none of them. The doctor believed she was physically impaired, but tests revealed that her hearing is above average, and that she could make sounds if she wanted. Indeed, one of the warders found her with a book that had been left in the bath-house . . .'

'A book?' I interposed.

'The minder did not know whether she was reading, praying, or simply mumbling. It was a German translation of the Torah.'

'What makes you think that she is Sybille Gottewald?' Helena's voice was calm, though I heard a tremor of impatience in it. 'Thousands of women have fallen victim to war and misfortune.'

Lavedrine smiled and his eyebrows arched. '*This* is the true Helena Stiffeniis that I remember!' he said with vibrant enthusiasm. 'She boldly says what must be said. Oh, I know what you are thinking. Such a waste of time. All this way for nothing. Forcing me to leave the children . . .'

'All this way, indeed!' I echoed sarcastically. 'Are you trying to suggest that this woman has walked to Bialystok from Lotingen? In winter? I remember examining a female corpse in an abandoned warehouse some time ago in Lotingen. We both agreed that the body was Sybille Gottewald's.'

He looked up at me. 'I recall why we presumed that it was her. In the first place, no other woman had been reported missing. In the second, Gummerstett's warehouse was an ideal place to hide a corpse. We concluded that the body was probably hers, because we were desperate to find her. Dead, or alive!'

'Are you suggesting . . .'

'We found what we were looking for,' he interrupted. 'We made no real attempt to identify that body. She could have been anyone!'

'A nameless woman who does not speak? Who may, or may not, be able to read? If you have nothing more than sand on which to build your castle . . .'

'I have these,' he said, putting his hand once more into the pocket of his apron. A moment later, he held up a pack of playing cards. They wore worn and torn, very old and dirty. He toyed with them, moving them from one hand to the other like a card-sharp, but not a very good one.

'I do not understand you,' I said, truly puzzled.

He flicked the pack with his thumb, looking at Helena, then set three cards face down on the table with an impertinent *snap*, as if we were about to play whatever game he had got into his head.

'These cards are grouped in suits,' he explained. 'Families, if you like. There is a family of farm tools, a family of farm clothes, a family of farm boots, and, well, a family of farmers. There are seven cards in each suit, and each suit is duplicated. Fifty-six cards in all. There are many ways to win the game. You may, for example, collect all the shoes, all the clothes, all the tools. Or . . .'

Suddenly, he looked from Helena to myself, patting those three cards on the table with his hand.

'What do you make of these?' he asked.

With a flick of his wrist, he turned the cards face up.

A cry escaped from Helena's lips. Blood began to thunder in my ears.

The pictures on these cards were rubbed, scuffed, faded. They had been handled endlessly, by numberless hands. Three children, two boys and a girl, each dressed in the rough clothes of peasants. The little girl was holding a bunch of flowers. Each child was grinning. I would have called them 'happy' children. But any notion of happiness had been cancelled out by a mark with a pointed stone, or a sharp fingernail. A gash at each infant throat had been incised with such force that the head appeared to be severed. There was nothing accidental in it. Those marks had been made with a destructive violence that was unequivocal.

'This deck belonged to one of the nurses,' he went on blandly. 'She accused the woman I was telling you about of having stolen her cards, and asked the inmate why she had ruined the pack. The nurse reports that the woman answered her. *Berit milah.* That was what she said. The warder is Jewish, she recognised those words. They refer to the ritual circumcision of infant boys.' He sought out my gaze. 'You realise now why I sent for Helena, do you not, Stiffeniis?'

Aaron Jacob had told me the meaning of that phrase. And he had described to me what had happened that night.

'Jewish women are no rare thing in Bialystok,' I said, unwilling to concede that Lavedrine might be right. 'Our driver called it the Polish Jerusalem.'

'There are more points in my favour,' he insisted, jumping to his feet, counting them off on his fingers. 'This woman has certainly given birth to children, but she is all alone. She reads German, and knows some words of

Hebrew. The cards show three young children—two boys and a girl. Consider the symbolic "slitting" of their throats. Think of her age, her state of person, her state of mind. All this may be, as you suggest, Stiffeniis, no more than coincidence, but . . .' He stopped, and turned to Helena. 'That's why I requested you to come,' he said. 'You have seen her, Helena. You can tell us if this woman is truly Sybille Gottewald.'

Screams and cries rang out all around us, muffled by the walls, but not a breath was heard in that room.

'What do you intend to do if she is?'

Helena was looking up at Lavedrine as she spoke. Her hood had fallen back onto her shoulders. The whalebone clip he had given her as a parting gift stood out starkly white against the chestnut colour of her hair. Lavedrine spotted it straight away.

He let out a loud sigh. 'I am not interested in justice, Helena. It is no concern of mine. I am only interested in my chosen field of study. I intend to examine this crime in all its aspects, and make public what I learn from it. Something that will shock the stuffed wigs of the Academy of the Sciences, and leave them gaping like fish. I mean to make a mark, and introduce new methods to the study of crime and criminals. With your help, I will return to Paris, and pick up my career again.'

Helena seemed to be turning over in her mind what he had just told her.

'If I do recognise her,' she said at last, 'Hanno, or some other magistrate, will be required to try her. She will be condemned. She will hang . . .'

Her breath died away as she said it.

Lavedrine closed his fist and tapped his knuckles two or three times on the table.

'Your husband and I follow different professions, Helena,' he said, finally. 'I hunt criminals with the aim of studying them. The magistrate's job is to judge and condemn without passion.' He turned to me for confirmation. 'Wasn't that what Kant intended when he put the idea into your head?'

'Where is the woman?' Helena murmured.

'In the bath-house,' he said. 'It might be best if you saw her there. She will be surprised to see you, but that will be to our advantage. I am counting on it.'

'Tomorrow will be soon enough,' I interposed. 'My wife needs to rest . . .'

'I am not tired. I have come for no other reason,' Helena interrupted sharply.

Lavedrine towered above her, offering his hand. His eyes were bright, attentive. Triumphant, like a hawk measuring his prey.

'Naturally, Helena. I knew that you would wish to help,' he said.

Helena took his hand, and rose. Her eyes never flinched from his for one instant. She did not immediately release his hand, as she stood before him.

'I wish to be alone with her,' she said.

I saw the shock register on his face.

'It is too dangerous,' I protested, stepping between them. 'That woman is being held to protect her from herself. To protect others from *her*.'

But Lavedrine regained his ascendancy quickly.

'I guarantee that nothing will happen,' he said. 'Trust me.'

'You are not obliged to see her, Helena,' I insisted, laying my hand over hers.

She slipped her hand from mine, touched my lips to silence me.

'I *want* to see her,' my wife said quietly.

·43·

WE SET OFF down a different corridor.

Low, barrel-vaulted, narrow, darker. There were no bars, no windows, very few doors, and everything was strangely silent.

From out of the twilight gloom, a warder came towards us. She was walking on tiptoe, and stood aside to let us pass. But Lavedrine stopped beside her, stepping closer, saying something in a low voice. The woman's eyes darted inquisitively at Helena, then at me, then back at Lavedrine.

She bowed her head in deference to his authority.

'I'll tell the bath-maid,' she whispered, glancing at Helena again, examining her from head to toe. 'She'll need a waxed coat and a hood. Those are the rules.'

'Very well,' Lavedrine replied, cutting her short. 'Come, Helena. Frau Barenstoft here will lead you in, and help you change. The atmosphere is hot and damp where Frau Gottewald is being treated. It would soak that fine cloak of yours in an instant. Stiffeniis and I will be close, I promise you.'

'Not *too* close,' Helena replied. 'I wish to speak to her alone. I told you that.'

'As we agreed,' Lavedrine assented.

'You must call for help if you need it,' I added sternly.

Frau Barenstoft smiled. 'There's no danger, sir,' she said, making a curtsy to Helena, inviting my wife to follow her.

As the door swung closed behind the two women, we stood in the corridor, watching through the window-glass. Frau Barenstoft stopped before a large cupboard, then turned to face Helena, indicating that she should remove her heavy travelling cloak. As she did so, the woman reached into a cupboard, came out holding a shimmering, sand-coloured canvas garment, and handed it to my wife. Helena looked bewildered as she donned the robe, and she put on a matching waterproof hat like a sou'wester with a peaked brim and a flap behind which covered her ears and neck. A moment later, they turned away from us. Frau Barenstoft stopped before a white door, went inside for a moment, then came out and nodded, signalling Helena to go in alone. Without a word or backward look, my wife pushed open the door of the cubicle and disappeared from view.

For an instant, a wave of panic swept over me. I felt as though I had lost her. She was out of my sight, beyond the range of my help, in an asylum for the mad. In a room where some mysterious medical treatment was taking place.

Frau Barenstoft came calmly out of the dressing room.

'Will there be anything else, sir?' she murmured.

Lavedrine shook his head, and she walked off quickly into the gloom.

'Come, Stiffeniis,' he urged. 'We must keep a watchful eye on our own dear Helena.' He took my arm, pushed open the door, and led me towards the one through which my wife had disappeared.

Our own dear Helena . . .

'You promised to leave her alone,' I protested.

Lavedrine held more tightly onto my arm. 'For safety's sake, we will not let Helena out of our sight.'

I needed no prompting to keep my wife from harm. And I was curious to see the woman that Lavedrine described as Sybille Gottewald. We sprinted towards the door that Helena had passed through. It was wider than a normal door, painted white, divided into two halves, a round spyhole of curved glass in each half. Lavedrine looked through one window, I peered in through the other, standing shoulder to shoulder.

There were three large metal boxes inside the green-and-white tiled room. They had been lined up against the far wall, each one like a large brass coffin mounted on a stand. The dull burnished metal was heavily studded, a variety of tubes set into the upper lid of the casket. The arms and the body of the patient were constrained inside, while the head protruded from a hole, resting on a sort of brace which held a pillow. There was another woman sitting in a chair by the far wall, who was evidently the guardian of the place. Her size reassured me, as did the fact that she was comfortably asleep, her chin sunk onto her breast.

Helena sat on a three-legged stool beside one of the contraptions, in which a person had been imprisoned. There was no other patient in the room.

'Frau Gottewald,' Lavedrine murmured.

I stared hard at the woman. Her head was tilted far back against the pillow. Through the billowing steam that clouded the atmosphere, I could see only her bare throat, the cusp-line of her jaw, and her distended nostrils.

'What's going on?' I whispered.

'This is the bath-house. Here they float in magnetic fluid,' Lavedrine hissed, 'oscillating between the positive and negative poles, washing away morbid disharmony, inducing a sense of warm well-being. The patient must relax and overcome all fears and anxieties. The conscious mind must surrender to the unconscious.'

A loud, rattling clink of pipes accompanied his voice. Vapour began to spout from the holes in the casket, enveloping the head of the reclining woman in a dense white cloud. The atmosphere inside the room was already hazy. Now, it seemed to swirl like fog. The mist clung to the inside of the window-glass, making it more difficult to see what was going on. I might have been staring into a vast aquarium. The hooded lanterns reflecting on the tiled wall made everything appear green in colour, melancholy in aspect, and I had to strain to see Helena.

She stood up, leaning forward over the metal casket. Her back and shoulders were partly turned towards the doors. I could only see the narrowest sliver of her profile as she bent her head towards the face of the woman in the bath. The bather had not moved an inch since Helena arrived. Her head was still reclining backwards, her lips barely visible, white steam puffing out generously all around her neck. Her disembodied head appeared to be floating on a pillow of rolling clouds.

Helena sat down again. She did not turn towards the door. She did not call to us. Yet she could have had no better view of that woman's face. I felt a sense of enormous release.

'Helena has no idea who that woman is,' I said, facing Lavedrine. 'She may be Jewish. She may speak German. She may even have murdered her own children, but she is *not* Sybille Gottewald.'

He laid his hand on my arm. 'Don't be so certain. They are conversing!'

I pressed my nose against the glass, struggling to see through the gloom and the steam. The woman in the casket had raised her head a fraction, and turned a little in my wife's direction. Was that why Helena had shifted? So that we might see the evidence?

'It is hard to see anything,' I murmured uncertainly.

'Now Helena is talking with the woman,' Lavedrine insisted.

I shifted position, but all I could see was a slender new moon of white forehead. Helena's cheeks and mouth were concealed by the curtain of her curls, which had fallen loose, probably made heavier by the moist air in that room.

'She has a generous heart,' I said. 'Her first instinct would be to comfort any woman in distress.'

Even so, I had my doubts. I looked once more. Despite what I saw, I felt compelled to deny it.

'It is a mirage, Lavedrine. You are imagining . . .'

'Helena would have come away,' he insisted.

In my heart I knew it, too. What reason could there be to linger so long beside a stranger?

'There! Did you see?' he cried again.

Suddenly, Helena stood up, and came towards us.

Lavedrine pulled the door open. He placed his hand on the arm of her saturated cloak as my wife stepped out of the treatment room. Her pale face glowed like a lamp. Her eyes were wide, her lips trembling. She caught her breath and gasped. Moisture ran down her cheeks and nose in streams, her matted hair glistened with liquid pearls. She looked at me. One instant only, then away again, as if she did not know me.

'Well?' cried Lavedrine expectantly. 'What did Frau Gottewald say?'

Helena turned to him. 'Frau Gottewald?' she murmured. 'What fantasy has possessed you, sir? I have never seen that woman in my life before today.'

Lavedrine gasped. His eyes shone with barely contained rage. The muscles in his face were taut, as if he meant to force her to tell him what he wanted to hear. He grasped her by the shoulders. 'I saw your lips moving, Helena. She spoke to *you*! In God's name, what did she tell you?'

I bridled at this harshness, but Helena's tongue was faster. 'Your desire to lay your hands on a monster has poisoned your wits, sir,' she replied sharply. She stared at him in silence, a tight smile tracing itself upon her lips. 'I did not hear a word. Nor any sound, except hot water bubbling through the pipes of that infernal machine. And the snoring of the matron. They were both in such a state of catalepsy, I doubt either one of them could have pronounced her own name.'

She paused for an instant, then she shook her head.

Like Lavedrine, I was astonished. By what she said, and the way she said it. I, too, had seen them speaking. Yet, she denied it absolutely. Their lips *had* moved. They *had* spoken.

Lavedrine was lost. He could do no better than accuse. 'But I *saw* you, Helena! We both saw you.' He spun around, and appealed to me. 'Hanno?'

The silence was as suffocating as the steam that filled the room beyond the glass.

'I saw my wife inside that room,' I said, like a child repeating his catechism. 'She was leaning over a bathtub. Her shoulders were turned to me. I could not see her face. The air was thick with swirling vapours. Can I honestly say that I saw her speak? Can you? Can you swear that it was not the distorting convex of the glass, or the effect of those vapours in the atmosphere? *I* cannot, sir.'

I darted a glance at Helena.

Half hidden behind his shoulder, her face was an open book. Her stunned surprise was evident to me alone. That look, and the smile that followed it, might have been ample repayment for the uncertainty I had expressed, but she did not hold my gaze. She turned to Lavedrine, as if to gauge his reaction.

The Frenchman's hand slipped from her shoulders.

'As you wish, Helena,' he murmured. 'As you think best.'

In that instant, in that place, so far from home and our children, so distant from all that we held dear in life, after all the trials that the investigation of the massacre had heaped upon us, I felt a sense of renewed hope. I was reminded of our unity of spirit after Jena, as we hid out in the woods from the French. It was a magic cloak that wrapped around us both. It had shielded us from all that had happened since the fourteenth of October, 1806. I tried to catch my wife's eye and share that emotion, but she bowed her head and looked away.

'The Gottewald case is closed,' I murmured.

Helena was quiet. Lavedrine seemed quashed.

'Nothing can keep you here, I suppose,' he said slowly. 'And yet, I owe you both the same warm hospitality that you offered me. I have taken a house in Bialystok. If you would care to rest and be my guests . . .'

It was a hollow invitation, and I left Helena to answer it.

'I would prefer to go home,' she stated.

'I must insist, Hanno,' he said, turning to me. 'It is getting late. You may have trouble boarding a coach. Better to leave in the morning.'

'You take too much upon yourself,' I replied, as one might reassure an old friend who is too insistently kind. 'My wife has a cousin living in Lomza. We'll be there before dark. How many years is it since we last saw Franziska?' I turned to Helena, inviting her to share the little white lie. 'She'll put us up for a day or two, don't you think?'

Helena did not answer me. Her eyes never shifted from Lavedrine's face.

'I am sorry to disappoint you, sir,' she murmured.

He smiled uncertainly.

'Sorry? Why should you be sorry for me? I'll find another case to impress the Academy of the Sciences, though it may not be so intriguing as this one.' Then, some thought wrinkled his brow, and he glanced at me. 'Hanno is not so stricken, I think. Now, he will not be required to try the woman for the murder of her children. Nor walk beside the hangman to her cell door. It would be hard to live with such a burden.'

He was silent for a moment. 'I do not blame you, Helena. If I could have you always at *my* side, I would consider myself the most fortunate of men.'

She did not respond to this declaration. But I saw signs of agitation lurking in her manner. A dull red patch lit up each cheekbone.

'What will become of her?' she asked him.

'She will remain here,' he said. 'They will take good care of her. One day, she may decide to tell her own story. Those images of children may be nothing more than damaged playing cards. Who knows?'

'Please help her,' Helena murmured, reaching out, touching his sleeve.

'I will, I promise you,' he replied quietly, offering her his arm. 'But come, *madame*, unless you wish to miss that coach, you must let me see you to the door.'

Helena took his arm with an acquiescent nod, and they turned towards the door.

I was a yard behind them, still struggling to comprehend precisely what had occurred that afternoon, as they passed out into the corridor, and the door swung closed.

I pressed my face to the glass and looked into the bath-house.

The inmate was still imprisoned in the casket. Steam spouted up around her head, then suddenly disappeared as if the vapours had been sucked back down inside the tub. Did she realise, in that instant, that someone was observing her? She raised her head and stared hard at the window. Her eyes were large and brown. Her nose was straight. The chin was delicately pointed. Her hair, soaked by the steam, was a wild tangle of curls. She frowned, and her eyebrows met in a sudden upsweep, like the wings of a gull.

The similarity was stunning.

Helena had brought that woman to life, directing my charcoal point over Aaron Jacob's rough approximation of a face. The woman that she had met while wandering alone outside Lotingen.

Before her head sank back against the pillow, a smile traced itself on Sybille Gottewald's lips.

Then the Mesmeric vapours swallowed her up in a cloud.

·44·

THIRTY MILES FROM Lotingen, that journey became something more
than listless staring out of the window at the monotonous white blanket of
snow, the boundless dark forests, the frozen lakes of Milicz, huddling
against the icy wind that raged and howled outside the carriage. My mind
was dull, my sight blurred by the endless succession of peasant villages,
each one identical, a church spire sprouting in the midst of miserable roofs
of blackened thatch, like rotting hedgehogs. I had long since ceased to
wonder what we would find at home, whether the children were well, how
Lotte had managed without us.

Helena sat in the corner of the coach and seemed to study my face.

I could make no sense of her sullen, fixed expression. I was waiting for
her to speak, waiting for her to tell me what was on her mind. But she did
not. The silence was intolerable.

'We will soon be home,' I announced.

Perhaps it was the closeness of Lotingen. The end of the voyage was in
sight. A line must be drawn, a closure made. If she would not broach the
subject, then I must do it.

'I saw her, Helena. I recognised Sybille Gottewald. As you portrayed her.'

She did not react immediately. She might have been waking up from a
deep, dreamless sleep. She stretched her limbs like a cat. Her eyes opened
wide and stared.

'Why did you conceal her identity from Lavedrine? She murdered her
children.'

'Does the name Gubermann mean anything to you?' she asked.

Mechanically, I began to answer. 'I read it in . . .'

I stopped, and stared at her.

I knew that name. Lavedrine knew it. Bruno Gottewald had known it. But
where had Helena heard it?

'She told you, didn't she?'

Helena's eyes gleamed feverishly. I saw her naked soul reflected in them. I saw uncertainty, fright, the desire to share her knowledge at last.

'We must talk now,' she said quietly. 'Otherwise, the Gottewalds will never let us be. They'll haunt us like ghosts.'

She shifted from her place, and came to sit beside me on the bench. The coach lurched and she fell heavily against my shoulder. She did not pull away. She raised her hand and rested it lightly on my arm. Leaning closer, her mouth hovered close to my ear.

On the opposite bench, a stout elderly gentleman opened his eyes and nodded approvingly, as if he liked to see two young people, a man and his wife, exchanging tokens of affection. A moment later, he politely closed his eyes again.

'She was not a figment of my fantasy,' Helena whispered. 'You thought that I'd invented her. That is why you never showed the sketch to Lavedrine. You feared that he would think what *you* had thought. That I had drawn myself, and that the drawing would reveal my own obsessions.'

What could I say? Helena had put into words the battle that had been raging in my breast for many days, and all the more since Bialystok.

'Tell me what you know of the Gubermanns,' she said again.

In my turn, I placed my lips close to her ear and began to whisper.

'Gottewald mentioned the name in his letter. But I have no idea who they were, or what they might have meant to him,' I admitted. 'I suspected that there might be a connection between those people and something that had happened in a place called Korbern, when he was stationed in Marienburg. But what link could there possibly be with two Jews who had been murdered . . .'

I did not finish. Helena's hands grasped mine. 'You said that fear pushed Sybille Gottewald to do what she did,' she whispered. 'It was worse, Hanno. You never really thought that madness could drive a mother to commit such a crime, did you? Not madness alone . . .'

The words that Kant had written in his report about the von Mandel case came back to me. The same words Lavedrine had taken over for his own use. Kant's conviction that love or affection could be more devastating than hatred. That the impulse to protect her offspring might push a mother to the extreme act. No man before him had ever dared to investigate such a crime.

'She slit her children's throats,' I protested. 'Was that atrocity *less* terrible than the punishment that she feared? What could be worse? What nameless fear . . .'

'I can name that fear,' she said. 'It drove that woman out of her mind. Bruno Gottewald was whom she feared. Her own husband.'

I was too stunned to reply.

'Samuel and Esther Gubermann were Bruno's parents,' she rushed on breathlessly. 'He didn't know the truth when Katowice ordered him to execute them. He obeyed without question, as he had always done. He was a Prussian soldier. He did what he was told, and he was promoted. But then came Jena. That battle changed the world for all of us, but the consequences were catastrophic in his case. He saw a glimmer of hope. He thought that he could be a soldier *and* a Jew. But Katowice was furious when he learnt that he had contacted the French. He called it a betrayal, and like a demon god, determined to destroy him. He told Bruno who those Jews in Korbern really were, knowing that the truth would crush him. But the knowledge that he had butchered his own parents was just the start of his punishment.'

I remembered what Katowice had told me.

Before I sent him out to die, before I set the hounds on him, I revealed to him how diabolical a creature he had become. Gottewald's hell began on earth.

'But why should Sybille be afraid of her own husband?' I asked.

'Just think what he was suggesting to her mind, Hanno! He sent her a letter. It was a warning. General Katowice could order Bruno to do *anything*. And he would! What greater sacrifice could that monster ask of his poor creature?'

Helena's insights were so intense, I was blinded by them.

'Could she believe such a thing? That Bruno would obey an order to murder his own wife and children?' I protested.

Helena closed her eyes and nodded her head violently. 'She did. Oh my God, Hanno, she did! He terrified the life out of her. That letter robbed her of her sanity.'

'But he was dead by the time she read it! Dead!'

I must have shouted, because the stranger opened his eyes and stared at me. What? An argument after so much tenderness? He closed his eyes again, resting his chin on his waistcoat, though I do not think that he was sleeping.

'She lied to you,' I hissed. 'Her folly is greater than it appears . . .'

'No one informed her of his death,' Helena interrupted. 'No one in Kamenetz bothered. She thought he was still alive. That he was coming for *them*, and would arrive at any moment.'

Again, the words of General Katowice seemed to deny what she had said.

I did not know that he was married until you came to Kamenetz.

'But Gottewald was talking of the punishment that he *himself* would have to undergo.'

'She didn't know that,' Helena insisted. 'She didn't know that he was dead until . . .'

'Until you told her. In the bath-house.'

A deep sigh escaped from her lips. 'You cannot imagine the relief on her face, Hanno. She need not fear him any more. She understood that he had never meant to sacrifice them. Her soul will never be free of responsibility for what she has done, but I gave her a grain of comfort. I broke a chip off the millstone hanging round her neck.'

I told her everything then. How I had glanced back as she and Lavedrine left the bath-house. I described the woman I had seen beyond the glass. The woman in the portrait. The woman who was so like Helena. Finally, I told her that I had seen that woman smile.

She gripped my arm with both her hands and hugged it.

'Did you really see it, Hanno? Did you see her smile?'

Her face lit up for the first time since leaving Bialystok.

In that moment, I think, we both felt as though the sharing of that terrible knowledge had drawn us closer together than we had ever been before. It seemed to make us whole again.

The sky over Lotingen appeared brighter as we climbed down from the coach, the wind less piercing. Spring would not be long in coming. Even so, as I picked up the bag and we began to make our way home along the road, I realised how much had changed for ever. The warmth of the days to come, the rolling blue of the sun-blessed Baltic Sea, the shouts of the children as we sat on the sand and watched the boats and sailing ships, the joys of summer on the northernmost shore of Europe: these things would never ever be the same again.

The chill of that hard winter would not soon be lifted from our hearts.

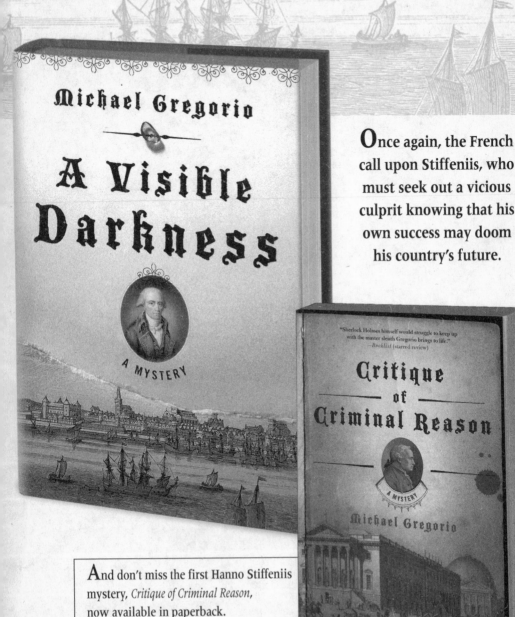